D0206941

The Seduction of Silence

The Seduction of Silence

Bem Le Hunte

HarperSanFrancisco
A Division of HarperCollins*Publishers*

THE SEDUCTION OF SILENCE. Copyright © 2003 by Bem Le Hunte. All rights reserved. Printed in the United States of America. No part of this book may be used or reproduced in any manner whatsoever without written permission except in the case of brief quotations embodied in critical articles and reviews. For information address HarperCollins Publishers, Inc., 10 East 53rd Street, New York, NY 10022.

HarperCollins books may be purchased for educational, business, or sales promotional use. For information please write: Special Markets Department, HarperCollins Publishers, Inc., 10 East 53rd Street, New York, NY 10022.

HarperCollins Web site: http://www.harpercollins.com

HarperCollins®, ®, and HarperSanFrancisco™ are trademarks of HarperCollins Publishers, Inc.

FIRST HARPERCOLLINS PAPERBACK EDITION PUBLISHED IN 2004

Library of Congress Cataloging-in-Publication Data
Le Hunte, Bem.
The seduction of silence / Bem Le Hunte. — 1st ed.
p. cm.
ISBN 0–06–057368–6 (paperback)
1. Himalaya Mountains—Fiction. 2. East Indians—England—London—Fiction. 3. London (England)—Fiction. 4. Young women—Fiction. 5. Hindus—Fiction. 6. India—Fiction. I. Title

PR9619.4.L4 S43 2002
823'.92—dc21 2002032843

04 05 06 07 08 RRD(H) 10 9 8 7 6 5 4 3 2

For my love, Jan.

This book is for you, for the faith you showed in my work.

Thank you for helping me find the silence to write it.

Acknowledgments

Nani, for having us to stay – all of us – and for sharing stories and memories.

My parents, for giving me such an unusual story. My family, for not forcing me to conform. Kathy Golski, for giving me three weeks to finish this book when it was only half written.

Ajay for renting us rooms in his Himalayan skyscraper. Sudhir for finding the heart to help us. My midwife, Mrs. Chawla, for comfort and support.

Nikki, my first reader, who stole the time to absorb this story whilst her three babies slept. Kerry Wood and Gaby Naher who gave invaluable advice so generously.

Marion Gluck, my doctor, who passed this book on to Julie Gibb at Penguin. Many thanks to you both.

My agents Fiona Inglis, Ali Gunn and Jane Gelfman. Fiona, thank you for the golden carriage and glass slippers.

Nicola O'Shea for an outstanding edit. Linda Funnell, Shona Martyn at HarperCollins in Australia, as well as the staff at Harper San Francisco, who has helped make this experience into such a fairytale.

Monika, for being a second mother to my children. Huge thanks to everyone who helped with Taliesin and Rishi – especially Kathy, Christopher, Rafal, Nadya and Rachel.

Thom Knoles for eleven years of meditation. Peter Sanson for being my Ashtanga yoga teacher during the months it took to write this book. Swami Ramachandra for prayers and fires.

Jan, for everything. Thank you for sharing my life. Your originality and strong spirit inspire me continually.

For all my teachers. For the writers of this world, past, future and present. For the great rishis and yogis of India. For Guru Dev, for Maharishi. For everyone who supports the evolution of consciousness and shares their inspiration with the world.

The Seduction of Silence

Prologue

"Do not think that life without the body is an empty one, my friends, for the spring from which we all draw life is here. We bathe in it, you and I. That same spring. You bathe your body and I my soul . . ."

"It is this spring – this Source – that supports every miracle, every phenomenon you see as ordinary in your world. You see it all. You are excruciatingly close to this Reality. But just as you cannot see your own eyes, only the visions they offer, this Reality evades you. Just as you can no longer see the water that makes the snows . . ."

[CLICK]

Rohini switched off her tape recorder when the voice started to fade. The contact was fractured. The spirit of Aakash was unable to animate the body of the medium for much longer.

It was always at this point that Rohini remembered to check on her own existence. She felt for the awareness of her own body, not just the soup of her thoughts. Her exact location on the physical plane. Second row from the front in a stuffy room in the Spiritualist Church of Great Britain, Belgrave Square.

Around her Rohini heard the shuffling of bums, searching out their ideal sitting postures. Coughs, whispers and other noises that interludes make. Dora's voice, too, could now be heard, a voice returned from its temporary exile, giving instructions in familiar tones. Rohini followed those instructions and then, like the fifty or so other people gathered there, she closed her eyes and held out her hands. Midwife's hands, deft with life, intuitive, capable, expectant.

What followed was what Fleur Heuspeth at the Spiritualist Church of Great Britain called "*a divine gift.*" At first it tickled, dancing patterns onto her palms, softly, like an angel landing.

Opening her eyes Rohini saw something quite ordinary: a fresh pink lotus. Ordinary perhaps if one of the ladies who collected donations was walking away all chuffed and cardiganed down the aisle. But there was no one there. And no way it could have been tossed forward from the small stage.

Tossed down from the heavens?

Maybe . . .

Or perhaps it had been pushed through the silent hum of the Infinite, to manifest first as sound, and then matter. Dividing, dividing, dividing the unity of existence until it found its own unique manifestation in waxy pink flesh.

For Rohini this was not just a minor miracle, it was a gift of love. Aakash, the spirit who had lectured on that day, was her grandfather in his earthly years. A grandfather she had never met. A man she could only know years later, through the soft, padded, feminine face of Dora Hindes, the medium who now channeled him.

Although he was unreachable on the other side of life, Aakash was closer to Rohini than all her family members who had deserted her. He had filled the gap left by her family by transcending the chasm between life and death. Only he could hold her pain and feel its weightlessness. Only he could be there for her in spirit, embracing her in totality. But at the end of every trance session Dora's head would droop and Aakash would be gone, back into the infinite recesses of his own timeless universe.

And Dora – she was left to feel her way back into her own form, slowly, timidly at first. Lifting her head and recovering her own eyes with their neighborly twinkle that defined her smile. Regaining her body's own lift, her unique relationship with gravity.

At the end of every session she was the same woman who had powdered her cheekbones that morning. Now she patted down her hair-do, smiled at the audience, using her very own wrinkles and her own cheery personality to communicate. Nobody could have been less related to the great Aakash. Nonetheless, she was the one he had chosen.

But not for much longer.

Aakash had announced at the beginning of this lecture that he was going to return to the world of the living.

Rohini was still disturbed by this revelation as she listened to Fleur Heuspeth's regular speech, thanking everyone for coming and sharing these wisdoms from beyond the grave.

"Of course none of this would be possible without the generous support of our fellowship. We're collecting now for the many urgent repairs that need to be done. And of course, we ask you once more to think of the work we do when you write your will. Think of the solace we provide for so many people in their time of need when loved ones have departed ..."

The room where Aakash had made one of his last visitations was called the Arthur Conan Doyle Room. Donated by Arthur himself, who made invisible guest appearances, taking advantage of his post-mortem privileges.

The spirits of the room sang of a former glory. The marble pillars and floors were patched up clumsily with cement, and the upholstery peeled itself from the seats as if it had no concerns in the material world.

Fleur was right. The church urgently needed repairs, but when the tray went around, the ladies from Knightsbridge who valued this service *so much* only chinked ten new pence each onto the metal.

"Oh well," whispered the spirits. "The day will come for our velvet curtains."

Dora Hindes stepped off the platform, ready for a cup of tea. Behind her was the usual sign: "Please do not clap until the medium has returned to his or her normal self." Today few hands clapped. Instead the hands held lotuses as their owners sat suspended in disbelief, in curiosity, in wonder.

In the next room people were starting to mill out of a regular seance meeting. Rohini tried to catch Dora's attention as she left Arthur's room and the two rivers of living human traffic merged with vanishing spirits moving toward the front door.

"Dora, can I have a quick word?"

"Of course, dear. I have a special message for you today," she said. Rohini followed, anxious to talk with the person who linked her back to her family through generations, through lifetimes, through different realms way beyond the divisions of Time and Matter.

Rohini had attended every one of Dora's trance sessions, and had booked so many private sittings that Dora knew her face as intimately as the face of Aakash. Sometimes when Aakash stood behind Rohini at a private sitting, with his spirit hand on her shoulder, she could see them as if in a family portrait. A photograph captured in ether, etched in ectoplasm. She with her beautiful high cheekbones, dark curly hair (only a little gray) and slim body in colorful clothes, human and fully sentient. He in white robes behind, an earnest expression, long white beard, more faded. The two of them made a noble pair, full of secrets.

Through Dora, Aakash had visited often, leaving behind prophecies like pieces of a jigsaw puzzle. Only he understood Rohini's state of aloneness. He was her guide and adviser. It was he who had first told her that she would have her own visionary experiences. And soon after, she started to decipher messages that rang in her ears like voices from a mixed-up radio frequency – clairaudience they called it, here in this church.

In the seance room, Dora sat in her usual seat, and swapped her usual set of senses with the extraordinary set she kept just behind the bones of her forehead. She looked through Rohini's intense stare and into her mind, waiting for the thought forms to settle. Letting the questions rise to the surface ... His talk had disturbed her. Was he really going to leave the spirit world? How could he?

One thought bubbled up and Dora read it in Rohini's mind: *He can't leave me. Without Aakash there'll be nobody to guide me. Eternity will be empty.*

Was she seeing these thoughts in the cavities of her eyes? Dark black Indian eyes, absorbing light into their chambers and throwing back only sadness. Eyes that used to look to life with all the greedy joy of a spoilt child, now looked only toward elusive spirits.

Dora couldn't help but notice.

"My dear, Aakash has told me it's time you turned your attention back to the world of the living."

Rohini shrunk back and another thought form emerged: *I can't rely on them.* Her world of the living was peopled with disappointment. A ghost of a husband who had deserted her. An only child. Elsewhere ...

But the dead were safe. They never went away. They never hurt you. And they looked away when you did. Aakash had no right to just get up and leave. To vacate his space in the Absolute.

"Aakash has told me that he is going to take birth again in your family."

"*What!*" Rohini's eyes were wide now, absorbing this information. Why her family? It seemed so inappropriate.

"According to the vedas, after a child is conceived the spirit will enter the body at around three or four months, when the mother first feels the child move. Do you know any of this?"

No. She was still absorbing the shock of it all. And no, Rohini had never studied the vedas. They just didn't seem as exciting and immediate as somebody speaking to you directly from the spirit world. The vedas were open to interpretation, but the voices from Infinity you could never argue with, although everyone had tried. Her daughter Saakshi had laughed at her preoccupation with receiving messages. "It's the fillings in your teeth," she'd said, "they're acting as receivers for radio signals. And all these people you think are contacting you from the Great Beyond are probably sitting at a microphone in a studio in Wimbledon."

Dora caught the thought and held Rohini's hand to bring her back to the present. She knew her role as Aakash's medium was soon going to end, although he hadn't told her exactly when. They had a quiet agreement with no expectations of each other, like spirit twins. In fact, somehow, Dora was looking forward to having control over her body at all times. It was time for her, too, to retire and return to the ordinary life of a woman in her seventies.

"My daughter has just discovered she's pregnant," said Rohini. "Is it Saakshi whom he has chosen?"

"Yes," came Dora's quiet reply.

Rohini's eyes took stock, smudged tears and blinked. Saakshi was living in Australia. Rohini would be closer to Aakash on the other side of life, she realized, than she would be to him on the other side of the world.

"Why does he have to come back when he was doing such good work in the spirit world?" As if she could have sent him back toward the Source with these words.

"Unfinished business. The same reason most of us are called back."

"He left nothing unfinished. He was enlightened."

"So doesn't the world need more enlightened souls in it?" Dora was insistent. "An enlightened soul returns to the world as an avatar. And Aakash will return with the wisdom of the ancient seers. He'll be able to shift mountains ..."

Of that Rohini had no doubt. But Saakshi? *What do I say?* she thought. *Darling, you're going to give birth to an avatar? She'll think I'm crazy. How do I ring her up with this news?*

Dora instantly pieced together the fragmented cloud of thoughts and continued Rohini's internal dialogue.

"Don't worry about your daughter or about how you will maintain contact with Aakash. There is so much support in the spirit world for coming events."

Nothing could have prepared Rohini for this prophecy. But she had this feeling, and she'd had it before in her life. *This feeling that everything happens for a reason.*

"Don't stop coming to see me," said Dora. "I'm always here if you need me."

Gripping her slightly sweaty fresh lotus, Rohini bade farewell to Dora. She felt an atmosphere of seriousness and importance as she left the eccentric haunted house in Belgrave Square and stepped out into London proper.

One minute out of the door and her focus on spirits was disturbed by the usual London concerns. Had her car been booked? Or even clamped? How on earth was she going to drive back to Chelsea before the rush hour?

Unreal London.

She drove, her thoughts in limbo, through London. Along Knightsbridge in the spitting rain. Past the parks filled with nannies and toddlers. Past the travel agent that always advertised fares to Australia and taunted all Londoners with pictures of how good life could be Elsewhere. It always made her think of her daughter Saakshi in Sydney. And wonder when they would meet up again.

By the time she reached Chelsea, Rohini felt a sense of relief. She closed her front door and cut out the world. Inside now she hovered, making small changes to the rooms whilst the big thoughts floated above. Lifting this, shutting that, closing curtains, checking her expression in the mirror and finding it too stern. Smiling at the mirror, and looking at the still space that surrounded her.

She turned on her answering machine and a voice broke her silence. One of her private home-birth patients was in labor. It was a third baby, and the mother was the sort of birther who popped out babies over lunch between courses.

She called them.

"Hello, Rohini here." Her involvement was so professional, nobody would have known that nowadays when she attended a birth she was more interested in the spirit helpers who gathered around than the new child taking its first breath of life.

The baby had already been born whilst Rohini's pager was switched off, as if to prove that time waits for no one, least of all a midwife. "But that's wonderful. The best births are always the ones where I'm not needed. How's Laura?"

She had switched off her pager and switched off from life. And during those few hours Laura's baby had been born. Whilst she was out of touch. Disconnected. Thinking about her own daughter and the loss of Aakash …

Saakshi, will I be there when you deliver your child?

Rohini knew she had already done too much damage to her family to have the right to ask for anything. Anything at all. She wanted so much to be there, but she had been given strict instructions to stay away. Her daughter didn't need her. And neither had Laura.

So what of it? And why should a midwife feel obliged to deliver her daughter's children? A child always delivers itself, if its destiny is to be born at all.

"Rohini, are you still there? We need you now. When can you come over?"

Needed?

She said she would come. She had to. She was still responsible for her patient, even though nature had made her redundant. She gave her usual advice about how to keep the baby warm and nourish the post-natal mother. And with all these reassurances, she climbed back into her car. This time going out into the world of the living, instead of returning from the world of the dead.

Part One

Go into the Silence and find the Reality that informs your existence. Then you will see everything as sacred. Your eyes will fill with tears for this life that you have been given. You will look at the blue skies above and know that there is more – much, much more to life.

I

Of all mountains, the Himalayas are the highest. They sit like a prayer table on the plains. The soil is closer to the Gods, the air purer, the mind clearer. There's a potency in the earth here – a quality of the Divine in everything that takes life.

It was in the Himalayas, in the holy mountains of Himachal Pradesh, that Aakash chose to throw his first seeds into the earth on some land that had arrived in his care through Divine Grace.

Many years earlier, when he was a boy, he had won this piece of land at a game of cricket in Chail. Not by winning the game, but by laying his hands on an injured hemophiliac boy and curing him of hemophilia altogether. An act of no consequence if the boy had not been the captain of the cricket team, and, more importantly, the son of the Maharaja of Patiala.

Years later, when Aakash went up into the hills as a man, he was mesmerized by the beauty of this God-sent land. Awestruck by the Silence as he walked the mountaintops and valleys, divining the perfect place to build his house.

There was one flat peninsula on the mountainside that begged for a home. From this place he could see layers of mountains on all sides, aspiring to greater and greater heights until they reached the snows.

Scattered in the distance down the mountainsides were terraces which circled the hills like green tidemarks, villagers grazing their cows and goats, people washing their clothes in the river, wooden makeshift dwellings, tall pines and Himalayan weeds with the power to heal diseases that usually carried death sentences.

The land he had been given was part of a mountain range whose tributaries trickled down to both the Ganges, river of Immortality, and the Indus, river of Civilization. In fact, if a tear was shed at the top of one ridge, it could have seeped through the soil to either of those two destinations. It was left for the Fates to decide.

Aakash built a farm in these hills, which he named Prakriti, and he had an elephant that he named Ganesh. He didn't have a wife yet, but the elephant, along with the seeds and the power of his vision, formed the roots of future prosperity. The century was still young, India knew no assurance of independence, and success was a scarce resource, owned mostly by the British.

Aakash felt lucky here, but the locals were too superstitious to call it luck. They always felt he had developed certain powers or sidhis. There was no explaining why rain clouds would hover over his farm well before the monsoons broke down in Delhi. No explanation why the household's vegetables were twice the size of those sold in any of the nearby market towns.

Then he also had the power of Ganesh. The villagers regularly came to give his elephant prasad from their fields and receive a regal salaam in exchange. Govinda, the mahout who looked after Ganesh, was always treated with great veneration. People said that he didn't just know the traditional pressure points to command this prehistoric force of a creature, he also knew where all the sacred points were to be found. The places between the thick elephantine folds where time immemorial was carried. Time so old, it could be traced back to its source and back to the controlling forces of the universe.

But success was a trifle for Aakash. He never sought it. He only thought how he could help his fellow countrymen. The planting of the seed was enough, and the shoots would be guided by the powers that be. His concern was to do his duty, and provide traditional medicinal herbs for those in need.

In those days Ayurveda was often the only affordable medical option for the masses. Western medicine hadn't been widely accepted and took its place amongst the other magical treatments the local people practiced. In fact, if anything, there was a far healthier scepticism toward it, as many a patient had escaped their bodies under the pioneering knife of medical science.

The seeds Aakash threw when he first planted Prakriti were later to be identified in Latin as substances such as *Withania somnifera, Carum copticum, Glycyrrhiza glabra* and many more. To Aakash they had greater affinity with the cosmic elements than with a botanical dictionary. They responded to the elements of earth, fire, water and air, and the way they replicated themselves as energy systems within the body. His ayurvedic herbs were the medicine of a nation that still held to ancient principles and trusted in the power of the Gods to potentiate their tinctures and cure their ills.

When Prakriti started to reap a handsome profit, Aakash was visited by his father Rahul, with talk of marriage. He was twenty-eight years old and had never questioned the inevitability of marriage. But then neither had he for a minute entertained any concept of a wife. His food was cooked by Hukam-Singh; Deepika, the cook's wife, cleaned his farmhouse, and a rotating assortment of local and migrant workers helped him in the fields. Every need he had was satisfied. And whenever he required conversation, he would spend a few hours on the verandah talking to Govinda his mahout, or he would take a stroll in the moonlight to visit his friend Xavier, the Christian headmaster in the nearby village.

When Aakash was visited by his father there were many long silences when Rahul turned their conversation to marriage. Many open-ended questions that hovered between thoughts. Rahul knew it wouldn't be easy to get an agreement out of his son. He knew also that no matter how well the farm flourished, it was his duty to find Aakash a wife. That there was no such thing as success unless a man was also "settled."

If truth be told, even Rahul found it hard to imagine his son with a wife and family. As a child, Aakash was like a deer: self-contained; poised; silently watching the world from the intensity of his own space. He never tugged at his ayah's sari palla like the rest of the brood. Neither did he feel the need to communicate with any of his siblings until he was at least four or five, when years of silence were ended with complete sentences that seemed to be spoken by a child twice his age. Nobody quite understood Aakash, and Aakash had never felt a need to be understood.

Like most parents in his situation, Rahul carried around the responsibility of his son's marriage like a piece of life's luggage. Only when he had successfully deposited this luggage would his load be lighter and his family responsibilities on earth be finalized. The weight of responsibility was far heavier than the feather-boned Aakash he had picked up in his arms the day he was born. And it weighed heavier still as his son's contemporaries garlanded each other and started having children.

Organizing a marriage for Aakash was like throwing a stick up high into a tree and hoping it would land. Even Rahul didn't dare think about what that married life might entail. The finality of the ceremony itself would satisfy him, like a handover.

The marriage he had in mind was with a family whom he didn't know too well, and that was not such a bad thing. They didn't know about Aakash and his unusual sense of detachment. The beard of a renunciant that he wore, and the eyes that looked only inward.

This unfamiliarity was also an advantage for the family of the bride. They too had an ulterior motive for marrying into a completely unknown family. It was like a marriage made on either side of a screen, with each family parading a shadow puppet for the benefit of the other.

When Rahul went to meet Krishna, the girl's father, he walked into a grand house in Amritsar, and was introduced to a beautiful, heavy-lashed, coy young Punjabi woman who held her head half-covered by her duppata and looked down at the ground. Sitting in the room with her was a cross-looking girl. The first one was introduced as Jyoti, or so he remembered, and the second one as Pyari.

The two of them were soon ushered out of the room without either girl speaking more than a few words, and the two fathers continued with more formal discussions of marriage over tea and a game of chess. The bride's father telling of the dowry he had kept aside for his daughter, and Rahul talking of his job in the Maharaja's service and Aakash's prosperous farm in the hills. They could have been any two ordinary men arranging a marriage, except that each of the chess characters they wielded had secret motives moving them across the board.

Krishna won the game, but nonetheless Rahul went away feeling elated with his own success and full of great anticipation on behalf of his son. He felt sure that this would be a match that would bring Aakash's attentions fully into the world. That he would be overcome with love for the gentle beauty who was soon to become his wife.

When Aakash was brought to the wedding, fully veiled by garlands of flowers in his sehra bandi, he stood veil to veil with his future wife, Jyoti Ma. The two of them, decked in marigolds and moongra, walked barefooted around the havan fire seven times, tied together by their garments. The union was made according to the Scriptures, and according to the Stars, and only after the ceremony, when they were bonded as man and wife, did Rahul realize that there had been a bride "switch." That Jyoti Ma had not been the woman he had been led to believe would marry his son.

The moment of truth dawned when the bride's veil was dropped, revealing the expression of someone caught between a bullfighter and a bull – angry, fearful and cross-eyed. Her warrior's wide nostrils were exposed. So too was her thin hair and the layers of ghee-filled flesh that fought their way over the hem of her sari blouse.

Rahul felt his heart gulp at his own blood. Gulp at the terrible mistake. He saw people whispering. What would they think of him for making such a choice?

He looked over to witness his son's disappointment, but saw only serenity. Aakash's eyes showed total acceptance, because his father's wishes were being fulfilled. Had Aakash turned his face to look at his father, on the other hand, he would have seen a helpless bystander, wiping the shameful sweat from his brow, panic in his eyes. A victim of a humiliating and heartless crime, looking around for the beautiful woman he had intended for his son.

He saw her, standing at the back of the shamiana with another man.

Later, Rahul enquired with guarded politeness about Pyari, Krishna's other daughter. Her father brushed him off, knowing that this was no time for lifting the curtains on the backstage drama. Pyari, he said, was betrothed. Krishna didn't want to reveal that she would soon be marrying a Christian, Anthony – a man of her own choice. It was shameful enough that she had found her own match, but more shameful still that she had reduced her father to such poor strategies to marry off Jyoti before any further scandals arose.

Krishna knew that Heaven had been their witness. The marriage was done. Over. It was meant to be. That was the way of destiny. And Rahul, after he had recovered from the shock of such a deceit, actually found himself quite relieved. If his wife had still been alive, maybe he wouldn't have been. But as things stood, there was nobody to object. Aakash, after all, accepted his fate as he accepted whatever was cooked and placed in front of him at suppertime. There was no question of wanting better or different.

Jyoti Ma was brought back to Prakriti wearing all her marriage bangles, and each day another of her new wedding saris. She did not look up at the hills, but concerned herself only with the farmhouse, carving her way around the land it occupied, making it her own.

She might not have been intimidating in her beauty, but she had a domestic austerity that terrified and humbled the servants when she appeared at Prakriti as a new bride. With her arrival in the house, the comfortable familiarity between master, chef and cleaner was doomed.

Jyoti Ma hated the way that Hukam-Singh the cook would always take instructions from Aakash, but feigned deafness whenever she commanded the dishes of the day. Yet Hukam-Singh's wife Deepika could call him from the other side of the house and he would always hear her. Why? And why did the cook and sweeper prefer to spend time together instead of attending to her needs?

She felt isolated being away from her family with a new husband in the middle of the Himalayas. And she hated the servants for feeling so at home in the hills. For feeling more at home in her house, with her husband, than she did. The servants could have helped her melt the snows, but her breeding dictated that she preserve all the boundaries between her class and theirs.

Jyoti Ma claimed her space by pushing away the people who served her, to the point where she hated them and resented their service. Even Govinda the mahout was divested of respect and tolerated only at the far end of the verandah. She started blaming the servants for her unhappiness and at every opportunity she would grumble to her new husband about the headaches they were all causing her.

In her anxiety to justify her authority over the servants she even found herself laying traps. Sometimes she would count out the amount of mithai in her cupboard so that she would know when some had been stolen. Almost eager for it to disappear. Then she would carefully empty packets of dust and soil in the kitchen cupboards just so that she could take up Hukam-Singh on the disgusting state of his kitchen.

The servants were no longer allowed to eat all the food they required. Only one dhal, roti and subjee was left for them, because that was all they deserved. Occasionally, when a piece of fruit was only minutes away from complete deterioration, she would donate it to the kitchen with great generosity and tell the servants to share it amongst themselves.

When she took over the accounts of the farm there wasn't a single minor corruption that was overlooked. Every poor farmhand's attempt to wangle a few extra paise out of the roaring profits of Prakriti was severed, like a hand chopped off for its crime. And with these extra savings, Jyoti Ma began her series of infamous shopping trips to Delhi, which were the talk of all the locals.

As a lady of means she invested the profits of Prakriti shrewdly in ornate sets of gold, diamond, ruby and emerald jewelery from every part of India. Then there were the Kanchipuram and Banarsi saris, threaded with heavy gold weave. When the first automobiles arrived in India she shocked everyone by announcing that she had bought one at the cost of three thousand rupees. "How could that be?" the other landowners pondered. "You can build a grand house for that much money."

Her next task was to dispose of the old servants altogether. If she could install a new batch, then none of them would ever question who held the scepter in the house.

Her opportunity came one day when Deepika was sweeping the floors and her back crumpled from the stress of having to watch every move she made around her new mistress. Jyoti Ma continued sipping her tea, rang her little metal bell, and called for her cook to come and carry away his crumpled-up wife.

"Aakash, these servants are absolutely useless. She's a jellyfish! Not made to work. No backbone. We must get rid of the pair of them."

The replacement cook was a villager from Uttar Pradesh who had left behind his new wife after just three days of marriage to go and work so that he could keep her. In place of his wife, the woman in his life became Jyoti Ma – a stern partner and exacting employer. The new sweeper was almost too old to work, but servants were hard to come by even in those days, especially as word had traveled about memsahib's treatment of her household workers. He had a few years of life left in him, though, and Jyoti Ma knew she could make him work for them.

She found herself humoring the sweeper as a way of keeping him from retirement. To make sure he didn't retire until he could bend no more, she saw to his numerous medical requirements. At first he never opened his mouth properly to talk, and she was always scolding him furiously for mumbling. When she realized that he was trying to hide the many gaps of missing teeth, she took him to Delhi and ordered a pair of dentures at great expense. This resulted in a sweeper with a permanent false smile, which turned the cook off cooking.

"Those new teeth memsahib bought for you are made from dog's teeth," said the cook slyly.

From that day on the sweeper went back to his toothless mumblings and Jyoti Ma had a new cause for complaint, this time about how the servants were still abusing her "after everything she did for them."

As was the tradition, from the very start of their marriage, Aakash gave his wife full jurisdiction over the house. He had no interest in the profits of Prakriti, so he was happy that somebody enjoyed spending them. However, sometimes he would catch the gaze of his mahout, and then sense Govinda look away, down at the ground, humbled at the thought that he had ever been allowed into the house. Aakash felt powerless to defend his old compatriots who had looked after him through his early bachelor days on Prakriti. And he didn't enjoy watching them stoop to dishonest behavior in response to Jyoti Ma's unscrupulous demands and wage cuts. Yet there was nothing he could say to stop her, so on a silent level he matched their downfall with his despondency, and detached himself from the house and all its inhabitants, including his own wife.

It frustrated Jyoti Ma no end, because after she had gained dominion over the household she wanted to gain full command of her husband's heart. The way things turned out this was never to be, because she could only accept Aakash if she accepted the whole of humanity. And there was simply not enough room in her house. So Aakash, without a word, stood back, an observer. And she forgot to smile at him. It was only when Jyoti Ma complained that she had none of the tenderness that other wives enjoyed, that Aakash dutifully spent a few nights with her to supply a son.

Nine months later, the birth of Ram was celebrated with almost as much spectacle as the birth of his namesake in the *Ramayana*. Sweets were distributed throughout the village, alms given, and if you looked hard enough, there were surely flowers being sprinkled from the heavens.

And with this, Jyoti Ma's heart softened a little as it sunned itself in the blessings of this god-given birth. She relinquished control over her household for a few months and devoted herself to enjoying these summer days. Ram was her biggest achievement. Her conquest over love. A person who returned her love, gurgling words that seemed to have real meaning as he pointed to the skies.

There was nothing short of worship in Jyoti Ma's adoration of him. An ayah was hired but she was hardly allowed to pick up the child. Her job was to clean the nappies, and for this she was given the highest status in the household, being the servant closest to Jyoti Ma's baby God. The only time she was strictly reprimanded was when she cut short any rules on hygiene.

With a baby to protect, Jyoti Ma's obsession with hygiene developed into a phobia of the outside world. Everything from outside became "dirty." Boundaries were marked out between the two worlds, which were violated by beady-eyed lizards bringing their reptile skins in from the dirt. By shoes, carrying clods of earth. By insects. Try as she would, she could never ban nature from her house. It continued to encroach upon her sanitised vacuum and entered her rooms with the freedom of air.

Once Ram was taken out for a walk and Jyoti Ma saw one of the workers kissing him and pinching his cheek. Immediately she summoned the baby back inside and rubbed his infant skin raw with disinfectant to stop the diseases from being absorbed.

There were diseases everywhere. Invisible, making them even more malevolent. Nature was diseased. The food in Jyoti Ma's kitchen was cooked until it was limp, in case a few germs remained. No fruit was ever eaten without being laboriously peeled and then dipped in potassium permanganate. Even the water was boiled four times before it touched the lips of any family member. (Of course the servants had to drink their water straight from the earth.)

Then there were the trees to worry about. A few grew too near the house and Jyoti Ma, through some error in her education, was convinced that they created too much carbon monoxide.

"We must chop down that jacaranda near the house," she suggested to Aakash one day.

"If you cut it down, my dear, I will leave and never come back."

"And where will you go?"

"Further into the mountains," was all he said.

So Aakash continued his life with his accidental wife, his earthly existence that is, while his spirit took on a life of its own. He allowed himself to slip further into Silence, because it was only in Silence that he felt fulfilled.

Every day he would chant and sing bhajans. He would do his japa on beads, immersing himself in the name of God with each bead held tight between two fingers. He would study the vedas, closing his eyes often to understand the intent behind each shloka. He would sit in silence and meditate after his regular yoga routine, which he practiced on the verandah every morning at dawn, with the pale orange hills watching every movement. Along with all this practice he maintained a strict vegetarian regime that sent his carnivorous wife into fits of desperation.

When Aakash made the rule that no meat was to be cooked on the farm, Jyoti Ma's craving for flesh took on obsessive proportions. Animals were slaughtered secretly by the migrant workers on the farm. Outings were always interrupted by furtive detours to the local dhaba to pick on a chicken leg or devour some masala'd mutton. Since dead flesh was forbidden in the house, Jyoti Ma had even savored the loins of the most forbidden meats – the holy cow.

Ram was brought up as a strict vegetarian, never knowing of his mother's secret fetish for meat. He grew up with the love of both parents in an absolutely ordered world. His father devoted a lot of energy to his son, taking time out from his work on the farm to teach him to walk and talk. And Jyoti Ma saw to his every physical need. Husband and wife were united through their son, their one point of mutual adoration.

Ram the Respectful, the Sensitive, the Earnest Philosopher, craved respect mostly from his father. His love for his mother did not alter or falter, but her respect was never required. Somehow Ram sensed that his mother's intense materialism was only a polarity of his father's isolation in matters of the spirit. Together, he felt they formed some kind of a balance. And anyway, he was the object of her love. Had he been a servant or field worker and not a son, who knows? It was never his destiny to find out.

Being his father's son he was always happy to spend hours learning to recite shlokas from the Rig Veda, or discuss the possibilities of an after-life and reincarnation, or even the idea of taking up a life of renunciance. The two of them would sit together, Aakash having esoteric discussions with a boy who wasn't much taller than his navel.

"Pitaji, if I were never to marry, would you try to force me?"

"If it is your destiny to stay a brahmachari, there is no question of force. Life is too short to live out your own desires, let alone the desires of another."

Life didn't seem so short in those days. But Ram always remembered the first time he learnt that people died. At first he didn't believe it, because it was so unfair. And where did they go? It bothered him.

"Pitaji, please live a long life."

"That is not in my hands."

"But please put it in your hands. It is your duty to me, nay?"

"It is my duty to help you walk the immortal path," Aakash told his son.

And together they walked it, as Ram continued to grow, a sapling by the side of a grand Himalayan pine. The day would come when they would have to face losing each other, but for now they were united at Prakriti, their mountain home where all paths ran together.

2

When Ram was very little he showed his father a picture book of Indian Gods and asked: "How many hands does God have, Pitaji?"

Taken aback by the question, Aakash decided on the spot to take on the role of his son's educator.

"Baba, take a deep breath." Ram did as he was told while his father watched, his intensity amplifying the silence around them.

"God was in that breath you took. Now do it again."

Ram took many deep breaths, until every cell of his body was filled with the life force that his father so wanted him to feel as his birthright.

"You see, it's got nothing to do with the pictures of God. God is in your heart. And surely you can always feel the presence of God when you breathe in and intend to feel it. God resides in you, my darling beta, and breath is the life force that's given to you. God is not in the statues or pictures. But you can love the images, just as you love the feeling in you."

After that day, a flame was fanned in Ram's soul, slow-burning out all attachments to the body that served as its vehicle. The same flame that burnt out all desires in Ram, ignited a desire in his father. The desire to teach. It was this desire that would follow Aakash beyond his last breath on earth. Not finding enough expression in the one lifetime, it sought its oxygen in the life beyond.

For two hours every day, Aakash would dismiss Ram's tutor. He loved the time when the mahout called him for his morning chai and he could leave the fields and herbs to grow on their own and go back to the farmhouse. Then he would go to the small study off the back verandah for some quiet time in meditation. This was followed by a philosophical discussion with his eight-year-old son.

In ancient times, if Ram had been the son of a prince, he would have been sent into the forest to learn the laws of the spirit from a sage or rishi. But there was no hermitage nearby, and Ram was not a prince, so Aakash took it upon himself to be the boy's guru.

"How do you know when you are doing something wrong, darling beta?" he asked Ram one day.

"It is something I know is wrong because I have been told not to do it," Ram answered, with the small voice of learnt wisdoms.

"Beta, it's like this. Each of us has the right to supreme fulfilment through right action. If our actions are guided by an inner Truth, then we are happy. So to be happy we must learn to trust that force that guides us. Consult it. If you feel that something you are doing is wrong, you will know. You *will* know. But you must be true to your Self."

"Pitaji, do you always do the right thing? Are you true to yourself?"

"It is a practice, beta. And the practice leads to perfection. But if you don't practice, you'll lose touch with the force that guides you."

"What if you think it's right to do one thing, and someone else thinks you should do something else?"

"Then you must try and find in you what would be best for both of you."

"Would it be best for Mama to come to class with me sometimes?"

"Mama has her duty, beta. She does her duty."

"But she thinks it is wrong to spend so much time learning these things. She thinks you are foolish."

"When you feel something is right, beta, you shouldn't worry about what other people think about it. It is your truth. And nobody can sit in your body and tell you that your truth is not real."

"She gets cross when you miss your dinner every time."

"Ram, these are small incidents in the ocean. If you feel the stillness inside you, it is like the feeling of an ocean. The waves come and go on top, but the vast ocean remains unmoved. We are like the ocean. The water may go into a katori, or into a thali. It may go into any vessel and take any shape, but it is still water. Like spirit in us all. You may be the katori and I the thali, but in truth we are both vehicles for the same substance."

"So Mama is the same as you?"

"We are our actions as well."

"So her actions are bad sometimes, hey nah?"

"I did not say that. But I want you to know that even though the ocean fills us all, we have the power to create the vessel that we use to hold that water. It's like this ... We are each of us a glowing light in a lamp. If we want to turn the light up high, we may. But if we wish to live in darkness, we dim the light. But we can never turn that light off. It is there at all times and will follow us through lifetime to lifetime. But if we light our torches well, we will for sure be born with a light to guide us in our next life, if we must have one."

"Pitaji, are you going to be reborn?"

"I hope that in this life I will burn out all my vasanas, all my desires. It is better that way."

"But I like this life."

"Your life will never end, beta. Just the body. The soul always has been and always will be."

And so they would go, deeper and deeper into the meanings of things. Aakash learnt a lot about teaching, getting better at handling the young enquiring mind that always tried to bring his father's abstract ideas back to his own experiences.

Aakash, meanwhile, thought about offering some of the villagers teachings from his growing body of knowledge, but his wife always discouraged him, saying that it would be like throwing pearls before swine. And although she felt that Aakash's interests were a little obsessive, she secretly approved of him taking responsibility for teaching their son. She would often advise him on what he should be saying.

"Ram is becoming too dreamy, hey nah? Maybe you should be teaching him some practical things, too."

"I teach him nothing but practical things," was Aakash's answer, which brought no satisfaction to the ever-fearful mother.

"No, I mean practical things like work in the fields, so that he can take over the farm and look after us some day."

"That won't be necessary."

"Aaii! You think we can ask your mahout to look after us all when we get old?"

"If he needs to learn these things, he will learn them, God willing, in good time. But I feel he will be a man of words. A man with a message. His understanding of spiritual matters is far beyond a boy of his years."

"Maybe so, but how will he support his family, let alone us? I want him to start thinking practically, so that if he doesn't take over Prakriti, at least he can become an engineer or something."

"Ma, you leave the boy to me." The tone in his voice was so firm, Jyoti Ma knew she could never challenge him. Till the end of their time together, she knew she would have to give all spiritual sovereignty to her husband as far as their son was concerned. But there were still his socks and kurtas to be washed, his food to be made and his hair to be brushed, and she took full charge over these things in her diminishing domain with all the authority of an empress.

3

Until Tulsi Devi arrived, Ram was an only child for many years. Alone, not just because he had no siblings for that period of time, but because there was nobody around but his father who could understand the world as he knew it. Unlike his sister in later years, he would never take to the fields and discover freedom away from the confines of his house. Instead, he built up a relationship with Silence and learnt how to enjoy its poise, like still water in a tub.

His studies were carried out in the main with a retired schoolmaster who came and taught him Hindi, because Jyoti Ma was determined that he wouldn't grow up illiterate in his own language as she had. The same master also taught him English and mathematics. Always courteous, he would squat on the ground as a sign of respect, whilst Ram sat at his desk. Looking up at his student, he would make corrections on the small slate and teach him facts, figures and skills that children three years his senior had difficulty learning. But then he would leave as silently as he had arrived, and Ram would have nobody to talk with except the servants and his parents.

A few times, the Master tested the water to gauge the level of happiness that his student felt. But always with modesty so as not to talk beyond his jurisdiction.

"Do you like living on this farm, bhaisahib?"

"I like it very much."

"Do you, muttlub, ever feel like leaving – getting out of here?"

"One day I will leave," answered Ram.

"If you are liking it, I can come and take you for a tour outside."

"That is very kind of you."

Having no firm commitment from his student, and not wanting any news of his suggestion to go back to the memsahib, the Master took the discussion no further. But he was still concerned that the boy never played like the other children, rolling a wheel along with a stick or practicing cricket throws. He had nobody to wrestle with, nobody to tease, nobody who could get him into any kind of trouble. So one day, the Master took the permission of the gods and brought his grandson Bahadur along to make friends.

Bahadur, usually a boisterous, happy, well-adjusted child, was immediately intimidated by the proportions of the farmhouse and the way the big people sat so high up from the ground. When his grandfather asked him to say hello to the bhaisahib, he opened his mouth, discovered that his voice had gone into seizure and instead put his hands together and gestured a humble "namaste." Immediately after, he squatted on the ground without looking up.

"I am thinking that the little boy might learn something from you, bhaisahib."

"What would you like to learn?" asked Ram kindly and willingly. There was no response, so the Master continued on, a ventriloquist on his grandson's behalf.

"He needs to learn how easy it is to study. Because you are so good, no?"

"Bahadur doesn't like to study?" It had never occurred to Ram that a child could not like learning. For him, learning was all there ever was.

"Just let him watch you, that will be honor enough."

Yet Bahadur's gaze didn't even reach Ram's feet, let alone watch what the bhaisahib could teach him.

The grandfather's face showed mixed emotions. On the one hand he was pleased that the boy was respectful, but on the other, disappointed that he wasn't making any headway in befriending saab's son.

"Let me teach him some English," suggested Ram, taking his chalk slate and squatting next to the dumbfounded child.

"Good morning, how do you do?"

The village boy's tongue slipped quickly around the new words. "Good morerning, how doo yoo doo?" Somehow it was easier communicating in a language other than his own.

"Would you like a cup of tea?"

"Wud yoo lika er cup of thee."

"Very good, Bahadur," coaxed the grandfather.

Ram started to get excited. "He must come every day, and I will teach him more and more. Say after me: I would like a toy car."

"I wood lika er toy kur."

"I would like a tin of sweets."

"I wood lika er thin of shweets."

The boy's grandfather started to look a little uncomfortable, knowing that it was no good to encourage all these 'wants' in a boy who was not destined to have his desires fulfilled. Already he could picture his daughter's unbearable sadness when her son demanded a toy car the next day. She would have nothing to give him but her love.

"Enough English for today. Let me tell you two the story of Ram Chandraji."

And so the teacher unfolded the story of the *Ramayana* as told by Valmiki. He was an excellent storyteller. Never sparing a gruesome detail of a bear's or monkey's mutilation in battle. Never restraining his fantasy about the many-headed demons whose heads were slain, only to reappear minutes later.

He told of the birth of Ram and his three brothers. How the Sun God stopped in his chariot for a month to rejoice at the new arrivals. How all the Gods showered flowers from the heavens. He told about the marriage of Ram and Sita. He told about the King of Ayodhya, Ram's father. How the time came for him to give his throne to Ram. Then he told of how Ram was cheated of his throne and sent to the forest for fourteen years.

"And there in the forest for fourteen years, Ram, Sita and Ram's brother Laxman lived in a humble hermitage, in total bliss, in nature, where everything they needed was provided. Until one day ..."

The Master told them how Sita stepped out of the chalk circle that protected the hermitage and was abducted by the ten-headed Ravan. He told of Ram and Laxman's journey to Lanka to rescue her and their return to the Kingdom of Ayodhya.

"And Ram, now that his fourteen-year exile was over, returned to celebrate victory in his home at Ayodhya. With lights, sweets, music and dance he was received as the new King ..."

The two boys looked at the Master as if he were Tulsi Das, the great sage himself, retelling the story. Ram's eyes reflected pictures of God-like men with bows and arrows, bare chests, golden crowns and armlets. He saw Ravan fight off the great bird that tried to stop his chariot from abducting Sita. He saw Sita shed her jewels to leave a trail for her husband. He saw the statues cry as the roar of battle was heard in Lanka. He saw the blood from the dead armies flow, and the final surrender and praise of Ravan when he recognised that he was being slain by the hand of God, and returning only unto him.

The story of Ram thawed the icy freeze in Bahadur's awestruck body. He became the same rubber boy he always was. He looked cheekily at Ram and said, "Let's go to the forest and play."

So they re-enacted the story in the gardens outside the house, using rulers for bows and sticks for arrows, whilst the Master sat squatting on the verandah watching. Ram wanted to be Ram, of course, and Bahadur was the ever-loyal Laxman.

That day Ram discovered the joy of play. For the first time in his life, he understood what it meant to be a child. He opened up the magic play chest of his imagination and out came kings, monkeys, bears, heroes, villains, chariots and a host of devas and devis, singing and chanting the glories of freedom, innocence and friendship. Never before had a dress-up box been so richly laden. Never before had a boy had fun as if it were he who was casting the very concept into creation. It was truly the Divine play that the Gods spun when they themselves took up incarnations as children.

The shrieks of joy could not be silenced. In a house where the servants had been tutored by the memsahib to talk in hushed tones only, the noise inevitably presented itself to Jyoti Ma's ears. The sounds made no excuses, showed no restraint and quite openly challenged her authority over the strict silence of Prakriti. It was a shameless disgrace, and she went to meet the onslaught of noise like all the armies of Lanka combined.

"Master! What on earth is going on?" shrieked Jyoti Ma. Her fury was so overwhelming, a few extra heads would have been required to contain it.

"Look, it's the wicked Ravan," cried the spring-like Bahadur with true abandon, and the authority worthy of the great Laxman.

"Then we must destroy him," shrieked Ram, pointing his stick into Jyoti Ma's thigh and tearing her sari. Yet he had love in his heart for her, as the true Ram would have had.

Ram's Master tried to grab the two boys, but they ran in different directions and nearly tore him in half. Being the only male who knew his place before Jyoti Ma, his blood was racing with fear.

"Stop them, you idiot. My house is not a bazaar! Ram, what has possessed you?"

"Bhaisahib, please listen to your mother. Stop it right now. Bahadur come here right now or you will get the biggest slap."

"Get out of my house."

"But Ma, we were only playing out the *Ramayana.*"

"Master, take that filthy boy and leave my house right now. And never come back again."

"Ma, what are you saying? He is my guru."

The Master caught Bahadur by the ear and pulled the half-inch of hair on his head. "Haram Zada, look at what trouble you've caused here," he muttered through clenched teeth. He was furious at Bahadur, but even more furious at his employer for showing no understanding for children. The two outsiders backed off like lepers into the gardens, and Bahadur ran the whole way back to the village so that his ageing grandfather could not catch him to give him the big slap that had been promised.

He was going to get the biggest hug he'd ever received instead, but at this stage he didn't know it.

When Jyoti Ma was alone with Ram she burst into tears.

"Look at my beautiful sari. My only son. And this is what you have done."

"Sorry, Ma."

"I never thought that you could do such a thing."

"We were playing."

"You're not going to play with that filthy boy ever again."

"But I am teaching him English. He must come every day."

"Ram, you don't understand. These people are dirty. You don't know where he's been and you don't know what you could catch from him."

"But his grandfather comes to teach me almost every day and he's never made me sick."

"Never again. That man has better sense than to come even to claim his last month's wages."

"Ma, it wasn't his fault. He is a good soul. His teaching is always wise. And he's never made me play any games before."

"But how dare he bring his people into my house without asking my permission?"

"Ma, if you like I will never play another game, but you cannot stop me from learning from my Master."

Ram was so humble in his reasoning that Jyoti Ma was forced to look at herself. How could she insist that Ram never played another game in his life? She felt so alone in her confusion. For the first time she felt she had no control over her own home and no control over the destiny of her child.

Moreover, she was wrong about the Master not coming back for his wages. That same day he came back, not to the farmhouse, but to the fields to find the man of the house. He found Aakash checking his notes, his mind buried in his theory of planting according to the movements of the planets, and in particular the seven rishis and the Pole Star.

"Saab, I am no longer able to teach your son," announced the older man, almost as if he were announcing his resignation rather than his dismissal.

"Master! We need you. You are not too old yet to give up on us! Come sit and talk."

"But Saab, I am unable."

"If it's a question of money," Aakash answered, "I can help you."

"It's my grandson."

"If he is sick, we can see to it that he gets the best treatment available. But you must keep teaching. It is truly your destiny."

"Memsahib has dismissed me because I brought my grandson to the lesson today and she caught them playing together. And so I am here for my wages."

Aakash fell silent for a moment in the face of the obstacle – his own wife. And then he faltered no longer, knowing that he could not let her get away with sacking yet another valuable employee. "Wait. Memsahib has no right to dismiss you. Arrive tomorrow, if you please, and be sure to bring your grandson. What is his name?"

"Bahadur."

"Master. From now on, Bahadur will be your student and mine.

He will have every privilege afforded to Ram, and I will double your wages for teaching them both. Just wait and see. *God will provide.*"

At first the Master was so taken aback at his sudden change of fortune, he fumbled with his overgrown stubble and thought only about how he could double the wages of his barber. His hand reached for a bidi, which he lit with great precision, inhaling a deep breath to consider the humiliation of returning, and balancing it against the golden future awaiting his grandson. He saw a grand wedding. A big dowry from Bahadur's future wife. He saw a respectable career in service for the wiry offspring of his daughter. And then he agreed.

"But memsahib has told me never to come to the house again."

"I will build a shed near this field where we can teach the boys," announced Aakash, being wise enough to render unto Caesar what is Caesar's. The house was Jyoti Ma's business, and he preferred to keep it that way. But the boy? He was his father's son from the start. As were the fields, the herbs, the sunshine and the open expanse of the hills.

Ram's Master, old as he was, skipped half the way home to his village, throwing loose paise over the precipices at the side of the road, kissing the coins before they leapt for joy into the valleys. On the way he stopped at a small Ganesh shrine carved into a rock facing the misty distances of Simla. There he offered his last handful of loose coins in joyful abandon. Already he was on the best wage he'd ever received in his entire life of service, and now it was to be doubled! Ganesh should be praised, for if he really was the remover of obstacles, he could not have found a greater one than Jyoti Ma. Oh blessed Ganesh. If Ganesh could do such miracles, he surely had the right to be worshiped in every home before any other God!

When the Master reached the village, he walked through the narrow cobbled streets in the bazaar till he came to his house at the top of the hill. Looking up to the window, he caught Bahadur's eye. With the lightning reflexes of an eleven-year-old, Bahadur jumped down from the top of the ladder-like stairs and brushed past his grandfather to find his friend Ajay, the son of the mattress-maker.

"Come here," cried the old man, but Bahadur was already as invisible as he was the year before he was born.

His good humor undiminished, the Master ran up the stairs as fast as his old legs would bend, to break the good news to his daughter. Since the death of her husband, she had returned to her father's home with her three children. All her needs were always met in her father's house, and now it seemed her desires could flourish as never before.

Bahadur was summoned back from Ajay's house and met the news with some trepidation. He had really enjoyed frolicking in the gardens of Prakriti, but even his richly fertile imagination couldn't entertain any possibilities of a return visit. Not to mention the prospect of studying under his grandfather, who would make sure that he was always on best behavior and never let him off any homework.

"But I don't want to study there, I like my school."

Bahadur's mother looked at him, her jaw dropped wide enough to hold a Himalayan apple.

"Nay, nay, bacha," spoke his mother, "the memsahib will be very nice to you now that you're her son's companion."

"She won't even see you, beta," added his grandfather, "we are making a special house for you to study in."

"If you make me study there, I will run away."

The old man laughed nervously and gave Bahadur a big hug.

"Beta, I know you would never disappoint your family," he replied.

So the next day, Bahadur and the Master set off down the narrow mountain road to Prakriti. The old man walked fast, because he wanted to get there and settle things quickly. He didn't know how to go about the new routine. Neither did he know where he would find Aakash and Ram. And there was always the possibility that his employer had changed his mind after discussing the previous day's events with his wife.

The Master's mind was immediately set at ease when, on arrival at Prakriti, the two of them were guided to the top terrace in the layer of fields, which pushed itself against a large rockface in the mountainside. Hollowed into the rockface was a cave, and inside it were three desks, chairs and chalkboards already laid out. Outside a latrine pit had been dug. Everything was ready and waiting in the new school. Only Ram was missing. So the two villagers squatted and waited inside the wide mouth of the cave for the lord of the lesson, watching the mountains stretching out to either side in the morning sunshine.

After an hour, Aakash appeared, holding Ram's hand.

"So this is your grandson Bahadur," spoke Aakash. "Welcome to your new school. Your nana is going to teach you here with Ram, and I will come every day to teach you some things as well."

Bahadur looked up doubtfully at his grandfather. This hadn't been the arrangement at all. But then the boy looked at Aakash and saw no anger in his face to match the fury of the memsahib's. Ram looked at Bahadur as if he were welcoming back a long-lost friend and the skinny village boy grinned with relief.

Aakash stayed for the first hour as the Master settled his two students into their morning Hindi lesson. On two chalkboards the Devanagari script started to appear: Bahadur's letters only one step away from drawings; Ram's letters as sophisticated as any adult's. But within the hour there was improvement, even though Bahadur's gaze kept returning to the spectacular view from the mouth of the cave, and the holy cascading mountains beyond.

Over the following months, Aakash grew to love the companion he had all but bought for his son. For the first few lessons that Aakash taught, Bahadur sat in silence whilst Ram answered all his father's questions. But Bahadur soon found his voice when Aakash presented the hungry boy with sweets freshly cooked in Jyoti Ma's kitchen. His tactics worked and before long Bahadur came and sat on Aakash's lap and tugged on his shirt with the same familiarity as Ram.

Every day the treats kept arriving. One day Aakash brought some fennel seeds from the fields for the boys to chew on.

"My papa used to eat this and I would smell it all the time."

"Take some home for him," Aakash said, handing over a large armful of buds.

"I'll have to take it a very long way," Bahadur said. "Papa has passed away."

Aakash looked at his small frame and thought about the man who had fathered this child, picking him up as an infant and loving him for every gram he weighed. He thought about how little he knew of the boy he taught. How different his life must be from his own son's.

"I can share my papa with you," Ram said in a voice so noble it melted his father's heart further. Bahadur went and touched the feet of Aakash, who pulled him up to sit on his lap.

That evening, when Aakash was having dinner alone with Jyoti Ma, he thought of his village student and wondered if his wife should ever be told about the cave at the top of the fields.

He hesitated. Since he had announced his plan to teach the two boys outside the farmhouse, Jyoti Ma had maintained resolute silence on the issue. On that particular day he decided to try to break the silence. He started to tell her about Bahadur.

"Ma, you know that Bahadur is not as bad as you thought. He is just a boy –"

No sooner had the tainted name passed Aakash's lips than Jyoti Ma's voice climbed a shrill octave higher. "Boys like him become murderers when they grow up!"

She was so angry her hands were shaking. The closest vent for her anger was a roti made too thick, and the next closest thing its maker, the cook. She screamed at him.

"When will the simpleton get it right? I've taught him a thousand times now. They're always either too thin or too thick." Jyoti Ma's accusations were sharp enough for the cook in the nearby kitchen to cut himself on a blunt knife.

The cook came in, took away his handicapped roti and backed off into the kitchen. Aakash felt overwhelmed with sadness that the people he treated with dignity and respect in the fields were treated as animals in his own house. Determined to make a petition on behalf of the cook, he started a lesson in such a simple tone, he could have been giving it to his two boys in the cave.

"Jyoti, it's not right to complain so harshly to the poor cook. He does his best, and you make him throw away the bread. Half the people he knows don't have enough bread to fill their bellies. And here you are making him throw away his rotis."

"You have no idea," answered Jyoti Ma, "how hard it is to get him to put anything on our table. When he came here he was absolutely raw. I spent hours teaching him and still he doesn't learn!"

"But before you came there was no problem getting food on our table. We ate in abundance on a nightly basis. You must give the servants the confidence to shop and cook themselves."

"And have them steal from me left, right and center? If I didn't supervise them they'd be taking half of the food back to feed their own families!"

"And what of that? They have nothing. How can people like you or I even begin to imagine what it must be like for them?"

"Oh, so would you like me to give them my gold jewelery? Or my collection of saris? And see their wives walking around the dirt in my clothes? No. I cannot agree. These people must know their place."

Aakash sighed and allowed himself the rare indulgence of imagining himself married to someone less harsh. Someone who could love humanity in the same way that he did. He'd met Jyoti Ma's sister Pyari on many occasions since their marriage and she seemed to have all these qualities, and more …

4

When Ram was almost a teenager, Aakash started talking about becoming a renunciant and taking sannyas.

Jyoti Ma, however, thought it was high time that her husband brought his thoughts back to his family. She was worried about a recent turn of events. Aakash was irretrievably absorbed in a fourth volume of spiritual literature that had arrived by mail order from an ashram in Calcutta.

"Already, Aakash, you have left for your blessed hills. Every wife in Himachal enjoys more company with her husband than I do. And every one of them has more children. I want to give you another child, before it's too late."

Jyoti Ma knew that to conceive once more, her timing would have to be absolutely perfect. To seduce Aakash out of his silence she would have to know not just her own rhythms, but the rhythms of the cosmos. She would have to know when the last leaf fell from his tree, and be there to catch it when it did.

One night, on the moon of Karva Chauth, she took the traditional fast of married women to pray for the health and longevity of her husband. Being so used to the good things in life, fasting wasn't easy, but this time she had strength of purpose to starve her senses. She watched for the dusk to fall into its red bed beyond the mountains and waited for the moon to rise. When she caught sight of it, she carried a bowl of water to Aakash, who was sitting in his room alone.

Jyoti Ma was dressed in her bridal sari and a newly fitted blouse (for she was several stone heavier than when she wore the matching blouse made for her wedding). When she entered the room she reflected the moon in the water, as was the tradition, and then her husband's face. Aakash looked down into the water, seeing the moon behind his head, fluid and rippling. He could see his expression shaking, his beard disappearing into the darkness.

Jyoti Ma, noticing how absorbed he was in the image, took the bowl away and fed him sweets before breaking the fast herself. Aakash attended to his wife's rituals and then went back to the fourth volume of spiritual writings that had been absorbing him completely over the past few weeks.

Jyoti Ma went back to her bedroom, that opened out onto the wide back verandah to a view of the cradle of mountains nearby. Thinking that she must try even harder, she dressed once more, this time in her most alluring pink and silver sari. She tied pearl strings into her hair and entered Aakash's room at a time she divined as perfect.

At that moment Aakash was reading about the responsibilities of a householder. About the workings of Divine Grace. The stupidity of assigning one's own efforts a greater place than that of self-surrender. The importance of seeking union with God at every opportunity in the home. The importance of woman as Goddess.

He was stooped over the books at his desk and the room was dimly lit when Jyoti Ma entered. She placed a handful of flower buds over the book he was reading and started to unwind the six meters of silver threaded sari that separated her from the bliss of a marriage she could only dream of.

"Jyoti, what all do you want? You are not tired?" Aakash asked, wanting to continue his reading without putting his lessons into practice.

Jyoti Ma had already started massaging him with some freshly made almond oil, and he started to warm to her. She undressed him more carefully than any Moghul concubine, and for several frozen minutes he was captivated in her spell – that of an extraordinarily beautiful seductress.

He breathed in the mountain air. A deep breath. And then, with the potency of a man who has been gathering up his powers in the practice of self-restraint, he surrendered. He was looking at her now and seeing all that she could be. Jyoti Ma welcomed his gaze. She looked beautiful, because she felt it. He finished undressing her so that the moonlight shone on her bare skin through the open verandah doors. And then he followed the moon as it covered her. She was his Goddess, raised on a cushion, as if on an altar, spreading herself open to the fertility of her God. She donated her body to his enjoyment and greater glory, and in doing so lost herself entirely in her own pleasure.

After such a consummation there was absolutely no doubt that a child would follow.

Ten moons later, to the very day, Tulsi Devi was born. Aakash waited for news in the fields with Xavier, his Christian friend, and Govinda the mahout. It was one of those rare open-ended nights when he was able to enjoy the company of his old friends without having to answer to anyone, because his wife was otherwise engaged. In the distance they heard the moans of childbirth, as they sat on a mound of earth discussing ways to unite the different religions of the world. At last, the midwife's helper was sent and Aakash left his friends to go and meet his new daughter.

The new baby girl was as radiant and beautiful as the moon of Karva Chauth that shone on the night she was conceived. She had none of the usual dried or red-patched skin. She stared wide-eyed back at her father, who picked her up and whispered in her ear, "My child, may you live to see through the illusion of existence."

Jyoti Ma, dressed now, the blood wiped away to look decent for her husband, watched the two of them with exhaustion and a hero's pride. She had hoped for a girl child all these months and cursed everyone who wished another son on her. She had been determined, too, that her daughter would have all the beauty her mother lacked. Every day whilst her belly swelled she had concentrated on having a beautiful baby girl, telepathically communicating the blueprint for her daughter to follow from the womb. The baby would have fair skin, dimples, angel's eyes and thick curly hair.

Tulsi Devi grew to be the very picture her mother had dreamed up – a mixture between Jyoti Ma's sister, Pyari, and Aakash. She had a moon doll's face, with eyelashes so thick and long they could have been painted on by a miniature artist. As soon as she took her first smile, two perfectly symmetrical dimples made their first indents.

However, in her determination to secretly create a beautiful daughter in utero, Jyoti Ma had given no guidelines for personality. So one of the first things Tulsi Devi realized, when she reached the age of realizations, was that she did not want to be like her mother. If anything, she wanted to be like Ram, because Ram occupied the exciting world of studies and her father's world of the farm. Ram was living proof that a child could grow up. That childhood itself was not a permanent disability.

As soon as she learnt to walk, Tulsi Devi started running free, with no role models to guide her. Everything was of her own invention. She played games on her own, drawing patterns in the earth. When Ram was not at his classroom in the caves with Bahadur, she would pull at his legs and make him shrink down to her height so he could occupy her world. And he would play along, a giant in the world of dwarves.

She was religious in her own way, but more ritualistic than her big brother Ram. When she was very young she created her own puja room in the farmhouse, making deities out of her various dolls. She would say her confused prayers, asking for the good health and happiness of each doll in turn.

But mostly she spent her time on the farm, because her mother's fear of the outside world only made it more intriguing for her. Going out of the house made her feel heroic, because there were all kinds of untold dangers beyond the verandah's edge. Anything could happen.

She was always a lover of animals and would spend a little time every day with Ganesh the elephant, and also with the mahout who took charge of him. Together they would lollop around the farm, with Tulsi Devi shouting instructions to the farm workers with the exact shrill frequency she'd learnt from her mother. She was a Boadicean-style princess, in charge of armies, empires, galaxies.

Being the only daughter of a well-to-do family, as a toddler Tulsi Devi was laden with gold jewelery whenever she went out of the house. But before too long she'd always be found rolling in the dirt, or falling out of one of the bushes in the orchard with bent bangles and broken chains.

And then the jewelery started to go missing. Some of the bangles were given as presents to the daughters of the migrant workers, who left as silently as they arrived, wearing gold instead of cheap white metal. One farm worker, at Tulsi Devi's suggestion, even managed to exchange a half-broken wheelbarrow for the child's gold choker.

Tulsi Devi was once given her mother's diamond ring as a diversion when the car broke down. When the car was fixed and Jyoti Ma asked for it back, the ring was nowhere to be found. The driver, mother and father spent the next hour on hands and knees, searching the roadside, scraping back layers of dust.

Only the ayah ever knew the truth of the missing diamond ring. She found it, along with half-digested dhal and subjee, in Tulsi Devi's nappy. As she was the only one who ever changed and cleaned nappies, she had no reservations about quietly keeping it aside as the Kohinoor of her own daughter's dowry.

After many such incidents, Tulsi Devi was left to roam unadorned, but she looked as glorious as ever with her dark mop of perfect curls, rosy cheeks, soft brown eyes and mud for jewelery. Whenever she was asked where her jewels had gone, she would smile sweetly and say she didn't know. Neither did she know what happened to the trail of ayahs her mother hired to look after her, who, like characters in a fairy story, lost their jobs for not giving the Queen the right answer.

Many years later, Tulsi Devi would recall how her mother made such a fuss over her beauty that it almost made her want to take a razor and scar herself for life. But life had a way of making its own scars, without too much conscious effort. And these scars Tulsi Devi learnt to disguise, so she maintained an aristocratic beauty, even into her old age. Such a good mistress of disguise she was, that nobody could have guessed what tragedies were sealed beneath her fair unwrinkled skin and warm smile.

5

By the time Bahadur was sixteen, the classroom in the cave had become a talking point in the village, making him a reluctant emperor amongst his peers. Everyone knew that fortune had smiled on his family, whilst laughing at the rest of the village. That it had swooped him up, like an eagle picking up a mouse.

Bahadur couldn't fit back into the village anymore than he could fit back into the womb that had carried him. Sometimes he felt as if he were living a double existence, with only a short stretch of road to separate his two lives. On his way home after class he would walk along that mountain road, slowly bringing his thoughts down to earth. Trying not to arrive in the village like a mortal returning from the heavenly palace of Indra.

Nobody except Ram and Aakash understood the boy's growing urge to break free from the life he had been born to.

When Bahadur turned sixteen, the inevitable discussions about his marriage started in earnest. A daughter of a hotelkeeper in nearby Kasauli soon became the pinnacle of everything he could ever achieve. Bahadur, as was the custom, was barely consulted about any of his future plans. Daunted by the thought that he would soon be a married man, swept up in the plot that surrounded him, he started to take days off school. When Bahadur hadn't turned up for three days in a row and the

Master was mute for excuses, Aakash and Ram left their cave and went down the road to the village to find him.

It was rare for the village to be visited by the landed gentry. The two people who walked up the narrow cobbled streets were the gods whom everyone served. And if they didn't serve them directly, they served someone, who served someone, who served someone who did. So when they passed the wooden shopfronts, the noisy, playful village life subsided as people performed for the two gods, on best behavior. Dutifully all the children and adults paid their respects with a gracious "namaste," and all the small children rushed off in a gang to find Bahadur.

Through the little passages at the other side of the village Aakash and Ram found Bahadur watching a visiting three-man paupers' circus. One boy, his eyes lined with kajal, was balancing on a thali and sliding across a dangerously hung rope. A little girl, with soot and lice in her hair, carried a copper plate around the small crowd. Ram caught Bahadur's eye and went round to greet his friend with a hug. The little girl pushed her plate into Aakash's belly and he gave her a generous donation: enough to feed the whole circus for six months. The urchin on the thali jumped down and grabbed the money, put it in a knotted hankie and stared up at his benefactor, his kajaled eyes framing a look of complete awe. Often, if a moneyed shopkeeper were watching the circus, they would cajole him into giving a second donation, but this boy knew that when the Gods rain flowers, you never ask for more.

Ram turned to his friend. "Come, Bahadur," he said, and the three of them left the circus and set off together.

"I can't live in the village anymore," Bahadur said, looking at nobody, simply setting his eyes in the direction of Prakriti.

"What's on your mind?" Aakash asked. "What did you do today that stopped you from coming?"

"I helped the mithai wala cook jalabis." And then he continued. "They want to start arranging my marriage. You see, I just can't live there anymore."

"If you don't wish to stay in the village, you may stay with me," Ram announced, as if it were he alone who lived in the farmhouse.

Thinking fast about the consequences of these words, Aakash made a suggestion. "You come and stay as soon as I've built that shed I was always going to make for a classroom. We'll put a bed in it and bring you food."

The prospect of a refugee on the farm appealed to Ram, who often wished for company at nights. Bahadur could be his sibling, closer in proximity than ever before. They could watch stars together, the way he often did with his father, picking out the constellations that influenced their lives.

"In our next life, Bahadur, we'll be brothers," predicted Ram. "But for now you must come and stay in our shed."

Bahadur's heart warmed at the prospect of returning to Prakriti. Since he'd stopped his education, the village had no charm for him. He had missed Ram and Aakash, but he felt too guilty to return with a wedding invitation. He loved them, and he knew his love was in good care, but he also knew he could never be what either of them was. For sure the ocean that bound together all souls would find it easier to unify a tiger and a rabbit than it could unite Bahadur with these two people that he so loved.

Before accepting the offer to stay at Prakriti, Bahadur thought about the prospect of being an outsider, watching the people he loved leave him every day to go to their big house. But then he thought about the outsider that he had already become in his own village. If his fate was to live always on the outside, so be it, he thought wisely. And with this insight he accepted the invitation to stay on the outskirts of Prakriti, in limbo, until fate decided his path in life and gave him a direction that was truly his own.

So the arrangements were made, but all the workers were instructed to keep the new resident's arrival a hallowed secret. That way memsahib would never find out, or be tempted to stretch her authority further afield.

Bahadur stayed his first night at Prakriti on a string bed in the cave. The sun fell behind the hills and Ram stayed as long as he could without being missed for the evening meal. Then Bahadur was completely alone, with only the stars for companions. The stars that pointed to other realms, far beyond the known world.

In the darkness he heard the bellows of Ganesh, followed by the sound of the mahout soothing him with a song in the darkness. Then silence fell and he was gripped with a fear that his life would never be the same again. He lay prostrate in the body of a youngster, not yet able to inhabit the full chest of a man, yet no longer a boy. He imagined himself walking on the road between the farm and his village. The safe middle ground which seemed to belong only to him.

It occurred to Bahadur that to be nowhere was actually the same as being everywhere. In this reverberating space he felt himself being called to move forward and take his first steps toward eternity. The calling was so loud it could have filled the entire night sky and the galaxies beyond with its wide-open invitation to explore further. Yet all that noise was contained in a shell of Silence.

The moon hung like an omen: detached, immobile and solitary, witness to the long night that lay ahead. Bahadur stared at the moon until his eyelids closed and the thin sliver of light imprinted on his sleepy retinas, only to turn into images of snakes that wove out of every nook and cranny of his dreams in the thick of the night.

6

A circle of conspiracy was established at the farm to prevent Jyoti Ma from discovering that Bahadur was camping out on the premises. None of the servants breathed a word to her about the farm's new refugee. A few sheds were constructed further down into the valley toward Simla, and when she asked what they were for, Aakash just told her that they were necessary, without offering any further information that could amount to a lie.

The bed he took from the house, he said, was simply to be used for rest. Jyoti Ma never left the house to wander the fields at nighttime, so there was no chance that she would ever find out exactly who was resting on it.

Ram often stayed out in the evenings at the sheds, but his mother was too preoccupied with his younger sister Tulsi Devi to worry about his whereabouts, and Aakash covered up well for his son. Only one person in the household had any desire to break the conspiracy, and that was Bulbul, Jyoti Ma's maidservant.

For some reason Bulbul seemed to be immune to the memsahib's torrent of criticisms, and she claimed the ground at Jyoti Ma's right hand as her mistress's indispensable ally. Whenever there was abuse to be showered on the servants, Bulbul let it roll off her as if she were a wax model. Only once did Jyoti Ma tell her to stop smiling when another servant was soaking up her outrage. Nobody quite knew why Bulbul was exempt from the ruler's tyranny, not even Bulbul. Perhaps it was her confidence that demanded respect. A confidence that came from the fact that her father had been a valued servant of a British officer, with many privileges way beyond those of his caste.

Bulbul was an arch-manipulator but, to all appearances, an angel (if you didn't care to look at the hooves that met the ground instead of feet). She often took pleasure in advising memsahib how to treat the other servants, and Jyoti Ma, not always familiar with the common law of the lower classes, would give in to her recommendations. She also ingratiated herself by pointing out every small misdemeanor and swindle, as if she herself were the memsahib instead of her henchwoman.

Thus the pages of the book that showed "how these people really are" grew daily in abundance toward the goal of being finally bound and presented on Judgement Day. Bulbul produced evidence on the dhobi, whose wife was caught wearing memsahib's sari to a local wedding during the time it had been taken to be laundered. Then the gardener was found guilty of being intoxicated at work on the bhang he'd cultivated on memsahib's very own soil.

Indeed, if caste hadn't separated them, Bulbul and Jyoti Ma would have been sisters in the cosmic courts of condemnation. They even took on the same proportions, with the same indignant gaze and mismatched eyes. But as it happened, the servant was to remain a servant and the memsahib the memsahib, due to constrictions of time and space that created a frozen snapshot, at least for this lifetime. Eventually Bulbul would leave like all the other servants, but her time of glory was a catalyst in the destiny of the family that owned the estate.

That destiny would have been different if Bulbul had not had a son, Raja, who was very similar to Bahadur in looks and intelligence. They were so similar, in fact, that Bulbul couldn't help asking why fate had snatched the one of them to put on a pedestal and left her own beloved son standing on level ground.

When she heard the story of how her memsahib had banished Bahadur from the house, her indignation grew even stronger. "Why, the two boys share the same caste, the same age and the same sky. And yet one of them commits an ugly crime and gets rewarded for it with special treatment from saab."

Bulbul couldn't help but feel that her son's life could be much improved if he too were allowed to consort with saab and Ram. If the young lord needed a companion, Raja would make an equally suitable one.

At every opportunity, Bulbul made sure that Raja accompanied her to the house in the evenings when Ram was around. She would tease Ram like a big sister, which he never much enjoyed. Her feigned playfulness always missed its target, as Ram felt uncomfortable that an adult should be acting like a child. Worse still, treating him as if he were still a child, squeezing his cheeks and cajoling him to eat his dinner as if he were a four-year-old, when he had always left empty thalis at mealtimes.

There was another miscalculation on her part. She assumed that Jyoti Ma and Aakash actually discussed plans for their children as other parents did. It was with this inkling that Bulbul asked memsahib if her son could also go to the classes in the cave. "We will see," answered Jyoti Ma, full knowing that the last thing she wanted was another parasite at Prakriti with expectations above his caste. Besides which, teaching was the business of her husband and she had created an apartheid system between his world and hers.

Unable to make headway with memsahib directly, Bulbul took the next big step she'd been planning and asked Ram if he could teach her son English. Ram hesitated, but then agreed, knowing that time wasn't counted in hours but in lifetimes. He knew, too, that his mother wouldn't tolerate Raja in the house, so the idea of teaching him floated around undecidedly, never having the material circumstances to land, take root, or flower.

Seeing that she could not propagate her plan in memsahib's house, Bulbul sought to promote her son's advancement outside its walls. Bahadur's move to Prakriti presented itself as the perfect soil for seeding her plan.

"This nobody," thought Bulbul, "has managed to cheat his way forward in life from nowhere."

Bulbul considered the audacity, mentally circumnavigating the event, calculating its dimensions and assessing its power and potential. She could see it take a physical form. Feel its heat. Give it a color and texture. It became a weapon for her, and one that she felt fully capable of wielding.

"Memsahib has a right to know what is going on under her very nose," she thought, working out exactly how she could unveil her latest discovery in front of her mistress.

The opportunity for Bulbul to sing her song, and to sing it sweetly, arose soon enough, but first she had to make a few rearrangements to the order of things.

Bulbul looked around for an object that would serve as Bahadur's shroud. Her eyes immediately rested on a small Kashmiri carpet in the guest bedroom. Without checking to see if anyone was watching, she folded it up, wrapped it in some saris and smuggled it out to her own quarters. There she presented it to Raja and told him to take it to Bahadur's room in the sheds and spread it out on the floor. "But whatever you do, don't let anyone see you."

Raja was quite unaware of his mother's plot, yet he agreed to be her accomplice, more through obligation than through any desire to become familiar with Ram. He didn't even question her purpose, thinking of his task as just another errand.

That evening Raja made his way toward the sheds at the far end of the fields, carefully avoiding all the seedlings on the way. When he arrived at the sheds, there was no need to burn any lights, because Bahadur was already there, lying on his bed staring at the ceiling in preparation for sleep, the only event left in the day after school.

"This is for you. I was sent to lay it down in your room."

Bahadur, pleased to have a companion at a time when he was often alone, asked Raja to sit down and give him news of his old school and the village. Raja told stories about their peers, and Bahadur listened like a man reliving his life in his twilight years.

When Raja had finished, Bahadur asked him, "Raja, do you ever miss the village?"

"It's much better here," Raja answered. "They look after you very nicely. Look, they're giving you a carpet for your room." Then he added, "Do you miss your family?"

The question made Bahadur's chest squeeze shut. Raja, sensing he had disturbed his old schoolfriend, said, "It doesn't matter. You are bhaisahib's brother. He and saab are your family." And with that, he left the carpet as consolation.

"Did you do it?" asked Bulbul as soon as she returned to their quarters from her evening duties.

"What, the carpet? Yes, it's in Bahadur's room."

"Good." The carpet was unrolled, and Bahadur's fate was laid down with it, she thought. Down on the ground where it belonged.

The next day she was oiling and brushing Jyoti Ma's hair. Just as she made a bun and stuck in the pins, a little more roughly than usual, she thought to drop the first piece of camphor into the fire.

"Memsahib, did you give permission for Bahadur to take that carpet back to his room on the farm?"

Jyoti Ma was familiar with the way Bulbul revealed information about the other servants, and she knew it was her job to tease the information out further.

"I didn't give permission for him to take any carpet. Has he taken it back to the village?"

"No, he was walking back to his room in the shed."

"He is living *here?*" Jyoti Ma brayed, her face so indignant a professional clown could have painted it on.

"I saw him leaving with it yesterday."

"Which carpet?"

"In your guest bedroom."

Jyoti Ma got off the bed clutching her bun, not waiting for Bulbul to finish speaking. In the guest bedroom she instantly noticed the oblong rim of dust which framed the empty space. No further evidence was required for her to file her case. She walked out of the house, through the garden and onto the farm. The farm workers glanced up at her and stopped their labors, knowing that it was almost as rare to see a walking scarecrow as it was to see memsahib taking to the fields.

Bulbul watched her from the front verandah: saw her hitch up her sari and stumble over clods of earth as her chappals slipped away on uneven ground. She saw her nearing the sheds and smiled as she anticipated Bahadur's dismissal from the farm. More than anything, Bulbul wanted to bear witness to that moment of shame, but she knew that her own sense of satisfaction would have given away the game if she had followed memsahib out on her mission.

Once inside the shed Jyoti Ma knew at once that Bulbul was telling the truth. There, unbeknown to her, Bahadur had been lurking, able to take whatever he wished from her house. As he wasn't in the shed at that moment, she searched around clumsily, pushing a small pile of the boy's clothes to one side, barely wanting to touch them in case she contracted his diseases.

Unable to find anymore of her possessions, she walked back into the fields, slamming the door shut behind her, and headed off in the direction of the cave.

Although she was aware she was transgressing boundaries, Jyoti Ma felt exultant with self-righteousness, confident that her husband would finally have to reconsider the waif he'd taken on. She knew with absolute certainty that this would be the end of Bahadur. That he could no longer show his face on her property till the end of his days.

And she was right.

If only she had accepted her carpet as a small loss, she would not have stood to lose everything else that she had ever been given. But how was she to know that? All she could sense was her fury, and that knew no consequences. She had a personal vendetta against that little villain, and even though years had passed since he first incited Ram to violence against her, she had not seen him to witness the changes in him. With her head held high she entered the classroom just as Bahadur was reading out a passage from the *Ramayana:* Ram's speech at his departure from Ayodhya.

> In his agitation he could not speak; grief overmastered him and wild anguish of heart. After most affectionately bowing his head at his feet, Raghunath arose and begged permission to depart. "Father, give me your blessing and commands; why so dismayed at this time of rejoicing? From excessive attachment, sire, to any beloved object honor is lost and disgrace incurred." At this the love-sick king arose and taking Raghupati by the arm made him sit down: "Harken, my son; the sages say that Rama is the lord of all creation, animate or inanimate; that God, after weighing good and bad actions and mentally considering them, apportions their reward, and the doer reaps the fruit of his own doings: this is the doctrine of the Scriptures and the verdict of mankind ..."

Jyoti Ma stood staring at Aakash. Her very gaze made Bahadur's voice fade into silence. It was the first time he had set eyes on his best friend's mother since she had banished him from the gardens and sent curses to track him back to his village. Seeing her made him feel as if he were back where he had started, a foot shorter and runny-nosed, not the man he now was. Just seeing Jyoti Ma made him feel as if he had committed an unforgivable crime.

Ram and Aakash stared back at Jyoti Ma with the amazement of two people looking at a night animal out stalking in the daytime. Aakash was self-composed, but to show his wife that she was acting incorrectly by disrupting this lesson, he addressed her as if he were a shopkeeper.

"And how may I help you?" he asked, searching out an explanation for her untimely arrival.

"You can help me by getting that thief off this farm." Jyoti Ma raised her arm and pointed her finger at Bahadur, as if she were shooting an arrow at his brow.

Knowing there must be some serious cause for her visit, Aakash was not alarmed at her accusation. If anything, he was slightly relieved, as was Ram, knowing that Bahadur would never be capable of stealing anything.

"Perhaps we can discuss this problem in the evening hours," Aakash continued, treating her revelation as a temporary impediment to the day's discourse.

"That rat is stealing things from under our noses and you are protecting him as if he were a member of our family. Good God, man, are you going to let these people walk all over you? Just go to his room in the shed and see the carpet he stole."

"On my honor, memsahib, *I tell you,* I did not steal that carpet," Bahadur answered, his innocence showing through in his look of concern.

"So, what? Did it fly into your room?"

Bahadur stared down at the ground, admitting defeat. He knew that this was the end of his time at Prakriti and he didn't wish to prolong it. Neither did he feel the need to clear his name by pointing his finger at Raja. With an unfaltering gaze of acceptance he looked up at Jyoti Ma as if to ask, "And what will you have them do to me next?"

"How dare you even stay on the farm. If you are going to keep him here just don't expect me to stay as well," continued Jyoti Ma.

"My dear, can you not contain yourself? There will be some explanation. Believe me," answered Aakash.

"Well then, keep him if he's so valuable to you. But just don't expect me to stay. Arré, take him, if it pleases you."

She glared at the three conspirators who all stared back at her dispassionately, and for the first time in many years, Jyoti Ma felt her place in the world commanded no power or respect, let alone love. If there was an instant when she might have felt abandoned by her Creator, it was then. All because of that stupid Bahadur. It had been a long time since she'd broken down into incontrollable tears and this time, when she did, nobody tried to comfort her. What she needed was to receive some small recognition – some love. More than that, she needed Bahadur out of her life so that she wouldn't hate the people she most wanted to love.

Bahadur looked at the Himalayan peaks that silhouetted Jyoti Ma's bowed head, as if to search out an answer. She noticed his unfocused gaze, and noted how the guilty can never look their accusers straight in the eye. And he did feel guilt, but not for the crime for which he stood accused: rather, it was the guilt of standing between two parties, like a border guard between two nations. It wasn't a situation that he'd ever sought. He had always seen his position at Prakriti as tenuous, always felt Jyoti Ma's presence whenever he walked past the jacaranda tree that brought the farmhouse into view. She was the woman who could look out of the windows at any moment, and to even come into her field of vision was more strain than he could ever wish upon her.

"I will go," he said. "I am sorry to have caused you so much trouble."

"You will not go!" Aakash's voice held a sternness that his student had never heard before.

"But I must, Pitaji," answered Bahadur.

"You must listen to your teacher," said Aakash, continuing to look at

Jyoti Ma, waiting for her to show some strength of character to match his. Instead she went, one last kajaled tear making a muddy river across her cheek.

Jyoti Ma walked back to the farmhouse, avoiding all the laborers so she could preserve her dignity and image of invincibility. Regaining her composure and haughtiness on the way home, she kept thinking that if she was going to lose, she was going to make everyone lose. She was going to pack her bags and leave that very night. That would show them. Then they would all be begging for her return when they saw how everything fell apart without her.

Ram, Bahadur and Aakash were already thinking about how to appease Jyoti Ma, but there were no simple apologies to be made. Her grievance was too old and too brittle to yield, and so following a long discussion, Ram surprised the small group with his conclusion.

"It is not you who must go, but I."

Aakash was not bewildered by his son's solution. He was quick to realize that if he himself could have got up and gone, he would have done just that. There were migrant workers younger than his son who had left homes higher up in the hills to work on the farm, and he trusted that Ram was equipped with knowledge way beyond his years to cope with the demands of daily life.

"If you are going, I will go with you, Ram," added Bahadur.

Suddenly the departure of Ram and Bahadur appeared to all three of them as if it were a forgone conclusion. It was as if their games as Ram and Laxman as children had been a prophecy, preparing them for this moment when they would have to leave the comfort of Prakriti and make their spiritual journey in search of peace – not just peace with Jyoti Ma, but with the laws that govern the universe. Like Ram and Laxman in the *Ramayana*, they would soon be going into the forest, stripping themselves of everything they knew, to discover who they truly were. Walking toward the Silence.

Ram's father felt a sense of pride, mixed with a longing to accompany the two young men on their adventure. In his own studies he was discovering the boundlessness of consciousness, but his boys were about to take off into the wilderness to experience its unadulterated substance. To bathe in the forest streams in the bliss of freedom. To scale mountains and see visions of grander realities.

"Where will you go?" asked Aakash, his question giving not even a hint of challenge to their suggestion.

"Rishikesh."

"Rishikesh, *yes!*"

"I must make some provision for you both."

"Pitaji, please do not worry about our welfare. You always said that God will provide and so far we have never gone without our needs being met. Why should we be deserted now?"

They walked out that afternoon. Aakash gave them all the money on his person and a promise to send more with a messenger should they need it. Ram did not go back to his room to pick up any clothes or to say goodbye to his mother or little sister, because he knew they would not let him go. Instead he set off on his journey in the clothes he stood up in, not knowing where he would rest his head at sunset. Like his namesake, who was sent to the forests in exile, Ram knew he would not return to Prakriti for some time.

Ram had total trust in his heart, fired with excitement and mixed with a sense of nostalgia for the only home he had ever known. He held his hands together and touched the feet of his father. When he stood up again face-to-face with Aakash he said, "Pitaji, I hope that one day I will be able to return the faith you have shown in me," then added, "Every step of progress I make on my path I make for both of us."

Bahadur touched Aakash's feet and said simply, "Pitaji, thank you for being a father to me. I will never forget your kindness and wisdom."

The three of them hugged and parted. Ram took one last look at his house and pulled Bahadur's arm to keep them both moving before they could change their minds.

Once Aakash had bade them farewell he went back to the farmhouse, filled to the brim with gratitude and wonder for life, for the son he had been given, and for this moment: a moment that comes but once or twice a lifetime. The courage he had witnessed had touched him deeply and he felt the importance of the event as he felt his own place in the infinite plan. Going home he sensed a deep connection with nature. The earth under his feet, the skies above and the etheric substances beyond it all. He felt that he was indeed a part of the diurnal course, which rolls the rocks, stones and trees through seasons and centuries.

When he arrived at the house, riding his thoughts like the crests of waves, he barely noticed Jyoti Ma ostentatiously packing her bags in the dining room. All her clothes were on the table and she was sorting a pile of saris into order of opulence. Next to her clothes was a neatly piled stack of frocks, cotton underpants and frilly socks for Tulsi Devi. Helping her was a puzzled ayah and a near hysterical Bulbul, who was acting out the inner turmoil that Jyoti Ma was too indignant to express.

Aakash met the scene with composure, expressing no objections or encouragement. Saying absolutely nothing he sat down at the table and started to eat the food that had been kept for him. Silent, thoughtful and as self-contained as the mercury in a thermometer that can gauge a temperature but do nothing to cool it down.

Yet it wasn't disdain that kept him from getting involved. It was just that his thoughts were walking down the road toward the village with the two boys he had been growing on his farm with the herbs and trees. The boys whose souls had taken flight, taking with them the biggest commitment he'd made in his life until then.

Jyoti Ma wanted to bring him out of the clouds and onto his knees: to let him know that she would never come back if he did not pay her the respect she deserved. But noticing his reaction, her expectations dwindled and she yearned for even less: just a little politeness, or even some kind invitation to make her stay.

She was met with nothing but a still pond. There was nobody to rise to the occasion, no friction to give her cause momentum, nobody to meet her where she found herself, so close to the cliff's edge. Her demonstration was like the sound of one hand clapping. As impotent as a toasted grain tossed to the earth.

Jyoti Ma wanted to scream, but she knew the noise wouldn't even rattle Aakash's eardrums, so very politely she pushed her wedding sari next to his thali.

"Here, I won't be wearing this anymore."

"What will I do with it, Patni Devi?"

Being addressed as his wife and goddess, Jyoti Ma broke down into tears once more.

Tulsi Devi, seeing her mother collapse for the first time in her life, felt that the walls that held up her reality were falling down. She took her side as only a daughter can.

"Pitaji, must we really go?" she sobbed.

Aakash picked his beautiful baby goddess up in his arms.

"No, beti. You can stay here as long as you like. You will always be safe in this house."

Her father's words were like the magic chalk circle drawn by Laxman around Sita when he left her in the forest hermitage. Outside was the land of the wicked Ravan. Inside was safe. From that day on, whenever Tulsi Devi left her father's house, she would be stepping out into another reality, where the light beams themselves would twist and turn before they reached their destination in her eyes.

"Patni Devi, our son has gone," Aakash said.

Jyoti Ma was jolted out of her senses. Left standing on the outside, looking back at her shadow and all that lay behind that had brought her to this moment. The drama she was staging revealed itself to be just that – an act put on in a living room; one that petered out when challenged by the drama of real life.

"Where has he gone?" she asked lamely, knowing that having caused his departure it would be nowhere she could possibly follow.

"Who knows. Maybe to Rishikesh."

"With Bahadur?"

"Yes."

For once Jyoti Ma could imagine herself kissing the feet of Bahadur, pleading with him to look after her boy. At least he would know the dangers in the world of the common people. He could make him dinner and make sure his clothes were always clean. She had lost her son. That much she knew. The shadow lying behind her told the whole story.

She wanted to apologize to her husband for her outburst, but the words didn't come out the way she intended them to.

"I should have been given the opportunity to talk him out of it."

"It is his destiny. Why challenge it? It was his choice and he had to do it."

"Why did bhaiya leave us?" Tulsi Devi asked.

"Beti, he needed to go on a journey." Aakash looked over at his wife. "It was nobody's fault. He decided to go and find out more about the world and his place in it."

"Does everybody have to go on this journey, Pitaji?"

"Everybody should go on it if they possibly can."

"Arré, what are you saying? What will he do for money? We must send someone after him to stop him. He won't have got much farther than Kalka tonight. And the train doesn't leave till midnight."

"We will send *nobody* after him. God will provide." Aakash's voice was adamant and Jyoti Ma knew she may as well have heard the will of God speak forth. She tried to imagine her son's journey and its destination, but could just see images of wilderness. Only a distant figure was visible to her now, dressed like a sadhu, wearing robes and carrying a staff, walking through the desert, not looking back for assurances or farewells.

Wasn't that the only way she could ever imagine a future for him, after all?

There was a certain appropriateness in his decision that even she couldn't fail to see. But the fear for her child remained. What Jyoti Ma did not realize was that the world outside would always look after Ram. Nature itself would conspire to protect him at all times. Never would fortune find the broken bones of her son under its wheels, for his was a life that needed to be lived.

The next day at Prakriti, memsahib's saris were surreptitiously returned to their abode in her bedroom and nothing more was ever mentioned of her departure. The sun rose, the laborers started their work, and Aakash found himself in the fields as normal. Yet the morning was long for Jyoti Ma. It dragged its feet slowly across her living room floor, as if to taunt her with its obstinacy.

That day gave her all too many hours alone with her thoughts.

She replayed her life as if it were a dance she could re-choreograph. She imagined how things would have turned out if she'd married someone else. If only Bahadur had come to play with Ram that day and left as silently as he arrived. She imagined seeing her son again, and what she would say to him. No words came to mind. Just a sad realization that she had not been involved much in his life for the past few years since Aakash had taken over his education. He had been stolen from her slowly by a thief named Circumstance. It was only the evenings they had spent together in recent times, and even they had been all too short.

Bulbul was scarce that day. She entered through the side door and made herself unusually useful in the kitchen. Her plan had backfired so badly she busied herself by ingratiating herself amongst her own people, gossiping about the previous day's events with the new cook, who didn't know her scheming nature well enough to keep his distance. She picked at food wherever she could find it to take her mind off the disastrous outcome of her meddlings. Being new to this house of abundance, and quite unaccustomed to a full belly, the cook joined in. Together they ate almost all the family's lunch and had to start preparing food all over again at midday.

Memsahib didn't call Bulbul for the usual preening duties that morning. Instead she supervised her ayah, who supervised Tulsi Devi, and Tulsi Devi, uncomfortable with so much supervision, took off to bed for a long morning snooze.

Jyoti Ma, now at a loss for any activity that was either useful or meaningful, sat by her daughter's bed for two hours, simply watching her sleep. She was painfully aware that Tulsi Devi was now her only child. A child she would protect to the ends of the earth, wherever those ends might be. *Ram always belonged to Aakash,* she thought. But Tulsi Devi belonged to her. So much so that Aakash could have relinquished responsibility altogether.

"You are mine," she spoke out loud over Tulsi Devi's dreams. "You are my darling little girl and nobody can take you away from me."

7

Ram and Bahadur stayed for one night at Bahadur's home before setting off. Needless to say, having saab's son as a guest was an imposition the family would never have wished upon themselves. There was only one room, which they all shared, so they could not easily vacate it for their honored guest. And to entertain their guest in the manner to which he was accustomed, Bahadur's mother was obliged to cook several extra dishes, stirring her tears into the spices to strengthen the two boys for their journey.

When it came time to sleep, she was embarrassed to show their guest his bed on the floor. She pulled out a light blanket and regretted instantly that she'd patted it as she watched a small cloud of dust rise, gather itself and then redistribute particles on all the other beds in the row. Ram hadn't noticed. He closed his eyes to the world effortlessly, with only a thin straw chatai between himself and the hard ground.

The following day, they left Bahadur's home as they had left Prakriti. But instead of the stalwart Aakash to wish them farewell, they had a trail of villagers following them, parading their different emotions. Some wagged their fingers, telling them how they were neglecting their duties in life. Others were excited by their sense of adventure and promised to do the same one day, if only they could get their relatives off their backs.

And the little children who followed tugged their clothes and asked for cuddles before the train arrived.

The stationmaster, who'd known Bahadur all his life, gave the two boys free tickets to Kalka. It was the first of an amazing series of gestures that would land them at their destination as if they had been transported by the hand of God.

The train swung around the hill and the figures of the villagers disappeared suddenly, leaving Ram and Bahadur waving back at mountains and skies.

They continued to stand, half hanging out of the train, feeling the breeze race backward toward the life they had lived. And then, just for a few seconds, an eagle with a wing span as huge as a dust-track road flew alongside, taking the width of their carriage under its wings before swooping down to a lower ledge.

"We are blessed," Ram muttered quietly as an offering.

As he said this he turned to notice an English lady whispering into the English ear of her husband – a man with a red leathery nose that seemed to have grown old too early on his face. The woman kept glancing at the boys, whispering, and then looking away. But the man stared at them and did not break his gaze. He glared at them as if they were two worms who had crawled out of the earth. Without getting up, he bellowed at them through a snuff-colored nose and pipe-smoker's lungs.

"This is a train, not a bullock cart!"

"And we are pleased to be on it," Ram answered with dignity.

"GET DOWN TO THE NATIVE CARRIAGE IF YOU WANT TO STAY ON IT THEN."

The woman was looking away through the opposite window to create an apartheid between the scenery appreciated by herself and the one appreciated by the natives. Ram and Bahadur looked out of their window and ignored the man.

"GET OUT OF THIS COMPARTMENT RIGHT NOW OR I'LL CALL THE GUARDS."

"If you get out of our country, then we will be very pleased to get out of this compartment," answered Ram sincerely, quietly, but firmly.

Bahadur winced. He was more accustomed to offering undue reverence, and he knew the cruelty of those who demanded it.

"They wouldn't even have these godforsaken trains if it wasn't for us," the Englishman growled at his wife, as if the two of them had personally constructed the train for the occasion.

The English wife whispered some more into the man's ear, and without giving the two boys even a glance, the Englishman got out of his seat and pulled the emergency handle.

The train driver didn't stop for about three minutes – the emergency signal was often pulled in the Ladies Carriage when a man so much as put his head around the corner. The train driver knew that by the time the train had stopped, the male intruder had usually disappeared back to his own compartment.

Nevertheless, the guard came, and when he realized that the Englishman had pulled the emergency signal he did not even ask what the problem was. "Goondahs!" he shouted at Ram and Bahadur, hitting them with his truncheon. "The only Indians allowed in this carriage are the cleaners." Every few seconds he checked to make sure that the Englishman was watching and approving.

The boys, holding their hands up to protect their heads, ran down the train to find some darker-colored seats.

Ram's face was flushed a furious crimson brown when they sat down in the compartment reserved for Indians. It was not simply the indignation of his own caste that he was feeling. He was outraged at all of humanity for setting up these hierarchies to hinder their own progress.

An older Indian gentleman dressed in British clothes sat opposite them and heard out the story from Bahadur, who felt more humiliated for his well-bred friend than he did for himself.

The man introduced himself as Shiv Kapoor.

"Believe me, these English are not like this in their own country. Something happens to them when they set foot on our soil."

He told them how he had gone to study engineering in London many years ago, and how well respected he had been by the majority of English who wouldn't have had much higher caste than the sweepers in the railway station. The story of his travels overseas unfolded.

"When my wife Rekha and I went to England," he said, "her parents insisted that our twin boys should be left behind. They were the only grandchildren, you see. Her parents couldn't bear to lose them, so they told us the boys would get in the way."

Shiv's eyes moistened as he continued. "Every day Rekha would yearn for those boys – how many times she fell sick from missing them. She even set her clock to Indian time to be closer to them. There wasn't an hour that went by without one of us thinking of our sons."

"When did you see them again?" Bahadur asked.

"We didn't," Shiv replied. "When we arrived back in Delhi our boys had died of malaria. Rekha's parents hadn't been able to put the words into writing, because this news was the only part of our sons kept alive for our return."

Ram wondered how Shiv Kapoor could possibly relive this story for their benefit. How he could share his devastation with two strangers on a train? Just as he was thinking this, Shiv added, "You know, my two boys would be your age by now if they'd lived."

Shiv went on to describe how he had started up an orphanage for abandoned children in the city. "We never had any more children of our own," he said, "but there was so much work to be done to help other children so we started an orphanage. The first one was small. It had a guard and a hole in the wall. Under the hole in the wall was a basket.

Just like that, in the middle of the night, the guard would hear a baby crying in the basket outside. Nearly always girls, I tell you.

"In the early days we teamed up with a nursing home where unmarried women came to complete their pregnancies and give away their children. The women were looked after upstairs in the nursing home and came downstairs to the delivery room when their time had come."

"How honorable you are, sir," Bahadur interrupted. "To make all of this happen by yourself."

"I make nothing happen," Shiv answered. "God supports us. We get donations from rich and poor alike. Money comes from where money is. Even the British support our orphanages."

The three of them shared stories. Bahadur and Ram told their new friend about their plan to journey on to Rishikesh, and it was Shiv who first planted the seed of finding a Spiritual Master.

"Let me tell you one thing. If you go to the hills with this intention, it will be easier to manifest what you are looking for. If you are wanting a holiday, all well and good. If you are seeking knowledge, you must find a teacher."

Being familiar with Rishikesh he gave the boys advice on the dharamsalas and ashrams there that would feed and house pilgrims from all over the country. He warned them about the bogus gurus and sadhus that performed spectacular feats in the name of spirituality. "Now tell me," he said, "how on earth will you gain enlightenment by wrapping yourself up in snakes? Or by standing on one leg for ten years, for that matter?"

"Beware of magicians," he warned. "They seek the manifestations of power, not the source from which it comes," and he went on to tell them about the caves around Rishikesh where they could listen to discourses and live in the forests with the holy men.

"Sir, how do you tell who lives the truth and who does not?"

"If you are devoted and wish to learn, your guru will find you. Do not simply look outward. Look inward, too, for you must be worthy of the knowledge you receive."

Shiv Kapoor reminded Ram so much of his father. As he turned to Ram and said, "God will provide," he could have been speaking with the voice of Aakash.

The train arrived in Kalka and there to greet them with the warmer air were two British soldiers. They were talking to the two British people from the train, and were united in their whiteness, eight eyes looking at their four. Ram and Bahadur walked past them with the confidence of visitors at a prison. But as they passed, they heard one soldier shout, "Oi! Come here," while the other said to the Englishman, "Are these the lads?"

The man with the leathery nose whispered something to the soldiers, while his wife stood slightly apart, her smug face pushing down a self-righteous double chin.

"Right now, which of you buggers thinks he's English?" Ram felt his fingers being twisted behind his back. A knee pushed him from behind. He said nothing.

"Arrest them both," the other soldier said, and they were marched toward a door on the platform marked in bold white English letters: STATIONMASTER. They were locked up for an hour before anyone came to see them.

Inside Bahadur said, "We should never have talked like that to those British people."

"You didn't talk at all. It was me, and I am prepared to take the blame for it," Ram responded.

"Arré, you don't understand. They could kill us!"

"I still feel we are blessed and protected by forces much greater than the British Army, Bahadur."

The two soldiers came in to execute their duties.

"Do you coolies speak any English?"

"Perfectly," replied Ram.

"And what about him?"

Bahadur was silent.

"He speaks equally well, sir."

"Don't you *sir* me, you little rat."

The larger soldier kicked Bahadur so hard in the knee they all heard the crack. Bahadur yelled and fell to the floor, holding his knee close to his chest.

Ram was desperate. "Please, sir, do not hurt him, he has done no harm."

"What do you mean, no harm? Trying to cause a mutiny on the train is a criminal offense!"

"But, sir, he said nothing on the train, *it was me.*"

"Stop trying to cover up for your mate. If you want the same punishment, just ask for it," said the soldier, throwing Ram to the ground and kicking him like a stray dog.

"Stop it, we've done nothing," Ram started. He looked up and saw a boot bigger than the man standing high above it. A thick leather heel came down squarely in his mouth.

"When I want you to talk I'll ask you, all right, coolie." Then he spoke to his companion. "You get the other bastard."

The second soldier took his command, and like a well-oiled machine started kicking Bahadur in the face. He didn't stop until Bahadur's cheekbone cracked, and pointed through the flesh like an arrow that only has the power to injure the one who wields it.

"Now take off your clothes."

Ram and Bahadur stripped with shaking muscles. The men searched their clothes and found the bundle of notes that Aakash had given Ram as a parting gift.

"Who did you steal this from?"

"My father gave it to me," answered Ram.

"Well, who did he steal it from?"

Ram didn't answer. The notes were tucked into a drawer in the office. Another small tribute to the empire.

"Well, bloody well get up and go, before we decide to lock you up!"

Ram looked over at Bahadur whose face was bleeding profusely. He grabbed his kurta and started to wipe off the blood.

"Get out of here. This isn't some kind of hospital department," barked the larger of the two British officers.

They put on their clothes and pulled themselves together. Bahadur's eyes were swollen and his chest had caved in. Ram put his arm around his friend and helped him out.

Back on the platform the passengers stared at the two victims, saying nothing in case the British soldiers spotted their collusion. Ram asked a porter when the next train to Delhi was due to depart. The man said nothing, walking away fast, knowing that if he spoke, his color would shine browner. The soldiers left the platform and the two boys collapsed on the ground.

"Do you still feel so blessed?" Bahadur asked.

Ram looked up at the sky, and looking down on him was the face of Shiv Kapoor.

"Yes," he answered.

And they were. Shiv Kapoor took them under his wing, clothed them, fed them and put them up in Delhi in one of his orphanages near the Red Fort. An ayurvedic physician was called to treat his guests and the wounds healed fast. Even the great gash on Bahadur's cheek healed and left a beautiful scar the shape of a bird in flight.

At the orphanage they often played with the many young abandoned children, who soaked up love like the desert sands. They reminded Bahadur of all the children who crawled around the streets in his village up in the hills, and made Ram think of his little sister. He wondered how and when they would next meet. And if she would ever remember their games of giants and dwarves.

Once Bahadur had recovered, they went out into Delhi and saw Britishers keeping a distance from their own people – the two races divided like two trains on their separate tracks, never to cross paths except in collision. Ram swore an oath then that he would never talk to a Britisher again, even if his life depended on it. They felt the presence of the British in their land as they never had in the seclusion of Prakriti or the village, and they thanked God that they had been born too far away to conquer. In a place too isolated to matter.

On their trips around the city, Ram and Bahadur couldn't help but notice the abundance of wandering ascetics who were gathering in their orange robes, ashes on their foreheads under long matted hair. They would sit and talk with the different groups, and the two boys discovered that the sadhus were on their way to the Kumbh Mela in Hardwar. Many had been before for the festival and they told stories about the huge crowds of pilgrims, saints and mystics who came together to feel God in the force of numbers.

It made them think once more about their destination. About Rishikesh that lay just a few miles further up the hills from Hardwar.

Every night they had dinner with Shiv and Rekha Kapoor, who never even hinted that they should move on. They had become part of the family already, replacing the two sons who had been lost to malaria all those years ago.

Knowing that they were in danger of never leaving Delhi, Ram and Bahadur started to talk to Shiv and Rekha about Rishikesh again.

"You will need money," was their host's first response.

The boys were silent, unwilling to ask for it, having already received so much generosity.

"Ram, you always said that God would provide," Shiv continued in the face of silence. "So surely you would not turn down a gift from God any more than you would refuse to breathe the air that is offered to you?"

Ram had no answer. He knew that he needed money, but he knew also that money could not make his heart beat nor his lungs fill with air, and that so much of what he needed was free in the environment that supported him.

He could only accept money if he was going to give something in return. He thought about what he could give Shiv Kapoor and only one word came to mind: "remembrance."

That evening they went back to the orphanage and slept above the newborn room, listening through the night to the cries for the mothers who would never hear them. By the next night Bahadur and Ram had left and there was nobody to hear the cries but an ayah whose dreams were hardened to the sounds. An ayah who continued on with her stubborn childless sleep as only an ayah can.

8

Getting off a crowded train at Hardwar, Ram and Bahadur soon realized that there wouldn't be a single dharamsala with space to put them up for the night.

The small town was brimming with mystics. Tridents, cloth, smoke, chanting, begging bowls and prayers all rolled and swayed together as they would have done at the beginning of Time, when the milky oceans were first stirred. Ram and Bahadur shuffled and squeezed past a sea of saffron and white robes. Past the different sects segregated like the bride's and groom's families at a wedding. Past the naked, ash-covered, matted-haired mystics who lived in the hills throughout the year and rubbed shoulders with the shaven-headed, clean-cut ascetics who visited only on holy pilgrimages.

They found themselves wandering through the crowds of orange, watching feats of miracles, prayer ceremonies and yagyas, listening to shlokas being read from the vedas and smelling the incense spiraling up to whichever Gods were being summoned. They walked past people who practiced everything from meditation to tantra, renunciation, tapasya, bhakti, charity and indulgence. They heard many wise and unwise words. They heard drums, cymbals and bhajan singers play louder and louder as they fought for supremacy. But wherever they went, they felt the Truth become more and more elusive.

They walked past people like themselves, not dressed as mystics. Novices. Villagers from around Hardwar making a day trip to the mela to practice austerities. Through the religious crowds they wandered, weaving their way past gurus, disciples, astrologers and magicians who made their fortune with psychic skills and trickeries. Past stray dogs, umbrellas and tents. Over squashed food and religious litter.

If Ram and Bahadur had wanted to go shopping for spirituality, this is where they would have come. They could have made their choices between bodily mutilations, penances or mangos here in the marketplace, where bangles, sweets and flowers were sold next to holy beads and statues of gods. Everywhere they looked there was something on sale. Everywhere except in one corner where a man had quietly died, unable to sell even his soul. Who was he? What had brought him to the Kumbh Mela? Had he died of disease or disappointment?

"What shall we do?" Ram asked.

"Nothing," said Bahadur.

"We can't just go off and leave him."

"Why not? He's gone off himself," replied Bahadur.

It was the first time that Ram had ever seen a dead body, and that amazed Bahadur far more than the sight of the dead man at the side of the road. In his village the dead were regularly taken through the streets on a stretcher, draped with flowers and followed by a procession of mourners. How had this experience evaded Ram? How could he have lived such a sheltered life? Bahadur pulled Ram along, fearing that he would want to go and sit in solace with the body that lay there.

In the face of death Ram tried to find Silence in his mind so that he could hear his father's words. What would Aakash have done in this place? What would his advice be now? He thought about his home. The Silence that sealed the hills of Prakriti from the rest of the world. He remembered how the rain clouds used to hover close to his father's farm when the plants needed to be watered. How much trust his father had in the forces of nature. How his father always repeated that "God will provide." It was then Ram knew that what they were searching for was the power and potential of Silence. It was the bliss of Silence and the prospect of a great and soulful adventure that had lured them from the hills of Prakriti, and it was Silence that now evaded them in this orgy of spirituality.

"If we were to look our Spiritual Master in the eye, we would not know we had found him," Ram spoke after a while.

Feeling overwhelmed they made their way out of Hardwar, past the holy fires and bathing pilgrims, up into the forests in the hills above the town where the air was thick from the invocations of fire down below. They camped out that evening on the periphery of the festival, hoping for some quiet, but through the night they were kept awake by enthusiastic mystical revellers entranced in chanting a single shloka, unable to stop their ecstasy. When dawn arrived there was a minute's break before a group of early morning bhajan singers arose to greet the new sun with even greater gusto.

It wasn't until the next day when they found a small Shiva temple in the very center of the mela, that they felt a sense of peace and balance once more. It was an inconspicuous retreat reached through a small carved archway. Ram and Bahadur had ducked into this pygmy's passage as a way of escaping a mendicant, his begging bowl and the rabid-looking monkey on his shoulder, which sat picking lice from its master's hair.

They stepped inside and the noise cut out.

Like the centerpoint of a wheel, this temple held a stillness that instantly distinguished it from the spinning world around. The air was cooled by marble, all sounds had been sucked out of the atmosphere, leaving it camphor crisp and still. It was as if the noise had spun into the center of a wheel and disappeared into nothing but a background hum.

"Who are those people?" Bahadur asked. Three men sat in meditation on deerskins spread across the gray marble floor. One of the men opened his eyes. His matted hair was tied neatly into a turban, his face was playful and charming. His smile welcomed them both to sit down without any words passing his lips.

Ram and Bahadur sat down quietly and closed their eyes to meditate. It took two minutes only for their world to lose all its dimensions as their minds settled down into the Silence. For the moments their eyes were closed the only world that existed was the one that vibrated in that inner stillness. And it wasn't even a world to speak of. More a consistent hum of smooth, uncluttered internal space where even the movements of the planets in orbit left no indentations.

Never before had either of them experienced such tranquillity or bliss. Such an alive sense of fullness – their bodies free of all boundaries. They had come from the dispersed, chaotic action of the outside world, and suddenly it fell away like a mist. They surrendered to that Infinite Silence and allowed themselves to be swept away to the center of all things.

Some time must have passed, who knows how long, before they came out of their meditation feeling hungry.

"If I don't eat soon," Bahadur said, "I won't remember that I have a body to feed."

Outside the light glared into their eyes and they walked unsteadily on their feet like two people who had just arrived from another lifetime. Bahadur was shaking with hunger, so they approached the first dhaba who was selling paranthas cooked freshly on the fire in front of them. There they sat, witnessing the spectacle of the mela and watching entranced as the rotis piled up to feed them.

When they had enough paranthas to feed everyone in the temple, they returned. Bahadur offered the food to Shiva, who was overseeing the small circle of seekers with the detachment of a god known for his austerities. Then he left the pile of paranthas in the middle of the mandir, and as the other men came out of their meditation, they all shared the god-given food.

The three men all seemed to know each other, but none of them talked. Their appearance, however, spoke of similar backgrounds. They were three men who had chosen the same path. All bearded, in white robes, with sandalwood smeared across their foreheads; one of them with a Shiva trident resting against the wall behind him. They looked like forest sages. Grand with Silence. Sincere and devout commanders of transcendence. Ram was so impressed he found himself thinking, *If these are the disciples, I must meet their Master.*

Together they ate, sharing the presence and the food, smiles but no words. Ram and Bahadur stayed with them for many days throughout the Kumbh Mela. They meditated, and then they returned to the outside world every so often to check on its existence. In the early evenings they would go down to the banks of the Ganges and watch the devotees cast their little leaf candle-boats into the river, filled to the brim with marigolds and rose petals. They would follow the flicker of lights on the water until the leaf boats disappeared out of sight, and watch the figures clothed and unclothed walking down the ghats and immersing themselves in the sacred water. When it was neither night nor day, but during that glimpse of twilight, the mela transcended its own traffic and noise to settle down into a magical evening serenity.

It was in Hardwar that the proportions of this adventure struck home. They did not know what would happen next: if they would ever find a Spiritual Master, or if there would be anything for them in Rishikesh.

Anything could happen.

After the stars had shifted on, the pilgrims started to disengage slowly from their gathering as they made their way back to hometowns all over India. But for Ram and Bahadur their pilgrimage had only just begun. They spent the last week of the mela sitting centered in their Shiva temple, until the three men started to roll up the few possessions they shared, ready for departure. Ram and Bahadur watched, until one of the sadhus spoke. It would have sounded casual if it hadn't been the first sentence that any of the men had spoken all that time.

"So are you coming?"

Ram and Bahadur nodded.

From that point onward their paths were transformed. No longer were they heading north toward Rishikesh. The forces had turned their heads around and made them face south, toward the jungles in the heart of India. There they were to search for a man some people claimed was the most revered sage of his time, the embodiment of Divine Consciousness. A rishi who lived with tigers, basking in the light that shone from his own soul.

At this point they could have continued on toward a different destiny altogether, but they didn't. Instead they joined the three men on a search party to find the man that the elders had determined would be the next Shankaracharya of the North.

It was a turning point for them in every sense of the word.

9

And so it was that Ram and Bahadur traveled through India down to Amarkantakas, the source of the holy river Narmada in central India.

With their three traveling companions they walked into a jungle to search for a mysterious swami. A jungle where plants bore leaves the size of human heads and banyan trees draped curtains of roots from branches high above. Thick with life left to its own devices, this sanctuary of nature yielded the seekers every luxury available in the natural world. Isolated waterfalls, caves as big as castles and solitude so perfect they could have been the first humans to cut through the thick undergrowth.

Quietly, curiously, they were being watched from the shadows of trees and vines by forest spirits trying to smell their purpose in the footprints they left behind them.

The man they searched for had never been found, although sources claimed he was alive and well, living deep in the forest in Silence and abundance. Whenever a search party had been sent previously he had evaded them, just like those forest spirits watching from the shadows, too still to be observed.

It was right that he should appear now, this rishi who had been chosen to fill the seat of the Shankaracharya of the North. If the other

Shankaracharyas knew this, then so too would the invisible sadhu of the woodlands. But there was still a small chance that he would outfox destiny, only because he had mastered its ways, learnt to pull its strings and make it perform whatever plays he wished to watch.

On the third day the search party stopped by the river to meditate, to find direction and strengthen their intention. When they came out of meditation the forest was dark and the flames cast shadows on the face of Arjun, the man who led the small party. He started to tell the story of the man they sought and the other four gathered around the flames and listened to this incredible tale …

"There was a man known to many people around India, who left a legend behind him in Uttar Kashi in the Himalayas where he went as a boy to gain the initiation of eternity. He was born into a well-respected Brahmin Zamindar family near Ayodhya, and when he was nine years old he left home without notice, a child ascetic on his way to the hills to seek enlightenment. He had nothing to eat. The only water he drank was from the Ganges, with the blessings of the River Goddess. Whenever he met a policeman who wanted to send him home he would question the policeman's authority and assert his Divine Right to push forward toward his destiny.

"This young sage was sent home by the authorities, where he argued with the family priest that he should be allowed to go back to the Himalayas and dedicate his life to learning the Truth that upheld it. At first they laughed at him, but when the priest was convinced that the child was not simply an upstart but a spiritual prodigy, he folded his arms before the boy and advised the parents that their son was acting on the Will of God. That it was not proper for anyone to stand in the way of such a sincere seeker.

"When the boy became a man he went to Uttar Kashi, in the time-honored tradition, to look for a guru who could instruct him on a path toward self-realization. He met a Dandi Swami – a stick-bearing ascetic called Swami Krishnanand Saraswati, a sage well known in that valley of saints, who took the responsibility for the young man's fervent spiritual aspirations entirely on his own shoulders.

"After proving himself to be an inspired disciple and a gifted swami, this young sage was sent to practice a special technique in a cave in Uttar Kashi, where he resolved to unveil for himself the mysteries of spirit and not stop until he reached fulfilment in its bliss. Little but legends are known of his life since, but some say that he lives here in this forest today ..."

Ram was so involved in the story of this swami that he did not notice Bahadur had left the fireside. The night had settled down into a quiet vibration of crickets and crackling fire. The men they traveled with made up their beds and went to sleep, but Bahadur had still not returned. Ram wondered whether he should wake Arjun and the others to set out on a search party, but instead decided to have faith that Bahadur would come back. And so he waited, alert to the noises of the night.

Lightning struck in the distance, electrifying Ram's fears. Raindrops fell in loud thuds onto the thick leaves all around. When Bahadur still had not returned nearly two hours later, Ram panicked and sounded the alarm.

By that time Bahadur was well and truly lost. The more he tried to find his way back to the campfire, the more the four directions flipped and swam around him, until he faced the dizzying darkness without a breath of hope.

The night was too black for Bahadur to see the moon. The forest foliage was too dense to allow any stars to illuminate his darkness. He shouted for help, but his shouts came back at him, dead and flat, as if they had bounced off the bark of the trees that trapped him in their own night dungeon. He sat down, irresolute, defeated. Slipping his legs out in front of him, he felt something pierce his foot, cutting through his skin, his last defense. He yelled as he heard the weighty slither of a snake sliding away along the forest floor, satisfied and poison-free. The noises in the forest were trapped now in Bahadur's head. The crickets screeched inside his ears as he felt the rush of poison numbing each toe in turn and pushing waves of dead pain up his leg.

Bahadur lay down, moaning, breathing fast with dread and desperation, willing the pain to stop creeping further toward his heart. He felt helpless now, reduced as he was to prey for every creature that mocked him from the shadows. Every noise in the trees made his leg ache with the awareness of danger. Only when he felt he could strain under the pain no longer did he remember to ask for Divine assistance. Only then did he remember to pray for his own survival. His last hope faded as he heard the noise of a large animal approaching. He swallowed some sweat on his lips and froze, unable to hide the smell of his own fear.

When he heard a voice, he was stunned.

"Shanti, Shanti, Shanti," the voice repeated and he saw a man appear in the night like a visitation. He seemed to be talking to the forest animals rather than to Bahadur, bidding them to hush, to leave in peace.

The stranger seemed to know exactly what had happened to Bahadur, but instead of attending to the wound he tore a piece of cloth from his loincloth and tied it around a tree. After doing this, he approached Bahadur and sat down next to him.

"The pain will start lifting soon," he said.

Bahadur looked at him and a sudden flash lit up the darkness. It could have been lightning, it could have been his imagination sparking, but as soon as he was struck by the sight of this man, Bahadur knew that his Master had been illuminated. He looked into eyes that were dangerous with life. At a forehead that was broad with wisdom. A beard that had grown untamed for many years.

"You must be Swami Brahmanand Saraswati?" Bahadur asked.

"Who is he?" came the answer.

When the man took Bahadur to his cave nearby, he was dazzled by further portents. There was food there waiting for them, warmed, even though there was nobody to have heated it. A fire appeared in the fireplace without his host having to light it.

These small signs convinced Bahadur that the forces had conspired to send him south to meet this man. He started to tell the sage about Ram, about how they had left their home in the mountains to go to Rishikesh but had somehow been brought down south before ever reaching their destination.

"Sometimes you have to come full circle before you can find what you're searching for," his host told him.

After a hearty meal, Bahadur was given a bed that was prepared for him in the corner and told to sleep. His host did not sleep. He watched the forest from the mouth of the cave until the dawn lit first the tips of the trees and then filtered through to the forest floor. After watching the dawn he went to bathe in the river and returned after his meditation to a meal that was already prepared.

When Bahadur awoke, the sage who had saved his life offered to take him back to his friends. As they walked together Bahadur thought about how it would feel to stay in the forests with this hermit and learn from him. He imagined with uncertainty what his friend Ram would think if he were to desert their party now. They had started on this journey together, but now Bahadur was feeling a magnetism in this forest stronger than his friendship with Ram.

When they arrived at the campsite, these thoughts vanished with the excitement of seeing Ram once more. Bahadur proudly introduced the sage who had saved his life. He started to show the travelers his wound from the snakebite, but when he searched for it, the fang marks had disappeared.

"Who are you?" Ram asked, looking directly into the eyes of Bahadur's new friend.

"I am," answered the man, without attempting to continue his answer.

When asked for the whereabouts of a swami by the name of Brahmanand Saraswati, this sage offered to give them directions and walked for the whole day through the forests with them. When they came to the edge of the river, he told the others that he would not be able to cross, but that they would probably find the man they wanted in a cave an hour's walk on the other side.

Bahadur was determined to stay by the side of this remarkable man, and in front of the whole party he lay prostrate at his feet and asked if the sage would take him on as his disciple. Much confusion followed as Ram considered whether he should continue with the search party or stay with Bahadur.

"I cannot leave the others," Ram finally decided. "But once we've found swamiji I will come and find you."

"I'm sorry," Bahadur answered.

"We're brothers," Ram said. "Distance can never change that. We'll meet again."

After Ram and Bahadur had made their final goodbyes there were four people left searching for the Shankaracharya, making their way back through the forest in the direction they had been shown. Meanwhile, after no more than a five-minute walk, Bahadur and the sage arrived at the cave in time for an evening meditation. They sat for about an hour in Silence and opened their eyes just as the four travelers arrived in front of them.

What followed was a realization that Bahadur had made before any of the others – that this was the man they had been searching for. Swami Brahmanand Saraswati, the man people said manifested food whenever he required it and addressed animals as if he were just one of God's creatures speaking to another. This was their Guru Dev.

When the three envoys from East, West and South of India asked Guru Dev if he could take up the seat of Shankaracharya of the North and shine some light on the vedas, he answered, "No, I cannot." They pushed him, knowing that they could not return with a refusal. Guru Dev continued, "How can I shine light on the vedas? It is like holding up a lantern to illuminate the sun."

Nonetheless, eventually Guru Dev did agree to take up the seat. What followed was a much-awaited spiritual awakening. He had the power to touch people deeply, and after seeing him they would go away inspired to live out their highest aspirations.

Ram and Bahadur, they too followed their Guru Dev on the journey north as he took the vibrant Silence that he had cultivated for nearly seventy years and became a spiritual leader who devoted himself fully to the dynamics of the suffering world.

10

The years passed and Prakriti became renowned far and wide for its exceptionally high yields and fertile soil. News about the farm even reached the British at their summer headquarters up in Simla, and they appointed a botanist to go and study the techniques, the formulas and even, daresay, the magic if there was any. A man from Yorkshire named Roy was sent with an array of Indian helpers to introduce himself and the empire to Prakriti.

Roy had an elfin quality, with green eyes that winked at the edges, light brown hair and a tip to his nose that bobbed up and down when he spoke, as if it too were speaking. He dressed a lot more casually than the uniformed British armed forces who stuck rigidly to their formalities in the unconquerable heat of their conquered land.

Roy had grown up on a farm in the Yorkshire dales, and shared that kinship between people who have lived off the land. But he had a brief, and that distanced him from Aakash. It was to let the native thrive on his property, but to make sure his secrets were learnt so that they could be reproduced throughout even the most barren and arid parts of this land.

There had to be some kind of fertilizer that was being manufactured for the exclusive use of this property. There was no other explanation for how the soil could be so rich, despite the fact that the crops were never rotated. Yet whenever Roy asked probing questions about fertilizers, Aakash gave philosophical answers, which shrouded the mysteries of Prakriti further.

"Take abundance from abundance and abundance remains," Aakash once told him, quoting from the Upanishads.

Roy asked about fertilizers again and again, but Aakash would repeat that nothing needs to be added when nature is, by itself, plentiful and complete.

"Nature is the universal abode of all possibilities," he would say. "And it can only be that because there is nothing missing. Every conceivable manifestation is held there in its unmanifest form. All it takes is good intention to manifest what is required."

"But you cannot just make plants grow by simply having the right attitude. Nature is independent of our whims. It is grander than all of us."

"Exactly. So we must make sure that we do her will. And we do that by perfecting ourselves so that there is no difference between nature and us."

"But you're talking about working on yourself here, and I appreciate that, but I want to talk about working on the land."

"But my friend, is the Self not the only real arena where we can work? And should not work on the Self precede all other endeavors in terms of importance?"

Roy was baffled and frustrated. Planting seeds and watching them grow was different from being a good chap and making sure you always did the right thing. He'd heard of the Americans with their Thanksgiving, and he'd celebrated harvest festivals dozens of times at his local church in the Yorkshire dales. But human beings couldn't be compared to clumps of earth. They simply could not. When he challenged Aakash over this analogy, Aakash started talking about the system of ayurveda, where all elements – Earth, Water, Fire, Air and Ether – operate at an energetic level in the body, making a universe within.

Roy tried, but never saw the truth in Aakash's words. Sometimes he thought that Aakash was as deceptive and tricky as the other natives, simply hiding his practical formulas behind rhetoric, and putting him off the scent. But whenever he looked in Aakash's eyes he saw no evasiveness, just a deep sympathy and a desire to be understood.

Whilst the land flourished, family life without Ram was like a chair with one leg missing. Manageable if the balance of weight was carefully distributed over the remaining three legs, but easily collapsed if too much attention was given to the missing one.

Without Bahadur to use for a scapegoat, Jyoti Ma couldn't help but shift the blame for her son's disappearance to Aakash. He took it well. Yes, he had given his permission. No, Ram had not written with details of his whereabouts. But he was all right. Aakash knew that much, in the same way he knew the functioning of his own body without insisting on glimpsing his liver or kidneys to confirm their well-being.

For Jyoti Ma, Ram's name was taboo, never to be mentioned by any of the servants. Only Tulsi Devi had permission to talk about her brother, but whenever she asked to hear stories about him, those stories would send him further away into a mythological realm.

Aakash encouraged this idolatry of Ram by telling stories of how he left home one fine morning to go and spend time in the forest. About how all the Devas and Devis attended to his every need wherever he traveled. How he met with wise men, slew monsters, learnt sidhis and conversed with the gods. There was no difference now between their Ram and the Ram of ancient legend. If there was a ladder that led from the sacred world to the profane one down below, Ram was well on his way to the upper rungs. Mythologized to the point where a few extra arms were starting to grow from his godly shoulder blades.

Having a deified brother made Tulsi Devi feel lucky and special. When she discovered the cave on the property and saw two desks and chairs laid out exactly as they had been left after Jyoti Ma's visit, she became curious. One of her friends who labored on the farm told her that Ram had studied in the cave and she was awestruck, insisting that her ayah take her there again and again so she could imagine the experience. When she finally announced that she too wanted lessons in the cave, Jyoti Ma told her "what nonsense," and changed the subject.

But Tulsi Devi's suggestion did not pass by without disturbing the peace. Jyoti Ma knew that Aakash would have happily conducted lessons in the cave for Tulsi Devi, but then her daughter would leave, just as Ram had. The fear of losing Tulsi Devi grew, as all fears do, into a monster that laid enough footsteps back to its lair to make it the only destination possible. Only by following those footsteps and fulfilling her mother's biggest fear would Tulsi Devi be able to slay it. But at the age of seven or eight she was still innocent of her fate. Like a child playing in the sunshine, not noticing the long dark shadows up ahead, cast by her future challenges.

The village school was not a serious proposition. Tulsi Devi would be like a lotus floating on a muddy pond filled with frogs for schoolfriends. And what if that lotus drowned?

No. The local school was out of the question, as was a local tutor with local ties. It had to be someone from far away with no history in the area to breed familiarity or contempt. Someone from far away, but someone absolutely trustworthy nonetheless.

The solution presented itself one night when Roy was invited to dinner at the farmhouse.

"It must be hard for Tulsi Devi, what with being an only child and living in this isolated part of the country," Roy commented during the meal.

Aakash looked at his wife. Her lips showed no movement, but without any words being spoken they agreed not to mention their missing son.

Jyoti Ma changed the conversation. "I am feeling the same concern. For so long I have searched for someone to teach Tulsi Devi, but these local teachers are not to be trusted."

As soon as Roy heard that a teacher was required at Prakriti he saw a future for himself and his old flame, Lily, whom he'd left behind in England when he was given a job with the government in India. "I may be able to help," he said with a smile, thinking of Lily, who had stuck by him in his memory even if she hadn't quite in reality. Throughout his long months in India she had remained with him – a picture of red frizzy hair standing out from the crowd on the Dover docks. She was the last image he'd gazed at when leaving England, as he lined up with the other passengers on deck to wave goodbye to everything they'd ever known.

A glowing reference followed. "Lily is one of the few women I know who has a university degree. She is also from a good family." (Roy knew that this was important to Indians.) And Lily's mother had been a famous suffragette, involved in organizing demonstrations and secret meetings until the moment Mr. Asquith granted women the vote. (He decided to leave this bit out.) "She is a highly skilled teacher and currently employed by a girls' school in West London," he added. "I'm sure that she'd love to come out and teach Tulsi Devi, if you're interested."

Aakash did not treat the proposition seriously, especially as they could easily find someone suitable from Delhi, and an English governess seemed such a short-term solution.

"You take care of these things," he said to Jyoti Ma. "You are in charge of Tulsi Devi's education."

For Jyoti Ma there was no question. To hell with the expense. She would make an employee of one of the country's rulers! The cost would be worth the currency she could trade in status … Jyoti Ma could already imagine herself mentioning her English governess at every important wedding or function she attended from that day onward – until her days were over. Slipping it into conversations here and there: *Oh, I'd love to come to Delhi, but my governess can't do a thing unless I'm around* … Yes she had joined the ranks of maharajas and maharanis. She was so excited at this prospect, in fact, that she didn't even stop to think of how her daughter may benefit from the education.

Roy picked up on Jyoti Ma's greedy enthusiasm. "I will write to Lily immediately," he said. It was a good excuse to actually send one of the letters he wrote to her. The other letters never made it onto the boat; instead they swam the complicated seas of his emotions, never to see the Dover shores.

Where would that letter find Lily? She was such an unpredictable girl. Feisty, spirited and independent. Would she even agree to board a ship and come to visit him? Roy thought about this and decided *yes.* Yes she would, because it was an adventure. An experience denied to most women. One to make her mother proud.

He was right. His letter found Lily on the verge of getting married to a fellow teacher. The letter from Roy, once read and digested, was redigested and rewritten as a "Dear John" letter to her fiancé. If Roy had known he might have considered her fickle. Either that, or himself very lucky. But Roy would never find out, because Lily's love was Lily's business. She set her sights on further horizons and in no time she had started her correspondence with Jyoti Ma and received confirmation that her passage to India was secured.

Tulsi Devi was as excited as her mother that an English lady was coming all that way to teach her. She practiced her curtsy every day, as if she were going to meet the Queen, and started wearing English frocks, that always looked a little odd because the local tailors had no conception of English ladies, let alone their garments. No exact dates could be given for Lily's arrival, because it depended on variants such as the skies and the seas. There was nothing to do but wait. Wait, and visit Lily's room-to-be every day to help make it perfect.

Thalis were replaced with plates and Tulsi Devi was taught how to eat with a knife and fork, which distanced her from her food enough to take away her enjoyment in eating. Not being able to touch her dhal, subjee and roti with her fingers removed an extra dimension of sensual enjoyment and she started looking a bit leaner in the face and arms. Jyoti Ma was somewhat distressed. Although she had no desire for her daughter to take after herself, she still would have liked to see the fashionable modest plumpness that distinguished the eating classes from the impoverished ones.

But these were trifling concerns. All things considered, Lily's arrival heralded a new era at Prakriti. A time when the orchards hung heavy with fruit and ripe possibilities.

11

Lily arrived in Bombay – stepping off the gangplank and into an embrace with Roy that raised eyebrows and tickled the curiosity of the onlookers.

From the moment she set foot in India, Lily felt aware of the color of her skin. She tried to explain this to Roy, but he was too well-adjusted to the easy inequality of the East. When they stopped off in Delhi, Lily insisted on making friends with as many Indians as possible, mingling with complete strangers in the bazaars, and buying herself some Indian clothes.

"I will wear this salwar chemise when I meet the family at Prakriti," she announced, and Roy shrank, unable to condemn her decision, yet unwilling to condone it.

Excited by her brief glimpse into Indian life, Lily was keen to push on and reach Prakriti. Roy made arrangements and sent a peon ahead to announce their arrival. They boarded the train and continued up into Himachal Pradesh, striking the mountains as if they were striking gold.

Lily had never seen anything so beautiful in her life, sensing immediately that she was in a holy place. The only mountain she'd ever visited before, in fact, was Box Hill in London's home counties, where she'd picnicked one summer. Nothing, absolutely nothing could prepare her for the magnificence and splendor of the Himalayas. These were the few folds on the skin of the earth that she'd studied on maps as a child. Now they towered above her like giants. But instead of dwarfing her, they made her feel exalted in every cell of her body. She felt as if she had finally arrived home. As though she had found the perfect setting for her soul.

Finally they arrived at the little station in the hills. The whole village knew that there was a guest due to arrive at Prakriti, because the only car and driver for miles around was waiting to pick them up. When they stepped out of their private carriage into the world, Roy nodded a welcome to the faces he recognized in the small crowd as a way of claiming familiarity. They were immediately surrounded by villagers who had no history with the British and no idea of their ruthlessness. Little children started pulling Roy's shirt out from his trousers, and when he saw the children starting to touch Lily he told them to "bhago." However, they stubbornly refused to go as Lily had produced a bag of boiled sweets and was distributing them to everyone under three feet tall.

The visitation of the white memsahib in Indian clothes became a talking point that formed part of the village mythology for years to come. But the car started up and drove slowly back up the mountain road, making her visit to their village a fleeting one. Lily was whisked off to Prakriti where she became "the big people's white lady."

Seeing the car approaching around the side of the mountain, Jyoti Ma disappeared into Lily's room. She picked up two small leaves that had somehow made their way onto the carpet, looked in the mirror, straightened her hair, and shouted for Tulsi Devi. Jyoti Ma was nervous, suddenly feeling inadequate; hoping that Lily would not be expecting the residence of a maharaja. Aakash, too, saw the car arriving from the fields and made his way back to the farmhouse.

When Lily stepped out of the vehicle, the first thing Jyoti Ma saw was a salwar-leg, and she expected an Indian chaperone to follow it out. Instead, Lily with her blazing red hair and Indian chemise stood upright, waiting to be formally introduced. It was a charged moment. Jyoti Ma's expectations fell the instant she saw that her English governess was wearing Indian clothes, and rose again when she heard the clipped tones of a perfect English accent. Tulsi Devi came running up and curtsied the way she had rehearsed all this time. Governess and child looked at each other and smiled – the Indian girl in a pinafore and the English one in a salwar chemise. The irony wasn't lost on Roy, who smiled too and gave Tulsi Devi a friendly hug.

The salwar chemise made the biggest impression on Aakash, who commented that if all the English took to Indian culture as quickly as Lily, there would be peace and prosperity throughout the land. Then he invited everyone inside to enjoy the best of Indian hospitality.

The party adjourned to the dining room and tea was served English style (without boiling up the leaves) and poured into cups ordered specially from an English shop in Calcutta.

"How was your journey?" Aakash asked.

"Much more exciting for being in India, thank you very much," Lily replied.

Jyoti Ma was overwhelmed by the unfamiliar feeling of respect, and muted by an unexpected feeling of inadequacy. Eventually she searched convention to find some suitable words. "How do you like our weather?" she asked, remembering that the weather was supposed to be a favorite subject for the British.

Roy laughed and relaxed, knowing that the decision to bring Lily to India would suit the needs of her hosts as well as it would suit his own.

Over the next few days Jyoti Ma fussed over Lily, asking her all too frequently whether there was anything else she needed. It was the closest that the memsahib had ever come to being a servant. There were absolutely no expectations made of the governess. She was treated as an honored guest who was just stopping off to inspect Prakriti as part of a grand tour. So much so that it was Lily who finally suggested starting the lessons for Tulsi Devi.

For Lily, friendship was the best way to encourage curiosity and learning, and so she set out to become Tulsi Devi's friend. She wanted them both to learn from each other, and began by asking her young student to teach her more about the Indian way of life.

"Tell me, Tulsi Devi, how are marriages arranged in your country?" Lily asked.

Jyoti Ma, who attended every class, answered, "Even in your country marriages are arranged." Tulsi Devi was about to add something, but Jyoti Ma finished with what she thought would be the most correct and suitable answer: "You see, all marriages are pre-destined and we must learn to love the person that fate has chosen for us."

Sensing that Tulsi Devi's voice was being squashed by her mother's, Lily tried again. "Tell me, Tulsi Devi, why are so many Indians vegetarians?" Before Tulsi Devi could open her mouth, Jyoti Ma answered: "Why should we kill an animal for just a few minutes of sensual pleasure? We do not eat meat because it is not pure."

Lily managed a defeated smile in response to the beaming Jyoti Ma, who all the time was wondering when the real lessons were going to start with instructions on writing, arithmetic, history and so on.

Later that day, Jyoti Ma took Lily aside and told her that if she wished to eat meat, she could help procure some for her. But Lily turned down the offer, saying, "When in Rome, do as the Indians do!" And took this opportunity of shared confidences to tell Jyoti Ma that she would prefer the lessons to be conducted privately.

Left to themselves, Lily felt far more relaxed and found that it was also easier to engage her student. Tulsi Devi told her all the stories that the workers in the fields and her ayah had told her not to tell Jyoti Ma. She asked endless questions about England, about Lily's childhood and her family. And Lily asked Tulsi Devi about her dreams and what she wanted to do when she grew up. It was an important question for Lily, because she had never been offered anything other than marriage as a grand prize, and after that a big full stop. Tulsi Devi wasn't any different, but within her restrictions she had a field day with her fantasies. Maybe she would marry a maharaja. Or maybe a man who owned a diamond mine. Or the king of all the pearl fishers. Or maybe even a prince who lived under the sea in a palace made of shells.

"Are you going to marry Roy?" asked Tulsi Devi.

"Maybe, maybe not. Maybe I won't get married at all."

"But what will become of you if you don't marry?"

"I'll become extremely successful and independent, and I'll set an example for all other girls of the future like yourself."

"And they will let you do this in your country?" asked Tulsi Devi, unable to imagine the sort of life Lily was describing.

Tulsi Devi asked Lily if she could go with her to England when she went back there, because it all sounded so very exciting. They talked about the places they would visit, and then Lily took Tulsi Devi on an imaginary tour around the world to places that she'd never seen herself. They imagined their way around Europe, Africa, China and the Americas. Lily would tell stories with drawings, illustrating the travels of fairies. There would be one fairy in front of the Pyramids, looking like a sphinx with wings; another under the Niagara Falls, with skirts tumbling down into the water. And then there were pixies who traveled to the Leaning Tower of Pisa and the Arc de Triomphe. When the fairies and pixies came home, Tulsi Devi had to write up their adventures as homework for Lily.

There was no doubt about it, Tulsi Devi was enjoying the most progressive education available in her country. And having only one student meant there was plenty of time off for Lily.

Often when Tulsi Devi was busy writing her stories, Lily would search out Roy in the fields to entice him on a long walk around the alluring hills. Roy, of course, was always willing to drop studies of seedlings and soils to follow Lily on her nature trail. When Prakriti was out of sight, they would sometimes spend a few minutes on a rock or by the stream, but Lily would always put a stop to his advances, knowing that even in the most remote corners of India someone is always nearby. That the trees up ahead of them could conceal a truant child, a cow girl or a sleeping grandfather.

One day when Lily came to seek out Roy's company, he took her not to the nearby valley but to the sheds where he had set up his temporary camp. The sheds where Bahadur had hidden his existence from the world. Once they were hidden and the door closed, Roy started feeling for the buttons on her shirt. His mind was racing forward. Lily was already naked, as she had been a thousand times before in his imagination.

"Stop it. Not here. Not now," she told him, speaking as a governess, not his lover.

"When if not now?" Roy said, feeling that if he waited for her any longer, he would surely be hospitalized with frustration.

Like a man drunk on his fantasies, unable to take control of his body, his hands worked their own will to continue undressing her. He was trying to free a bird from its cage, but the bird simply refused to fly. Lily reached for her clothes to assert herself, and just as she was doing so, the door opened.

It was Aakash who walked in, saw things exactly as they were and walked out again, wordless.

In an instant, Lily's self-respect deserted her.

The two of them searched for their fig leaves, putting on their clothes as swiftly as if Aakash were still standing there watching them. Lily feeling shamed and powerless; Roy embarrassed but cross at the interruption.

"Don't worry," Roy assured her. "He's a man. He'll understand. He was just coming to call me for lunch."

Lily sat down and started biting her nails, a habit she had neglected for over fifteen years. They tasted dreadful, and the thought of the eyes watching her whilst she ate her shameful lunch made her feel sick. Roy put his arms around her, but her shoulders seized up under them. This was how he had caused all the trouble in the first place. How dare he!

"Relax. Do you think he's never done this before?" Roy's words made Lily feel angry, as if she had undressed for a crowd of men who had all "done these things before."

"We have disgraced ourselves. We must leave Prakriti immediately." She said it again and again, as if the words alone could fly her out on a magic carpet without having to face another person on the farm. The humiliation of leaving in such disgrace made her nerves tighten further.

Roy promised to sort things out. He knew he could – he had calculated that the odds were in his favor. Aakash may have been older than him, but they would be speaking man to man, and Roy possessed the implicit advantage of belonging to the ruling nation.

As things turned out nothing was straightforward when the two men met in the fields later that day. Aakash did not show any reaction when he saw Roy. He was quite willing to continue their friendship without any discussion about the incident. Roy started off the conversation by telling Aakash that he wanted to propose to Lily.

"You mean you haven't already?" Aakash responded, making Roy feel instantly guilty.

Roy continued on undeterred, and told him of his love for Lily. He asked Aakash to keep quiet about events he had witnessed for the sake of Lily's honor and his own. As Aakash responded well to this request, he made another one – to borrow Ganesh and the mahout for one moonlit night.

Lily was unsettled over the next few days. Nobody was treating her differently, so she presumed they did not know about her public display in the sheds. Nevertheless, she avoided Aakash, even though he showed her as much respect as he always had.

One night both Roy and Lily had dinner with the family in the farmhouse. When the meal was over Roy stood up, took Lily's hand and asked her if she would come with him for a walk. Everybody was smiling at her and Tulsi Devi was giggling, making her feel extremely conspicuous. She turned Roy down, saying that she should stay behind and get an early night, but Aakash said, "No, you must go."

No sooner had she stepped off the verandah, she saw the elephant crouched on the ground in the darkness and was helped up onto its back. Roy hopped up with her, and the mahout followed. The four of them advanced up the hills and into the night, Ganesh as sure-footed as a mountain deer. A Yorkshire farmer, a London girl and an Indian elephant tamer on a mission to secure a life partnership.

Roy did not know just when he should pop the question. If truth be told, he did not know *when* because he did not know *if* Lily would say yes. She was capable of anything, he knew that much. But if he didn't procure her love for always, he knew that she would remain forever tantalizingly out of reach. Even if she had reservations, he had one thing in his favor: since Aakash had discovered them undressed in the sheds the pressure was on to make their match respectable.

So the moon bore witness, and the mahout looked the other way as Roy kissed Lily passionately. His urge to undress her was so strong that he proposed there and then, so he could claim the privileges of husbandhood for the rest of their lives.

Lily knew he was going to ask. Otherwise, why the elephant? And because she didn't know what to answer, she thought she'd leave it to her instincts at the very last minute. It would be a gamble – like a dice thrown the minute the question left his lips.

The dice spun ... Lily analyzed her thoughts for clues. The first thing that came up was her conversation with Tulsi Devi about how she needn't get married at all. No, she would say "No."

And then another thought bubbled up from the depths. It was the realization that every single suffragette she knew was married.

Without thinking any further she said "Yes." The rolling dice landed and Roy breathed a sigh of relief. Then he belched. The after-dinner tension had been all too much.

On their return they were congratulated by Aakash, Jyoti Ma and Tulsi Devi who had stayed up late to discover the outcome. Tulsi Devi knew all along that Lily would say yes, but she remained awake just to see if the face of her governess had changed in the two hours she had been gone. Jyoti Ma felt as if a historic event had taken place in her house. She distributed sweets and made the betrothed couple place mithai in each other's mouth.

During the festivities Aakash took Roy to one side and told him for the first time that he had been unsettled by his discovery in the sheds. "I am not talking about morality," he said, "my concern is for the souls of the unborn." Roy wasn't about to start telling Aakash the details of his precautions, so he accepted the advice in the good spirit that it was given, and the party continued.

A few days later Roy was called off to Delhi to offer landscaping advice and help plant trees that would see India into the next century. He left Aakash to plant a new hybrid herb that would start saving lives the minute it was first harvested.

Meanwhile, Jyoti Ma was experiencing a spell of happiness and contentment that she had never known before, feeling the romance in the air as if it were her own. There were no troubles in the house and the servants were allowed the grace of forgiveness for all minor misdemeanors.

Until Lily finally left to marry Roy, Tulsi Devi became like a younger sister to her governess. It was a friendship that explored a world outside of the farm – a world where men and women kissed and fell in love. A world where Tulsi Devi, too, could imagine herself kissing and falling, falling, falling, without ever reaching the ground.

12

A long time had passed since Lily and Roy had left the farm to get married, and a twelve-year-old Tulsi Devi had started to turn feral again. Jyoti Ma had stuck to Lily's rigorous teaching schedule for a few months, but the task of supervising the household and the servants was so tiresome, she could barely fit it in. Besides which, now that Lily had reinvented the concept of education, captivating Tulsi Devi's imagination was like trying to catch clouds with a fishing net. She may have been sitting poring over her books, but she wasn't fully present in her body. Once or twice Jyoti Ma saw her concentrating hard over a story, only to find when she looked more closely that the book was turned upside down.

To do things slightly differently and make up for Lily's Westernized system of education, Jyoti Ma started teaching Tulsi Devi Indian history. Together, mother and daughter devoted as much attention to the Moghul emperors as Jyoti Ma had devoted to the wives of Henry the VIII when she herself was a child, being taught in a convent.

But rote learning didn't come easily anymore to Tulsi Devi and she started getting most confused. She always muddled up her emperors, remembering Aurangzeb as a kind old man whom the people loved, instead of the tyrant who killed anybody who was in the slightest bit decadent. When Jyoti Ma asked who built the Pearl Mosque, Tulsi Devi answered Bahadur Shah Zafar.

"Ma, wasn't Bahadur Ram's friend?"

"What sort of a friend would take you away from your family like that?"

Thus the lessons continued to take off at tangents. Jyoti Ma would leave the class to make sure the servants hadn't stopped working, and when she came back, it would be Tulsi Devi who had stopped working. Either that or she had run out into the fields to go and talk to the women workers, who could teach her all the wisdom of the world that doesn't dare walk into any classroom.

Tulsi Devi learnt what it meant to have problems with in-laws, problems with money and problems with your reputation. Her women friends in the fields made her help them tend to the crops and harvest the fruit in the orchard so they could claim Tulsi Devi's work as their own and earn some extra money.

Aakash knew that they were making money out of Tulsi Devi, but he knew also that she enjoyed the work so he let it pass. What he didn't know was that Tulsi Devi also robbed the coffers to distribute spare cash to the women in the fields who entertained her with their stories.

All the women learnt to trust saab's daughter as a secret source of supply and they began to approach her with many and varying stories of woe. She contributed discreetly to increase the dowries of their daughters so they could find a better match. She helped their cousins escape from bonded labor on nearby farms, and she helped support elderly relatives of the workers whom she had never met.

Once when Jyoti Ma was going through the books with her usual microscopic attention, she discovered that one worker was consistently being paid twice. When Aakash was cross-examined by his wife, he confessed that his workers occasionally earned wages for the labor of Tulsi Devi.

"You are knowing of this all along and doing nothing?" Jyoti Ma cried out.

"It's just child's play," Aakash answered. "She's just pretending."

"It's not play – it's deceit. You are letting all the workers know that it's just fine to rob us."

"A few paise here and there. That's all. It's my dharma to work, not examine the fruits of my labor," Aakash told his wife.

"But what of your daughter? Will you have her married off to one of their brothers, uncles or cousins? Do you want to see her live her life with someone who crawls in the dirt for a living?"

Aakash argued that their daughter needed the company of other people. She could not be reared in isolation, just because they lived in the Himalayas so far from anywhere. Jyoti Ma, forced to agree, was left to work out yet another strategy for creating the "right" kind of company.

She thought about who could be trusted to provide good company for her daughter, and an idea slowly evolved. She would invite her sister Pyari and her children to come and stay.

At that time, Pyari and her husband Anthony were building a home in Delhi, enduring the discomfort of temporary quarters until such time as their house was habitable. They had two angels for children who were a little older than Tulsi Devi – David and Joyce. The more Jyoti Ma thought of them, the clearer the solution became.

Very soon she wrote to plead with Pyari and Anthony to come and stay until their house was built in Delhi. She wrote beautiful things about the mountains, the healthy air and the wonderful nature of the mountain people. She seduced them with the comforts she could offer and talked about plans for a school they could set up together.

Jyoti Ma's sister didn't need any persuading. It was a dry hot summer in Delhi and the children were listless. She organized the move to Prakriti within a few weeks, bringing dozens of Delhi luxuries, her entire wardrobe and an abundant amount of enthusiasm.

Anthony stayed to supervise the builders and continue his work, but Joyce and David came with their mother to enjoy time on a farm in the hills. Tulsi Devi was thirteen. It was just about the time when she was starting to see men as handsome, and her cousin David was, in her opinion, most definitely handsome.

The farmhouse was transformed into a living, breathing, noisy home. David soon became the playground hero by learning from the mahout how to instruct Ganesh. With their new trainee mahout, the children would take off into the mountains, singing at the tops of their voices, saying "faster, faster" to Ganesh, who continued to plod on slowly, trusting his ancient wisdom rather than the rash eagerness of his underage riders.

When it appeared that the guests were there to stay for quite some time, Aakash gave David a plot of land to call his very own. David planted it with flowers and vegetables and supervised the mali to dig out any seedlings that had taken root in his own little kingdom. Not content with his own piece of Prakriti, he went out into the fields to learn about every plant and every tree that grew there.

Aakash grew very fond of David and his wild spirit. This boy, he felt, belonged to the mountains, belonged to the land. In the city he would grow old in a chair and his eyes would grow short-sighted from not being able to see far enough into the distance.

The little gang of raucous privileged children commanded attention wherever they went. Together the three of them went regularly to the markets in the nearby village, and David showed them all how they could distract the shopkeeper to steal sweets. Once they were caught and escorted home to Prakriti. Aakash managed to buy off the shopkeeper with enough money to supply his store with sweets for ten years. But first he asked the shopkeeper what he suggested as punishment.

"The children must learn what it is like to be poor," he told them all. "Send them to me and I will show them."

Aakash sat them down to tell them once, and once only, about stealing. He knew that they would all be compassionate as adults, so he let their shame work its own course without dwelling on their misdemeanours. Neither did he tell their mothers.

Far from learning the meaning of a life of poverty, with David as their ringleader the children had the family fortune at their command. When David announced that he wanted to learn to ride horses, three horses were bought from another farmer. When David declared that they should have fireworks for Diwali, a peon was sent to Delhi to buy a big basket of fireworks for all the children.

That Diwali was the most magical any of them had witnessed. The children were sent off to light the fireworks far away from the house, in case they set fire to the roofs. They rode Ganesh up to a nearby mountaintop, after painting him in elaborate designs with the clay colors the mahout saved for such occasions. They looked like renegades from an ancient royal parade, commanding the King's elephant to take them Elsewhere.

They arrived at their mountain on top of the world and David supervised, letting them each light one firework in turn. Sprays of gold and silver burst over the trees, making Ganesh startle as if he'd just seen a wild tiger. They laughed and shrieked and gasped whenever they saw a big explosion. When all their fiery delights were done with, they marched Ganesh back down to the farmhouse as if they were Shri Ram and his entourage arriving for a homecoming feast after fourteen years. Away down in the distance they could see all the little lights in the village and all the lights around Prakriti illuminating the night sky.

Tulsi Devi couldn't help but think about her brother Ram and wonder if he would ever return to play with them and their fireworks, now that Prakriti was so much fun.

With Pyari for company, Jyoti Ma loosened the bridle on her servants and spent many hours doing nothing but talking with her sister.

"You live in a paradise of bliss," Pyari told her. "We could be in the Kingdom of Heaven, Jyoti. You are so very lucky."

"This place is out of the way. In the middle of nowhere. I long for Amritsar. For Delhi. There's nothing you can buy here. Nobody worth talking to."

"If Anthony didn't have work in Delhi I would pick up and buy a farm next to yours tomorrow."

Whenever Pyari thought of her husband she would start to weep, and then Jyoti Ma would weep too, both of them shedding tears for the husbands who couldn't be there to meet their needs. Once Pyari read a letter from Anthony out loud.

"My darling heart, my Pyari," she said, her voice imitating her husband's deeper tones. "How I long to hold you. How I miss your kind words, your gentle presence. I long to sit our children on my knees and laugh and play ... We will be together before long, I promise. And I will be a husband for you once more."

Jyoti Ma was so enchanted by the voice of love she asked if she could keep the letter. Pyari gave it to her, but not without crying some more, this time for Jyoti Ma who was herself shaking with tears.

Those were good days for the servants. There was never anything to do when the mistresses of the house were absorbed in their sobbings. Instead they sat on the kitchen floor and entertained each other as if they were the lords of the cooking pots.

Everything changed dramatically, though, one day when Jyoti Ma discovered that the tea was finished. According to her calculations there had been enough tea in the tin to last for another month. Where had it gone? When she realized that her servants had been sitting around drinking endless cups of chai for the past few weeks, she picked up her iron scepter once more and reclaimed her formidable status as ruler of the household.

Pyari let her get on with it, spending time learning about ayurvedic herbs and formulations. In the evenings she would talk with Aakash for hours about the herbs. Some that could kill, some that could cure, and others like amla, which prevented diseases. She learnt that a cough was not just a cough, but often an off-balance of vata, and could be soothed by talking less and sipping ginger tea. She learnt how diseases of the heart, lungs and kidneys went together, because they were all linked by the element of air. She learnt how to detect a vata complaint when long thin people complained of itchy skin, sleeplessness and poor digestion. She learnt how to diagnose diseases by feeling a patient's pulse.

"I marvel at your knowledge," she told Aakash one day, "but you must use this knowledge for the benefit of others. This is why you have your farm, nay, to help people? So why just send the herbs elsewhere? We should set up our own clinic here at Prakriti."

It was a thought that had already occurred to Aakash, so it sat quite naturally on the seat he had allocated in his mind. What turned the thought to action was the way Pyari said "our own clinic." What he had been waiting for all these years, he realized, was a companion to help him in this mission.

"If you help me," Aakash said, "I will set up this clinic tomorrow."

"It would be the greatest honor," Pyari replied.

Aakash was true to his word. The next day an ayurvedic clinic and dispensary was set up outside the house, and the following day the first patients came.

The dispensary was popular and Aakash was charmed by Pyari's kindness to the villagers. She always called the village children beti and beta, as she did her own children. After seeing a patient she always said, "God bless you and make you better. Have faith. That is the main thing."

Aakash often skipped his supervision in the fields to help her prepare combinations and pass on more of his knowledge. Sometimes he would lay hands on patients and effect an immediate cure, just as he had done with the maharaja's son in Chail so many years earlier. Everybody would be amazed, but Aakash would say, "Disease is not a final outcome.

Unless the patient is dead, energy is always free to move, and so is the disease that blocks it."

Pyari appreciated his support and looked after Aakash, sending him endless treats from the kitchens and making sure that he was welcomed home a hero every day. She was saturated with admiration for him. And he, too, admired her. He admired the way she threw boundless affection at the children, teaching them lessons in the most informal and effortless fashion. And he loved the way they all adored her, bringing her strange products of nature as their offerings: once it was two guavas that had joined together as one; the next day it was a scorpion found in Joyce's salwar chemise that had been left on the ground. Then the children found elephant hairs as thick as twigs. None of these precious natural miracles was lost on Pyari and she dedicated a shelf in her room as a shrine to amazing artifacts that the children had given her. "Without children, who could truly teach us joy?" she would say, as she treasured the rewards of her devotion.

One day during Pyari's stay both Jyoti Ma and Aakash fell sick with fevers. Pyari took over the supervision of the children and the household without losing any of her sweet nature, still finding time to run her morning ayurvedic clinic and nurse the two of them. "Just sleep," she told Aakash. "You have been working too hard and this is nature's way of forcing you to take rest." When she started to pat Aakash's head with ice and a towel he held her arm in his delirium as if she were his own. Her presence was so soothing and reassuring he almost wished to stay forever on his sickbed, receiving this endlessly loving attention. When his fever was high he often found himself imagining that married life was the most blissful of all experiences, but then he would cool down and realize that Pyari was not his to hold.

Aakash was a noble man, and he allowed himself to love Pyari for who she was – his sister-in-law – constantly reminding himself that desires should always be checked. Nonetheless, Jyoti Ma could not help but notice his admiration for her sister. It filled her with a warped kind of pride in her family, together with a hatred for her husband, and herself. She was unable to take Pyari's lead and appeal to her husband's affections herself, because the more he warmed to Pyari, the less deserving, in Jyoti Ma's eyes, he became.

Aakash couldn't help but feel pleased that Pyari was staying long-term at Prakriti. Their plans to build a house in Delhi were always being thwarted by the British, who kept commandeering their laborers with higher salaries to help them build what was soon to become India's new capital. Anthony would despair and take a month at a time off work to come and stay at the farm. Pyari would dote on him as she doted on everyone, showing all the little signs of affection that had been rarities in their household up till then. "Come, let me press your feet," she would say, and always waited for her husband to eat before eating herself.

Aakash liked Anthony. They would discuss philosophies and religions at length into the evening hours. Anthony was a Christian, but an open-minded one who didn't care to adhere too closely to the dogmas of his faith, because he refused to believe that most of his good friends and his much-loved wife could possibly end up in eternal damnation.

The two families became one for four years. The clinic that Pyari and Aakash set up soon began testing remedies of miraculous potency. Joyce was to receive her first offer of marriage at Prakriti when she was seventeen, from a friend of her father's whose son was seven years her senior. She turned down the offer because she was enjoying her life on the farm too much to leave. Anthony was pleased, although he couldn't tell his friend. It wasn't so much that the boy was unsuitable, but that he wanted to spend a few years together in their new family home in Delhi before saying goodbye to Joyce.

When the house was finally ready, Pyari went alone to Delhi to prepare her new home. Life went on for everyone as usual. The children, now a little older, managed to continue their self-sufficient form of schooling. Only Aakash found himself missing Pyari and the time they spent together in the mornings. And the villagers who came for their medicines – they too missed her. Aakash felt as if they had shared a vision together that was all gone. But he carried on their clinic in her memory, as if she were deceased.

One day when Aakash was a little late to start the clinic, he heard Jyoti Ma screeching at a small group of villagers who had lined up along the back verandah. He marched out to the clinic and, for the first time in his married life, he found himself shouting at his wife. His language was restrained, but his volume so loud that Tulsi Devi, David and Joyce came running to see who was hurting him. The small crowd of villagers soon dispersed, feeling guilty for being sick, and Jyoti Ma continued to vent her venom at her husband.

"I am sick to death of these people lurking around our house every day. Pyari's gone now and you should be getting back to work instead of wasting your time on them."

"How dare you take it upon yourself to destroy these charitable works?" answered Aakash. "If you had even one ounce of compassion in you we could have set this up years ago."

"Oh, come, come, how much compassion have you shown me after all these years? Haram Zada, you don't need a wife, you need a donkey!"

Tulsi Devi had never seen such a display of emotion between her parents, and she found herself almost enjoying it, simply because for once they were really interacting with passion.

But all this passion was making Jyoti Ma giddy, and she felt blinded by loathing for the man who had brought her to this despicable state of self-hatred. She screamed at the children to go and pack their bags.

That night they all left for Delhi. All of them except for Aakash. David and Joyce, nostalgic already for their country life now that it was over, and Tulsi Devi with a strange feeling in the pit of her stomach that her family would never be the same again.

Jyoti Ma was silently incensed that her husband had humiliated her in front of the villagers and in front of the children. She was serious this time about staying with her sister and never returning to see this man who had offered her nothing in marriage but money.

Aakash had time that evening alone.

Once the servants had cleared up the mess left by the exodus party he sighed, sad that the person whom he missed most after the departure of his entire family was not Jyoti Ma, but Pyari.

13

Several weeks had passed since Jyoti Ma and the children had left Prakriti. However, far from feeling robbed of his family, Aakash was now starting to experience the freedom of a true renunciant. His life was as it had been before he married, only now he was more experienced. Instead of the usual noise of active young teenage children, he heard the sounds of the mountains. He started to hear life in its more subtle dimensions. No birds, because birds were rare in those hills, but distant calls, the winds and the sound of Silence itself, vibrating in its fullness. It made him feel alive and complete. His body, which was older now, felt charged with life in spite of its outer signs of ageing.

There was no feeling of loss. If anything there was anticipation.

Prakriti became his garden of Eden and he felt as if he were at the beginning of a new life. Without Jyoti Ma he experienced a greater sense of love and compassion than he had ever encountered in their time together. There was no stopping him from giving abundantly to the deserving and undeserving. There was no looking back over his shoulder for fear of being checked. Nobody to challenge his sense of purpose and his vision for Prakriti. He was free to bring anyone he wished into the house. Not that he ever did, because he found his freedom most profoundly in his experience of solitude.

The night after Jyoti Ma and the children left there was a freak storm up in the hills. Nobody had ever seen the likes of it before. Hailstones the size of bricks fell from the sky as if there were a bunker full of them suspended in the air. Several people were killed and houses destroyed as icy bricks fell through shingle roofs like warnings from the heavens. Even Ganesh fell to the ground concussed and was unable to get up on his feet again for several days.

The storm could have been a simple coincidence, but Aakash couldn't help but link the two events. The spontaneous reaction of nature to events of human consequence.

After the storm Aakash surveyed the devastation and then resolved that nothing is lost where experience is gained. Plants had been completely uprooted. Bushes that were four feet tall lay flattened on the ground. Buds had been severed from the sap that fed them. Whole branches lay on the ground, snapped off wherever nature had created a fault line. Everywhere the ground was thick with a carpet of green debris.

Many of the workers stayed at home after the storm, trying to bring back order in their own lives and repair their own dwellings. The ones who didn't have homes were sent off by Aakash to help the ones who did.

Aakash himself did not go out into the fields, because he had an idea that if the plants were left to themselves their instinct for life would triumph. He went instead to Ganesh and he stayed with his hands on the elephant until he saw the first stirrings of life in his trunk.

From then on the weather improved, the downtrodden plants raised themselves with the strength of their own inner vitality and desire for unity with the sun. The debris soon turned to compost and the farmland was nourished as never before. Prakriti started to experience unprecedented growth.

It was around this time that Aakash started receiving orders for herbs from ayurvedic centers and factories around India. He had never before envisaged such demand and questioned whether he should be embarking on such a lucrative expansion of his business. In fact, he had never intended Prakriti to become a business at all, only a service. The integrity of Prakriti, he felt, would survive this stage of development, but perhaps his interest in it would not.

Regardless, Aakash ordered seeds and waited for the new life that would come with them.

One night Ganesh became unsettled. He bellowed and trumpeted and paced and would not rest till dawn. Aakash stayed up the night with him to try to fathom the reason for his heightened reactions, but could not cure him. In the morning the mahout arrived and whispered calming words into the tip of his trunk. Ganesh held his trunk up to the mahout's ear and snorted.

"We must decorate him," announced the mahout and went to look for the paints that awaited special occasions such as Diwali.

Once the mahout had started his soothing brushstrokes Ganesh settled down. Before too long, there were circles of intricate ochre patterns around his face and decorative designs all over his head.

Aakash, as always, was stunned by the man's symbiotic understanding of the elephant. He had thought that Ganesh was still suffering from the storm like the rest of Prakriti, but no, he became settled as soon as he was wearing his ceremonial adornments.

The mahout then advised Aakash that Ganesh needed a walk, and so Aakash sent them both off to pick up the heavy bags of seed that were scheduled to arrive on the morning train.

They were gone some time, but when Aakash saw Ganesh returning, he walked out to the road to see how he had fared on the journey. In the distance he saw the painted elephant with two figures riding. Closer it came and the second figure became clearer. He was wearing a white shawl and white robes. Closer still and the face became familiar. A man with uncut hair and beard appeared. Ganesh stopped and crouched down on his knees. Bedecked in his regal designs, he lifted his trunk to the prince, who started to dismount. The two figures climbed down and then Aakash saw him. Ram.

"This is where we said goodbye fourteen years ago, Pitaji," Ram said.

For a second Aakash lost contact with the ground that he trod on. His arms quaked as he opened them to embrace his son, but Ram touched his father's feet for a solid minute before they held each other tight. The mahout burst into uncontrollable fits of tears just watching them. Aakash, speechless, put his arm around his son to lead him back to the farmhouse. He ordered the cook to prepare a banquet and he sat down to study the years that had passed in the face of this striking man.

Ram was a pure beam of light. A light that traveled so fast it could have been an image of Aakash himself as a young man. His son's clarity was awe-inspiring and his presence was mighty. Aakash immediately saw in him the vision he himself had sought out in early life. Ram hadn't wasted a minute of life without asking the question: "Who am I and what am I here for?" His focus was unerring. It showed in the intensity of his very Being.

Aakash was intrigued by his son's path. His destination. His profound understanding of the very sap of life that feeds and unifies the whole of creation. Ram was no longer the curious and earnest young boy Aakash had known. He had traveled ever closer to the source of all knowledge in his adventure. His questions had transformed themselves into living answers. They were there in his veins and in his cells and every part of him that drew a different life from the heightened state of consciousness he now held.

They discussed philosophies and mysticism. Aakash told his son about his struggle between his desire to renounce the world and his passion for life. Ram gave him his answer, telling him that they were one and the same, only separated by intellectual activity of the mind. He encouraged Aakash to look deeper. Not to think, but to go beyond thought to the quietude of inner experience, where he could feel for himself how pure consciousness unites all distinctions.

"Pitaji, your passion for life does not diminish when you renounce the world. It increases. In truth you are not giving up anything, but rather embracing everything."

"You make it sound so simple."

"Actually, Pitaji, it is simpler to surrender your desires and your concerns than to hold on to them with all your strength."

Aakash listened and marveled at his son. He asked more about Guru Dev, and the more Ram talked about his life with his Master, the stronger Aakash's own beam of light was drawn in that direction.

If there was one thing Ram said that clicked a switch in his father's head, it was this: he described his feeling on arriving for the first time in Jyotir Math, a remote little town in the Himalayas. Instead of feeling as if he were living his life on the periphery, he felt as if he'd finally landed in the very center of the universe.

He continued to talk of life at the centre of all things – and described how his dedication to this pure state of consciousness was a way of preserving the infinite knowledge that was held there. It was the place where all diversity met unity.

"If consciousness precedes all matter, I can dedicate my life to no higher purpose than to its illumination," Ram told his father with the sincerity of a man who had questioned a thousand outward directions before finding his most instinctive inward one.

The two men meditated together. They walked the fields of Prakriti. They talked about old times. About Bahadur.

They visited the cave where this big adventure had begun. Sat down at the old desks and looked far out at the mountains, as they had first done when the significant questions of life started to arise.

There in the cave Ram taught his father a meditation technique from the holy tradition of the Shankaracharyas – the same one he had been taught by his guru to bring his thoughts back to the source of all life. It was his gift, Ram felt, to return all the support and knowledge that Aakash had given him in early life before he left to live in Jyotir Math.

Aakash came out of his meditation feeling as if he had traveled down to the depths of the earth and returned with great treasures of the soul. He didn't want to speak to break the profound sense of silence and bliss that had seeped into his body.

Realizing the depths from which Aakash was returning, Ram chose this moment to express the real purpose of his visit. He turned to his father.

"Are you coming back with me?"

The answer was incontestable.

That night Aakash wrote a letter to Jyoti Ma in Delhi and explained that he was going to take up sannyas and live a life of renunciance in the hills. He left instructions with the mahout on how to manage the farm till Jyoti Ma's return. He gave thanks and said prayers for the continued life and success of Prakriti, his family, and the successors he was leaving behind. He took leave of everyone he knew at the farm and blessed the bags of seed that were left now for someone else to plant.

14

Jyoti Ma looked over the few pages that marked the end of her married life. Unable to read the words out loud, she passed the trembling sheets to her sister – a sad exchange for the love letters that Pyari had shared with her in earlier times.

Pyari's support was unfailing. The whole family, including Anthony this time, made their way back to the hills to settle the affairs of the farm. And Jyoti Ma, like a widow, returned to Prakriti ashamed of her new status. "If Papa had known what sort of a man I was marrying," she told her sister, "he would have demanded to talk to his father. Made him see some sense." Jyoti Ma had forgotten that she was the one who had left her husband, her daughter in tow. "Now I have nothing," she sobbed. "Who is going to help me?"

Help was all around her, but she was blind to it. Pyari was patient. "Jyoti, you married a good man," she assured her sister. "You'll be fine. I'm here. And Anthony. We'll look after you."

Anthony found the affairs of the farm in perfect order, but when he took the time to show Jyoti Ma all the orders for herbs and remedies from around India, a river of tears erupted and she told him to throw it all away.

It wasn't as if Aakash had done something dishonorable. Taking up sannyas was a respectable sequel to a life of dynamic activity, if he had only waited just a few more years. No, the shame came from the fact that everyone around her suspected that she had driven him to it. That the loudness of her discontent had driven him into the arms of Silence.

One part of Jyoti Ma desperately wanted to see Aakash again, so that she could have the opportunity to show her husband she was capable of change. Yet, after the insults that she had flung at him at their last meeting, there was also a small, desperate sense of relief that she didn't have to face him again. But nothing compared to the burden of desertion. Whenever she thought of Aakash her eyes burnt and swelled with tears of self-loathing.

It was a turning point for Jyoti Ma. Her life had come full circle. It had returned to zero. She felt as if she had arrived at a dead end in a nowhere land where nothing ever happened. "If God takes me now, I will go willingly," she began to say. From that time forward, Jyoti Ma no longer vented her frustration on her servants, but on herself.

Pyari saw to all the household affairs whilst her sister sat looking at the mountains for the first time in years, incapacitated. "You cannot give up," Pyari told her. "Look at how much you have. Look to the world. See how much you still have to do here."

Slowly, by virtue of her headstrong nature, Jyoti Ma arose from her own ashes and started to participate in the business of Prakriti. At first she simply went out into the fields to stare at the workers, unable to issue a single decree. Then she started noticing the missing seeds, the long chai breaks, the excuses made for absent laborers, and her insistent habit of command forced her back into action, if only to stop the workers from taking advantage.

She did not grow remedies; she grew plants. She was more interested in filling orders than serving people, but she saw to it that Prakriti was considered one of the superior sources for ayurvedic supplies around India. Over the months to come, her involvement turned to obsession, and she could often be seen walking the fields that had hitherto been the private domain of Aakash.

Without a husband she never quite recovered her sense of purpose, and became a very distant mother to Tulsi Devi. Jyoti Ma devoted endless hours to proving that Prakriti could be a success without the mystical influence of Aakash, which left less time to supervise her daughter.

Tulsi Devi held a quiet resentment against her mother for making her father leave. She missed Aakash intensely. He had left nothing of his presence, no reminder of his love, but she could see very well why he had gone. It was nothing to do with selfishness, as her mother always claimed. She knew nobody as selfless as her father. No, the reason was far beyond that.

There was only one good thing to come out of all this for her, and that was the fact that she was united once more with her cousins on the land that she loved more than anywhere else in the world.

Tulsi Devi, Joyce and David spent their time out of the house – nobody seemed to care too much for their daily routines. They went to the cave to play "future games," where each of them would take it in turns to imagine a future for the others. It was a retreat from the horribleness of the present, but served its purpose in shrouding the reality that they found themselves a part of. In the futures game Joyce told Tulsi Devi, "You will marry an Englishman and go with him to London, where you will run his small castle and sometimes visit the Queen. Your children and your children's children will be famous heroes in their time and you will die in a grand wooden four-poster bed."

Tulsi Devi wasn't interested in endings. At least not yet. There was no happy ending within sight, so she would rather have heard nothing. For now she was content to sit inside her chalk circle in the confinement of the present and wait.

15

Standing in the Ganges at Rishikesh for the first time in his life, it occurred to Aakash that he had never so much as dipped his feet in the holy water before. He had never made this pilgrimage even once. His life had not allowed it, until this moment, and now he was at a threshold. The last threshold before crossing into Uttar Kashi, the valley of the saints. He stood under the Laxman Jhula swing bridge. The last bridge. And there in that garden of Eden he saw his last challenge in the material world – the return to Prakriti of his wife and daughter. He felt their shock, fear and pain as his own. He shrank back at their realization, weighty with his final responsibility to the world. He walked further out into the river to find his answer, until he was up to his shoulders in cold Ganges rapids, with Ram watching from the banks. There he held his hands together, his long thin fingers trembling and wet, and mumbled, "It is so so very beautiful here."

"Pitaji, there has not been a day when I haven't thought of you, or seen these hills through your eyes," Ram said. "For so long I've wanted to bring you here ... if it wasn't for Mama ..."

The water flowed relentlessly forward and Aakash looked up. He saw a sage sitting in meditation further upstream. The man's hair was tied in a topknot. He wore a string around his thin waist, a small loincloth and, apart from these things, only ash. Above him rose a high cliff to separate him from the world. At his feet the water ran into a still pool, small and green. Behind him, just near the river, was a simple dwelling. A home that Aakash would have been all too happy to call his own.

Ram walked out into the water and put his hand on his father's shoulder. "Pitaji, if you can believe and trust that you will be taken care of, then you can trust that your family will be taken care of too," he said.

Aakash found himself weeping, not through regret so much as joy, and his tears joined forces with the holy river. He was ecstatic with the freedom that rushed through his veins faster than the gushing tide that flowed around his body. Cupping a handful of water high above his head he offered himself as a libation. "Good Lord, I am yours now. Do with me what you will," he said, laughing with the glee of a young boy skipping down a hill, exhilarated by his own momentum, his unstoppable surrender.

"Let us cross the Laxman Jhula and make our way to Jyotir Math," Aakash said, pulling Ram's elbow in the direction he had always been heading, further up into the hills. They crossed the bridge together and made their way onward.

As Aakash traveled with Ram toward Jyotir Math, the seat of the Shankaracharya, they met other holy men. Some living in the hills permanently; others making pilgrimages, just passing through. They were offered shelter and food, and Ram introduced his father to the people he knew. One evening they sat around a fire with two other sages. A man with a wiry beard and weathered face asked Aakash, "What makes you think that you can find salvation here if you could not find it on your farm?"

"My friend," said Aakash, "I have found everything I needed to find on my farm, and I am sure that everything I need to find here, I will find. It is not a question of *where* I am, but *who* I am. And while I am still in this body I intend to discover that eternal essence, here in Uttar Kashi."

This answer gave Ram all the assurance he needed that his father had made the right decision to leave his former life behind.

On that journey into the mountains, Ram often heard his father say: "God, give them strength. God, give your protection." He did not need to ask what Aakash had meant by these words. He knew that his father was petitioning for his family in the only way he knew how; speaking words in faith, the only language he could guarantee would be heard.

The ashram at Jyotir Math was high up in the hills, in a world of its own. The walls marked out a space that was virtually empty, except for the inhabitants. Aakash touched the stone on the floor where he entered, and breathed a sigh of relief. "It's so peaceful," he kept repeating, relieved that there were no traces of the humdrum world lingering in that center of calm.

That evening he saw Guru Dev for the first time. It was a communion of Great Souls, and Aakash immediately sensed that he was in the company of someone he had been destined to meet. "We have been expecting you," was all that Guru Dev said, and from that moment Jyotir Math became Aakash's home. A home where his only obligation was to sit in Silence and experience pure Being – the force that gives life to the world.

Part Two

Although your body may exist on earth, your soul is always in Silence and knows no other home. It is never separated, even when you find yourself spiraling outward with nothing but the memory of Silence pinned to your consciousness – even then, remember the badge of Silence, for your true residence is written here, in the indelible ink of consciousness.

16

Well before partition, Tulsi Devi was sent to a convent school in Lahore "to pick up some Punjabi culture." There was nothing for a young girl on a farm. Living on her own with a beautiful daughter, Jyoti Ma felt the increasing pressure of the world Outside watching her exquisite flower grow. The truth of the matter – and what was most frightening for Jyoti Ma – was that this fair flower may one day intertwine with some local weed, and then any hopes for the future would be dashed into the pebbly earth.

She hoped that a change of air would bring Tulsi Devi down to earth and stop her acting like a villager, all too familiar with the junglee creatures in their tattered clothes, whom Tulsi Devi called her friends.

After all these years, Jyoti Ma was still repelled by the locals and by the filth that covered her whenever she left the house. Even now, when she laid her hands in the earth every day, it still represented an unknown world of contamination. She wanted her daughter to have a different life. A change of air, a change of company and a change in discipline would pull Tulsi Devi into shape, or so she thought.

She did not realize that this change of air up in Lahore would have the power to change Tulsi Devi's life forever.

As Tulsi Devi and her mother boarded the train for Lahore at Amritsar, Jyoti Ma felt as if she was introducing her daughter to the world. But then again, there was a nervous suspicion in her heart that the young girl who sat next to her in the first-class carriage, with the breeze in her dark curls, was not quite ready to see it. Or at least, not through the sedate gray lenses with which Jyoti Ma wished her to view things.

Little villages flew past the windows. Other lives, other concerns, other faces met theirs as they stopped at the stations and saw the beggars and peddlers hawking along the corridors and forcing their wares through the bars on the windows. Jyoti Ma slammed the window shut, nearly chopping off the last two fingers one beggar possessed.

At least her daughter was going to be looked after by nuns, she told herself. She, too, had benefited from a convent education. She had learnt French and English history and could recount any number of facts about Henry VIII and his six wives. But she had never officially learnt a word of Hindi. Ironically, the fact that she spoke "servant Hindi" instead of the pukka version was a mark of status in the colonial era.

It was a cool day when they arrived at the convent gates. The chowkidar looked Tulsi Devi up and down, and quickly decided she would not last there. The daughter looked far less determined and robust than her mother. There was a dreamy quality in her eyes, a layer of gelatine that filtered out the real nature of things. Even the mother seemed to be unsure of whether she should be leaving such a pretty one behind.

Once inside the gates of Loreto Convent the two were welcomed by the sisters and introduced to the young ladies who studied there. The emphasis at the convent was on learning etiquette rather than learning facts and figures. The girls were all dressed in the fashion of the time, with saris hitched up high to expose a variety of ankles, and feet clad in European buckle-up shoes instead of chappals. With their hair swept back flat where possible, and parted in the middle, the girls uniformly spoke of a dainty and civilized life.

Jyoti Ma left for Amritsar the next day, after Tulsi Devi had befriended a nice Punjabi girl by the name of Rashmi, and felt that maybe she had nothing to worry about. This life in the convent, although it was far from home, was more appropriate for a girl from her class. Without a father to help raise Tulsi Devi, the child would inevitably run wild on the farm, but here within the walls of the convent, she was safe.

The girls at Loreto Convent seemed to have respect for the nuns, always seeking out their advice on matters such as the future marriage partners who were being suggested to them. From their limited experience of life in a village in Ireland, the nuns would advise and reassure, laugh and cry with the girls in their care.

There was no overt missionizing, but if any of the students showed even the slightest interest in Bible Studies, they were welcomed into the inner circle of nuns with open robed arms. From that time on they were made to feel like part of a special secret freemasonry. What Jyoti Ma didn't realize when she left Tulsi Devi, was that her daughter's new friend, Rashmi, was one such convert.

"Do you ever wonder about all these idols that our families worship?" Rashmi asked Tulsi Devi one day.

"They just represent God. If God is everywhere, why can't God be in the idol too, hey nah?"

"But isn't it better to believe in a real person?"

"But what about our great gurus?"

"There was never a guru any greater than Jesus Christ."

"Rashmi, you're talking like you're going to become a nun. They'll keep you here and make you teach and you'll never get to leave school."

"This is what my life is for, Tulsi Devi. I'm going to become a nun."

"So you won't get married?"

"I will get married. But I will marry Jesus Christ and nobody less."

"Why don't you first get married, and then when your husband dies, take up sannyas and marry Jesus Christ?"

The discussion went no further. But the two girls were to have a meeting point soon. It came in the form of David De Souza, a Christian Goan who'd been called up north to teach maths because none of the sisters could count much further than a hundred.

This swarthy Goan took Loreto Convent by storm. Suddenly Rashmi wanted to marry David De Souza instead of Jesus Christ. As for Tulsi Devi, she was ready to replace all her idols with the Cross, the Holy Mary and the gaze of her latest idol, David utterly-butterly-delicious De Souza.

Suddenly it became extremely important to take an interest in mathematics. Both Rashmi and Tulsi Devi started asking for extra help, and managed to get David De Souza working overtime on their equations and square roots.

"These logarithms just don't add up, sir. How to do such complicated sums?"

The two girls became mathematical experts before long. For Rashmi, this encounter with David De Souza would stand her in good stead later in her married life, when she was taking hisaab from her servants and accounting for every paisa overspent on sweet limes and bitter gourd. For Tulsi Devi, it added up to a whole lot more, as she found more frequent occasions to talk with Mr. De Souza alone.

The day David De Souza summoned the gall to invite Tulsi Devi outside the convent grounds into the depths of Lahore, everything took a more serious turn. Only trusted college girls were allowed to go out into the city, and Tulsi Devi would have qualified, had she been out with Rashmi. But on that occasion, nobody was privy to the meeting that was set up, except for the two clandestine figures who made their historic departure from the haven inside the convent walls. It was raining heavily so nobody cared to look out into the gray to see them leaving separately. Tulsi Devi covered her head, and if anybody had been looking out of the window, they wouldn't have guessed who it could be slipping so quietly through the gate.

Only the chowkidar gave them each a knowing glance, being from a society where such liaisons were more readily accepted and expected. The teacher and student, however, knew that should their rendezvous in Temple Road be discovered, they would both be in water deeper than the puddles that splashed around their ankles.

Looking back on that day in the years that followed, Tulsi Devi would wonder how she could have found David De Souza so handsome. His eyes were framed by a single eyebrow. He had a good head of hair, but he was still only thirty-three. Maybe it was the fact that he was called David, just like the cousin she so admired? Whatever the attraction may have been, she never saw him for what he was – a single man in a school full of girls. But those realizations came too late. By the time the whole story was told, she had learnt the moral, and had paid for it. It was a story she would have to live with, and there was no looking back.

17

Tulsi Devi learnt a lot about men that rainy day. And she learnt how to hide her feelings about herself in a very deep corner of her being.

She met David De Souza at the corner where the chai wala set up his kettle and stove. From the moment she saw him, she started to feel a little unsafe. There was no hint of mathematics, nor a charming interest in her studies. He was nervous. Looking around like a criminal with no alibi. The adoration she had hoped to see in his eyes was smothered by a sense of urgency.

And then circumstances fell into place that made the situation an emergency.

Hindu–Muslim commotion was heard from the nearby bazaar. Blood-curdling screams of women drowned out the sound of the rain that smashed onto the streets.

David De Souza hurried Tulsi Devi into a nearby fabric shop. The owner, who was known to David, locked up the front door and the three of them decided to lay low until the disturbance subsided.

The events of that rainy afternoon in Lahore left no room in Tulsi Devi's memory for the face or features of the shopkeeper. All she knew was that her admirer gave him some money and he disappeared discreetly.

David De Souza, meanwhile, paced the empty shopfloor, peering out of the window every now and then to look out for street fighting. When Tulsi Devi asked when they should go back to the convent, he told her, "If we went back now, we would be going back in a coffin."

How they ended up "taking a siesta" upstairs in the storeroom was a leap in events that could only have been achieved by a man who had done such things before.

"Come, we'll be safer upstairs," he said. But Tulsi Devi climbed the stairs knowing that the territory she was about to enter was anything but safe.

The storeroom was filled with rolls of cotton fabric in every shade and hue to help the ladies of Lahore make blouses that were a perfect match for their saris. Stacks of rolls and multi-colored selections of cloth were piled up at bed height in almost every square inch of the room, with the top two or three colors covered slightly in dust and faded by the light of the sun.

"We can lie down here," David said with confidence. He picked up a few slightly faded reams of cloth and turned them over to show their dust-free side. Then he shut the curtains, but not to stop the cloth from fading further.

In the darkened room his breath sounded hungrier, coarser, more predatory. Tulsi Devi panicked and started to make her way out of the room as he began patting down his newly made bed.

David De Souza grabbed her arm. "You're not going anywhere, Tulsi Devi. Understood?"

"But we can't stay here. What if we get caught?"

"If we are caught, I am in this as deep as you are."

And then they were both silent until Tulsi Devi whispered, "Help me, I'm scared."

David looked at her with a cool brown stare, contemplating how best he could help her. In his plan for the outing, this had been the best possible outcome. Now this situation was here, presenting itself. A young girl, alone and trapped. The Lady of Situations had brought him here to this moment in time and he was the Master of Events. He surveyed the scene as a fox surveys its prey. And then he decided to pounce.

In a slow, calculated approach, David put his arm around Tulsi Devi's waist and started to untuck her sari at the top of her petticoat. Tulsi Devi startled and froze.

"Relax, and you won't be at all frightened," he tried to reassure her. Thinking fast, he realized that things would be a lot easier for him if she were a little more willing.

"I thought we liked each other?"

"Yes, I like you, sir, but they might be wondering what's happened to us at the convent. I have classes . . ."

"Just try and relax . . ."

The authority that David De Souza held over his student was enough to render her helpless. No amount of shame or guilt gave her the power to challenge her mathematics master. Her shame materialized into the shape of her mother, watching her with disgust from the corner of the room. Blame incarnate. Tulsi Devi could look away, but her mother never did. To distance herself from her humiliation, Tulsi Devi found herself watching the scene as her mother did. She found herself sitting on the fan that revolved slowly above them, counting out the seconds until the lesson was over. The only time she came back into her body lying on the bed of colored cottons was when she stopped to think, and was overwhelmed with a sense of shame and guilt, the unbearable feeling that this was all her fault. She could almost hear her mother's thoughts from the corner of the room. Her fears for her daughter's future after such an incident.

David De Souza had not even slowed down enough to undress his victim, who lay there with her petticoat lifted, and sari blouse buttoned tight. Without even taking off his trousers, he lifted himself on top of her and spread his weight over her body and the rainbow of fabrics below her.

Tulsi Devi was deflowered unceremoniously and abruptly. It was a loveless mating and all her illusions about her man of the future were crushed on the pile of cottons that lay beneath her. There was no pleasure in her eyes, and very little in his. Her mouth was dry and tasted of bitter almonds. She did not make a sound, just held her breath in case she created too much intimacy by exhaling over him. He breathed his hungry, constipated breath over her face. The sound sickened Tulsi Devi. When he finally pulled out of her, his eyes for the first time met hers and another personality appeared on his face. A momentary look of reflection and guilt. Seed spilt; urgent now not to use her up but to get her out of there.

For a moment there was nobody in control. And in that moment, Tulsi Devi vomited over David De Souza's trousers.

His guilt turned to revulsion as he pushed her away; became the master once more and instructed her to leave.

"You must get back to the convent. Take this money and call a tonga."

Tulsi Devi put on her sari, buckled up her shoes and walked slowly to the shop door, aching and wet between her legs. With her head swimming she arrived at the convent gates with the look of someone who has just stepped over a major threshold to enter the next stage of her life.

The chowkidar looked at her with pity and sympathy combined. She returned his gaze, and glancing beyond, over his shoulder, she could see her mother, still blazing with a fury so severe that every muscle of her face was contorted around her purse-like mouth.

Tulsi Devi felt as evil as someone who had just committed a cold-blooded murder. Whenever she looked at anybody that day, she felt that they knew what she had done. They could see it in her eyes. It made her want to put an end to her life, except maybe that wouldn't be a great enough punishment. Better to live with it and allow the punishment to linger. Let that black cloud of shame rain over her again and again, every time reminding her of that rainy day when she stepped outside the gates of Loreto Convent, outside the chalk circle and into the world of adults.

18

At first Tulsi Devi felt such repulsion toward herself she could tell nobody her unbearable secret. But it lingered inside her, aching, swelling, squeezing, until she had to say something. Just once.

As soon as she saw Rashmi the secret climbed out of her body, like a spider walking over her skin as the words spoke themselves.

"Rashmi, something dreadful has just happened to me," she said.

"Where were you? I had to tell Sister that you were sick."

"I've been out with David De Souza."

"Did you kiss?"

"I can't live anymore. He was sickening." Tulsi Devi collapsed onto the bed, convulsing in tears of self-hatred.

"Kya? What's gone on?"

"You promise you won't tell anyone?"

"I promise. What happened?"

"No, you must really promise."

"I promise on the blood of Jesus Christ."

"I have been insulted by David De Souza."

As soon as Rashmi had heard the whole story, she wished she had never been so curious. Her innards digested the images that her friend was dwelling on and a temperature started to spread across her brow. She could not vomit and she knew that there was only one way to get this sick feeling out of her stomach. She would have to tell one of the nuns. Better than letting it fester in her own thoughts. These thoughts could breed diseases, she was sure of it.

She left Tulsi Devi staring at the ceiling, listening to the tick-tock sound of an old clock, which marked the passage of time that would unfold all the consequences.

There was one maths lesson the next day, and Tulsi Devi sat staring down at her buckle-up shoes throughout it, as David De Souza continued the education of his Loreto Convent girls. His pride unscathed, his confidence unshattered.

"Looking now please at the calculations on the board. You can see how number nine is the very last of all single-digit numbers. The most complete one. Pick any number over ten, add up the digits in that number and then subtract the total from the number you started with. Your new number will surely be divisible by nine. It is the very last stop before infinity."

Tulsi Devi could not stand to look up into those almond fox eyes that kept trying to catch hers to see if she was going to disclose their secret. She could feel his questions on her skin. She knew that if he looked straight into her eyes, his gaze would penetrate into her body, just as his flesh had.

She looked away.

If her life had ended in that classroom, she would have welcomed the new one that lay ahead. But soon the bell rang, the class was over, and Tulsi Devi was forced to recognize that her existence in this nightmare would have to continue.

19

Sister Mary knew from the moment she heard the knock at her door that she was going to hear of some trouble. Rashmi did not know how to even broach the subject that was eating at her insides. She knocked only once, so so softly, in case Tulsi Devi were to hear.

"Come in," welcomed the nun in a high Irish shrill.

"Sister Mary, I have something to confess."

"Well go ahead, dear. I've listened to many confessions in my life."

"But I have promised silence to the friend who trusted me with her story."

Sister Mary had the extra senses of an eagle, and decided to make the confession a little easier for the quaking girl in her informal confession box.

"So tell me. What story did Tulsi Devi tell you?"

There was a long silence as the unspoken words lingered in the air, looking for the most genteel form of expression. The feeling of shame had been so powerfully transferred that Rashmi felt she had done the unspeakable deed herself.

Sister Mary took a deep breath. This was no ordinary confession. No tale of sweetmeats being stolen from a fellow student, or white lies being told about studies. This was a story of life rarely heard on the lips of any girl at Loreto Convent.

"Take your time, dear. It's hard to tell the truth, but you'll feel better for it once it's done."

"Sister Mary, is the carnal experience out of wedlock an everlasting sin?"

"Go on, my dear. No harm. Take a big breath now." She sat Rashmi down, so that the young girl would not feel as if she were reciting lines at the front of class, and put a comforting arm on her shoulder.

"Tulsi Devi has had this experience with our mathematics teacher . . ."

"And . . . *and* . . .?"

"She went out with him. To Temple Road. And he took advantage of her. Now she will not speak. I'm scared. What is going to happen to her, Sister Mary? Is her life over now?"

"Don't speak so," said Sister Mary, but then gathered herself together when she realized that speaking was exactly what she wanted.

"Go on, my dear. Have no fear at all. The good Lord is not going to punish you. Or her, for that matter. She's not to blame, the wee girl." Sister Mary had the good sense to know that no amount of Hail Marys or Our Fathers could dissolve the feelings of guilt that swelled up in her study that day.

"He is utterly horrible. He told her to be quiet about it and now she will speak nothing. What is going to happen? What will her mother say?"

Between her shock and her anger, Sister Mary had already considered how she was going to explain such an incident to the mother of this distressed child in her care. She was willing to accept total responsibility for Tulsi Devi and bear the consequences of her fate. Even answer at the gates of salvation to petition on her behalf. But Tulsi Devi's mother? Would her ears and heart survive the news?

When the whole story was out, and lips were sealed again, it was decided that Jyoti Ma must find out from a personal messenger. One of the senior nuns was sent by train to the farm to inform and counsel the girl's mother and request her presence immediately at the convent.

Sister Agnes packed her bags the same day and headed toward the holy hills of Prakriti, rehearsing all the way her unwelcome news. Whilst thoughts of chastity, tragedy and duty percolated in her mind, she could not help but notice how the poorer travelers on this same line laughed and smoked up on the roof of the carriage, with the breeze of freedom in their hair. When the train stopped at stations, her eyes could not help but rest on the undulating bodies of the third-class travelers making love under blankets whilst waiting for their trains to arrive.

At Kalka, where the mail train stopped and the plains met the Himalayas, Sister Agnes had to catch the little steam train up the windy hills. The fast swings and non-stop chugging of the train made her feel hideously nauseous. But every time she felt she would vomit, a mountain rhododendron would sweep in through the carriage window and shock her out of herself, until she was spinning with the pines, jacarandas, flame trees and jasmine. Transported not only higher into the hills, but closer also to her own soul.

It was a precious moment. She was so far from the familiar life she knew. So distanced from mundane concerns, intoxicated by the Himalayan air. It was a moment of pure Being. The kind that follows you through lifetimes, because the images themselves are framed in archetypes of the imagination.

When Sister Agnes arrived at her train station, a man with a donkey agreed to carry her black-and-white form the half-hour journey to Prakriti. The donkey was so small the nun's feet almost dragged on the ground. A very strange sight indeed. Like the virgin on her way to Bethlehem, to tell not of a birth but of a death. It did not take much for Sister Agnes to realize how easily these images distorted to find their opposite meanings in the worldly plane.

Jyoti Ma was out in the fields supervising the laborers when she saw the donkey in the distance heading toward her house. It was a sight so telling that there was hardly any need for a story thereafter. A nun from her daughter's convent, and no daughter. She knew when she saw the vision that her daughter had died.

Jyoti Ma's first reaction was to think of someone to blame. Her heart was racing and she cursed her husband for leaving her and going to live in his beloved ashram. For shirking his responsibilities. For taking sannyas before God ordained it. How dare he!

She ran back to the house and looked in the mirror. Even in her panic, she looked like a woman of great standing. All the more to prove one of life's most shattering lessons: that something like this can happen to anyone. Everybody is reversible. The victim and the victimizer. The memsahib and the servant.

Ganesh, the family elephant, went to meet the donkey and raised his trunk in a solemn salaam, turned, then walked back to the house. Sister Agnes was so amazed at the sight, she thought she was witnessing a visitation of God.

So wrapped up was she in this unworldy encounter, she almost forgot her mission. Until she saw the look of fear and numbness in the eyes of Jyoti Ma, who was awaiting the messenger on the verandah, her sari palla wrapped around her head in preparation for mourning. She did not want to hear the words, for they were already all said.

The black-and-white figure followed Jyoti Ma like a ghost into her husband's bedroom. She summoned the nun to sit at her side, on the bed where Tulsi Devi had been conceived.

"Just say it," she ordered, like a Queen.

"I do not know if this will be of any solace to you," started Sister Agnes, passing over her cross into Jyoti Ma's hands. "It's been a great support to me for many years."

"Just tell me, Sister, what has happened to my beti?"

"God help me. The news I bring is not easy to bear. But it has come to our attention that your daughter left school premises and met with a man."

Somehow the realization that her daughter was not actually dead softened the blow of this news. "So she is no longer at the convent?" Jyoti Ma asked.

"Oh no no no, she's there, she's there ... But we fear for her."

If blame could be distilled, it was held in its purest form in the silence that followed.

"She is the only one left for me now, Sister. Do you realize what you are saying?" Jyoti Ma said eventually.

"I know, I know, and it's not easy."

"You know nothing. Just tell me one thing, for God's sake – how is my daughter?"

"Well, it's hard to say now. Tulsi Devi hasn't really spoken since the incident. Not to me, not to anyone."

"So nobody knew of this? And nobody at the convent tried to stop her leaving through the gates? Sister, I studied at a convent, too, and I sent Tulsi Devi to Loreto because I understood that she would be safe in your care."

"Yes, yes, that's right. Under ordinary circumstances she would have been. However, it seems she was drawn in a different direction. She stepped out of our protection."

"Well then I'm going to bring her home personally."

"And that's why I'm here. She's gone so much inside herself, we don't know what she's going to do next. She needs her mother. Simple as that."

Jyoti Ma handed back the crucifix. "Here, take this. It is no compensation. I have nothing anymore. If your God had any power whatsoever, you would not be here now."

Sister Agnes accepted her crucifix, sanctifying it again with a kiss and a prayer. She began again, undeterred, inspired by the holy hills and this moment of testimony.

"Now if this cross has any power, and I believe it has, I would like you to hold it just once more and ask God to provide you with what you most require."

Taken aback by the sudden strength in the nun's voice and the abrupt screech of brakes as time stood still, Jyoti Ma took hold of the cross once more and offered the universe the biggest challenge she could flaunt at it.

"I WANT MY HUSBAND TO COME BACK."

Crisp and clear, the words were jotted down in ether by the invisible hand that records all desires and offers them fulfilment; often long after they have become redundant to the person who thought them up in the first place.

20

Nobody in the world knew what it was like to be behind the eyes of Tulsi Devi in the days that followed. To witness the world in silence, with all sensory information rebounding against the walls of her subconscious. People had tried to talk with her, but everyone had given up with the feeling that the sounds they made hadn't even registered.

Sister Mary took it upon herself to put Tulsi Devi in the Lord's charge, as she was no longer able to keep control of the situation herself. She went into Tulsi Devi's room and started a monologue, which was more like a chat with a stone idol.

"Come here, Tulsi Devi. Now it's time to snap out of this. You haven't given your clothes to the laundry. Will we take them now? And what about these curtains? Open them up and let a wee bit of light in, will you."

Sister Mary opened the curtains with great zest and the light tipped into the room, turning it into a stage set ready for a show to begin. The light found Tulsi Devi sitting immobile, like a Japanese actor, waiting for meaning before action could take place.

"Now I don't know what you'll think of this idea, but you're not even going to answer me anyway, so I won't ask you. We're taking a wee walk down to the chapel and we're going to say a few words together, because nobody in this world is given a problem without also being given a way to solve it."

Sister Mary took Tulsi Devi's elbow, and walked her out of the room and down to the chapel, where she offered her a cushion for her knees and gave them each a little tap at the back to make them bend.

"Almighty God, we pray and beseech thee for your presence today. May you take this young girl into your arms and clothe her with light and blessings, so there is no shame in the world that could disrobe her. Please forgive all our sins, for it is not our intention to stray from the holy path. And do not deny us the life everlasting. Just as you gave your only son, do not forsake your daughter. Give us today your grace and salvation, so that this young girl may be brought unto you as pure as the day she was born."

With the intensity of Sister Mary's pledge it was hard to feel like an outsider in the House of God. A single tear broke the levee of restraint in Tulsi Devi's face. The first tear in the river of purification that would follow.

Sister Mary got up and hurried to the back of the church to bring back some holy water in cupped hands to perform an informal baptism.

"Water will purify you of your sins, my dear, just as your tears will wash away any curses that Satan has laid on you. Water is what you need. Water. And lots of it. There isn't a stain on our souls that can't be washed away."

The darkness had begun to settle in the chapel and Sister Mary lit a few candles on the altar.

"I'm going to leave you here now, my dear. You'll be safe. Now take your time and allow the Lord to come into your soul and make you his own. And pray. Your prayers will always be answered. Even if you pray the most selfless of prayers – 'thy will be done' – it will be so."

21

There were two striking differences at Loreto Convent when Sister Agnes and Jyoti Ma arrived. The first and most noticeable was the fact that there were now two chowkidars guarding the gates.

The original chowkidar, who had worked for thirty years at the convent, had been asked to leave. In his place were two brothers from the same caste and village as the original chowkidar. It was clear to all but the nuns that the former employee had made certain that the vacant position was put to good use.

The two brothers took it in turn to roam the streets of Lahore, visit the whorehouses and entertain vagrants at the convent doorstep. As a result the saintly whitewashed walls were fast turning a spattered red as more and more paan and betel-nut juice were spat at the school.

The second and most striking difference was that Tulsi Devi had vanished. Upped and left, in the dead of the night, whilst the original chowkidar was fast asleep at the gates. Neither Jyoti Ma nor Sister Agnes had been informed of the above changes, and Jyoti Ma insisted on going straight to her daughter's room before paying a visit to the principal.

Jyoti Ma knocked at the door with great authority. "Tulsi beti. It's Ma. Open up."

The door was opened by a timid Rashmi. Inside everything was just as Tulsi Devi had left it, except for a Bible next to her bed, open at Corinthians:

When I was a child, I spake as a child, I understood as a child,
I thought as a child: but when I became a man, I put away childish things.
For now we see through a glass, darkly; but then face-to-face:
now I know in part; but then shall I know even as I am known.

"Hasn't Sister Mary told you what happened?" Rashmi said, with some hesitation.

"Sister Agnes, has the whole convent been told of my daughter's misfortune?"

Sister Agnes interrupted. "Nobody knows except Rashmi. Tell me, Rashmi, where is Tulsi Devi?"

"She's gone."

"Like the rest of her family. My God."

Thinking there must be a mistake Sister Agnes shuffled Jyoti Ma off to Sister Mary's office in search of an explanation.

Sister Mary's office faced east and let in the morning sunshine to make a halo around the nun's earnest and concerned face. It was the moment that Sister Mary had dreaded – meeting Tulsi Devi's mother to offer one empty hand of solace and with the other accept total responsibility for her student's misfortune.

"Now if it's any consolation to you at all as her mother, I know that she left with the grace of God," said Sister Mary with as much poise as she could muster.

"What sort of consolation is that? I leave my daughter in your safe care and come back to find that she has left one time with a man and the second time with the grace of God. She is a young girl, Sister. Do you not understand the dangers?"

"My heart bleeds for you," answered Sister Mary, "and I have tortured myself pondering how I could possibly bring news of this further turn of events."

"But I'm her mother. Sister, you have never had a child yourself, so you will never know. My husband has gone. My son has gone. Now you are telling me that my daughter has gone. Why don't you just kill me now? She is my own flesh."

"I promise you that the Good Lord will bring her back to you. She could not have gone far. She'll come back to her senses and return. We've informed the police. The whole city has been sent on a search party."

"Sister Mary, both you and I know that this town is filled with scoundrels. And what if she's left Lahore? India is a huge country. She will be like a drop of water in the wide open sea."

"That drop of water will come to shore, I give you my word. It's the way of water. Just give it some time."

"I knew I should have married her off as soon as her father left."

"A girl who's old enough to be married is old enough to be able to take care of herself. Legally she is no longer a minor and if she wished to pass through those gates she is old enough to take responsibility for her actions."

"I do not know if I'm hearing this conversation or dreaming it. I know you people do things differently over there, but this is India. How dare you let her go! You're not talking about a maidservant, you're talking about my daughter!"

"Ahh, but I'm not just talking about your daughter. I'm talking about the power of the Lord. She will return. All we require now is patience."

Patience was all that was on offer, and had to be accepted as a muslin plug for a sink that was emptying fast down to nothing. Jyoti Ma felt like doing some kind of violence to herself in protest, but she could not face the loss of dignity, nor the blemish of any physical scars on her body. But the thought was there. And if the thought counted for anything, there were already a million gashes on her skin caused by the loss of her beautiful daughter.

22

The sickness that Tulsi Devi had felt when she was first violated remained with her over the following days and it soon became evident there was something growing in her body. Something alien, something invasive that wished to take over her whole Being and make her step to one side for a while. She knew the act of love begot children, and she had no doubt that she was with child, even though there had been no love at all in the act as she had experienced it.

One night soon after, she lay in her bed at Loreto Convent. Her thoughts preyed on her flesh, first closing doors to create an insane kind of privacy, and then feeding off the claustrophobia.

She felt trapped in her body and had to get some air into the corridors of her mind where she crouched, immobilized. The smallness of her own mental space was terrifying, for she had no connection with any grander vision outside her own walls. Her thoughts breathed their own stale air, distorting slowly into monsters to punish the master that trapped them there.

This sense of desperation drove Tulsi Devi to dress herself, throw some clothes into a small case and walk out through the gates of the convent, past the sleeping chowkidar. It was easy. So much easier than staying where she was.

Outside in the open air, the labyrinthine corridors of her mind straightened out again and she could get some sense of distance and freedom. There was a world outside her thoughts and she was glad of it. Her heart released itself from its cramped position and she was filled with a sense of love.

It was the love of God and the love of her brother Ram combined.

The minute she caught herself thinking about Ram she realized that she was now stepping in his footprints. He had laid them out for her all those years ago so that she would not be alone in her own journey. If there was anyone in the world she wished she could be with right now, it was him.

Tulsi Devi cried as she thought about how she had never really known her brother and was only now beginning to understand him as she set out on her own rite of passage. She remembered the stories her father told her about her brother and his mystical quest. He was the magical figure of her childhood, capable of lifting mountains and flying with the winds. Ram the believer, Ram the conqueror, Ram whose compassion would move people to follow him wherever he went.

As soon as she found herself in the streets of Lahore, Tulsi Devi had a yearning for mountains. But not the familiar ones she knew. Not Prakriti. She knew that the tattle of the villagers and the pity of her mother would have driven her to a grief far more remote than the one she felt now.

There was no doubt that she should go to Rishikesh, as Ram had done. Not to find him, because his existence as a human being was questionable, but simply to be near him.

Her instinct to follow Ram brought her to the railway station where she sat down on the darkened platform wrapped in her shawl. When her eyes started to close and her head dropped forward in unconsciousness, Tulsi Devi surrendered to sleep and allowed her body to lie down on the hard floor for the first time in her life.

The morning train arrived for Delhi and Tulsi Devi went without hesitation to the third-class Ladies' Carriage where she sat on a hard plank of wood. The other women all huddled around asking her questions, for she was so obviously not from their ranks. Her sari was starched, ironed and clean; theirs were dirty, crumpled, shrunken and torn, used as they were to wipe babies, sit on the ground and carry trinkets. And then there were her feet. Buckled-up, polished European feet that had never walked barefoot on the soil.

"Where are you from?" they asked. "Do your parents know that you've gone away?" "Is your father in business or service?" "Where are you going?" "Have you got any family?" "Do you have a husband?" "Do you have any children?"

Getting no answers, they presumed that Tulsi Devi was deaf and dumb and they started talking openly about her.

"Aiii, she's a runaway."

"Badly treated by her husband, and she can't speak to tell anybody."

"She's going back to her parents' house."

"Poor girl. Her life is over now."

"Far better at home than with a husband who beats you."

"See, her parents are having money. They can afford to take her back."

"He made her leave their children behind though."

There were no bruises on Tulsi Devi, but her very presence in their compartment was testimony to her history. She continued to say nothing, simply looking out of the window and pulling her sari over her head.

Soon she ceased to be the object of discussion as the women, mostly strangers to each other, told stories about their husbands, children, in-laws, sisters and brothers. Each story had a prompt that would trigger another story until a rich tapestry of lives had been spread out before them. Lives where a few rupees made the difference between love and hatred. Where in-laws ruled, children over-ruled, and husbands came home intoxicated.

When the women ate they shared rotis and vegetables with Tulsi Devi, gesturing to make her eat.

"Make her eat some more," yelled one woman, "she's brought nothing with her. She must have been kicked out in the middle of the night."

The guard came to collect tickets and Tulsi Devi looked blankly at him.

"Arré, leave her alone. She has no ticket, she's deaf and dumb and she has no money because she's running away from a wicked husband."

The guard, feeling like a grand philanthropist, nodded and went on, not wanting to interfere too much in the business of ladies. There was obviously something wrong with the woman for her to end up in the third-class carriage, and if she'd been dealt such a blow by life, he wasn't going to add to it by knocking her down further.

As soon as the guard left, Tulsi Devi vomited out of the window.

"She has a baby in her belly!" said one of them, patting her tummy and smiling toothlessly.

"This is one that the wicked husband won't be able to keep."

"I hope it's a boy. That will show him."

When Delhi arrived, the third-class companions picked up their bundles, which were tied together in large old saris, and guided their prized deaf and dumb beauty through the human jungle of hawkers, passengers, beggars, children and the occasional British soldier. They wove their way around the people and parcels that lay on the floor, and around the coolies with five cases on their heads and sweat dripping off their muscles, who bumped into everyone on the platform. Everywhere, all around, the world was on the move.

Outside, under the shadows of the Red Fort, the women started talking about what they should do with Tulsi Devi. At this point, one of the grandmothers who had been in the Ladies' Carriage saw a wealthy-looking Indian woman nearby supervising three coolies and a horse tonga. She approached the woman and started telling her about Tulsi Devi's predicament. Glances were cast over and eventually the woman came over and took Tulsi Devi's hand. She led her up into the horse carriage and then signaled the third-class ladies to move on.

Up above the human traffic, the two elevated women made their way out of the throng. Tulsi Devi looked sideways at her chaperone and realized that she was a vertical person. Every groove on her face ran in vertical lines. Two thick vertical furrows above arched eyebrows, and two vertical lines dropping down to her chin from the corners of her mouth. She was thin and had the iron-rod posture of a village woman.

Along the roads they traveled, behind the clicking heels of an emaciated white horse, to pull up outside an elegant bungalow near the university. The woman pulled out a small chit of paper and started writing in English.

"I am Anjali and you are welcome to stay here with me for a short while only. What is your name?"

Relieved at not having to speak, Tulsi Devi took the paper and wrote: "My name is Tulsi Devi. I am trying to reach my brother in Rishikesh."

The conversation continued in scribbles.

"So you cannot return to your husband?"

Tulsi Devi thought about what words she could use to describe her circumstances and finding none, scratched out an undecided "No."

There was no more talk of husbands or returns. Once inside the house it was evident that Anjali did not have a husband either. Had he died? Run away? Tulsi Devi was not prepared to request answers from the woman who had begrudgingly taken an absolute stranger into the house. She started to regret her own willingness to be shifted, like a human parcel, piled up with the others at Delhi station.

Her time there was spent in a purposeless daze, hanging around the kitchen and the living room. At least twice a week there would be visitors. In particular one Englishman and one German who would always be entertained in strictest privacy. Anjali would scribble that a business acquaintance was arriving and she should be left alone. This would be Tulsi Devi's cue to go and sit downstairs on the lawns, waiting for the tipped-hatted departures before she was free to go back upstairs.

In the evenings Tulsi Devi was sent to sleep on one of the verandahs, because there was no spare room in the house, in spite of its enormous proportions.

She soon discovered why when a man arrived one day with some shapes tied up in muslin and jute. He carried them over his shoulder and unlocked one of the doors in the house. Tulsi Devi followed him and watched him untie his figures. There in front of her eyes, an ancient stone temple image of Lakshmi was unveiled without ceremony or respect. Lakshmi, the goddess of prosperity and wellbeing, was held hostage by a man with crooked teeth and a bent back, who had chopped her down as a prize from a temple, cutting her off from her dignity and her past. Here she was now in a dusty room filled with other deities, shrunken down to rock objects of artistic merit.

Tulsi Devi crossed herself as she had seen the nuns doing at Loreto Convent when they had heard or seen something that they wanted to protect themselves against.

A few more days and it soon became evident that Anjali was trading with the British and Germans to smuggle these Indian gods to foreign shores, where they would sit alongside pot plants and coffee tables to bless the bookshelves and fruit bowls of wealthy homes. These idols that were the guardians of prayers and wishes invested over the centuries in caves and temples throughout India.

From that time on, Tulsi Devi could not look Anjali in the face. She would glance just to the left of her and catch her vertical form cut across the horizontal floor in the corner of her eye. For three months it continued this way, with Tulsi Devi staying as an unwanted guest.

To excuse herself from any contact with Anjali, Tulsi Devi started to write and draw. Her stories were taken from her imagination and her home; her drawings all hybrids of fantasy and reality. Every single picture sported a pregnant belly. There were fairies like the ones Lily had drawn, and Devis and even nuns with bellies under their gowns. Once or twice Anjali noticed her etchings and tut-tutted. Then she gave her a piece of letter-writing paper and told her to inform her brother that she was on her way.

Sitting down to write, Tulsi Devi bit the end of the pen, not knowing if the words would come out as she really felt them.

Dear bhaiya,

I pray to you to help me. I am coming to Rishikesh to get away. Something dreadful has happened and I am needing your assistance. I don't know what all will happen next.

Your always loving sister,

Tulsi Devi

Anjali took the letter, taking the pains to read it first before putting it decisively into an envelope. She signaled to Tulsi Devi to write an address on it.

Tulsi Devi started boldly, first writing her brother's name. Then she suspended her pen over the envelope, as if her brother's whereabouts would simply write themselves onto the paper. When no inclination came, she simply wrote "Rishikesh" under the name and handed it back to Anjali.

Anjali sighed. So the brother had been a figment of the girl's imagination. The girl was mad after all.

Her hostess had hoped that she could pack off her guest to a known address, but now she understood that she would be sending her off into the mists. But whose business was it anyway? None of hers. The girl would simply be going off to her fate. Does one take an ant off the pavement to prevent it from being trodden on? No.

When Anjali's friend Vachala arrived, they drank tea together whilst Tulsi Devi sat on the floor, writing at a low table.

"The girl is mad, yah, so why are you keeping her? It's not safe. She could do anything to you in the night."

Tulsi Devi did not look up. She continued a drawing of Vachala's face, which she had memorized after letting her in – eyes bulging out of their sockets over a parrot's nose.

"She has nowhere to go. Just a make-believe brother in Rishikesh. I was just trying to offer some charity."

"Anjali, since when have you ever entertained charity? You keep a goondah at your gates to chase away anybody who comes asking for alms."

"But this girl is not from that class. It is quite evident."

"Worse still. If she were, at least you could ask her to do some washing or sweeping."

Underneath Vachala's face, Tulsi Devi was starting to draw a body now. On it was a belly at least twelve months pregnant.

"Good God, I can't ask her to do anything. She's pregnant for goodness sakes!"

"Then get rid of her now, or you'll have two of them on your hands."

Vachala, as an act of generosity, offered to send her peon down to the station to buy a ticket to Rishikesh, and it was delivered the next day. Anjali wrote a message to Tulsi Devi that she was free to go and see her brother on the morning train. Her ticket had been bought, a peon was instructed to accompany her, and she would also receive one hundred rupees' charity to see her through. Tulsi Devi wrote a deaf dumb "thank you," without looking up, and Anjali took that as some kind of agreement, thereby wiping her hands of any commitment to this stranger.

That last night in Delhi, Tulsi Devi decided to try and take a last look at one of the rooms of deities. She crept along the verandah and climbed through an open window, and there in the moonlight was her Lakshmi, lotus and garland of flowers in two hands to greet her, the other two hands offering and receiving blessings. She dropped onto her knees before the idol and prayed.

"Lakshmi, if this is the last prayer you will ever hear, please hear it well, for it is of great importance to me. Please look after me and help deliver me from these circumstances. May I live to look Ram in the eyes once more. May my suffering be my salvation."

She kissed the broken feet of the goddess and swallowed the small flake of grit that remained on her lips – the symbol of Lakshmi's own suffering when she was axed off at the feet.

"And may you always keep your power, wherever you go," she added, suddenly feeling for the goddess as a mirror image of herself.

The two goddesses faced each other with equally unsure destinies. They would go on two separate journeys, even though both had been born to rock-solid foundations. There were dangers up ahead for both of them. Either of them could be smashed before reaching their destinations, or survive intact, to be admired and appreciated at some distant moment in Time.

23

On the train to Rishikesh, Tulsi Devi found her mind hovering over images of suicide the way flies hover over a piece of dead meat. She was possessed by fear. Not fear of the outside world. She could take anything from it now that she had stepped over the chalk line, transgressed its boundaries and become an outcast. It was the fear of the thoughts inside her head.

She fell asleep on the train and started dreaming of haggard wizened creatures stalking the corridors of her convent, opening doors to see virgin students in their beds. When she woke up and tried to swallow her fear, the images did not go away. The nightmare continued. She saw specters with her eyes wide open, with the same acute fear of her dreams, only now heightened by a fully conscious mind.

Tulsi Devi could not think her way out of it. It was her thoughts, after all, that had broken down the doors dividing her nightmares from her reality. The only solution was to finish off the body that hosted this parasite of a mind.

How?

Images came to her. Lodged themselves in her body. She heard the whispers of women who had died from setting fire to their saris. So easily. *(The fire starts. It bursts out loud, breathing its red breath over the layers of cloth.*

Then you just run ...) But what if the fire burnt out, leaving her shriveled up and alive, with raw open wounds?

The thought penetrated her body as if it had already happened. It hijacked the oxygen in her lungs and replaced it with panic. Her head was down on her knees and the other passengers kept looking at her and offering water to ease her travel sickness.

She felt envious of them as they looked out of their safe railway carriage and all saw the same scenery, doors shut tight against the oceans of subconscious life down below. If only her thoughts would go away. If only she too could close the doors and shut out the monsters that trailed her.

In desperation she turned to her nearest fellow traveler and confided in him in her panic, just so that she could hear some words come out of her dumb mouth.

"I want to kill myself," she said, feeling the sounds shaping her tongue.

"Drink some more. You'll be feeling better once the train stops."

Tulsi Devi remembered Sister Mary saying that she needed water, and lots of it. She drank the water that was offered to her and prayed to Jesus, the God of Sanity. It was soothing, so she continued invoking him. She imagined her way back to the chapel at Loreto Convent. The monsters were outside the door now, too scared to come in, leaving her in the quiet of the chapel's sanctuary. She lit a candle and poured holy water over herself until she had absorbed it all like a spongy vessel, and then she lay prostrate on the floor in front of Jesus, who guarded her with one hand on his heart and his eyes up in the air. It was a safe retreat. She was glad that she had found this mind corridor that led back to the convent. If she kept her eyes closed for a while longer she could stay there.

The train stopped at Hardwar but Tulsi Devi did not wait on the platform for a train to Rishikesh. Her body demanded the distraction of walking. She stepped off the train and for a few minutes walked purposefully through the streets of this pilgrims' town. Past the roaming cows and the grandmothers who fed them before feeding themselves.

Past the flower-sellers, the eunuchs, the holy men. All the time her sixth sense guiding her toward water, toward the Ganges.

The monsters were tracking her again. Small shriveled limpets with large teeth and tangled hair. She knew they would not survive water, so she carried on walking, imagining herself inside the thoughts of the shopkeepers who watched her from behind big sacks of dhal and rice. She looked normal. Like a married woman on the way to the bazaar. There was nothing odd about her from the outside if you were blessed with eyes that were blind to the creatures that trailed her.

When she arrived at the ghats she stepped down fifteen steps to the holy water of the Ganges. She counted them to distract herself from her fear of insanity. *One, two, three, four, five, six, seven, eight, nine, ten, eleven, twelve, thirteen, fourteen, fifteen.*

Her feet had touched the water.

She was witnessing the water touching her feet.

Up to her knees, to her waist, to her neck.

She could see herself holding her breath and then down went her head.

Now she would stop breathing. Just stay there. In a few minutes the thoughts would all stop. She could feel the blood rush to her head.

An image of Aakash appeared in front of her. He was saying something, but she could not hear it because her ears were plugged with water. He was in the water himself now. Immersed. His beard floating like water weeds. Was it her father, or the ghost of someone whose remains had been tipped into the water that day? She heard something now. *You are drowning the temple . . . how will you understand your own Divinity?*

Tulsi Devi took in a deep breath. It was water. She started choking. She took in another breath and then she was delirious. *Death ends nothing.* She wanted to surface, but did not know which way was up, so she floundered until she rose, floating with her mass of black curls loose and drenched, on the surface of the water.

Spluttering, she lifted herself out of the water and onto the ghats, where she fainted. A young woman and man, around the same age as Tulsi Devi, helped to clear her lungs.

The two of them had come to throw the burnt remains of their mother into the Ganges at Hardwar. As they were emptying the hessian bag, they said their prayers. The girl's thoughts when she first noticed Tulsi Devi were of her mother. As she looked at the ashes falling into water she caught a glimpse of her mama when she was alive, saying goodbye to her after her marriage. They were both weeping and she had said, "If you do not leave, then how will you have the joy of returning?" It was this mama they were saying goodbye to now.

The hessian bag was half cleared of the ashes and bones when they caught sight of Tulsi Devi. There was something strange about her. Usually it was the lower classes who immersed themselves completely in the Ganges. The wealthier pilgrims simply cupped their hands and moistened their foreheads daintily with the holy water, without this dramatic display.

Then they saw Tulsi Devi struggle to breathe underwater and come up spluttering, only to faint on the ghats. There was no question of whether or not they should help. Their mother's remains were left, half in the water, half on the earth, whilst they helped this strange woman teeter on the threshold between life and death.

Tulsi Devi was taken, along with her small bag of possessions, to a humble but fairly respectable halfway-clean nursing home down one of Hardwar's side lanes. It was such a hot day that by the time she arrived there her clothes and hair were dried through.

The first thing she noticed when she regained consciousness was not the world outside, but a strange movement, like the flapping and gurgling of a fish inside her. She stayed with the feeling for a while, before she herself emerged from the depths and came to the realization that this was the child that she was carrying. It was a strange time for it to signal its insistent presence. From its own water world, it had shared the experience, feeling the temptation to return painlessly to the blissful Source from whence it came. But the possibility of returning had also prompted this soul to try and fully occupy this unfamiliar body. And when it did, it raised its first question: *What about me?*

"Feeling a little better, madam?" asked a voice from the world she'd left behind. The nurse in her white sari and little white hat was holding Tulsi Devi's hand, even though it seemed to Tulsi Devi to belong to someone else. She met the eyes of the nurse, then vomited and choked as if she were emptying not just her stomach but her lungs as well. The nurse helped her, holding the metal sluice bowl whilst also supporting her frail body. She did not need to ask Tulsi Devi if the incident had been intentional. Neither did she need to ask if she was pregnant. The two just went together and made sense of an unspoken story.

But she did need to know just what to do next.

"Do you have family here in Hardwar?"

Tulsi Devi told her that she knew nobody and that nobody knew her. The nurse told her to rest. A few more days of trying to keep down food and she started to recover some strength.

Then the question of what to do next became louder. So far the nursing home had taken in an emergency and did not know if she was even capable of compensating them.

Tulsi Devi didn't think too far ahead. She felt safe in this place where the nurses all wore white and smelled of disinfectant.

Her baby kicked more as it gained confidence in its demands of life, and every time she felt that flutter of a fish jumping, she thought positively about life. She imagined that she had been saved from drowning by Jesus, to play her part in this miracle of nature. Positive, that is, until she remembered that to have relations with a man outside of wedlock is a mortal sin.

Could mortal sins be washed away?

Instead of saying her prayers to Jesus, she hesitated and said them to his Mother. Hadn't Mary become a mother unintentionally, like herself? She tried as best as she could to remember the prayer that the nuns had taught her to invoke the Mother. "Hail Mary, Mother of us all, you are the most blessed of all women and blessed is the fruit of your womb. Mary, Mary, mother of Jesus, pray for us now and when we must die as well."

Praying to Mary the mother was more reassuring. The power of intercession overcame the finality of mortal sin, because Mary understood these things. Maybe Mary would understand that Tulsi Devi was raised a Hindu, and that half her family had turned into rishis. She tried explaining it all to Mary and waited for an answer. The one she received was this: that in the same way we eat when others starve, when we have a child there are others who cannot have them, so we must count our blessings. That simple.

A few days after the incident at the ghats, a eunuch came to the nursing home to enquire about whether any babies had been born that day. He wore a gaudy red wedding sari with gold borders. He had men's feet and ladies' make-up. His face wore the expression of a smiling cat, with cat's eyes and a cat's smile – a cat with its whiskers shaved off. He wore his earrings and necklace with such extreme feminine pride, only a man could carry it off.

His name was Bubbly and he had just done the rounds of Hardwar on behalf of his eunuch clansmenwomen to create a log of births and marriages to add to their extortion list. Bubbly was the most daring and outrageous of the eunuchs in his clan, going to any lengths to taunt the locals into giving bakshish to his people on auspicious occasions.

Nobody who had just had a child could get away without an offering to the eunuchs. He would start off by telling them that he would bless the child so that it became strong, wise, healthy and successful. If the parents shooed him off, he would threaten them that their child would die before it reached five. If they still ignored him, he would simply follow them home and ring a loud bell all night outside their home until the screams of the newborn baby demanded that some bakshish be paid.

Some nursing homes sent their chowkidar to beat him if he tried to hop over the fence. However, the chowkidar at this nursing home was in the habit of humoring the eunuchs, because his wife seemed to fall pregnant if she even looked at her chowkidar. By keeping the eunuchs sweet he had saved himself a fortune on payments. The eunuchs were his foster-friends, and he was their informant.

The chowkidar at this nursing home was also very superstitious. Bubbly knew that if he threatened to curse his next child to the life of a eunuch, the guard would always let him through the gates.

So the chowkidar kept an eye out for any women who visited with big bellies and took a great interest in parents who left the nursing home with newborn babes, always asking them where they lived and how they intended to get home.

That afternoon when Bubbly arrived, he stopped for his usual chat. The chowkidar told the eunuch about the strange lady who had arrived with a child in her belly after trying to drown herself. Bubbly sat down, smiled his red-toothed, paan-addict cat smile at the chowkidar. This news was intriguing enough to get a little closer to his informant. The chowkidar felt uncomfortable with this level of familiarity. The man was a eunuch, after all, and they were always creating such a tamasha.

Armed with information, Bubbly strutted confidently along the corridor, smiling appealingly at the nurses as if he were one of them. He told them that he was there to look after the lady who had risen from the Ganges, and was guided to Tulsi Devi's bedside.

Tulsi Devi was asleep when he took her hand. She awoke startled, as if she were coming out of a deep coma, and stared in shock at what she thought was a groom wearing a bride's sari.

"If you are having a baby, and you do not have anywhere to go," he told her, "we can look after you. If it's a boy, he stays with us, and if it's a girl, we will give you money to look after her. If this suits you, I can talk to my guru and make arrangements."

Tulsi Devi was overwhelmed. Her thinking was fifteen steps behind this manwoman's. She was only just starting to register that she was talking to a eunuch and she was already being propositioned to move in with him and his people.

"I cannot stay with you," she said.

Of course she could not!

"I am on my way to meet my brother," she continued.

Bubbly's thoughts had not been swimming in water like Tulsi Devi's and his responses were dry and sharp.

"Beti, you will not find your brother at the bottom of the Ganges," he answered.

Tulsi Devi looked at his odd maternal smile and told him slowly that she could work and look after herself.

"Then I will offer you a job."

But the job came with a contract – that if she should give birth to a boy, it would be his.

Bubbly talked as if he knew everything about having babies. As if he had fathered half a dozen with his own faulty equipment. He made her laugh by telling her how hard it was to work whilst being pregnant, patting his belly as if there were a fetus in his intestines. How did he know how hard it was for single women to raise children? What gave him this interest in nutrition for the expectant mother? It was entertaining to hear him fussing over her, and it made her think of her own mother.

An image of Jyoti Ma appeared, looking disgusted, disappointed, disgraced. Then her mother turned her head, having just witnessed her daughter's shame in Temple Road. Tulsi Devi realized then that Jyoti Ma would not be as compassionate as this eunuch, but she still could not accept his offer.

"So what will you do with your child?"

It was a startling question, simply because Tulsi Devi had given it no consideration. The reality of a child had only just started to stir inside her, and her first thoughts were that she would have to give it away. But still, it was a long time yet, and she could think no further than sunset on that particular day. The very notion of continuing her life still required more foresight than she was capable of.

Bubbly cooed and cajoled, touching her belly and giving her his best mother-cat smile. When the food came he wouldn't even let her sit up for it, spoon-feeding her lying down so that she almost choked to death once more.

Later on in the evening a doctor came round to see Tulsi Devi and told the eunuch to "bhago." Bubbly refused, saying that he would lift his sari and shame him if he was forced to leave.

"Lift your sari all you like, you will not be showing me anything I haven't already seen."

When the doctor had ascertained that the eunuch had no connection with Tulsi Devi he summoned the chowkidar to drag him off, so that he could talk about more important things, such as money. The chowkidar arrived, put on a mock show of bullying, and patted Bubbly off when he was safely on the other side of the fence.

The doctor then asked Tulsi Devi how she intended to pay for their services. She told him she had one hundred rupees. He calculated another three days for her budget and then checked her pulse, looked at her tongue, into her eyes and her ears, examined her outwardly healthy appearance and diagnosed her fit to leave – in three days' time, once her money was up. Tulsi Devi felt indignant at his sense of satisfaction and lack of care. Her baby kicked her and she could feel that it was on her side.

So the next day, Tulsi Devi dressed herself in one of the saris her mother had packed to send with her to Loreto Convent. It was creased and stained now, but it was the best she had and she wanted to feel her best as she faced the world once more. After tipping her favorite nurse a generous five rupees, she counted ten more to last her till God knows when.

As she left the nursing home wondering where to go next, a peacock appeared before her like a mirage, its hundred feathered eyes looking out toward a hundred different directions. "Where are you going?" the chowkidar asked. "To Rishikesh," she answered. As long as she had a destination, her life was still ahead of her, so she clung to her only sense of purpose and walked out onto the streets of Hardwar and into the blazing heat. The strength that she had put into storage in the nursing home was being seeped out of her now by the sun – as if it did not have enough energy of its own.

She walked the streets, but had to stop at a water-seller before the hour was up. After quenching her thirst she got up to pay the paani wala, but her costs had already been covered. Tulsi Devi turned around to see Bubbly there with three other eunuchs, waving a few rupees in his hand, singing a song about being a rich man in love, whilst his big feet tapped the ground under his sari.

"See, I'm already looking after you," he said.

It was so absurd and playful. They sat down together and had another paani, and another, for no sooner had the water been absorbed than it evaporated through their skins, back into the sky, to the rivers and back into the paani-seller's clay pot.

This was good business. For Bubbly as much as anyone, because he could see that he was making progress. His eunuch clansmen were making Tulsi Devi laugh, telling her that she needed a little more make-up, and a little red parting in her forehead so that everyone knew she was married. Then she could walk the streets singing and dancing like the eunuchs did and nobody would touch her.

It wasn't Bubbly in the end who persuaded Tulsi Devi to come back to the haveli and meet their guru, but the other eunuchs. Bubbly just sat and watched as she was charmed into submission. All the while Tulsi Devi was wondering what in fact she had to lose. The women she had met in the third-class carriage on the train from Lahore were so much more hospitable and caring than Anjali in Delhi with her stone cold statues. These were people who could understand her status on the Outside. She was not a eunuch, but she may as well have been.

Tulsi Devi followed the eunuchs back to a large haveli around a central courtyard. It was a beautiful house, with mirrorwork on the walls and painted patterns on the floors. Waiting there in the courtyard, the eunuchs combed out her hair and tried to make her look respectable to meet their guru. "We don't want Mata to think that we found you in the streets," Bubbly said.

"Stand up straight and smile sweetly," another eunuch instructed, making Tulsi Devi believe that she was about to meet an examplar of decency.

When the matriarch of their order appeared through a small wooden door, Tulsi Devi nearly laughed out loud. He was bigger and hairier than any of them. Surma smudged so far down his sleepy eyes that it almost reached his cheeks; his thick dark stubble making a mockery of his delicate matching gold earrings and necklace. Somehow he, too, had Bubbly's cat smile, although it was absurdly clear that he could not have been his father.

"Mata is an excellent dancer and teacher of dance," Bubbly told Tulsi Devi. "Do you dance?"

No. Who would have taught her? Jyoti Ma? Lily? Tulsi Devi admitted to having feet with no rhythm and they promptly started teaching her how to dance, clapping their hands and counting "digdadigdadhee, digdadigdadhee, digdadigdadhee." They were now teaching her the most flirtatious dances, for women – their favorites – the popular folk dances, not the classical Kathak. They pulled duppatas coyly over their faces and peeked out from behind them with innocent big male eyes. Suddenly they were all cow girls, outraged and charmed by Lord Krishna who had stolen their saris as they bathed in the river.

Later, whilst two eunuchs still danced, Tulsi Devi was shown to her room and asked if she wanted to stay. Her head was still spinning from dancing in circles when she answered "yes"; mostly because there was no other possible reply.

A few days passed before Tulsi Devi asked if she could do some work. After all, that had been the original premise for her stay there. Bubbly, with his dark maternal gaze, returned to the implicit terms of their contract, assuring her that having the baby was hard work enough. They did not need a cook. Nor a cleaner. And how could she dance at weddings? She had none of the enchanting feminine grace of a eunuch!

Nothing was required of her. She was served her lunch every day like a little memsahib and scolded if she spent too long out of the haveli. When her belly really started to bulge, the eunuchs were all convinced that it would be a boy. He would be called Ravan and he would be theirs. Tulsi Devi need never worry her sweet little head again.

Bubbly asked Tulsi Devi how she got the baby into her belly in the first place. Tulsi Devi did not say. They coaxed her, promising to tell all their lustful stories in return, but still she did not say. After hours of teasing, she finally said that she would tell them once and then she never wanted to hear them talk about it again.

The story was told in the dark after dinner, around the light of a few dias. The faces of the eunuchs were lit from underneath, making their large painted eyes even bigger as they heard an edited account of her rape. "It was like he was doing this thing to someone else. My body was no longer my own," she told them.

Silenced by the story at first, they soon broke out into a moralistic condemnation of the man who had abused her. "Why did he do it? Why did he not go and see a prostitute? Or why not some dancing girl? Why his poor student?"

"It will come back to him. See how much he enjoys it when his own daughter gets molested."

Bubbly stayed quiet at first, and when they had all settled down from their outrage he announced that he was quite certain now that the baby would be a boy. There was an unbecoming seriousness in his eyes, as he told of how the conception foretold the fate of the child. He spoke to Tulsi Devi in a voice so sinister that, with the dia light shining underneath his chin, he intimidated even his fellow menwomen. He told her that he would look after the boy. That soon she would be rid of the whole incident.

"And your boy? He will be the most legendary eunuch to have ever set foot in this haveli."

Tulsi Devi shuddered. The others changed the subject to talk of the boy's birth. Together they plotted her delivery at the same nursing home where she had recovered recently. The only alternative was a midwife's delivery at the haveli and that was laughable. Which midwife in the whole of Hardwar would come to this eunuchs' haveli – the only home in town that had never welcomed a new soul into the world? And which of the eunuchs would the midwife choose for her assistant?

All the eunuchs were laughing loudly now, but this talk of birth set fire to a forest of fears that Tulsi Devi had not yet considered. It was too late to talk about these things. Too dark. Women died in childbirth all the time. What chance of survival would she have with this ill-fated child?

She remembered then that if she were to die in childbirth she would just be completing a process she had already started. Everyone in the room was dying. Only slowly. Wouldn't her baby die, too, one day? If not tomorrow, within a hundred years?

No, it was too late in the night to think about the birth for the first time. The monsters started knocking on the door again. Tulsi Devi started shivering and crying. That night she begged one of the eunuchs to stay with her, just so that she would not be alone. Bubbly offered. They lay together on the single string mattress: he in his bright red wedding sari and she in her white convent sari that Jyoti Ma had bought for her in another life. Bubbly put his dark arm around her, feeling her blood journey underneath her skin while she slept. He didn't close his eyes until the morning, thinking again and again about how his little Ravan was resting now in Tulsi Devi's womb, waiting for the moment when he would join the world, join the clan and become his.

24

Tulsi Devi lived the next three months in denial of her pregnancy. Unlike most expectant mothers she didn't once try to think of a name, imagine a relationship with her child or even think about the birth. She knew that any such thoughts would start to raise questions that could not be answered by anyone but the monsters of her imagination.

To maintain her seclusion in the present moment in time, she entered the most fervently religious period of her life. Her thoughts were permanently occupied with images of gods – white ones, black ones, blue ones. Any god would do. Their only role was to distract her from her future or any thought of it.

Whenever she felt a pain, she asked the closest god at hand to help make it stronger, so that she could feel some form of distraction in the punishment. And it always got worse, because it was always within the realm of the gods to amplify any kind of experience.

When there was no pain, she would chant Hail Marys to mark out the passage of time.

Only when her belly hurt in the ninth month did she start to think about the birth, not through any concern for the future, but because she simply had to get this huge weight out of her. It was not possible to grow any bigger. There simply wasn't any room. Although the eunuchs all watched her eat every meal like eager grandmothers, she could never persuade the baby to roll over and let her fit more than half a roti alongside it in her belly.

The eunuchs were pleased that she was big. It meant the baby would be a boy and a healthy one at that. One of the eunuchs cracked a joke that she was walking around like she had a cucumber between her legs and the others chided him, forcing him to show respect for the mother of their baby.

Tulsi Devi spent her last day of pregnancy lying down alone, looking over the most enormous belly at her feet that were propped on a pillow. Every now and then the baby would stretch out a limb and distort her perfectly round shape to suit its final fetal movements.

Seeing the shape of a limb brought her closer to the reality that this was a child, and she allowed herself the liberty to think of the man who had put it there. That day in Lahore. His eyebrows that joined together and furrowed to make a triangle at the moment he released his seed. The wet feeling came back again.

She thought about how Jesus had been born in a manger because there was no place for him at the inn. She thought about how Krishna had been born in a prison because his wicked uncle had heard a prophecy that he would be slain by the God-baby. She thought of how she lay here now, in a eunuchs' haveli, because there was nowhere else to go. In those last few moments before her time was up, she started to feel that this creature she had hosted all this time might actually be someone quite special.

That night when she got up and squatted on the toilet, she felt the most enormous tug up along the sides of her tummy. The pain collected itself just underneath her ribcage, seethed and squeezed and tightened and then just as suddenly, released itself. Water started to run down her legs and she felt a sense of urgency, fear and excitement. She went to lie down again, but the pain was too severe to lie horizontal, so she started quietly pacing the courtyard of the haveli.

Instinctively, as she had done when she first arrived in Hardwar, she decided to make her way down to the ghats. She had an urge to be in water and a lucid intuition that she could cleanse herself of mortal sin if she were to bathe in the holy water of the Ganges.

So Tulsi Devi walked through the streets to reach the ghats. Whenever she felt one of those pains she walked through it, so that if there were anyone awake to watch her, they would never even imagine that she was in labor.

A thought struck her that a dacoit could jump out of the shadows and discover that she was with child. One man walking the streets did notice her and wondered why a pregnant woman was out at this time without a chaperone. But her sense of purpose was so strong he did not approach her. He simply gave her a comfortable distance so that she would not feel too threatened by the presence of a lone man in the streets at this witching hour. Tulsi Devi noticed him, felt one of her pains and walked faster through it until it surged so hard against the top of her belly she felt like doubling over. Instead, she just kept on walking. Fast.

At the ghats she lowered herself into the water and felt its warmth soothe her back and belly, making her feel lighter and more buoyant. She lowered her head below the water, her liquid midwife, and submerged herself to the experience, praying to be cleansed. Her practice of asking the gods to intensify the pain was working for her, allowing rapid progress. Whenever it built up she laid herself bare at its crescendo until there was no greater pain it could offer her. And she would open a little more.

Things were moving fast for one so fearless.

Then, out of nowhere, the most unbelievable sensation possessed Tulsi Devi and made her let out a muted lion's roar. A plough was pulling itself down her insides, forcing its way out of her. She had never felt so powerful before in her life, feeling as if the forces that made this very river flow were active in her body to help her push out the baby. It was a force field of gravity, the power of a hundred elephants pulling down a tree, but coming from within. Right down her center and out through her legs. She could feel a huge mass at her entrance and she let out a muffled scream as her baby broke free and slithered its way out into an even larger waterworld that would cleanse it of the last taint of mortal sin.

Tulsi Devi reached down and guided the baby up to the water's surface. It was then that she was taken aback by the most surprising and inexplicable emotion. The feeling of Love. Pure, boundless, accepting, unquestionable.

The pain disappeared and all that was left was a delirious joy.

Tulsi Devi stepped onto the banks of the river as if she were returning to a new world of people who had played their part in this mystery of life by becoming parents. She sat with the small naked creature clutching its birth bag in her lap. Her heart was racing from excitement as much as the process of the birth itself. She adored her baby so much, she wanted to kiss it and caress it, so she held it close, bit the cord and then she noticed – her baby was a boy.

Her exhausted body was gripped with fear as she suddenly remembered the eunuchs. She could not bear the thought of losing love so soon after she had found it. Nor the idea that this perfect creature could be castrated if she left it a minute too late to act. So she walked, her nude infant in her arms, wearing her drenched and bloodstained convent sari, through the night to pick up her belongings at the haveli.

When she arrived there, everyone was too sleepy from smoking opium the night before to hear the whimper of a newborn and the departure of Tulsi Devi.

Once more she headed to the station to await the train – any train – forcing herself to walk until she could finally collapse at her destination. Time was running out. The sun was starting to rise and the light would trace her escape route all too easily for the eunuchs who had waited so long for her deliverance. The train to Delhi arrived at six in the morning and she had to wait for thirty painful minutes before it would take her and her new baby safely away.

When the wheels started turning, and she could see there was nobody she knew in a red and gold sari on the platform, Tulsi Devi took in a deep breath and held her baby tight.

She would call him Jivan. He looked as if he would suit that name, although he still had his eyes shut to the world and his dramatic escape through the prison gates. Tulsi Devi fed him and held him against her heart, feeling the responsibility of his total trust in her. He had surrendered to life, she thought, and was now totally vulnerable to whatever kind of an experience she could create for him.

Tulsi Devi decided there and then that Jivan would have the best life if they went back to Prakriti, and she had no hesitation that it was now time for her to return. She thought of her mother and how she would respond to their arrival. She even prayed that maybe Jivan would replace Ram in her mother's heart. But it was not something she could even begin to wish for until she had met with her mother once more. And that involved perhaps the biggest challenge that she had faced up till now.

25

Stepping off the train with her newborn baby, Tulsi Devi was quick to attract the attention and pity of the entire village. There was no car to greet her, not even Ganesh. No husband to assist her. No fanfare for her arrival. Her clothes were tattered and her hair was unmade. This was not the same girl whom every tailor had made garments for throughout the early years of Prakriti.

There was a story that walked with her down the cobbled streets, demanding to be told, but the curious villagers knew that they would never be the ones to hear it.

Tulsi Devi passed the shop where she used to steal sweets and looked down to avoid the pity of the shopkeeper who had wished an experience of true poverty upon her. Sure enough, that curse had found its target and clung with tenacity.

When she could walk no further she sat down at a chai shop and summoned over a young boy who looked no less ragged than she. Promising him rewards at a later date, she made him run an errand to Prakriti to inform Jyoti Ma of her arrival and request a car.

From then on, all she could do was wait, sip tea and talk with her little creature to avoid making conversation with anybody who might try to discover what had happened. Jivan opened his eyes for the first time to see unfocused dirty walls, a dirty table and a mother sipping chai, her face holding back total fatigue only because she had found love.

She saw his face and smiled. He tried to focus. She kissed him and he closed his eyes again, to shut out the light that came from this disorientating, complicated world.

Jyoti Ma received the news of her daughter's arrival with great composure and sent the mahout, who was now the driver of cars as well as elephants, to bring Tulsi Devi from the village.

Since Tulsi Devi had left Lahore, Jyoti Ma had become practiced in the art of living alone: resigned to her fate and completely occupied with the affairs of Prakriti. Nevertheless, there hadn't been a day when Jyoti Ma hadn't wondered where her daughter was. She would think of her, then force the girl out of her mind. It was simply too painful to believe that Tulsi Devi had rejected her like the rest of the family.

Now that she had come to terms with her new state of affairs, a shabby worn-out boy had arrived to tell her to make room in her life once more for family. She felt her heart pump in her chest, but subdued the excitement of anticipation, because she was now at an age where nothing should be expected of life.

Jyoti Ma wondered what she was going to say to her daughter. She prepared a lecture and decided that Tulsi Devi would be restricted from going out for a few months as punishment and not allowed any of her usual favorite sweet dishes or any new clothes. It was too late to continue her education so she would start up correspondences to find a suitable match.

In spite of her prepared severity, something inside of her wanted to jump up and down with excitement. Her daughter had died, and now she had come back to life. That meant new life for Jyoti Ma. She was a mother once more. It was her second chance.

Jyoti Ma ordered tea as soon as she saw the car swing around the hill and literally ran out to give her little girl a big welcome. The car pulled up under the jacaranda tree and a village woman with broken European buckle-up shoes and matted hair stepped out of the clean car, carrying a miniature creature with a shock of dark spiky hair.

"Kya ka kya hogia?" Jyoti Ma muttered in her throat. *What could have been*? She didn't feel disgust, simply disappointment that she no longer knew her daughter. The young girl she had dropped off at Loreto Convent would always be a hostage of the past. Something had killed her, just as Jyoti Ma had always suspected.

Tulsi Devi, the guilty and the famished. Jyoti Ma, the mother now of an adult, held her daughter's hand and then hugged her. The only thing that came between them now was the smell of the Ganges, which made Jyoti Ma pull away in revulsion.

"Ma, this is your grandson, Jivan," Tulsi Devi announced as she made her only oblation.

"Beti, you both need a bath," was her mother's reply.

The maidservant prepared the bucket and the hot water. Then she took the baby, giving Tulsi Devi the first sense of release she had experienced for what seemed a lifetime. Prakriti was an indulgence she had almost forgotten. The feeling of safety and comfort was sewn into the very bed linen.

After her bath, Tulsi Devi, having surrendered her baby, relinquished responsibility and allowed her body the luxury it had been born to.

The maidservant bathed Jivan and placed a small black tikka under one cheek to ward off the evil eye that had surely been cast on him to have arrived at Prakriti in such a condition. Then she brought him in a clean white towel to play with his nani.

It had been a long time since Jyoti Ma had handled a babe so small and she was most unprepared. She examined him to make sure that he was completely normal to all outward appearances. Only a pungent black stump on his navel deformed him. A tiny little hand grasped her finger, but she felt no connection with him. No, he was not hers and had no right to claim her. He had brought misfortune on her daughter. It was almost irritating that he was so small and appealing.

There was nothing in the house that made it a home for a baby. One servant was sent to summon a tailor; another was instructed to start cutting up an old cotton sari to make into nappies. The baby screamed, but nothing could wake his mother. He screamed and screamed until he could sustain his cry no longer and fell asleep, rocked in the arms of his new ayah to the tune of a Pahari folk song.

Whilst Tulsi Devi slept, her mother, forgetting her previous resolution, prepared a section of her own wardrobe to clothe her daughter and ordered all her favorite sweet dishes to be made in the kitchen for her evening meal. She also sent the cook to buy lotus seeds, more almonds, ghee, wheat and all the other ingredients necessary to make panjiri, the traditional recipe she had been taught in former years for strengthening new mothers.

But Tulsi Devi wasn't about to get strong fast. Fifteen hours later she still had not woken up, and she was weaker than ever when she did. Her eyes had turned yellow in her dreams and her head was spinning. She could hardly pick up the baby when he was handed to her. When he sucked on her breast it felt as if her very life force was being sapped out of her.

The doctor was called and Tulsi Devi was diagnosed with jaundice. He recommended coconut juice if they could get some from Delhi, plenty of water, pomegranates, radish and as many sweet things as the patient could eat.

Tulsi Devi could not touch a thing. Only warm soups and the occasional piece of fruit. She fostered her child to the ayah and gave in to her body's desire for total collapse. The illness had waited for this moment when she could hand over all her responsibilities and allow it to claim her body as its own.

"Mama, will you promise to look after my child?" she asked once through her delirium. But Jyoti Ma never answered.

It took months to recover her strength. Jyoti Ma kept calling the doctor, who said, "Nothing, absolutely nothing can be done about it. Skin must return to normal color, that is all."

When the color started to look as if it were a permanent yellow dye, and the cook was sick of cooking up tasty morsels of every description just to have them all rejected, he suggested an alternative. "My mother has been afflicted by the yellow illness too. There is a man in the village who can get rid of it. Five minutes is all it takes."

Jyoti Ma had no interest in herbal remedies, even though she maintained the profits of Prakriti at dizzying heights by selling them. For her, a doctor trained the English way was the only trustworthy solution. She continued to call her trusted doctor, but diverged her strategy by calling in an artist also, to record the varying shades of yellow that Tulsi Devi turned each week, in the hope that the color was slowly fading.

Desperate now that she may be forced to become the mother of Jivan, Jyoti Ma called in her cook and asked him for more information about this man in the village who cured jaundice. The cook offered to bring him to the house the next day. "Memsahib," he said, "I must tell you that in the village this man is considered to be the wisest of us all." It was his way of saying that the healer was accustomed to being shown greater respect than any Jyoti Ma had ever allotted anyone.

The man arrived and silently prepared a shallow clay bowl with white lime powder. Then he threw in a mystery leaf, chanted a mantra and beckoned Tulsi Devi to put her hands into the milky white water. Tulsi Devi obeyed and, feeling giddy from the effort, closed her eyes. The man started to massage her wrists downward and a few seconds later he nudged her. She opened her eyes and saw the yellow color leaving her hands and coloring the white liquid. Her giddiness lifted and she breathed in a deep lungful of pure health.

"I'm better, Ma," she announced.

Jyoti Ma reserved her judgement, saying "Let's see." She'd heard of this remedy before, but it didn't make any sense. She gave the man a modest amount of money (just in case the cure was only a temporary one) but he refused it, saying that he was not able to accept money for work that was done by God. It was the first time Jyoti Ma had come across a villager who did not see Prakriti as some kind of cash cow, and she was quite taken aback. Even more so when Tulsi Devi sustained a genuine recovery.

By the time Tulsi Devi was well enough to play with Jivan, the baby was crawling around, driving Jyoti Ma into a frenzy every time he licked a shoe or sucked on his ayah's sari. Tulsi Devi could tell that no great friendship had grown between her mother and her son during her prolonged illness. It was almost as if Jyoti Ma never wanted to get close to anyone again, in case they too had the opportunity to reject her.

As much as Jivan was disowned, Tulsi Devi still belonged to Jyoti Ma. She had experienced some things that a girl should never have experienced, but it was not her fault. In fact, Jyoti Ma liked to dismiss "those convent days" – everything that had happened to her daughter between leaving Prakriti and returning. After she had extracted the whole story, she said only these few words of consolation: "Do not talk about these things to anyone!"

Tulsi Devi's own inclination was to say nothing about what had happened. Even to her own cousin. Joyce brought her baby Tara with her to visit Tulsi Devi in Prakriti, but soon found that her cousin had drifted off into a strange silent sea, the waters between them now too deep to fathom.

For Tulsi Devi, Joyce represented the great expectations of the past and the many failings of the present. The difference was that Joyce was married. Her husband may be away at sea in the merchant navy, but she still *had* a husband. Her legitimate child made her a legitimate mother.

Was Joyce coming just to pity her? Tulsi Devi remembered how they had been so egalitarian in their futures game. All it had taken was a few years for these hierarchies to stake their claim. Just a short period of time for their young fantasies to meet the future as it really was.

It was Tulsi Devi who was stopping Joyce from becoming a close friend and confidante once more. Joyce loved her cousin as much as ever. But somehow the carefree days they had spent together as children and their common bond in motherhood were simply not enough to ignite the friendship once more.

Over the next few years Tulsi Devi focused on her child, and on trying to make amends with her mother. Jyoti Ma, however, made it clear that amends could not be made in this lifetime alone. Jivan, whom Tulsi Devi had so hoped would bridge the gap, only served to widen it further. No amount of company or help with the business of the farm could bring any comfort to Jyoti Ma.

"You have no idea, absolutely no idea what I have had to go through," she always told her daughter, accentuating her own misfortune over all others.

What Tulsi Devi did not realize was that she was trying to compensate for every tragedy in her mother's life, and it was simply not in her power to do so. Jyoti Ma's happiness was a stubborn hermit. She never gave in to her daughter's attempts to make her happy, yet she did not allow Tulsi Devi the relief of stopping the great effort. It was simply a daughter's duty to look after her mother. So Jyoti Ma absorbed all her daughter's efforts without it showing, in the same way that okra soaks up oil, sticking to the pan all the while.

There were times when Tulsi Devi spent more energy trying to please her mother than she did looking after her own son. It was on one such morning that Jivan went missing.

That morning Tulsi Devi awoke to find her bed empty. Presuming that her son had woken early and gone off with his ayah, she spent the whole morning in the fields helping her mother. Paying some further dues. The ayah, meanwhile, had taken the morning off, thinking that her mistress had taken the child with her.

When the two came together, childless and immediately guilty, a search party was sent around Prakriti, with Tulsi Devi all the while imagining her son pale and lifeless, face down in the soil.

Jivan was found in a gully of prickles quite some distance away from the farmhouse. He was quiet, his eyes wide open and thorns piercing his skin. Tulsi Devi's first reaction was utter relief. Delight that he had been attacked only by thistles and not scorpions. But then Jivan's stoic acceptance of his thistle bed worried her. His eyes showed that he expected life to be cruel. She wondered – as he grew would he let others pierce his skin at will?

Tulsi Devi tried to discover how long he had been in the thistles – maybe he had even slept in them, because nobody had seen him since he awoke, and there had been a few nights when he had walked in his sleep.

For the next few nights Tulsi Devi slept with Jivan in the same bed, a thin cotton thread binding together their wrists. Whether that would be enough to keep mother and child together in the future, when the forces of destiny pushed them apart again, even Tulsi Devi did not know.

26

Ever since she first set eyes on Jivan, Jyoti Ma never once thought of a marriage partner for Tulsi Devi. She had already decided that no man would ever have her, or her little boy. If something had happened to the child, maybe she could have been married off once more to a man with equally unlikely prospects. But as things were, Jyoti Ma resigned herself to a future with an unmarried daughter, and the hope that the boy would grow to look after them all in their old age. Nothing changed until one day a letter arrived.

It was from a retired army officer named Colonel Chopra. Through a twist of fate, he was visiting a friend in a Gurkha regiment nearby. Over several rums in the officers' mess, he had confessed that since he had left the army he had no interest in life and was thinking of taking a wife. When his friend had asked if he was serious he had answered, "Why not? I'm not fussy. I can find a wife in a nearby village if it pleases me. There will for sure be some father who cannot marry off his daughter and will be pleased to get rid of her."

And so Colonel Chopra learnt about this beautiful girl with wealthy parents who lived further down the road to Simla. He was instantly intrigued. There was no need for her to be a virgin – he had already notched up more virginities amongst village girls to last him a lifetime.

But the prospect of marrying someone from his own class was far more appealing. Someone who had a few life scars like his own.

Tulsi Devi and Jivan were playing on the verandah, throwing pebbles and seeing how far away they landed, when there was a knock at the door. Siesta time was an unusual time for visitors. It was a sacred three-hour period in the afternoon, when not one of the servants or workers would disturb memsahib during her slumber snores. Tulsi Devi rushed around the bungalow to meet the visitor, but he had already been shown in. Apparently her mother was expecting this guest. So she went back to her game with her son, condemned, as she was, to a sleepless siesta with a fully alert child and no ayah awake to look after him.

Through the cracks in the wooden doors, Tulsi Devi heard a conversation about her future that was so blunt, it verged on obscenity.

"She may be beautiful, but there's not another man in the land who would have her," spoke a man with an accent so British he could have been mistaken for the Queen's husband.

"She is welcome to stay here for as long as she likes. This is her home and always will be," responded Jyoti Ma.

"But the boy needs a father, and all your wealth will not buy him another one. The dowry I am asking for is so small compared with what you have. It will set up your daughter in a manner to which she's accustomed. And within the right caste."

"Caste is no bar, sir, we are Arya Samajis. And you are thirty years her senior."

"In thirty years of searching, she will not get another offer."

"Maybe it is possible, but you ask for too much. What will I survive on, now that my husband is gone?"

"I am not asking for your farm. It is yours, and it will keep you well."

"I can give you five lakh of rupees, not ten."

"Ten lakh and nothing less. Do you wish to bargain for this marriage like a pound of dhal at the market? Isn't it enough that a gentleman has come to you with a proposal?"

"We still need to ask the girl."

"Will that really be necessary?"

Angry at these words, Tulsi Devi threw a stone for her little Jivan, and went to the window to look at the man who was making the preposterous offer. Jivan was so excited at the throw he ran off in glee to return it to his mother for a second go.

Peeking through the slats at the window, Tulsi Devi saw a crutch before she saw the man who leant against it. There was no leg. Just a sewn-up kurta pyjama, with a chemise drawn up so high you could see the string that held it up. She instantly felt pity for the man, and with it some sense of respect that his words did not warrant. The leg itself spoke of tragedy, and with that tragedy she could feel a certain affinity, because however tragedy befalls you, it is your humanity that is exposed in the process – that which we all share in common.

The next thing she noticed was an army jacket with some badges of dignity on the shoulder. None of these indicators seemed to go with the words that she had heard, so she searched for the lips of the man who had spoken them. They were found under a moustache that had been barbered for the occasion half an hour up the road. Thin lips which lost their balance mid-way, undecided over happiness or sadness. His hair was thin on his head, dyed black with a millimeter of gray roots.

Then she looked more closely at his eyes and a shiver of fear made her nipples stand on end. They were gouged so deeply and set so close together, the sculptor who had created them surely had no one to model them on. *Were* there even eyes in those huge valleys under his brow?

Tulsi Devi knew when she saw his eyes that she would be marrying this man. No matter what resistance she may offer, the sacred marriage fire had already been circumnavigated and the knot had already been tied.

For this was the marriage that would atone for her sins and make certain that her quota for tragedy would be used up fully in this one lifetime.

Jyoti Ma called for her daughter, her tone urgent and commanding. Both daughter and grandson entered the room of audience from the back verandah. Tulsi Devi kept her eyes lowered, like a virgin bride. And Jivan, with love in his heart and excitement in his legs, sprang onto the man's lap and embraced him. Without even looking at her daughter, Jyoti Ma said, "Jivan beta, give your papa a big kiss and he will look after you always."

Jivan took no notice, but somehow registered the word "papa." He leapt off Colonel Chopra's lap, grabbed his crutch and shouted at the top of his voice, "Look, Papa's got a stick! Papa's got a stick!" He took the crutch and waved it around his head. The weight of it sent him off balance and he fell like a cripple to the floor with his new father's crutch crashing down on him.

Colonel Chopra took one look. His army instincts told him to take the boy outside for a flogging, but his better judgement and sense of occasion elicited a half-smile on the happy side of his face. Even that was not so much for the boy, but at the sight of his bride-to-be, who was even more beautiful than the picture painted of her by his officer friend. *What a stroke of luck,* he thought, *that one so beautiful could be so readily available for me at my age.*

27

Being the only daughter of wealthy landowners, the wedding of Tulsi Devi would ordinarily have taken place as a homage to the family's status. From the time when her daughter was born, Jyoti Ma had imagined herself taking her pick of the country's most eligible suitors, as if she herself were choosing a prince at a royal swyamvar. The groom and his baraat would arrive on Ganesh, the family elephant, who would come decked like a royal vehicle, his eyes, face and trunk decorated with paints from the earth, his back draped in a bejeweled cloth. She had even designed a set of silver anklets for the elephant that she had intended to have made on the occasion of her daughter's betrothal.

In Jyoti Ma's vision of excess, the bedi for the havan fire was to be made not just with garlands of flowers, but with strings of pearls as well, so that it would be a canopy fit for Sita, the earth Goddess of virtue and purity. She was going to import a sweet chef from Bengal to offer every kind of mithai known to the palate. A shenai player would be summoned to the farm to play his humming melodies to the hills not just for the day of the wedding, but for the month before and the month after. The country's best mehndi wala would be called for a week to paint henna onto the hands of every girl and woman for miles around. All the workers, for once in their lives, were to receive not just a set of clothes, but clothes made of finest silk. Her daughter's in-laws would receive jewelery far beyond their wildest expectations. In fact, if she could have organized the heavens to rain flowers on the day, she would have booked each and every god months and months in advance for the occasion.

As it happened, Tulsi Devi's wedding was far truer to the Arya Samaji reformist spirit than any extravaganza cooked up in Jyoti Ma's imagination. The pandit called to perform the sacred rites was the only guest invited. Even Jivan was not present, because by the time the pandit had arrived and set up, he was well and truly tucked into bed. Jyoti Ma was pleased: if Jivan were asleep, maybe the gods present for the ceremony would neglect to notice that her virgin daughter was already a mother.

There were no canopies of flowers, only a handful of buds for the offering, and two strings of flowers for the couple to garland each other. The bride wore a simple red South Indian temple sari, with only a modest amount of gold woven into the border, red dust in the parting of her hair to show that she was betrothed, four new gold bangles and two simple frames of black kajal around her eyes. Her natural beauty did not require anymore augmentation. Her hair was plaited with a rose at every rung, and an intricate array of little plaits wove their way down to her waist.

Tulsi Devi was resolute, composed and totally present. When the shlokas started, she looked directly into the eyes of her husband and had no thoughts for the future. So few people had managed to penetrate deep enough to catch his gaze, that the Colonel was momentarily taken aback. Yet her eyes were not challenging. They accepted him as he was, whether his intentions were honorable or not.

He knew then that these were the eyes of the bride described by Manu in the ancient texts. One who would accompany her husband loyally, even to the brothel. Indeed, Tulsi Devi did see her salvation in the Colonel, but only in terms of penance and tapasya.

The pandit tied Tulsi Devi's sari palla to her husband's sash and they stood up to circle the fire seven times. Jyoti Ma noticed how sturdy the

Colonel's leg stood. In most weddings she had attended, by this stage every young boy standing on two legs would be quaking with fear. For the first time she thought positively about her new son-in-law. It was true that he was old enough to be the girl's father, but seeing as she no longer had one, it wasn't such a bad thing.

The couple were now united, not just for this lifetime but for many to come. Colonel Chopra touched the feet of Jyoti Ma for her blessings, then they all sat in silence as the pandit packed up his sacred paraphernalia. Usually he was able to do the task invisibly, but on this occasion there were no festive distractions and all eyes were solemnly awaiting his departure. He hurriedly ate the sweetmeats he was offered and threw the sacred ornaments into his bag. *Strange,* he pondered to himself. *And why choose this inauspicious season for a wedding?* But he dismissed the thought swiftly and considered instead how auspicious it was for him to gain some employment at this time when things were usually so quiet.

After the wedding, there were no young children awake to ridicule the new groom, steal his shoes – or even the single shoe, in this case. There was no henna on Tulsi Devi's hands for her new husband to search out his initials amongst the ochre lattice designs before taking her to bed. There was not even a bed made up for the couple to retire to, let alone one decorated with flower buds and petals. In her minimalist preparations, Jyoti Ma had quite forgotten about any nuptial consummations, thinking only up to the moment when she would finally hand over Tulsi Devi's welfare and be freed from the burden of a spinster daughter. So, tired as she was, she called in one of the servants to make up a bed in the spare room.

Shankar, the cook, arrived, and knowing that in this house he could not protest about chores beyond his duty, duly made up the bed. Only when he was told to bring in Tulsi Devi's clothes from the cupboard in the other room, did it strike him that a wedding had taken place in the house. *How strange these big people are,* he thought, knowing that he would be unable to keep his discovery a secret.

The next day he told the mahout, who told the local shopkeeper, who told the doodh wala, who brought the news back to the farm. When the farm manager discovered that a wedding had taken place, he personally went to the memsahib to insist on a customary gift. Jyoti Ma begrudgingly offered him one of the kurta pyjamas that had been left behind by her departed husband. And that was the end of it.

After Shankar had made the bed and transferred the clothes to the bridal chamber, Tulsi Devi walked directly into the room without even saying goodnight. Taken aback, the Colonel stayed a little longer to talk pleasantries with Jyoti Ma, looking for the first time a little uncomfortable. But when he realized she would much rather put an end to the arduous day, he bade his new mother-in-law goodnight and let himself into the impromptu honeymoon suite.

Inside was his new wife, fast asleep. Wondering why the woman had no sense of occasion, he dropped his crutch noisily to the floor. Then he sat on one of the two single beds that had been joined together in holy matrimony and leant over the sleeping beauty who was still fully dressed in her sari and modest wedding jewels. For a moment he wondered if he would ever be able to win her love, but dismissed the thought, thinking that it was hardly necessary. What he felt was a lust so strong, that even love would have respected it as an equal suitor.

Ideally he should have waited the prescribed ten days before any act of love, but he knew that given the circumstances there was no need for obligation or pretense. So he lay down next to her and started to unwind the six yards of silk between him and total consummation, kissing the cloth as it passed through his fingers.

Tulsi Devi felt the force of strength above her before she opened her eyes to see the man who wielded it. Determination and power were so concentrated in his body that they instantly summoned awake a sleeping goddess of sensual pleasures from within her. She reached out for him, but then pushed him away slightly, remembering that day with David De Souza.

Undeterred, the Colonel pressed down on her with the weight of his eyes alone, and she held him, this time running her hand down to feel his missing leg. She felt for a moment as if the two of them had no history and no culture. They were innocent and unrestrained. Tulsi Devi surrendered to him as if she were handing over ownership of her own desires. It gave the Colonel a lion's appetite and he took his fill, leaving hardly a scrap of flesh on any bone that was not fully and utterly devoured. Afterward, the three legs lay entwined amidst the unraveled sheets.

Sweet sleep ensued, until just after midnight when the newfound serenity in the house was torn by a blood-curdling scream. It was Jivan. In his dream he was climbing a tree to pick apples, red and plump. But as he picked them, they grew thorns to stab him. He had to let go, and in letting go he fell further and further down the tree, that scratched and ripped him until he was no longer recognizable.

Freefalling to the ground, he yelled. Yelling first in his dream and then wide awake, unable to stop the sound escaping his mouth. When he opened his eyes and saw that his mother was gone, he ran out of the door and met her on the verandah, where he fell into her arms.

Tulsi Devi picked him up and took him back to his bed to cuddle him close to her heart. It was the last time the two of them would be allowed to sleep together, but not realizing this at that moment, their rest was undisturbed.

28

After the marriage, Colonel Chopra took his new wife and her child down to Delhi, to the house of his dead parents. It looked, on the outside, like a very Indian, very Delhi, flat-roofed house. Inside it was a little England.

Over the years, with no family to spend his money, the Colonel had invested in English artifacts to prove that he was a loyal servant of the British Army. There was not a single ornate or exotic influence. There were paintings on the walls of thatched cottages in Suffolk, and a portrait of an aristocratic English lady, rejected by the client because the shadows on her face looked like a moustache. Victorian furniture decorated the rooms, the bookshelves were filled with English classics.

All this love for the British on his walls, and yet no love had been returned. Tulsi Devi found out some years later that the Colonel had been asked to leave the army when his leg had been damaged whilst quelling an anti-British riot. "It was that Gandhi," he told Tulsi Devi. "He's getting us to kill our own people. The British are not our enemies. We are our own enemies."

After taking early retirement, the Colonel had to moderate his lifestyle considerably. "You have met me in my shadow years," he always told his wife. There was a time in service when he had ten servants to attend not only to his needs, but the needs of the other servants. There was a cook, someone to grind the masalas and wash up the dishes, two chowkidars, a sweeper, a dhobi to wash clothes and four peons to run errands. But now there was just one man: the perpetually faithful Dhruv, his original cook, who performed all the household functions and still had time to spare.

When Colonel Saab arrived with two extra bosses, Dhruv's workload was extended further, and he was now also an ayah for the little boy. As things turned out, this soon became his favorite form of employment, so Tulsi Devi was happy to help Dhruv in the kitchen, and the Colonel ate chappatis made by his wife's own fair hands.

Tulsi Devi was neither happy nor sad; she seemed to exist outside the parameters of standard emotions. She simply performed her duties for her husband. Unlike most newlyweds, she needed no period of adjustment and there were no in-laws to please. She was immediately the lady of the house, without having to produce the obligatory son to deserve respect.

Up till now Colonel Chopra had been quite happy to spend most of his time in the house. But since his marriage, staying at home seemed a lady's thing to do, making him feel redundant in his own environment. If anybody needed to do any adjustment, it was him, and he preferred to do his adjusting outside of their domestic boundaries.

He would spend all morning at the army canteen, buying discount provisions. Then he would continue on to the club designated for Indian officers, where he would feast on pakoras and Chinese noodles for lunch. In the afternoons, when everybody was taking their siesta, he would read newspapers in the club library. None of the other retired officers who sat with him ever knew that his life had changed so dramatically in later years. Nor did they know of his new wife. He lived the frugal life of a bachelor, without spending a paisa of the ten lakh of rupees he had been given as his wife's dowry.

Husband and wife led very separate lives. As soon as the Colonel started going out in the daytime, Tulsi Devi also went out to explore the city with Jivan.

In the evenings they would meet over dinner, or sometimes in the early afternoon over high tea if the Colonel was home in time. Dhruv would serve the food on fine bone china instead of the thalis that Tulsi Devi was used to, and offer each of them a napkin made at Fortnum & Mason in London. The Colonel would then instruct Tulsi Devi on how she should behave and what she should wear.

Tulsi Devi found her freedom through regular adventures into the city. She was not interested in the grandeur of Lutyens' Delhi that was being constructed before her very eyes. Her favorite venue was the old Chandni Chowk, where she and Jivan would explore the bustling bargaining labyrinths of the old Moghul market. The sweets dripping with fresh syrup, the garlands of pearls. The gold, fingered and weighed. The firecrackers wrapped like sweets. The multi-colored bangles that stretched out like rows of arms, their glittering mirrorwork catching the sun. The havelis, the alleys. The daze of heat and action.

One day after Connaught Place had been newly opened, Tulsi Devi took Jivan there for an informal lesson on the English, as if the regal pillars and walkways would speak stories of their own, letting him into the British inner circle.

Tulsi Devi walked for an hour while Jivan ran with his arms out like an aeroplane, weaving his way around the pillars. It all looked so new and grand. She couldn't help but marvel at how well the British knew how to make themselves comfortable in this land that wasn't theirs.

Just then she saw a shock of red hair. Absolutely recognizable. It was Lily, her governess from that time before everything happened. The singular difference in her appearance was that she now had the body of a mother. Next to her to prove it was a girl of about seven years of age, with Roy's forest-pixie face and her mother's frizzy hair, only a few shades closer to ginger.

Tulsi Devi was so overwhelmed with joy that for a moment she felt as if nothing had happened in the intervening years. That she had never been robbed of her girlhood. She was the student and Lily the governess once more – only this time they were both women. She took Jivan's hand, skipped up to her governess and curtsied as she had the first time they met.

Lily burst out laughing, eyes alive with delight, and the two of them stood on the walkway wrapped up in a hug, whilst Jivan and Lily's daughter looked at each other suspiciously. Nothing as suspicious though, as the looks they were receiving from other voyeurs who had never before seen such a union between East and West.

"So you must have been married very young?" said Lily, admiring her student's son who was only a foot shorter than her own daughter. "What's this beautiful boy's name?"

"Jivan," replied Tulsi Devi.

"Juliet, shake hands with Jivan."

The young girl shook Jivan's hand, a little self-consciously.

Lily insisted that Tulsi Devi came home for tea, and so they left everything, hopped into Lily's car and drove to a mansion not far from Connaught Place.

The house was designed around a set of domes and archways, with servants' quarters that would make any ordinary house in Delhi look like a hovel. Jivan felt shy and unworthy, but Tulsi Devi, on the other hand, stepped out of the car as one accustomed to such splendor. "This could only be Roy's house," she said. "It has the most beautiful garden in the whole of Delhi."

Afternoon tea was served on the lawns by two servants who looked so elegant in their crowned turbans and formal uniform that Jivan thought they were princes. Juliet, who had obviously known no other life than this one here in India, looked like she had been born for the Raj. She may have had Roy's face, but there was nothing in her personality that harkened back to the Yorkshire moors.

Tulsi Devi and Lily talked about Prakriti, about Roy, about Tulsi Devi's education since Lily left. But not about what had happened at the convent, or afterward. Tulsi Devi skirted around it like someone walking past a urinal in a park, giving it plenty of distance to disappear into the loveliness of its surroundings.

"I didn't even know you were married," Lily said, not quite bold enough to comment that she hadn't received an invitation. "I've been to a few Indian weddings now and they really are the most splendid occasions."

"We only had a small wedding. Mama wanted it that way since my father ..." Tulsi Devi realized that Aakash's disappearance was yet another incident that required explanation. "My father spends a lot of time at his ashram nowadays," she finished.

By giving Lily a highly edited version of her life since they had last met, this occasion allowed Tulsi Devi to revisit the story of her youth and the golden days of Prakriti, without casting any clouds over her memories.

After a few hours in the lap of British luxury, the driver was ordered to drop them home and Lily insisted that Tulsi Devi drop by regularly now that they had rediscovered each other.

When they arrived home, Tulsi Devi told Jivan not to mention Lily to his papa. She knew that her husband would demand an introduction if he knew of Lily, simply because she was British. Whatever else, Tulsi Devi felt the need to keep the two compartments of her life entirely separate.

But Jivan never talked to the Colonel anyway, so the chances of him finding out were very slim.

Tulsi Devi's husband knew nothing of her adventures into the city, thinking that she was always at home, too shy to leave the house and explore her new surroundings. Neither did Tulsi Devi think to tell him how she spent her days, because he never stopped to ask her questions.

Jivan's first few months in Delhi were without any schooling or any friends, except for Dhruv. Sometimes Tulsi Devi tried to discuss Jivan's schooling needs, but the Colonel always said, "He is your son, you school him." Then Jivan would cast his invisible eyes toward his mama to see if she still loved him.

Nonetheless, Tulsi Devi made sure that he had all the fun a young boy should, stopping every dancing monkey show that passed by on the street to perform for her little boy. At every private performance Jivan would jump up and down with glee, pointing at the monkeys dressed in their wedding clothes: a hairy somersaulting bride and groom playing their tricks to the sound of a rattle drum.

His education was informal, a kind of hearsay in the Big City, partly from Dhruv, partly from his mother. Having never left the country before, Jivan was amazed by the grandness of the city. To say nothing of all the white people who walked around so proudly you would have thought they owned the whole world, not just India.

For him, the Colonel was like those white people. Arrogant, aggressive and powerful. One day when Jivan was out with his mother, they passed an Englishwoman who was trying to walk by on the narrow pavement. When Jivan did not move swiftly enough, the woman took her sun umbrella and whacked him hard to force him to one side. Neither mother nor son said a word. Not a tear fell from Jivan's eyes.

Tulsi Devi watched like an impartial witness, unable to express her horror as she heard the thwack on her son's backside. Jivan accepted the abuse as a sign of the absolute authority and superiority of the British in his country, and he felt a warped and complicated kind of respect for the race that validated its authority so freely.

Tulsi Devi pulled down his pants in public to inspect the red slash, patted it lovingly and told her son that he was a very brave little boy.

"Ma, Dhruv says that English madams don't wash their bottoms after they do coo coo on the potty. Is that really true?"

"What has that Dhruv been teaching you, beta? You must start going to school soon." Tulsi Devi was trying not to laugh, but school was becoming a bit of an issue for this homeling.

"But is it true?"

"I don't know." Tulsi Devi did know. And it was a much-discussed abomination of the country's rulers. "And anyway, it's not nice to say such things."

"They must really smell if they don't wash their bottoms."

"Don't talk such nonsense, beta."

"Does Papa refuse to wash his bottom like the English?"

Tulsi Devi's amusement turned to horror as she imagined her son repeating these words to her distant Anglophile husband.

"No, no. Stop it! Do you want a bara thappar?"

Jivan had never been threatened with a slap from his mother before. It made his fresh slash from the umbrella sting with fear as he felt his only real supporter in the family slowly defecting to the other side.

That night they heard news that Britain was going to war against Germany. The Colonel, who had war in his veins, knew the implications better than anyone.

"This means that dreadful Gandhi is going to take over the running of this godforsaken country. It will go to the dogs."

"Can they call you up if you are retired?" Tulsi Devi asked.

"And have me hop out the battalions?"

The Colonel may have sounded self-deprecating, but the truth was that he hated his missing leg and he hated having to leave the army. His heart was with the soldiers who were going off to fight their war.

"If England is going to war, I would like Jivan to go to school," Tulsi Devi said. The two things didn't quite go together, but she was talking fast, searching for conversation with the Colonel, and at the same time trying to calm her own bewilderment at the prospect of war.

"Who knows if there will be any schools left? If the English leave us to go to war this country will fall apart. Indians are hopeless at running their own country. They always have been."

Tulsi Devi did not agree. She knew that the British had to go. She felt angry at what had happened to her own son, and she felt angered too by the fact that the Colonel was not allowed to go to the club for English officers, in spite of his high status in their army. Then there were the wanton killings of Indians – innocent demonstrators most of them.

Jivan shuffled around on his sore bottom and Tulsi Devi felt impelled to tell her husband of the incident that had happened earlier that day.

"Serves him right for taking up too much space on the path," the Colonel answered without the slightest hint of indignation on his stepson's behalf.

Tulsi Devi did not stand in Jivan's defense. She only acknowledged her husband's reaction and placed it in a neutral compartment amidst many other perceptions she'd gathered of this man she had married.

That night, as nations lined up for war, and the graves of many men awaited them, the Colonel felt a shiver up his spine as he crawled into bed. It was the awakening of the spirit of war in his physicality – a combination of instinct, fear and camaraderie refueling his obsolete sense of purpose. He saw that Tulsi Devi was awake beside him on the shadowy side of the bed and decided to make her his concubine. If he could not go to war, at least he could taste the rewards of the victor.

His wife submitted as she always did, feeling herself the awesome heat, the anticipation of war, and the beckoning of the unknown, all of which hung thick in the air that night.

29

"A special report from Delhi follows . . ."

Three anxious faces sat listening to the wireless for news of war – Tulsi Devi, the Colonel and Jivan – waiting for any scrap of information that would help them understand what was happening in their country, and in their lives.

"Not only are the British in the process of making Delhi their capital, there are events taking place here and in the rest of this country that will have far more profound repercussions for Indians than any taking place in Europe. The future of the world may be uncertain, but the spirit of the Indian nation is evolving fast."

It was true. Souls usually happy to sit at home eating rotis and ghee had been galvanized into highly emotional and active states of patriotism. A newfound dignity and pride was being kindled. The battle had been all but won for India, even though it had only just started in Europe. War meant that the British would have to leave. Every day, people huddled around the nearest wireless to listen to stories of the war, and news of the Quit India Movement.

"Gandhi will for sure make those smelly English leave," announced Jivan one day.

"Inshallah." God willing.

The Colonel, keen to stamp out this ignorance, wheeled out his usual speech. "The English are going, that's true. And they'll be better off without having to run this cumbersome country. It's the beginning of the end. You'll see. We'll have goondahs for rulers and not one person will be able to hold it all together."

He did not like his wife to have a different opinion. It sent acute memories of betrayal down his severed leg. If it weren't for Gandhi, he would still have his missing limb. It was Gandhi who was responsible for inciting violence against British rule, even if he spoke the words of peace.

But Tulsi Devi's love for Gandhi was like Mary Magdalene's love for Christ. She knew that he was willing to die for his cause and so too was she. Only she was committed to a husband in the British service and quite unable to touch the feet of Gandhiji, the man she most admired. The rest of the nation may have been wearing homespun garments to protest against the British monopoly on cotton, but she was condemned to wearing saris shipped to India from the Lancashire mills. If she could have burnt her English cloth in the tall flames with other protesters, she would have, but she was a British subject through marriage, or so it seemed.

When Jivan started studying at a nearby school, Tulsi Devi went every day to drop him off in the morning and help him with his books and tiffin carrier. For several days during his first term there was a silent demonstration of holy men outside the nearby police station. It was unlike any of the other Quit India demonstrations Tulsi Devi had witnessed. There were no crowds of men bellowing and sweating, fists in the air and burning meteorites in their eyes. Just a group of men wearing white robes, with long dark hair and beads, sitting in silence. It was a demonstration of humility and strength combined.

Every time Tulsi Devi passed the men she covered her head with her palla to show respect for their mission. These were Gandhi's men, she was sure of it. They were selfless and non-violent, but more than that, like Gandhi they realized that it was a spiritual struggle. The very soul of India had to be freed.

She was taking Jivan to school one day when he wanted to stop and urinate outside the police station.

"Ma, I want to do shoo shoo."

"Not here, beta. It's really not proper." Tulsi Devi was embarrassed by the presence of the holy men and did not want to disturb their silence with the spray of a young boy's business.

"But Ma, I have to go."

"You will not!"

"I'm going to do it on *you* then."

"Hari Ram, would you ever even dream of doing such a thing at Prakriti?"

"Let him go," said a voice. A man in the circle of holy men stood up and came over to her. "You do not know who I am?"

"I am so sorry to disturb you. My son is being difficult."

"I did not know that you had a child."

"Should you know?"

"Ma, I've finished."

The man took her hand. "You are my sister."

"Come, Ma, or I'll be late for school."

"I am very sorry," Tulsi Devi said, letting go of the man's hand, "but I have to go now. I wish you well."

She hurriedly dropped Jivan off at school, thinking about the strange encounter all the way. She was used to being called "sister" or "mother" by every shopkeeper in Delhi trying to ingratiate themselves, but this time it had sounded so sincere. On the way back from the school, the man's true identity dawned on her, like a black-and-white photograph developing slowly in her mind. Finding the face, the eyes, the cheekbones. It was an image she had seen on the mantelpiece at Prakriti.

A photograph taken of her brother Ram before he took up sannyas. Before he even left the farm. His hair was cropped now, but the face was recognizably the same – an echo of her own.

Her heart raced with anxiety as she hurried back toward the police station. Would he still be there? "Ram," she heard herself whisper his name. This had been her dream – to see her brother once more – and now she had met him! She had no thought for the Colonel, for Jivan, for anyone. Just her Ram. She wanted to fall into his arms, dismissing the years that had parted them.

She kept matching the face she had just seen with the one on the mantelpiece at Prakriti, until she was absolutely convinced she had found him. Ram had survived! He would save them all.

In the distance between the school and the police station, the face of Ram that had appeared before her just a few minutes earlier became the most beautiful face she had ever seen. Ram had spoken. He had remembered her even though she was so small when he left.

Tulsi Devi was breathless when she arrived at the exact same spot where Ram had stood before her.

The holy men had gone.

She felt like screaming in frustration. Had it been a visitation of spirits? Was it some form of torture for her brother to appear after so many years and then to just vanish before she could hold him? She stared at the empty space in front of the red wall where the holy men had been, and then walked over the ground where they had sat, feeling the cruelty of the vacuum they had left behind.

She followed her body as it took its own course down the road, her legs setting down each foot in front of the other to make progress toward Ram. He was close. She could feel him. Who could know where he had been all those years? It did not matter, because now he was surely just a few streets away. Only a thin illusory veil separated them, and if her faith was strong enough, she would find him.

Tulsi Devi walked into a nearby market, searching for faces, for white cloth. "Have you seen any sadhus nearby?" she asked, talking fast like a woman who has just lost her child in a crowd. Not waiting for answers, but walking on and asking again. Asking again. Asking again. "There's a man . . . he was here . . ."

Anonymous blank faces met hers.

She asked a street barber. The man stopped shaving his customer for one second, considering, his razor suspended over the frothy-bearded man in his chair. "Over there, try over there," he pointed and Tulsi Devi cut through the crowds, following his razor's direction.

Now she was shouting at the people selling vegetables, coconuts, digestives from their trolleys. Shouting at everyone: "I'm looking for my brother. For God's sake, someone help me!"

She was creating a spectacle, she realized, but all she knew was that she had to find Ram, because this was the time decreed by God for them to be reunited.

But Ram eluded her, like the deity that he was.

Tulsi Devi went home and sent Dhruv to pick up Jivan from school. Then she left the house again and walked aimlessly around Delhi to search out faces. She could feel Ram from afar, the way she could feel the rains before they came to Delhi. He was somewhere in the city, but more importantly he was in her heart, where he had been all along.

To find Ram she would have to look inside herself.

Tulsi Devi passed a Hanuman temple, saw the deities lined up facing the main entrance, and decided that this was her last chance. It was the services of Hanuman she required. Hanuman, who had been sent by Ram to the Himalayas to find rare herbs and bring them back to where Laxman lay dying. Hanuman, who had searched for the herbs, but not finding any had lifted the whole mountain and flown it down! He had the power to do these things. He had the power to find Ram, because he too had to be reunited with him.

After she had prayed to Hanuman, she prayed to Aakash, wherever he may be. Her father who believed in the unity of all things was now being petitioned by his estranged daughter to believe in the unity of his family.

Somewhere, somehow, Aakash felt her request like a dimple upon his Silence. He gave her his blessings from a cool ashram up in the hills, where blessings can spin down to the plains like winged seeds from giant sycamores.

One thought came: go to the police station and ask there.

On this advice, Tulsi Devi deposited all the money she had on her person at the feet of Hanuman, touched his mountain for blessings and then touched the feet of Ram who stood next to him. The monkey god had a sweet smile and Ram, too, wore the painted smile of a girl. So happy and blissful and beautifully dressed in their glittering temple clothes. It made Tulsi Devi feel cheerful and positive as she made her way home to the Colonel and Jivan.

Tulsi Devi spent that night already living the next day. Her son and her husband both talked to her separately, as they always did, but neither was able to get the expected response. Now there was nobody else in the world but Ram.

30

The next morning Tulsi Devi dressed Jivan so quickly for school that his shorts were put on back to front. Later on in the day he would be teased for having "oolta poolta shorts" but right then it was the last thing on Tulsi Devi's mind.

They ran the whole way to school and Jivan arrived half an hour before any of the other boys. Tulsi Devi left him squatting on his own in the playground, drawing in the dirt. She blew him a kiss and ran out of the gates before he could demand she stayed.

When she arrived at the police station she went to where the holy men had sat, as if she were visiting a shrine, holding her hands tight in prayer to find them. A sweeper was watching her, wondering why this lady had come to say prayers to the police. He stood against the front wall, his face the hideous face of a gargoyle that protects a temple, waiting to assist her, to answer her prayers.

"The sadhus were arrested, sister," he called out to her.

The only word Tulsi Devi heard was "sister." It startled her. She looked up and saw the man's bulging eyes and buck teeth. For a split second she forgot about Ram.

"What?"

"The one who spoke English refused to speak to the English soldier, so they were all taken away."

Ram spoke English. It must have been he who had refused to talk. If the sweeper had put his hand on Tulsi Devi's chest, he would have felt it pounding.

"My brother was one of them," she told this man, not knowing if he was to be thanked or detested for giving her this news. "Is he being kept inside?"

"No, taken away."

"Where?"

"God knows."

Was this gargoyle performing some kind of ritual to test her sincerity before letting her into the temple to meet Ram? Tulsi Devi walked indignantly into the police station, her head held as high as the long steeple of handwritten files that lined the walls. She chanted her brother's name inside her head, as if it were a mantra to give her the power to find him.

A chaprassi saw her and asked what she wanted.

"I am looking for the group of sadhus who were protesting outside yesterday," she said out loud. *Ram, Ram, Ram, Ram,* she continued in silence.

The man went off to talk to some officers in the depths of the police station. He came back and told Tulsi Devi, "Nobody has seen any sadhus. If they had, they would have informed me, and nobody has informed me, so I know nothing of their whereabouts."

They hadn't existed. Nobody had been arrested.

The man was talking as if he were reading out a statement in court, using someone else's words. Words that covered up the identity of the officer out the back who had spoken them.

Tulsi Devi left without saying anything. Without telling the chaprassi that he was a liar with an Englishman's tongue. Without screaming about the insanity of British rule.

As she walked she carried on repeating Ram's name so that wherever he was he would feel her searching for him. Just by chanting her brother's name, she was protected from her own outrage, cocooned from the gargoyle by the entrance who watched her as she left.

She so needed the power of Ram now. And the power of Gandhiji. Her Ram had been arrested because of his silent protest. Did they not know whom they had captured? She felt as if she should give up everything she had secured in life and join the freedom struggle right there and then.

Instead she walked home. She thought about how she could find Ram. How she could bring down the British as punishment for taking away her brother. The closer she came to her home, the further these thoughts traveled until she realized that she was unable to do a thing about her situation.

It seemed an absurd idea at first to tell the Colonel about her brother's capture, but then she remembered that he had a double life – the officers' mess. All those other officers who were still serving the British would be able to locate Ram's whereabouts as easily as the chaprassi in the police station.

That night Tulsi Devi broached the subject slowly. First she introduced the fact that she had a brother. The Colonel hadn't known that. Then she told him that her brother had joined an ashram many years ago. And then she told him the rest. "My brother is in jail," she said. "And there is nobody I know who can help him, except you."

The Colonel looked at his wife's anxious expression, held his chin and thought. There was an heir to Prakriti other than Tulsi Devi. That was not good. But it *was* good that this man was behind bars.

"How can I help you get someone out of jail whom the British have put in there for good reason?"

"You can help me because you are able. And because he is my brother."

"Do you want me to go against the law?"

"I want you to act for your family and for your nation," answered Tulsi Devi, determined that her husband would show some compassion.

"My loyalty is first and foremost to the British throne. Are you asking me to go against everything I have worked toward in my entire life?"

"I am asking you to be human."

The request landed on ears of stone. Her search would have ended there, but at that same moment an image appeared in her head of Lily at Prakriti. She saw her former governess bathed in light, as if she were looking at her red hair through a crack in a darkened box.

Seeing Lily, Tulsi Devi realized something crucial – that every obstacle she had overcome in her life up till now had given her the boon of its power. She knew, too, that she needed a boon more powerful than ever before, because she was about to face an obstacle bigger than the seas between India and Lanka. Bigger than the seas between India and England. A wide ocean that took lives at will and flung bodies back onto random sands.

31

When Jivan was at school the next day, Tulsi Devi caught a tonga to Lily's mansion. The horse and cart wove through town, away from the crowded Indian streets toward the rows of spacious British homes. The horse snorted when its master stopped it in front of the house fringed with frangipanis and palm trees and an armed guard at the gate. Tulsi Devi stepped down from the cart, looked at the chowkidar and wondered why they should need a gun to protect a man who grew trees and flowers.

Then she looked at the enormous house with its tall pillars, endless verandahs and abundant gardens, and she repented her decision to approach Lily. Tulsi Devi had always considered Lily to be her senior, but her equal nonetheless. Lily had known her in her splendid mountain home, where she had looked down on the world like a princess with a kingdom at her feet. Now here she was, begging a favor of her governess because her skin was the wrong color to achieve anything in her own country.

Reluctant but needy, Tulsi Devi commanded the chowkidar to let her in, and he opened the gates, knowing that this Indian lady had arrived once before with his memsahib.

When the chowkidar went to call Lily, Tulsi Devi found herself thinking of Prakriti, just so that she could match Lily with a sense of place – meet her on common ground, make the mansion her own. But when she saw Lily's face, she realized that no such pretensions were required. Lily was delighted to see her, making such a fuss that she could have been a visiting maharani.

It was enough. All that was required for her to relax and start telling Lily her secrets again, as she had when she was a girl at Prakriti.

They sat for tea on the lawn and Tulsi Devi began to tell her story from the very beginning, from the time when she had known her brother Ram all those years ago at Prakriti. Lily knew that Tulsi Devi had a brother: he had been the enigma of the farm, missing long before she arrived. Aakash had talked about him quietly. Tulsi Devi had told her about Ram back then and even shown her the cave where he had studied. So when Lily heard that Ram had been found, then arrested, she made it her personal mission to help Tulsi Devi find her brother.

"Leave it to me. Roy will know someone he can ask," she told Tulsi Devi. "I will find him for you if it's the last thing I do before I go back to England."

"Go back?"

"Everyone will be going back before too long, Tulsi Devi. You wait and see."

"But not now?"

"No, but soon."

On the way home in Lily's car, Tulsi Devi thought about Lily's words, spoken as if they were a prophecy predicting the end of the world. So many changes and uncertainties lay ahead. Lily would soon be gone, and with her any chance of finding Ram. She prayed to Ram in the car, just as the ancient rishis used to pray to the gods to manifest before them.

That evening Tulsi Devi watched the tension between her son and husband come to breaking point, and wondered if Ram would ever have the power to resolve their differences.

Jivan had a habit of diverting his mother's attention to his own needs whenever he found her talking to his stepfather. He thoroughly resented the Colonel, because the man had stolen love from him in so many ways. First by taking his mother, and then by putting him down at every possible opportunity.

That night, the Colonel caught his "fake" son pretending to have a crutch, imitating him hobbling around the house.

"Take this good-for-nothing out of my sight and punish him! He should be beaten out of existence," he yelled at his wife.

Tulsi Devi rushed Jivan to his bedroom. When the Colonel found her sitting on the bed, holding Jivan's head in her lap and catching his tears instead of flogging him, he grabbed the boy and started thwacking him with his wooden crutch until Jivan was lying curled on the ground. Seeing Jivan so weakened made him feel even stronger, and he continued hitting the small body as if he were trying to tenderize some meat.

Jivan screamed, "Ma, Ma, Ma, Mama, Mama, *help!*" but Tulsi Devi could do nothing but watch, unable to stop the madness.

She had tried so hard to protect her son. When Jivan had broken one of the china plates with a cricket ball, Tulsi Devi had quietly thrown the evidence into the bin and told Dhruv not to say a word. When the teachers told her that Jivan wasn't studying hard enough at school, she came home and told her husband that Jivan was the star pupil. She had even bought sweets from the market and asked Jivan to present them to his papa.

The Colonel, however, had thrown the box of mithai back at Jivan, scraping his eye so badly he had to wear a patch for two days. "Good God, woman," he had shouted, "the boy hates me, and I'd prefer you to stop the pretense so that I don't have to like him any more than I do."

Now, lying on the floor and crying after the Colonel had left the room, Jivan asked his mother, "Who was my papa before Papa?"

Not wanting to break his heart any further, Tulsi Devi told him the story of the legendary Queen Kunti who had been given a boon by the gods to grant any wish she held dear. One day when the God of the Winds appeared, Queen Kunti told him that she wanted him to father her child:

"And so she fell with child, even though she did not yet have a husband."

"Was my first papa a god?"

Jivan asked the question so innocently, Tulsi Devi had to swallow her tears to protect him from the brutality of the truth. How could she liken herself to the much-honored Queen Kunti, who had practiced such great austerities to make her wishes come true? How could she now tell her son that there wasn't a man in the world who loved him as his own?

The following morning Jivan was not well. He had come down with a terrible flu, which was followed by a dead kind of pain in his left leg. Tulsi Devi was terrified, but the Colonel dismissed it, saying, "He's impersonating me as usual to get attention. I'll give him another good beating and he'll get better, you'll see."

Tulsi Devi forced him to feel her son's forehead. The heat was so strong the Colonel's hand was like a pot on the flames. Feeling the heat, his next, less radical suggestion, was the treatment he offered every sick soldier who wasn't ill enough to be dead. "Cold showers for a month and no food for three days."

In the next few days, Jivan's illness got worse and worse. Tulsi Devi called several doctors to the house, but none of them knew what disease could have possessed him. Then he started falling down whenever he got up to go to the toilet.

"It's my leg," he told his mother. "The sickness is coming from my leg!"

This strange insight was like a child's hallucination – enough to make Tulsi Devi feel sick, too. Sick at the thought that this was all her fault and she was too weak to protect her little boy. Jivan was too heavy to carry, and the only person who helped her with him was Dhruv, in between cooking, cleaning, swabbing floors and dusting.

Things were deteriorating in all aspects of her life. Jivan was so sick that Tulsi Devi had no time for her other life: no time to see Lily and discover if she had found Ram.

It was around this time, too, that Tulsi Devi discovered she was pregnant again.

32

Ever since the war started, the Colonel had wanted a child. It was the instinct of the threatened animal in him. Just like the cockroaches that laid eggs whenever they were sprayed with chemicals, the Colonel wanted to lay down his own seed for the future. Otherwise, why go to all the trouble of having a wife?

Up till now he had not been able to get Tulsi Devi pregnant, and it was not through want of trying. Obviously the woman was capable of bearing children – the brat was the living example. When the finger of infertility pointed at him, he stared at it in disbelief, his manhood and sense of virility quaking with indignant anger.

Why couldn't the soldier in him, who had commanded so many souls in his career, not command the presence of a single one now?

Unbeknown to Tulsi Devi, it became an obsession with the Colonel. He visited a myriad of doctors in his countless hours of spare time, without telling anyone, least of all his colleagues in the officers' mess who were all still in service and presumably fully fertile. No, he had taken on the burden of conception single-handedly, fighting his own battle with the medical profession.

One specialist, Doctor Mazumdar, suggested that they take sperm from a donor and insert it into his wife. He thought of Jivan, his albatross, and flew into a rage, slapping his crutch so hard on the doctor's desk it smashed in two, sending a large splinter spinning off fast enough to crack the doctor's spectacles.

"Who do you bloody well think I am to look after someone else's child?" He bellowed the words so loudly the doctor feared violence and slowly pushed his chair away from his patient.

Then the Colonel read an advertisement pasted onto a discolored wall, telling of a specialist who could assist. The advertisement read: *Help your unbearable wife with fruit.*

When he plucked up the courage to face the medical world once more he was told that he should have brought Tulsi Devi along to be examined as well.

"You want me to make a mockery of myself in front of my wife, as well as in front of you?" he'd shouted, and stormed out once again, furious that the world was offering him the insult of infertility.

"Let those doctor bastards father children by the hundreds," he thought as he left, wiping his hands of the terrible responsibility of having to father a child of his own.

But the pursuit of fatherhood did not let him go. It made his lower back ache and swell. One day he mentioned his pains to an acquaintance in the officers' mess, who recommended a famous ayurvedic doctor in the thick of Chandni Chowk.

There was no harm in visiting a quack, the Colonel told himself as he prepared for his visit. He wouldn't even have to take the medicines if they did not taste good.

When he met with the ayurvedic doctor and told him of his pains, the doctor asked without any side-stepping: "Are you able to have children?"

Stunned by the question, the Colonel told the physician that he wasn't, and was given a potion to take away discreetly in a bag made out of newspaper.

Only when he arrived home and went immediately to the bathroom to take his first dose, did he read the label. It had been made in Prakriti! What it did not say was that Aakash had pioneered this exact remedy nearly twenty years earlier.

The result was a severe bout of sickness, not for him but for Tulsi Devi. An illness that started almost as soon as their child was conceived.

Tulsi Devi could never have wished another pregnancy upon herself. At first she hid the nausea, vomiting as quietly as she could in the bathroom. It wasn't that she feared having another child. She knew now how to face the unknown and accept its phantoms. But she feared for the life of the child, and feared her husband's anger more than any other obstacle she had encountered up till now.

But there was no need for worry.

One day soon after her realization, just as some delicious food was put down on the table, the Colonel saw Tulsi Devi cover her mouth with one hand and run out of the room. It alerted his suspicions and he followed her to the bathroom. After she had finished retching he asked, "Is that my baby in your belly, my Patni Devi?"

Tulsi Devi said "yes" and looked the other way. And in doing so she missed the first deliriously happy smile that had ever touched the Colonel's lips. It was the look of absolute, unadulterated, glorious victory.

Even though they had been married some time, Tulsi Devi had never truly had a husband until now. Suddenly all that changed.

Now the Colonel would stand up whenever she entered the room, showing the same respect he would show a senior officer. When she lay down at night he would spend the last few minutes of each day gently touching her belly and telling his baby about the joys of life and the great future that awaited.

The new life insisted on a future, and the Colonel went to an auction to buy a large plot of land in Sundernagar, a new colony next to the Old

Fort. The house would be huge – a mansion like those constructed for the senior British officers. He withdrew funds from his dowry payment and made plans with eagerness and devotion. "This child's birth will be the start of a new life for both of us," he said. But none of his efforts made Tulsi Devi happy. It was as if he were showing a grand future to someone in the last few years of life. When he asked her what was troubling her, Tulsi Devi spoke to her husband about Ram once more.

"How can I be happy about my future when I know that my brother is in jail," she said.

Seeing that the Colonel did not seethe at the mention of her brother, she continued, like a heavy urn of water that cannot sit upright until it has emptied its load. "I dream about him," she said. "If I don't find him it will haunt me for the rest of my life."

She told him about how she had prayed to meet Ram once more. How she had searched the whole city to find him. She even told him about Lily in her mansion.

Her husband stood firm on his one leg, listening and supporting her as she wept. Then he came up with a simple solution that caught his wife by surprise. Why not find out which prison Ram was being kept in and go there? He would dress up in his army uniform and enquire what was happening with her brother. What was the problem?

Tulsi Devi looked up at the Colonel to see if he had really said those words, and seeing some gentleness in his face, she cradled his head in both her hands and squeezed her cheek against his until her eyelashes kissed his skin.

For the first time ever, she felt love in her heart for the man she had married. Equally, he felt her soft hands on his skin as if she were touching him with the trepidation and tenderness of a new bride. A tear gathered in the corner of his eye, like a lake in a deep valley, and they held each other in that moment of revelation, hijacked by an overwhelming sentiment in the general direction of happiness.

33

It was Lily who discovered where Ram was being held, and sent a messenger around to the Colonel's house. When she heard the news, Tulsi Devi knew that it was time to introduce her husband to her former governess. To marry her two different lives and allow a union between her past and present.

She knew exactly what Lily would think about the Colonel, and she was right. Lily's first impression was that Tulsi Devi had been married off to a man too many years her senior. Then she thought, "He must be rich," and after that, "Either that or Aakash chose him for his spiritual strengths."

None of this showed on Lily's face as she told the Colonel how charmed she was to meet him and introduced him to her husband Roy.

Lily did not hesitate to loan them her car and driver and so the two of them left as if they were envoys of the British seeking asylum for her beloved brother – the Colonel feeling like a resurrected hero in his full military regalia.

The prison was just outside Delhi. They talked on the way, and the Colonel told Tulsi Devi about a military base not far from the ashrams in Rishikesh. If Ram had gone back to the hills he could be found by sending a message to an officer there, no problem. Tulsi Devi laid her head down on her husband's uniformed shoulder and thanked him, and the Colonel thought then how he too would move mountains to find Ram – if he could always be rewarded with such warmth.

When they reached the prison, Colonel Chopra walked confidently on his one leg and demanded to see the records of his brother-in-law who had been mistakenly arrested. When one of the prison guards told him that the man in question was already free, the Colonel's voice boomed even more confidently: "For God's sake man, where is he? I know he's free. He never committed any crime to speak of in the first place!"

The Colonel was shouting so loudly that he didn't hear the timid words that followed.

"He's still here."

Tulsi Devi insisted on seeing Ram alone. This was the moment she had lived through a thousand times in anticipation and she did not want to share it with another soul, except the one inside her. A prison officer showed her the cell and she let herself in, for there were no locks on the door.

Ram was sitting on a straw chatai on the floor of an immaculate room, sunlight streaking over the hard floor, imprisoning flecks of floating dust. Tulsi Devi's face caught the sun and she squinted at the figure whose face was too bright to see.

"Ram?"

"Sister, come," he said, so casually Tulsi Devi wondered if he knew who she was. She sat down on the ground next to him, and he held her hand whilst her eyes adjusted to the sharp light, and the years that had passed.

She said nothing and he continued. "Have you come to see someone here?"

"Yes."

She watched him, knowing that he had mistaken her for someone visiting a prisoner. *Ram, I am your sister, don't you know it?*

"So how can I best help you?"

Remember me. She answered him in silence, staring, willing him to see his sister where she sat.

"Sister, there are many people in this prison whose bodies are confined here, but whose souls are free to reach the greatest heights."

"The man I have come to see is such a soul. He is my brother." She waited and looked directly into his eyes, longing for recognition. Then she spoke again. "I am your sister. Your parents are my parents. I grew up for many years at Prakriti without you, playing in the cave where you used to study with Bahadur."

She said the words fast, as if they were her claim to him. All the evidence required for flesh and blood to reunite.

"Tulsi Devi?" She heard him speak her name and that was enough. He was giving her the honor of remembrance.

She continued, seeing that he was the one silenced now. "We met outside the police station and ever since then I have wanted to find you."

"Tulsi Devi!"

He held her hand tighter and they embraced each other in the sunshine, all illusions now parting. For a moment they were the same age, having shared a childhood together. Remembering each other even though there was precious little they had shared in the few years that they had lived together.

Tulsi Devi spoke again, but this time about things closer to her heart.

"I missed Pitaji very much when he left us."

Ram squeezed her hand and she saw her father in him. Large eyes with whites that hung low below their dark centers, and a long beard that pointed like an arrow down to his heart. Everything she had ever loved about her father was in her brother's face. Looking at him now, she could tell why Aakash had left. He was not from this world. His tread was softer than a butterfly landing on a flower. If he had stayed at Prakriti his wings would have folded over and never flown to the great heights he yearned for.

Ram could say nothing. Aakash had fulfilled his life purpose: there was no blame. But he allowed himself to feel his sister's pain for a few moments, as if it were his own. He felt his father leaving Prakriti, but instead of experiencing a sense of freedom, he experienced his sister's loss. It was heavy, cloudy and complicated, feeding in on itself. He observed the feeling and then felt his way outward, back toward the light that filled the room.

"You have a child now?"

Tulsi Devi told him everything. She told him about the man with the almond eyes who gave her a child whilst she was still a student at the convent. About her return to Prakriti. Her marriage to the Colonel. She spared no tears and no details as she told her story, unlocking emotions that had shied away from the light for years.

She talked about their mother, whom she could never please; about her husband who had only just learnt to love her; and about her precious son who was both loved and hated. Ram listened, knowing that no one else had heard these words, feeling the intensity of her need for him.

"I am a renunciant," he said, "but I will always be your brother."

Tulsi Devi wanted to know so much more about this brother. Ram, sensing that his sister needed this information to make sense of her own experiences, started telling her about his life, about the mountains where he had spent all those years, and about his brothers in Silence.

"The day I left Prakriti I knew that I was walking away from the world before I'd even joined it. I was walking away and yet nothing could have made me happier ..."

Ram told Tulsi Devi about his travels to find the Shankaracharya of the North. The utter joy he had felt when he met his Master. He tried to describe how the years slipped by in meditation and discourse at the feet of Guru Dev. He told how he had been given the gift of Silence to explore and how he enriched his senses with the power of transcendence. He told stories of the saints he knew in the mountains. Talked of men who grew their hair six feet longer than their bodies, and of men who were said to have lived as long as the hills. He told stories of other sages who could disappear and then manifest in two places at once. All mythical people who inhabited his extraordinary world in the forests of the Himalayas. And then he told her more about Guru Dev.

"Imagine a person, Tulsi Devi, whose power and intention is so strong he could lift the illusion of life from before your eyes. Imagine, just for a moment, if you could stand outside all your experiences up till now as if you had never had them, and see who you are without your pain ..."

If Ram could have given the gift of Guru Dev to his sister he would have done. But what he gave was more important still. The gift of himself. He gave her his journey to the highest mountains, and allowed her to add it to her own voyage to the bottom of the deepest oceans. Together, for a moment, they bridged the unity of all experience.

"Did you miss us all those years?" she asked her brother.

"How could I? You were always with me. I missed nothing."

"And Pitaji?"

"Pitaji simply followed a choice that had already been made long, long before he was born."

"Ram, why has it been so easy for you? Why have I had to struggle so?"

"Tulsi Devi, everything will make sense to you when your life comes full circle. Imagine there's a woman holding a treasure behind her back. You are traveling around the world to see the treasure that is hidden in her hands. But once you have circled the earth, you will have wisdom enough to realize that *everything happens for a reason.* And you will see the treasure that was kept for you and recognize it as Divine Grace."

Ram told Tulsi Devi about their father. How he had been favored by Guru Dev and given his own ashram in the hills. "He is himself one of the greatest living saints in Uttar Kashi now. No matter how hard he tries to renounce the world, more people come to hear him talk in the afternoons when he gives an audience."

"And Bahadur?"

"Bahadur is the reason for my being in prison now," Ram answered. Tulsi Devi heard how the two of them had studied together with Guru Dev. At first Bahadur was given pride of place whilst Ram was made to sweep the floors of the ashram, as a way of redressing the balance of nature. When they had achieved equilibrium, they experienced a true brotherhood, without the bondage of caste or birth.

"When Bahadur heard about progress in the freedom movement he wanted to serve the political prisoners who were being held down here in Delhi, and Guru Dev gave his blessings," Ram told Tulsi Devi. He went on to tell her about his decision to stay and work with political prisoners for a while, with the people who were profoundly affecting change from India's spiritual core. People like Gandhiji, like Shri Aurobindo.

Tulsi Devi listened and understood why Ram's calling had taken him to a life beyond the short history that they had shared together. He was everything their father had ever told her he was. Even as he sat there in front of her, a free man in jail.

There was a knock at the door. It was the Colonel, reminding Tulsi Devi of her other life. She introduced them.

Ram brought his hands together and then held the arm of his brother-in-law, looking deep into his set-back eyes, scanning for the soul of this man whom Jyoti Ma had found for his sister.

"Ram, I will come back," Tulsi Devi told him, although now the need to see him was no longer so urgent. She had fulfilled one of her greatest desires simply by finding him. Ram had the ability to touch her life and make her feel that he would always be with her from that time onward. They were together again, and somehow there was a new sense of balance in the world.

34

Tulsi Devi's second pregnancy was, in many ways, more challenging than her first. Even though she now had the security of a supportive husband, the tension caused by Jivan's very existence in that house left her utterly exhausted. Not to mention the worry about his inexplicable illness.

Her husband didn't even notice her exhaustion. Instead he kept demanding her attention to make plans for their grand future – their house in Sundernagar. It was the last thing on Tulsi Devi's mind, but aware that their new relationship needed nurturing, she created enthusiasm out of her concerns.

"Should we have a squatting toilet for servants immediately outside the house, or shall we have it only in the servants' quarters?" he asked. She gave him the answer he wanted to hear. "In the servants' quarters, of course."

"And should the baby's bedroom be adjacent to ours, or down the hallway?"

Tulsi Devi noted there was never any mention of Jivan's bedroom. That had become "the spare room." Looking back on it many years later, after going over this period of her life again and again, she realized that this was the point when Jivan was first alluded to in abstract.

Tulsi Devi oscillated between her roles as nurse and architect. Concerned by Jivan's continuing sickness, she called yet another physician. This new doctor was better qualified and more experienced than the others, but within five minutes of meeting him, she wished he had never come. His verdict was final and disastrous. Jivan had polio.

Tulsi Devi held her son's hand as the judgement was pronounced and her grip loosened slightly as her eyes poured tears of guilt and helplessness. She knew in an instant that this was no disease picked up in the air at school or out in the streets. It was caused by the enormous weight he had carried with him from when he was a pea-sized baby in her belly, and now his small frame was collapsing under the burden of his stepfather's oppression.

Jivan hadn't heard of polio, but he did know about polo, because he'd seen a painting of maharajas playing it from the backs of elephants. He asked the doctor if it meant he would be good at sports, and the doctor and Tulsi Devi looked back at him silently, offering only pity as an answer.

Throughout the rest of her pregnancy, Tulsi Devi felt traitorous at bringing another life into the world when she had failed her first child. Her guilt and fear kept her up at nights and she frequently visited Jivan's bedroom to make sure he was still breathing. Sometimes when she heard him breathing erratically she would wake him up with her reassurances.

After a while Jivan started to walk on the outside of his left foot. The Colonel was irritated, because the boy's lameness reflected his own hated missing leg. Worse still, since the illness had been diagnosed, even more attention was being diverted into the lost cause of his stepson.

With Tulsi Devi overcompensating and the Colonel ignoring the whole business, the only person who still treated Jivan normally was Dhruv, who had grown up in a village where one in five children had this affliction. It was nothing to fuss about. Just the way life is. He would pick Jivan up on his shoulders, even though he was a little too heavy now, and continue cleaning dishes and pounding masalas. Jivan would pretend that Dhruv was the elephant they used to ride at Prakriti. He would wave one of the cooking spoons and suddenly he was a famous princely polo player.

The Colonel had hoped that their house next to the Old Fort would be ready by the time their child arrived. Tulsi Devi's belly was growing, yet the house was still only one story high, surrounded by bamboo frames. Every day he visited and watched the bare-chested laborers carrying plaster and concrete in baskets on their heads, backward and forward, stepping over rubble to reach the house. Trying to meet the Colonel's deadline.

The house was still open to the elements when Tulsi Devi's waters broke and she was taken to the military hospital for her delivery.

The Colonel sat outside her room. Ready to spend a long night in a long corridor. He heard her half-conscious groans and thought there may be some problem, then dismissed his fears. Whatever was happening in there, his wife was in safe hands. After all, the military hospital had an excellent reputation, and he knew that Tulsi Devi, as the wife of a Colonel, would be given extra special attention.

But then it started getting dark and nobody came out of the room to make any birth announcements.

He sat absolutely straight in his chair. Waiting. This was taking a lot longer than he had expected.

For once the Colonel was grateful to Jivan, not so much for being born, as for opening the passage. His wife was going to be fine, he kept telling himself. How could he expect a child to be born in just a few minutes? This was birth. Women's business. Even though he suspected that it was more threatening and challenging than any military exercise, it was survivable.

His composure did not last long. Soon a nurse rushed out and called for three more to follow her in. Hearing Tulsi Devi's piercing screams through the open doors, the Colonel felt the nerves in his missing leg come alive as if they were being severed all over again. He could tell that this was an emergency and that his child's life was in danger.

Feeling an urgent need to act he marched into the hospital room, to see a dozen eyes turn to question him over green masks. But the Colonel felt justified. He had gone to such great lengths to plant his seed, he was not prepared to have it tossed out like a weed.

"What are you doing in here?" asked one male voice through its mask.

"I am a Colonel and I intend to witness the birth of my child," he answered.

"Then please stay away from the sterile area," another mask snapped.

The Colonel realized that he was standing between his wife's legs, leaving no room for the doctor who was at that moment preparing to wedge metal forceps around the baby's head.

The Colonel looked at Tulsi Devi's face. Her eyes were closed and her blood vessels were bursting at the surface of her skin. She was oblivious to his presence, holding the hands of two strangers at either side of her.

During his army days, he had seen surgery carried out without anesthetics, but never had he witnessed anything as grueling as this. The tongs went inside, between his wife's legs, and clasped the child's head. The doctor pulled, leaning back with his whole body weight, but the head did not shift. The Colonel knew then that only he would be able to deliver the child.

"For God's sake, it will suffocate in there. *Move!*" he commanded.

And pushing aside the doctor, he took the tongs himself and gave the baby's head the most almighty tug.

"Wait until she's having one of her pains," came another voice.

The Colonel looked at Tulsi Devi, who started building up toward something.

"Now push," he ordered, and with the full force of his years he pulled the head out. "Again," he ordered. And the body slipped its way through.

The child came out screaming at the audacity of being forced into this world of the living. Two sharp indents from the forceps were planted onto its small malleable skull.

One of the assistants looked over his mask with questioning eyes to see if the Colonel was disappointed at seeing that the baby was a girl. The smile he saw on the father's face was conclusive. Nothing in the world could have been more momentous or extraordinary for the Colonel than the tiny girl baby who was being lifted up to the doctor's scissors, about to experience the first separation of many.

35

Baby Rohini was brought home to the old house two weeks after her birth. Tulsi Devi had needed the rest, and her husband, wanting to make full use of military privileges, had insisted that she stayed in hospital until she had made a complete recovery.

It was the first time he had lived alone with his stepson without a go-between, and he managed just fine as long as Jivan was neither seen nor heard.

Jivan, on the other hand, moped around as if he were the one with a sliced umbilical cord. Without his mama he felt like an ant – so small, insignificant and vulnerable. He stayed out of his stepfather's way to avoid being trodden on. Always confined to the small space of his bedroom, because since the Colonel had been given a child of his own blood, there was nothing that could possess him to sit in an officers' mess all day long.

Jivan missed his mother as badly as if she had been lost in childbirth. He thought of her as soon as he opened his eyes in the mornings, trying to picture her face. Whenever the image became clear, he saw his mother at Prakriti, with mountains and fields all around.

Every day when the Colonel went off to see her in the hospital, Jivan stood at the doorway, hoping that he would be taken as well, but the invitation never came.

When his mama was brought home and Jivan came to the door to greet her, he was shooed away by the Colonel and told to let her get some rest. He spent the remaining two hours of that morning crying into his mattress. When the sobs became louder and more distressed, Tulsi Devi heard him and came in to talk whilst her husband lavished attention on the new baby.

"I don't want to be here anymore," Jivan sobbed. "You only love your new baby."

Tulsi Devi tried to console him. "Baba, you will always be my first baby. Nothing can ever change that. You're number one."

Tulsi Devi went to her bedroom and came back with Rohini in her arms. "See, she wants to meet her bhaiya!"

She placed the tiny bundle in the lap of her tear-struck little boy.

The Colonel, who was shadowing his new infant, objected. "Don't give her to Jivan. She's not a toy."

Hearing the interference of his hated stepfather, Jivan scowled and pushed the baby so hard she rolled off the bed and landed on her head, screaming.

Things moved so fast, there was no time for anybody to think. Tulsi Devi rushed to pick up the poor bundle of baby and the Colonel took Jivan by the wrist and flung him against the wall, where he punched him until two teeth fell out of his mouth.

"Mama, help me, I'm scared!"

Jivan was screaming. His stepfather was screaming, and Tulsi Devi, too, was screaming at the top of her voice as she tried to calm down the situation. She grabbed Jivan, pushed herself between the two of them, and dragged her children off to her bedroom, where she locked the door.

Outside the Colonel raged, shouting and kicking his antique English furniture. Inside Tulsi Devi gave her baby her breast, to calm down at least one of her children, whilst Jivan sat sobbing next to her, covered in blood, holding his mouth with one hand and his mama and baby sister with the other.

After a while they heard the unbearable sounds of the Colonel's remorse, as he wailed and wailed, asking God to help him take control of himself.

That night he was surprisingly tender. He told Tulsi Devi of his shame, and of his love for her and the new baby. He spoke of their future together and asked her for forgiveness.

"You must apologise to Jivan, not to me," Tulsi Devi replied coldly, unwilling to soften and bend. "It's he who has to live with the scars."

The Colonel agreed to apologize, but only when he was ready.

"I will do anything to make our lives happy," he told her.

Then he dropped the bomb in her lap. "We must find some other place for Jivan to live for a while."

At first she was too furious to hear him. But then the penny dropped, and landed in a pool of murky water. Plop. The fiery loathing she felt for him was replaced by a cold fateful numbness. She realized then that she had, in fact, heard his words correctly. He was talking about her son.

"I have so much love for Rohini," he continued, "but I cannot express it with Jivan around."

Her heart was thumping. There and then she knew she could not subject her son to this man any longer.

"And what if he gives Rohini polio?"

"No, stop it."

Tulsi Devi was stricken by the grief of losing her only son before it even happened. The boy she had gone to the ends of the earth with. An image of David De Souza came into her head out of nowhere. He was older now too and had a family …

She looked across at the Colonel, who could not return her blank gaze. Instead he turned to rock the baby, who was sleeping quietly in her jhoola.

Tulsi Devi couldn't say anything. She had lost in life.

She raced back over her thoughts, backtracking to eradicate any inkling of the Colonel's suggestion. Her son would never ever be sent away. She would leave this man tonight and then the three of them could always be together.

But it was just another thought, without any power to create the impulse of action. She knew that she could never do it again – run away like a convent schoolgirl with two children in tow.

"But why can't he stay?" Her voice was as impotent as one already defeated. She already knew the answer. Something had to switch off – everything that she had ever invested in her own happiness.

Tulsi Devi started to tell herself that Jivan would have a better life without her, and that she had failed him, but she could hear the contradictions as she tried to persuade herself. No, it was not true; and neither would she have a better life without him.

Nevertheless, they were being torn apart, because their love was accidental.

Tulsi Devi never agreed out loud to sending her son away, which meant that the Colonel would return to the issue again and again, as if presenting her with a bowl of food she'd left uneaten weeks ago.

"I cannot bear the way he looks at me when I'm holding Rohini," he told her. "Why don't you make some arrangement with your brother to take him for a while?"

Her brother.

Tulsi Devi, in her total paralysis, had not dared to venture to think, even to consider, where "elsewhere" could be. Until now …

To save her son she would have to ask Ram to take care of him. She realized that this was the first time she had thought of her brother with any sadness.

"Yes," she replied flatly. "I will ask him."

36

When Tulsi Devi went to the prison to ask for Ram's help, she told him the state of affairs matter-of-factly. She made certain that Ram understood he was her last hope. She reminded him of the obligations of a brother and how he was the one who had promised to love and protect her at raksha bandhan all those years ago at Prakriti when she was more or less a baby herself. Now her son's life depended on him. She had to make sure that Ram realized the seriousness of her plight.

Ram listened to her story, took a deep breath and then spoke. "Jivan cannot stay in a house where his physical, mental and spiritual growth are endangered," he told her.

His advice was the voice of wisdom. It soothed her, somehow easing the burden of her decision.

"But you will not live another day of your life without regretting what you have had to do," he continued.

His words were like a bullet in her head, leaving her with the cold senses of the dead. She felt tortured by her brother's wisdom, and yet utterly relieved that he had agreed to help.

The help Ram had promised was to "take care of things." She did not dare ask what that would mean, because she knew the truth would cut her even more deeply. She would have preferred to know that Jivan would be brought up by his uncle, but another part of her knew there could be no place for a young boy in an ascetic's life.

Over the next few days Tulsi Devi showered attention on Jivan. Her husband let her, knowing that this was the last week he would have to put up with supporting a child who stole blood rights from him without deserving them.

Instead of bonding with her new infant, Tulsi Devi spent her time reconciling herself to the loss of her son. She stroked his hair, kissed his cheeks and told him how much she loved him every few minutes of the day.

"And I love you, Mama, as high as the highest mountain," Jivan would reply, holding her hand and stretching out his other one to show her just how much.

It was a happy time for him, like the old times at Prakriti when they spent endless hours together. There was no school, the weather was warm but not hot, and he was allowed any treat in the world he wished to have. But nothing could have been more of a treat than these never-ending hours with his mama, who was entirely his own.

They went to their old haunts. Down to the sweet-sellers in Chandni Chowk, and up and down the stairs at Jantar Mantar, the ancient sun-dial monument that counted the hours out until their separation. Jivan played as joyfully as a lamb before the slaughter, not noticing Tulsi Devi's intermittent cramps of grief whenever she thought of his life ahead.

Jivan was sweet to his sister during those days when he felt confident about his place in his mother's heart. "Mama, how long before Rohini can walk and come with us?"

Tulsi Devi could not take any more. Jivan was expected by Ram on Sunday, but she decided to take him one day early. The torment of dragging out the time was too much for her.

Many years later Jivan was to recall that Saturday. He remembered being excited, because he'd never met his uncle Ram before. And he remembered not knowing why his mama was packing a bag. There was something else he remembered too. How his stepfather had said sorry to him just as he was walking out the door.

That Saturday Jivan met Ram and was taken to the orphanage run by Shiv and Rekha Kapoor to make some nice new friends.

One of those friends asked him if he had lost his parents and he said, "No, of course not!" He felt lucky that he hadn't. He still had a mama who was waiting for his return. And he had an uncle, too, who always came to play with him. The others had no one.

Then one day Mr. Kapoor told him that he was especially lucky, because he wasn't just going to have one set of parents, but two. Jivan would always remember that first meeting – the happiness he felt that at last he had a father who was warm and kind.

"Set number two" became special people in Jivan's life. In the years that followed, there was no question in his mind that they were his parents, because they were the ones who had invested their love so freely in him. It was a long time, though, before he realized he would never live with his mama again. Throughout his childhood he continued to believe that she would come for him. He did not know when it would be, but deep in his heart he never lost his trust that one day he would see her again.

Part Three

Many paths will lead you home, but with every decision you make, every action you take, you will be creating the path on which you must walk. So be silent and yield. For in Silence you will find all answers and all directions. You will never be lost, for you will always be at the center of all creation.

37

Tulsi Devi treated the loss of Jivan as if it were a death. She mourned him for the year and four days that the soul is said to hover around the earth. Every night she lit a dia for him and prayed for his soul. God knows where it was, but she felt his body still walked the same earth.

The Colonel never talked about Jivan again. Not even to console his wife. He tried instead to encourage her total rapture in the new baby. It did not come easily at first and Tulsi Devi found herself letting her husband tend to her daughter – to become both father and mother to her.

Rohini was lovely, but she wasn't enough. Tulsi Devi was a mother of two. Rohini may have needed her, but her deserted Jivan needed her more. Rohini couldn't talk, but Jivan could. Tulsi Devi missed their conversations together and his childish perceptions of the world. The way he used to say things wrong in his sweet loving voice. The way they used to cuddle up and tell stories. She missed his boundless affection.

Then she tortured herself for comparing her two children, feeling like a loveless mother to her poor baby girl. To make up for it she kissed Rohini endlessly, and always held her close when she missed her son. Tulsi Devi made the most of the fact that Rohini was a girl – special and nurtured. But a girl. Not a boy.

The huge house in Sundernagar was completed and they moved in. It was alien territory for Tulsi Devi. There were none of the usual cracked and discolored walls that told of history and life. The rooms all seemed like large whitewashed boxes, the air inside dull, lifeless and smelly. After some time of maladjustment Tulsi Devi decided that her place was the garden, and started to plant it with trees that would grow taller than the house by the time her grandchildren were born to see them.

She never had any time to herself in those first few months, because the Colonel hardly ever left the house. If Tulsi Devi wanted to go outside, she had to present him with a suitable excuse. If she said she wanted to look at things for the house, he always went with her. If she went to the shops to buy food she was expected home within half an hour. The only place where he could not follow her was the Chinese beauty parlor, which soon became her favorite venue.

This was the place where she and Jivan were alone together in her memories.

After her eyebrows had been threaded, the girls would ask if she wanted anything else and then Tulsi Devi would not let them go until they had performed every beauty treatment imaginable to give her more time alone with Jivan. After a pedicure she would have her legs waxed, and then a facial and then a massage, haircut and henna. Usually Tulsi Devi left looking a little less beautiful than when she had arrived, because she had the kind of looks that were hard to better.

Her husband, however, would look at Tulsi Devi on her return with complete adoration in an attempt to rekindle the small flame that they had once lit together.

When the house was properly equipped, Jyoti Ma often came to stay with Tulsi Devi instead of Pyari. She was losing interest in Prakriti. Its profits had slowed down and the farm had started to experience freak weather conditions once again.

It all happened around the time the mahout died and the Colonel helped her sell Ganesh to the Delhi Zoo.

Ganesh was sent to the zoo by foot, lolloping all the way down the mountains and along the long roads to Delhi, stopping to eat leaves from the shady trees planted by the Moghul emperors for the shelter of the common man. The day he left Prakriti there was a snowstorm in the summer and the crops started to fail.

But that wasn't the reason why things had stopped working for the farm, according to Jyoti Ma. How could she believe the suspicious nonsense of the workers? Prakriti was failing because she was losing interest in the place. That was it. "How can I be expected to do all this work at my age?" she complained. "I'm too old to make sure the workers aren't stealing from me left, right and center."

Besides which, she had discovered something that she loved even more than life itself. Her new granddaughter Rohini.

Jyoti Ma was a surprisingly loving grandmother. The distance of one generation allowed her to indulge this little girl as she had never indulged her own children.

Rohini absolutely adored her grandmother. From the time she could walk she would follow Jyoti Ma from room to room, clutching her sari – she even followed her to the toilet to watch, saying, "What are you doing, Nani, shoo shoo or coo coo?" Jyoti Ma pretended to be cross, but she utterly adored this little girl who gave her so much more company and affection than anyone else ever had.

In her later years she realized that what she missed most after all this time was a sense of family, and she found it in her daughter's home. She had also developed a great deal of respect for her son-in-law in recent years and approved of the way the Colonel had invested the money she had given as a dowry payment. "That money is better in a house than in a bank," she told her daughter wisely.

Tulsi Devi felt as if she had finally gained some sort of approval from her mother by having Rohini, but it made Jyoti Ma's rejection of Jivan split open like a fresh wound. When Tulsi Devi told her mother about finding Ram and asking him to look after Jivan, Jyoti Ma said: "Good for you. Imagine what your life would be like if you hadn't." She didn't even ask about Ram's welfare; she had wiped her hands clean of him and her previous life.

But Tulsi Devi could never wipe her hands clean of Jivan. The memory of him was impossibly real. She held the most painful recollections of him close by at all times. His little body in the thistles. His loving face saying goodbye at the prison – an image that remained close to the surface of her consciousness throughout her life. As close to the surface as her own name. Yet, within a few years Jivan would forget the face of his mother.

Being without her son meant that Tulsi Devi could only ever live half a life from then on. She could be enthusiastic about her daughter's development, and even completely involved, but that only fulfilled the half of her that was Rohini's mother. There was another half. The half that still lived at Prakriti, picking flowers to show Jivan. Calling out his name and hearing it echo against the hills.

Every family occasion Tulsi Devi wondered what Jivan was doing, and thought about how he would have enjoyed meeting his sister, who was growing up to be as playful and affectionate as he had been.

When Rohini turned three, she received more presents than Jivan had received in his entire life. Although Tulsi Devi shared her delight, she also felt strongly for the relative deprivation that Jivan had experienced in the time they had spent together. How Jivan had been born without a garment waiting to be placed on his little body.

And it wasn't just material comforts. Rohini also received so much more attention than Jivan ever had.

Jyoti Ma came down from the hills especially to attend Rohini's third birthday party. She ordered a range of little frocks to bring with her – three from every tailor in the village. Every one of these frocks had the number 3 embroidered onto the fabric somewhere.

Tulsi Devi had been three when Ram left home.

A small group of family, children, ayahs and parents gathered around the cake to blow out the candles.

Like her mother, Rohini was going to grow up an only child, with a brother lost to the world.

"Mama, I want four candles on my cake. One for good luck." Her daughter's demands brought Tulsi Devi back to the present. The need for good luck. She brought an extra candle out of the kitchen, feeling as if her entire life were a pretense. Sometimes it took everything she had to stay in the present moment, and not remember the life she had lived with Jivan.

Her daughter grew fast, and suddenly she was the older sibling, because in Tulsi Devi's memory Jivan was always a small boy. No matter how she tried to put an adult face on her memory of him in later years, she could never quite imagine how he would look. Jivan was frozen in time, never to get older than the day she had dropped him off at the prison, full knowing her betrayal.

Often she thought of ways she could contact Jivan to apologize and arrange a meeting. She wrote letters to the ashram at Jyotir Math to ask what had happened to him, but she never sent them, knowing that she did not deserve to have him back.

Rohini grew up to be an absolutely charming child. She had Tulsi Devi's dark curls ringletting around her shoulders, doll's eyes and a round doll's mouth. An adorable little girl, but also an over-indulged one. Every day her father took her to the sweet shop a few hundred yards away and let her choose whichever mithai she wanted. If she hadn't been so skinny, the excess would have given her Jyoti Ma's figure. But Rohini could put away any number of sweets and they only ever made her taller.

The Colonel was a reformed human being. Many people who met him in those later years would never have recognized him as a military man. Rohini was allowed to play with his crutch as much as she wanted, and he would laugh at her games. She could even smash his antique English washbasins and get away with a short but even-tempered scolding.

However, he still occasionally flew into a temper at a servant or inanimate object. If Rohini was around she would watch with a look of absolute disbelief, pouting an immobile lower lip. After he had settled down, she would disarm him by climbing onto his lap, holding his head in her hands and asking if he was all right.

In their relationship, Rohini was always the one in command. It was the Colonel's duty to fulfill her orders. If she wanted to visit her grandmother at Prakriti, he always made the arrangements. Once, when his daughter hadn't liked a teacher, her father went to the school principal and demanded that teacher's dismissal. And when the zoo was being built inside the Old Fort just opposite their house, she insisted that he sit on the committee so that she could decide which animals became their neighbors. In the early days of the Delhi Zoo, it was Rohini who was responsible for placing the deer next to the hyenas and lions, making a farce of their biological differences.

Tulsi Devi's new life demanded that she retire her old one. None of it had happened. If it had, none of this could be working out as it was now. The war was over, the British were leaving, India was divided, and Gandhi was dead. There was nothing to fight for anymore. Even the Colonel had left his army days behind. The only thing that the future demanded of her now was that she be a good wife and mother.

Tulsi Devi was a very good mother, and to make sure that she didn't destroy the life of her second child, she took the utmost pains to be a good wife. It was an effort, and it involved playing a role, but that role-playing would eventually make her into the person that she acted. She had observed her auntie Pyari being a good wife, and she tried to make her responses to her own husband appear as effortless.

It worked.

"If I had known that married life could be so sweet," the Colonel told her once, "I would never have waited until I became an old man to enjoy it."

Tulsi Devi was the perfect wife and the mother that every child adores: making little treats for all of Rohini's schoolfriends, organizing picnics in Lodi Gardens, and sharing tea with the other mothers, as if her life too had been an endless round of social events and shopping trips.

There were always other children in her house, unlike the days when she and Jivan lived in isolation from the world. Rohini adored people. She would play with anybody, or anybody's cousin's sister's friend. She consumed people entirely, and would have to be fed another batch of friends by the end of the day once her first lot were exhausted.

Tulsi Devi sometimes tried to imagine how her daughter would play with her big brother if they were to meet one day, but it was useless. Somehow she couldn't even picture them in the same room together. The two of them belonged to different compartments in her life, and in this one Rohini would always be an only child.

"Papa," Rohini would insist. "I've decided that I should have a baby brother or sister."

It was one of the few wishes that the Colonel could not fulfill. How could he tell his daughter that she was a miracle never to be repeated, having slipped through the fingers of fate as she had?

To make up for her singular existence in family life, the crowds continued arriving. As a teenager Rohini had a posse of schoolfriends – all girls who went to the cinema together. They would talk about their heroes endlessly: Kirk Douglas, James Mason and Errol Flynn.

"Kirk Douglas is sooo handsome," declared Rohini's best friend Damayanta.

"I will marry Clark Gable," Rohini announced, trying to imagine what life would be like if she were married to an older man. She was fascinated by the concept of romantic love, and imagined that her mother had fallen in love with her father because he was handsome and older than all the other boys who had been introduced to her. Her papa had come and charmed her grandmother at Prakriti and won the heart of her daughter.

Following her suspicions she pretended she was a spy, making innocent investigations.

"Mama, did you kiss Papa before you married?"

"Nobody kissed in those days," answered Tulsi Devi.

"Hold hands then?"

"Chup, what nonsense."

Tulsi Devi felt the incredible weight of the past most when she was challenged by Rohini. Her daughter knew nothing of the time she had spent in rags. Nothing of David De Souza. Nothing even of her own brother. Which kept Rohini's speculations regular and confronting.

There was nothing for it but to provide endless distractions for the young girl's inquisitive mind. Music was often the key. It served to fully absorb Rohini and she excelled at every instrument she picked up. The sitar was her favorite, and the favorite of her parents, too. She would play the most soulful melodies, bending poignant notes to express her yearning for love. But it wasn't enough. She had to learn the harmonium, too, so she could sing all the romantic ghazals and put words to her passions.

The Colonel would encourage her, saying, "Wah, Wah, arré Wah. We have a gandharva in the family!"

Next, Rohini learnt to dance. After a week of lessons, her father bought his daughter her first pair of ghungroos and her dance guru blessed the bells before she put them on her ankles.

"The dance is sacred," the teacher told her. "If you are playing Radha, you are becoming Radha. You are joining in her cosmic play."

Rohini took this to mean that she could grant wishes, too, and she would often dance her way up to her papa as if she were Shiva as Natraj, dancing the world into existence.

"Papa, Papa, make a wish and I will grant it for you," she told him adoringly.

Without fail, he would answer, "I wish that you will always be as lovely as you are now."

Rohini took to the steps as if she had been born with bells on her feet. And she could dance with her eyes, they were so expressive. She sang and danced at every opportunity, and even when there was no opportunity, simply as a way of speaking the language of her heart.

When Rohini was a teenager, the Colonel decided as a treat to take his family on the boat to England. Tulsi Devi felt as if she had traveled enough distance in her lifetime to have a rest from it, but nevertheless braved the waves of the endless journey for the sake of her family.

Every night on the high seas, the Colonel told his daughter stories about England and the British – glorifying their values, their conventions, their protocols, their sense of decency and style. Never saying a word about how they had raped India's land and made prisoners of India's heroes.

As the Dover docks drew nearer, Tulsi Devi felt grateful that her feet would once more walk on ground that did not sway beneath her. For that she was delighted to be in England. But for Rohini and her papa, they were arriving at last in the Promised Land. This place that crawled with the people the Colonel used to serve.

They traveled up to London by train. Looking out of the window, Tulsi Devi felt quite unable to share her disappointment with her enraptured family. How could they not notice? All the houses were built so close together, without any splendor or vision. *They are huddled up in their own country, how they must have enjoyed spreading out in ours,* she observed. She felt herself wishing that she could have shared this realization with Jivan, who would have willed the British out of his country if he could.

Sensing her mother's lack of enthusiasm, Rohini commandeered her father for long trips around the city, making him show her *everything*. One day they were stopped by an English couple on the way to the Houses of Parliament and Rohini was asked if she was wearing her sari with trousers.

"No, this is a salwar chemise," she told them. "Only the gypsies in India wear these. We are from an ancient caste of gypsies!" And then she dragged her father off to yet another famous sight. When she had exhausted her father, Rohini took her mother out with her instead. Tulsi Devi was younger and Rohini knew she could persuade her to go further afield.

They often caught the train out to London's suburbs. One day they saw two young lovers kiss on the top of Richmond Hill. Rohini made Tulsi Devi stop and watch.

"Look, Ma, they're kissing in front of us! Let's follow them."

Tulsi Devi tried to stop her daughter, but she was off, camera in hand. Years later Rohini found the old black-and-white photograph – two angry faces that looked directly into the lens like a couple of Spanish dancers, with the Thames valley and its meadows in the background.

For Rohini, England was the most exciting place in the world. Not in the same way as it was for the Colonel, who respected it as the center of the empire; the thrill for her was that this place was the center of the free world. When it was time to cross the seas once more, Rohini promised herself that she would come back here to England. She knew that she would somehow return to this country of fun and freedom.

Tulsi Devi didn't know if she would ever come back again, so she made plans to meet up one last time with Lily.

Lily picked her up from Guildford station, recognizing her instantly because she was the only woman on the platform in a sari. Lily was harder to recognize – her red hair had turned gray and her face was rounder and older.

"You look just the same," Lily said, but Tulsi Devi knew that neither of them did. They were just exchanging compliments as women often do. They hugged and Lily drove them to her house. Tulsi Devi thought that they were just stopping there for her governess to make a quick delivery. It simply could not be Lily's home.

"Come out, Tulsi Devi, we've arrived," Lily told her, and Tulsi Devi found herself walking down a short garden path into a small and very plain home.

"I've made you scones, because you used to love them at Prakriti," Lily said, pushing back a few strands of gray hair. It was at that moment Tulsi Devi realized that she had traveled further than across the oceans and a few years in time. Here she was sitting in an English living room in another era. Prakriti was a faded memory. Glory was something of the past. The British had retreated to their cold little island.

"How is your son? He must have left home by now," Lily asked, making Tulsi Devi regret this visit in an instant.

"Our sons don't leave home. They stay with the family," she found herself answering.

"Is he here in England with you?"

"He died."

Tulsi Devi continued to talk of her daughter, and Lily, sensing that she had all but run ashore, took tack in a different direction. They talked pleasantries and Tulsi Devi left, somehow feeling deprived of the experience she had expected. Nevertheless, she was glad that she had visited. It had burst the bubble of illusion that the British had created for her.

She thought about how her mother would have felt in her shoes at Lily's house.

Her mother.

Suddenly Tulsi Devi, for the first time in her life, was overwhelmed by an urge to see her mother. She did not know where the cold feeling under her skin was coming from. All she knew was that she had to see Jyoti Ma very soon.

When they arrived home in Delhi they received news the same day that Jyoti Ma had died.

The Colonel held Tulsi Devi's arm as she was given the news by Pyari. He was expecting her to crumble but it was Rohini instead who collapsed, crying like a child deprived of her favorite toy.

Tulsi Devi just asked emphatically, *"When?"*

Jyoti Ma had supposedly died two days earlier, but Tulsi Devi, with the instinct of someone who shares the same blood, knew that this was not the truth. She had known in London nearly three weeks earlier that something had happened to her mother. Something, Who knows what. Not even Tulsi Devi was ever to hear the real story of how Jyoti Ma fell with a heart attack one day as she was sorting out the final pile of her husband's possessions.

It was a swift and fairly painless parting, and Jyoti Ma was found on the floor by the maidservant, who called the cook. Together they dragged her body out into the thick snow and buried it so that she was well preserved. Then the cook, the sweeper and the maidservant entered into a conspiracy that allowed them to run the household for a few days as if it were their own.

That night the three servants each took a room in the house and slept like maharajas in real beds. They ate their food on the dining room table, sitting on real chairs instead of on the kitchen floor. The cook made grand meals for them to share for the first few nights, and then insisted on reversing roles with the other two so that he too could enjoy the luxury of a life on the receiving end. Just like the memsahib. Just as long as it could last.

They continued the conspiracy for three whole weeks, until the farm workers started coming to the house for wages. Then the three servants pocketed all the cash in the house and called a nearby farmer to send a telegram to the relatives of the deceased. Finally, Jyoti Ma was dug out of the snow and defrosted before the family's arrival.

Jyoti Ma's death was a major turning point in everybody's lives.

Suddenly the farmhouse was peopled with figures from Tulsi Devi's childhood, only now there was another generation tagged on. Pyari and Anthony, David and his children, Joyce and hers. And the ever-sociable, wildly excited Rohini who entertained all her generation as if she were the new memsahib.

A surprising number of people attended the prayer ceremony. They came not just to pay their last respects to Jyoti Ma, but to be present at the end of an era. They came to witness the gathering of the children and grandchildren of Aakash. To pay homage to the man who had started Prakriti and lived to become a legend of his time and place.

Jyoti Ma's body was bathed by Tulsi Devi, Pyari, Joyce and Rohini and dressed in a white cotton sari that would have left her shivering if she still had the senses to feel it. The body lay on the living room floor, decorated with flowers that had made a pilgrimage up from Delhi. The family sat around her, sang shlokas from the Bhagavad Gita and then took her body to a specially prepared dais some distance from the farmhouse.

Neither eldest son, nor grandson was there to light the fire, and their absence at this crucial time was noted by all. The funeral party looked around, wondering which man could be asked to perform these last rites.

Tulsi Devi's lost eyes landed on Anthony. He nodded, and then her Christian uncle passed his flame under the Hindu logs.

Tulsi Devi cried not just for her own loss, but for her mother's. How could it have turned out this way? How could she have lost all the men she most needed in her final hour?

Apart from Jyoti Ma's husband, son and grandson, the only other people missing around the funeral pyre were the three household servants, who had slunk away, guilty that the taste of the good life still lingered in their mouths.

The flames flickered and Jyoti Ma's family watched the fire silently, until it burnt to embers.

It was the last time they would all be together at Prakriti.

38

Tulsi Devi and Rohini cried all the way back to Delhi. Not just for the loss of Jyoti Ma, but for the end of everything. The Colonel comforted them both, knowing that he was their only future now.

Pyari came round the next day with her sister's ashes to say that she would accompany Tulsi Devi to Hardwar so that they could place the ashes in the Ganges.

Hardwar.

Tulsi Devi started sobbing violently at the thought of it.

Pyari looked at the Colonel. This was Tulsi Devi's biggest outburst since she had heard the news of her mother's parting. They both felt the urge to distract her from her tragedy – so that she could look everywhere, but not in the face of death.

"Maybe Rohini can take your place on this journey," Pyari suggested, and the Colonel nodded.

Yet that single word 'Hardwar' lodged itself in Tulsi Devi's ears and rang too loudly for her mind to decode. The others tried to persuade her that she was being irrational. The ashes would have to be deposited and it was their duty as a family to go.

"I will not let my nani be thrown into the water unless I am there to dance," Rohini announced. But that was even more absurd. The whole affair was turning into some kind of circus.

Tulsi Devi listened to them all, feeling a familiar sickness in her stomach, her body's memory of the fifteen steps down to the Ganges. She felt herself submerged in the water.

"How can you dance at such an occasion?" Joyce interrupted.

"But masi, it's a sacred dance. It will be my last gift."

"No, no, she must be allowed to dance," asserted the Colonel, surprising everyone with his support.

Tulsi Devi closed her eyes. Her body was swaying. She allowed it to drop to the ground. She could hear Bubbly's voice in the distance, talking with some nurses …

As awareness of her body started to prickle her skin once more, she started to hear the voices outside her head as well as the ones inside.

"Quick, get some water. She needs lots of it."

Tulsi Devi was given water with a homeopathic dose of camphor, and put to bed with her feet up. There was no more talk of Hardwar. Nonetheless, when Joyce left, she went ahead and joined the ladies' queue to buy three tickets for the morning train.

Pyari, Anthony and Rohini went off on the train the next day with as much cheerfulness as they could muster. They were going to make it quick. Just a day trip.

Their plans started off on the right foot. But then the train was held up and they waited in the middle of nowhere for so long that one of the local villagers set up a new business selling roasted sweet potatoes to the passengers held hostage by engine failure.

When they finally arrived at Hardwar, it looked as though they would have to find a dharamsala and stay the night. But before making any arrangements they sought out the ghats and found a platform over the river where they could stand to throw in the ashes.

Rohini held the clay urn containing her grandmother's remains close to her heart. The three of them sat on the side of the river, looking across the water to the banks on the other side. Anthony stepped back, respecting that he was a Christian and did not have the authority to supervise this final ritual. Pyari put her hands together to pray and Rohini lifted her hands into the air and started to dance.

Within two minutes they had started to attract a crowd of pilgrims, mourners and locals. They stared at Rohini, who continued oblivious, making mudras with her hand, casting her eyes this way and that, but not once looking at the spectators.

Pyari wanted to cast the ashes into the water and get going so that they could put an end to the spectacle they were creating. She tipped the urn halfway over the water and a clump of ashes fell to the ground. She felt rushed by the multitude of watching eyes. How could she just hurl the remains of her sister's body into the Ganges in such haste and run off like someone disposing of a murder victim?

She felt embarrassed, and a strange thing happened. She imagined how it would have felt to have lived her sister's life. She thought how Jyoti would feel now if she could watch this scene. And then she picked up the urn with one hand, grabbed Rohini's hand with the other and marched her off mid-twirl to escape the scene they had created. Anthony helped push aside two or three people to create an escape route, but as they were walking away an arm grabbed Rohini's.

"You dance well, sister."

"Thank you."

Rohini turned around to see an ageing man with a bright yellow sari and a cheesy lipsticked smile. He winked at her, and Pyari pulled Rohini's hand to draw her away from the eunuch. The manwoman stayed behind slightly, but followed them with his eyes.

Anonymous again, they walked around Hardwar until they found a small dharamsala where they were offered rooms for the night. Pyari made her niece stay indoors for the rest of the day, and the three of them sat and waited until nightfall when they could finally put an end to their mis-spent day.

It wasn't where they had intended to lay their heads down for the night. The rooms were humble and decent, but they were in anonymous beds. The best thing was just to sleep, and in that sleep they would not know where they were.

Rohini had already been asleep for five hours when she woke to a knock at her window. She lit a match and walked to open it. Standing there was a man with matted hair tied into a bun above his ash-covered face. There was nothing frightening about him except the hour at which he knocked.

"What do you want?" Rohini asked sharply with the confidence of her grandmother.

"You never threw away the ashes," answered the man.

"But that's none of your business."

"Your nani wants to speak with you."

"Go away, she's dead."

Rohini was about to start getting abusive with this man, but before she shut the window she had to ask him: "How did you know she was my nani?"

The man held out his hand and opened his fist. Inside was a small gravelly pile of ashes. He held them close to her face so that she could see what he saw.

"Come."

She hesitated.

It was dark and the man was a total stranger. But he had raised so many questions. What if her nani wanted to say goodbye? What if there was an important message? What if this man took her into an alley and tried to kill her?

And what about her parents? What would her mother say if she knew her daughter was out wandering the streets of Hardwar on her own this late?

Nobody in the world would let her go off with this stranger, and in the middle of the night. Nobody could give their consent now except her …

Rohini started climbing out of the window, and the decisiveness of her movements stopped her mind from questioning her actions any further.

The man had very little to say. She asked: "What is your name?" He said nothing. She asked: "Where are we going?" He did not answer.

She followed him through the unlit streets, noticing how the town seemed smaller at night, as if the sky were closing down on them. She kept her distance from him, this mute stranger who carried her dead grandmother in the palms of his hands. Just enough space to give her a head start if she had to run. He did not notice, continuing to weave through the streets and along the river like a nocturnal animal.

The man arrived at a dark funeral ground and went straight through the arched entrance with the confidence of one who walks freely between two worlds. Rohini looked up above the entrance and saw a statue of Shiva, God of Destruction. She realized now that this man was an aghori – a man who lived in funeral grounds. She knew nothing about aghoris except that they worshiped Kali, talked to the dead and ate their meals out of human skulls.

Through the gates Rohini could see a fire. Who knows, it could have been burning the remains of someone who had lived just a few days earlier.

Squatting around the fire were another two men, dark, smoky, covered in ashes, watching her.

She took one look at those coal-dark aghoris and saw herself suddenly as a victim: a young girl alone, captured by three strangers burning the dead in the thick of the night. Another step further and it could be her on the fire. She froze, staying close to Shiva at the gates. And then she saw the aghori turn and start coming back to get her.

"Come," he shouted over to her.

Without thinking Rohini turned the other way and ran faster than she had ever run in her life. She chose only the wider roads, looking frantically at all the houses to see which doors she could bang on if she had to. Searching the streets for life. Every few minutes she looked behind her, expecting to see skulls flying through the air.

When she arrived back at her room, she climbed through the window, locked it tight and covered it with a duppata. She opened the adjoining door into Pyari and Anthony's bedroom to be nearer to them. But then she locked it again, thinking that if the aghoris were going to come back to kill her, at least her relatives would be spared.

The whole night Rohini stayed awake with the bedcovers pulled up tight over her head, imagining footsteps outside. There was nothing in the room she could throw at them. Nothing for protection but her prayers. She willed the morning light to come, but when it did she found herself with an oddly regretful feeling. She had been offered an extraordinary experience and she had turned back at the last minute.

In the morning it was not what her mother might say that haunted her, but what her grandmother had not said.

It was early when Pyari came to wake a sleepy Rohini to go down to the ghats and then to catch the early train. Walking through the same streets in the daytime Rohini found herself looking for the mystery that had begged to be solved during the darker hours of the night. Yet she saw nothing but ordinary life. The people of a small holy town going about their daily lives: trading, gossiping, playing. Watching those ordinary lives she swore that she would never again deny herself an opportunity to experience something uncommon.

At the banks of the Ganges Pyari insisted that there was to be no dancing, and Rohini agreed, sitting down like one defeated by her own lack of daring. The last of Jyoti Ma's ashes were thrown in the water and they went back to the dharamsala to pick up their bags.

When they were all standing outside the building, saying goodbye to the man who ran it, the aghori who had lured Rohini to the funeral grounds the night before came walking down the street. He looked so different in the morning. Less deathly, with a spring in his step, fresh ash on his face and alertness in his words as he delivered his message.

"Your nani says you must meet your brother."

That was all he said.

Suddenly Pyari was speaking loudly. "Why are you talking to him, Rohini? You mustn't go attracting all this attention to yourself."

The aghori continued down the street, not feeling the need to stay any longer now that he had delivered his message in the light of day.

"Pyari masi, which brother must I meet?" Rohini asked.

Pyari went into such a state of confusion Rohini was puzzled.

"Did Mama have a boy before me who died?"

Her aunt dismissed the whole conversation with uneasiness. Anthony watched his wife, uncomfortably silent.

From that moment onward Rohini was convinced that she must have had a brother who had died, but sensing their discomfort, she decided to make her own enquiries at a later date.

When they arrived back in Delhi, Tulsi Devi asked nothing about the trip to Hardwar. But she listened to their story attentively – or to Pyari's version of it, which focused on the long and terrible wait in the train and the uncomfortable bed in the dharamsala.

Rohini said nothing of her late night escape to the borderland between two worlds. Nonetheless, it became her quiet obsession and she looked up what little information she could find on aghoris whenever she went into a public library. She discovered that they were renunciants who used mantras and rituals to commune with the dead. Their path to enlightenment was considered fast, but dangerous. They wore the ashes from the funeral pyres and had the help of spirits whenever they needed it. And yes, they ate from bowls made of skulls and used intoxicants to free their minds of their daytime realities.

It was enough information to set her imagination off. She became obsessed with aghoris, little suspecting that her fixation would take a different form over the years and become the carriage to transport her freely between the two worlds in her later life.

39

The Colonel was glad when Rohini started college to study medicine. It would be good to have a doctor in the family, he thought. Ladies were doing all kinds of things now that they had never done before, and he wanted his daughter to have all the privileges of the new generation.

More importantly, he was getting old, and he knew that Rohini's skills, if learnt well, would be useful before too long. Already his only leg was starting to swell in the joints, and his sleep was disturbed like one who knew there was not much time left. There was also his smoker's cough. Although he had not smoked for years, the tar from his army days had clung so surely to the porous insides of his lungs that the thick black coating had become a part of his anatomy.

He never complained of any ailments, just as he had never complained about being a cripple for as long as everybody had known him. The only time they realized the man of the house was getting old was when he stopped dyeing his hair.

After two visits to the barber the Colonel's hair turned completely white. Soon after, his stoop became more pronounced, and his deep-set eyes sank even further back into his skull. He never said a word, but his white hair was his way of telling the family that he had now reached the stage where he would need some looking after.

The only reference he ever made to his state of health was with regard to Rohini's marriage.

"We must start looking. I want to see her settled in my lifetime," he would tell Tulsi Devi, but instead of setting off thoughts of marriage his words made her think of nothing but widowhood.

There was nobody in Delhi society except Pyari's brood who knew the full history of their family, so they were highly respectable in a disguised sort of way, and after the sale of Prakriti they were more affluent than ever. Moreover, Rohini was beautiful and educated ... and her father had been in service ... and both parents were still alive ... at least for now.

Rohini herself was happy to think about marriage. She understood her body well enough to know that it would not last out its passions in the singular for much longer. She wanted to fall in love, even if it meant that her love would have to be found for her.

The Colonel started going back to the officers' mess to rejuvenate acquaintances and to enquire who had sons of a marriageable age. In the past he used to assess his fellow officers according to rank, but now he saw them solely as future in-laws for his daughter. He thought of how his daughter would rank them.

During this time, Tulsi Devi talked to Pyari. Pyari talked to friends. Those friends talked to friends and a small circle of matchmakers was set up. Before long Rohini even started receiving offers directly from the parents of her old schoolfriends who wanted brides for older sons.

Several introductions were made. There was Gokul, who had finished studying surgery and was practicing in the big government hospital. (Handsome, fair-skinned, tall, good family.) He seemed to be the most likely candidate at first, as Rohini and he talked for hours when they were left alone to get to know each other.

Everyone in the next room thought that things were going well and that the young couple had started to discuss matters of the heart. In actual fact, if they had put their ears to the door and heard the conversation, they would have discovered that Rohini had spent that entire meeting extracting information from Gokul on the subject of autopsies.

When she was asked if she liked Gokul, she said, "Yes, he is such a knowledgeable person." When she was asked if they should talk to his parents about arranging a marriage, she answered, "How can I marry someone in medicine? We will talk of nothing but cadavers!"

Three more boys were introduced: an engineer, a young man with great prospects in the Foreign Office, and the son of a General. When Rohini was asked which of the three she preferred, she said, "I like all of them."

"But which one do you like the best?" asked her father.

"Rohan, I think. I talked with him for at least an hour more than the other two."

Her father was delighted. Rohan was the son of the General and was known to him. They would have a military-style wedding with a full brass band playing. In marrying off his daughter he would be reaching a pinnacle in his military career, the Colonel thought, even though his army days were long gone.

It was good that she liked Rohan. Strangely, it was good that she liked all three boys. It meant that his daughter was easy to please and that she would make an accepting wife no matter whom they found. "There's many a slip between the cup and the lip though," he would say, knowing that Rohan may not be the last boy that they would have to consider.

Rohini and Rohan. Even their names went together. But that was in those few moments when the cup and the lip were still coming together. Before the cup was smashed into too many pieces to glue back together and fill with tea.

Everything changed the day Ram arrived at their house in Sundernagar.

Tulsi Devi was told by her maidservant that there was a man at the door, dressed in white robes, who claimed to be her brother. (A beggar, maybe, dressed up as a holy man?) Tulsi Devi looked around to see if anybody had heard, patted down her hair with a nervous hand and quickly took her handbag to go out to meet him.

"Ma, I'm coming with you." It was more of a statement than a question.

Tulsi Devi was about to insist that she be left alone, but Rohini had already picked up her duppata and was walking ahead of her mother in the direction of the door.

That day Rohini found out more about her family than she had done in a lifetime of observing them. It was the day when all preconceptions of her mother, of morality, and of her society were changed forever. The mask of the world as she knew it fell to the ground.

For Tulsi Devi it was Judgement Day. The day of all revelations. Nervously she witnessed her two lives collide, shatter and reveal the truth that she had been hiding all these years. It was an exposing and humbling experience, and if she had not been in the company of two such compassionate people, it would have been impossible to continue.

They were at a small restaurant close to their home. Tulsi Devi felt intensely vulnerable even before she heard the news that had brought her brother to the city.

"Pitaji died two weeks ago." Ram spoke the words softly, looking across at his sister who had her face cupped in her hands, hiding from the sight of her own shell as it cracked.

In her shock Tulsi Devi searched her memory for the last image she had of her father. He was angry and they were leaving Prakriti. When she had returned to the farm she remembered crying for him as if he had passed away. All this so long ago, and now he had died again.

"Your nana was one of the greatest and most noble souls to walk this earth," Ram said to his niece, sensing his sister's acute vulnerability, trying to overcome it with his gentleness.

"How did he die?" Rohini asked with unnatural curiosity. She could feel the awesome presence of her uncle and, faintly behind him, the presence of her grandfather whose spirit had trailed Ram to this small restaurant to help break the news.

"Sometimes Pitaji would call me and tell me the exact experiences he was having, describing this feeling of dying ..." Ram looked at his sister whose whole face was now directed down at the table. "He would always say that the body knew how to die ..."

"Did he know exactly when it would happen?"

"His soul slipped away while he was sitting in meditation ... Your nana was an inspiration, beti, believe me."

Tulsi Devi lifted her face and said, "Ram, we have lost everything now."

The three of them held hands. Rohini tried to imagine how it would have been to have a grandfather, trying to feel him through Ram, but no image appeared. Instead she thought of her grandmother, and remembering the aghori at Hardwar she asked Ram straight out: "Ram uncle, do I have a brother?"

He looked at his sister. Her eyes begged him to break the news, and then Tulsi Devi cupped her face in her hands once more as Ram told Rohini about Jivan.

What followed for Rohini was a sea change of emotions. A shift in her understanding that required every memory to be reinvented. She listened, her face immobile. Only her eyes blinked as she heard the catastrophic story, spoken by an uncle whom she was meeting for the first time. Under the table, her fingernails dug into her legs, and her feet twisted around each other.

"Mama," she said finally, "if this is all true, there's something wrong with this world."

The seriousness in her uncle's face let it be known that the facts were all real and, if anything, it was life itself that was illusory.

Rohini felt for her mother. She felt her mother's shame as her own and she knew then that nothing would ever again be as it first seemed. No ground beneath her feet could ever be called stable.

It was the first time in her life that she was conscious of feeling respect and gratitude toward her mother. All these feelings, combined with a sense of confusion toward her father.

As she heard Ram talking she had an important realization that helped her make sense of this new order. A realization that *everything happens for a reason*. That everything eventually makes sense. Otherwise, why would she have met the aghori? Why were these revelations designed for her and no one else?

Realizing that her mother was bowed down through embarrassment as much as grief, Rohini tried to console her.

"Mama, we must try to find Jivan."

Tulsi Devi cried and cried, the two of them comforting her. She cried for the loss of both parents. For the loss of her son. For the loss of her disguise. For the shame she was bringing on her daughter. Rohini watched, for the first time seeing her mother for her failings, and loving her still.

Rohini and Tulsi Devi walked back into the house bigger people. The Colonel, who had sat reading the newspaper during these dramatic changes, looked up to see the two women in his life in tears. Not able to get up quickly, he called Rohini over to tell him what had happened.

"My nana has died," she told him. That's all. But he could sense by the devastated expression on his daughter's face that the news went far far deeper than that. She had not even known her grandfather, so how could she look so bereaved? He got up to embrace his wife, who turned away, wanting to grieve alone.

Not wanting to think about how much Ram had told them, the Colonel considered instead the implications, wondering if Rohini should marry so soon after a death in the family. If she waited, what of Rohan? Would his parents wish to wait, too?

There was no need to worry, as Rohan's parents called around the next day to talk about the match. It was clear that their son had been captivated: Rohini's charms had worked like a love potion.

The Colonel invited them in for tea and ordered it to be served in their best porcelain cups. The deal was made and the two families agreed to a match, but in a year's time, to show due respect for Aakash. An engagement ceremony was to be held and that would end the looking. After that, the young couple would be free to go out occasionally and meet in private to get to know each other a little before the marriage. Rohini agreed, and even Tulsi Devi was pleased, knowing that if her daughter did not marry soon, they would all be undone.

There could be no certainty about the future, but somehow everyone felt it taking a different course. Nothing was straightforward anymore.

Ram came back two days later. Thankfully Rohini was at medical school and so Tulsi Devi took her brother to their small secret restaurant alone. She could tell that Ram was not a messenger of auspicious news. He had gone to the orphanage to try and locate Jivan's foster parents, but the family who had adopted him had moved – to England, the neighbors said.

"Rohini has her heart set on meeting him," was all that Tulsi Devi could say. To mention nothing of her own aching heart.

"The two of them will meet one day, if it is to serve a greater purpose," Ram assured her.

Tulsi Devi saved these words for her daughter, but Rohini tossed them out without question.

"How can these things be left to fate? We must go to England and find him, otherwise he will think that nobody ever bothered. And I will live my whole life walking the same earth as my brother without meeting him."

Tulsi Devi took the blame entirely, but could not conjure up the missing person they both so badly wanted to hold. She felt for Rohini, remembering her own search for her missing brother, but also felt powerless to make another miracle happen. How could they go back to England now? Especially with Rohini's papa in such ill health and no clue where to find Jivan.

Rohini knew that it was unfair to vent all her frustration on her mother, so she decided to target her father instead. In her eyes, the father she had loved and worshiped all her life became a tyrant responsible for all the world's woes.

When the Colonel tried to talk to Rohini about her marriage, she said, "What do you know about marriage? Look at how you've made Mama hate you. I'll be damned if I ever marry somebody you've chosen for me."

"Listen to yourself, girl. *I'm your father,"* he answered, unable to understand how the sweet daughter who had always charmed him could let these insults trip so freely from her tongue.

"How can you call yourself my father when you all but murdered my brother?" she screamed. But her fury landed on a little old man with a missing leg and no strength left to find an explanation, even if there had been one to be found.

Worse still, no amount of rage could bring Jivan back.

40

The hostilities in the house were unbearable – oscillating between war, cold war and icy cold battles of eyes. Rohini spent most of her time at medical school, but when she was home she would talk to her father only if she had some barb she could add to the conversation. Tulsi Devi, on the other hand, found herself overcompensating by tending to all his needs and showering him with piteous affection, making him feel hideously undeserving.

Her husband's frailty made Tulsi Devi feel weak. She hated herself for not fighting to keep Jivan. She hated herself for letting down her daughter. But she could only show that hatred by loving the man who had instigated it all.

The Colonel, in his dotage, cried tears of both love and sorrow. If he could have produced Jivan, decorated him in gold and begged for his forgiveness, he would have, because to suffer for his sins at the eleventh hour was too great a punishment for his shrinking bones.

Just to stay in the house was unbearable.

In the midst of all the hostilities, there arrived a single young man walking through the battlefield waving a white flag.

His name was Gordon.

His arrival had been expected after Tulsi Devi received a letter from Lily in Guildford, telling her about a friend who was making a trip overland to India. Gordon had heard all about the family and Prakriti, Lily said, and he was really looking forward to meeting them and having friends far from home. Tulsi Devi had mentioned the letter to her husband and daughter some time earlier, but was totally unprepared for the visitor who arrived at their door, blond-haired and unshaven, with bushy sideburns disguising a handsome face. He wore kurta pyjamas that looked more like baggy pants and an untucked shirt. His only possessions were carried in a multi-colored cloth bag.

If Gordon hadn't been white, there would have been no room in the house for him. In fact, he probably wouldn't have even been allowed to get through the front gate. But Gordon was gloriously white. Not the kind of white that the Colonel had ever encountered: he was used to seeing suited or uniformed white skin. Not white people in Indian clothes. But Gordon had the same familiar accent, the giveaway signs that he was from a good family. Very polite, highly thoughtful, perfectly cultured. Yes, Gordon would be most welcome to stay.

The usual questions were asked to assess his status and background.

"What do you do in England, Gordon?" asked the Colonel.

"I'm a student of philosophy at Cambridge, but I'm taking study leave."

What Gordon didn't tell them was that he never intended to go back to studying again. He'd been studying Jack Kerouac and Hermann Hesse instead of Kant and Galileo. Smoking opium instead of going to lectures. Spending time in London going to clubs in Chelsea instead of making friends at university.

One of his London friends, who called himself Dylan after Dylan Thomas, had gone off to India. Dylan was from Elephant and Castle, from a family of criminals and football players. In Gordon's eyes, he was working class and he was free. Dylan left his flat in Peckham with three months' rent unpaid and hitched his way through Turkey, Iran and Afghanistan to get to India. Meanwhile, Gordon was left behind to write tedious essays on subjects such as "Can God make a bowl of porridge too big for him to eat?" The bigger question facing Gordon was: "How can I get the hell out of here and get my arse over to India?"

His parents had tried to persuade him that he could do it later. That he would receive an all-expenses-paid round-the-world holiday when he graduated. But that wasn't enough. Gordon didn't want to "go on holiday." He wanted to "do the journey."

"What does your father do?" asked the Colonel.

"What all have you seen in India?" asked Rohini.

They were all talking at once in their enthusiasm at having Gordon to stay.

"My father is in the British air force," Gordon replied, immediately stepping up another dozen rungs in the Colonel's estimation, to leave his shabby clothes well behind. But the stories of what he had seen in India were not for the ears of the entire family. They were tales that Rohini would extract from him later when nobody else was around.

Gordon was shown to his room, asked about his culinary preferences, and later that day Tulsi Devi took him out to buy another six smart kurta pyjamas. She liked this boy. His curiosity about India and Indian customs reminded her of Lily when she had first arrived at Prakriti.

That evening, once her parents had gone to sleep, Rohini – who had waited for an opportunity to be alone with this curious foreigner – started spouting the questions she'd been saving.

"Why do you wear your hair so long?" she asked.

Gordon told her it was actually short. It had been longer three months ago, but he had to cut it to get into Nepal.

That was the first of many stories he told her – about the strict border guards who had insisted that only smart people were allowed through into Nepal, which was fast attracting undesirable travelers. He told her about the one suit that ten beatniks shared to get their visas, and how the man in the visa office always recognized the suit, sometimes with the legs a little too short, sometimes a little too long. He told her stories about how he had been spotted in Bombay and given a part as a British soldier in a Hindi movie. Then he told her the story of when he gave two hundred rupees to a beggar, but not without insisting that the beggar first took him home and made him a meal.

The stories of his travels unfolded like the rich patchwork tapestries the Gujurati women rolled out to sell on the streets of Jan Path. He told Rohini about the time he befriended a sweeper caste in Mysore and joined them to help clean the bourgeois homes. On every occasion, the owner of the home would stop him doing the work and invite him in for tea.

Rohini laughed. She thought about what her friends would think of Gordon. They would think he was crazy, for sure. Either that, or just talking nonsense.

"India is the most awesome place on this planet," Gordon told her that evening. But instead of making her feel proud, it made her jealous that she would never be able to see her country like a foreigner could.

"Why did you bring only one small bag with you?" Rohini asked.

"No matter what you bring with you, you're always unprepared," he told her. "This is a country where anything can happen."

Rohini nodded knowingly. Fully aware that nothing had ever happened to her in India, except for that one time in Hardwar, but even then she had shied away from the experience that had been offered.

Gordon was free at all times. He was free to travel on top of the trains instead of inside them. Free to catch a bus without knowing where it was going. Free to visit anywhere without asking permission. His willingness to experience freedom had taken him on wild journeys. He'd slept in temples, in stables, on beaches, on roofs, in boats, in whorehouses.

"Don't tell your parents any of this stuff," he told her. He needn't have bothered. Rohini knew there was nobody in the whole of India she could share his stories with. They talked of unknown quantities of freedom and absurd transgressions of acceptable behavior.

Instead of feeling challenged by Gordon, Rohini was intrigued. She envied him his freedom and his fluidity. He was like an English god on holiday in India, free to play, to imagine, to create. He described the temples in the south where he'd seen goddesses taken from their shrines to be immersed in water. He'd seen the tea-pickers up north. He'd been to Kanyakumari at the southernmost tip of India to see the three seas meet. He'd seen the spice markets of Cochin, the prostitutes in cages in Bombay. He'd spent the night in the Ajanta and Ellora Caves in Aurangabad, climbed to the top of Palitana in Gujurat, visited the mining towns of Orissa and stayed to make friends with the tribal people in the forests.

He knew India and she knew only Delhi. He was a man of the world, and she a little girl who knew only one corner of her city. The more she heard him talking, the smaller her world shrank, until she had almost nothing to say to him. What could she say? She couldn't start talking about medical school. He didn't want to know about which teachers made the students laugh. Neither was he going to want to hear her stories about girlfriends rejecting marriage partners. The only tale of any mystery she had to tell was her story about the aghori in Hardwar, so she told him about what had happened, adding several shades of color to paint an even more dramatic picture of the funeral ground she visited.

". . . And then, through the gates I could see two more naked aghoris, with skulls in their hands, sitting next to a fire blazing with bones, ready to raise the dead there in front of me . . ."

"Well, did they manage to do it?"

Rohini continued, telling him how through the dark shadows she had seen a faint transparent image of her grandmother. The figure beckoned.

The three ash-covered messengers watched. "I walked up to feel fingers of ash and hear the words: 'You have a brother. It is your destiny to meet him.'"

A chill of cold fingers ran down Gordon's warm back and he was captivated. He too had spent the night in a funeral site, in Calcutta. He'd even meditated in a Parsi cemetery, opening his eyes occasionally to see the odd crow picking eyes out of skull sockets. But Rohini, she had taken this mystical experience one step further. She had become one of the inner circle.

Then there was the story of the brother. It intrigued him. Gordon asked more questions about Jivan than Rohini could answer. After she had revealed as much as she knew, it was her turn to swear him to secrecy.

"If my mother knows I have told you all of this she will never be able to look you in the eyes again."

Gordon assured her that they were conspirators together.

"Come to England with me and find Jivan," he said.

The two of them stayed up until the sun rose in the sky and the kabari wala had started his rounds, shouting "kabari wale" the way the cock crowed at dawn in Gordon's country.

Gordon would have kept talking, but Rohini knew that they would have to make themselves scarce before her parents had their morning tea. Getting up, Gordon leaned over to kiss her good morning and good-night.

It was unexpected for Rohini. The kiss lasted a little too long, and their eyes met for a few seconds more than they should have for a simple good-night.

Gordon took Rohini's unwillingness to move as permission to kiss her again. This time with his body pressed to hers, as tight as two flowers pressed into a book, preserving the memory of that night for the years to come.

Like a released prisoner taken to the gates of the jail, Rohini's legs started to tremor at her newfound sense of freedom. There were a few moments when she didn't know what to do, and then her sensuality took her forward. She ran her hands through his long blond hair and touched his open pink lips and white cheeks, just as she had seen in the movies. She pushed herself even closer to her liberator, as if she were adorning him with all the melodies of love she had sung for so many years in anticipation of this event.

But the dawn was insistent. The crow was warning of her parents and their wakefulness, and warning too that such a state of arousal was inappropriate in their living room. Rohini kissed Gordon softly on the cheek and told him she would not sleep, but just wait an hour and then emerge so that she could see him again.

Lying on her bed on her own, Rohini couldn't have slept even if she'd been dosed up on the sleeping remedies they used to grow at Prakriti. Her heartbeat was racing. Her cheeks felt hot, and the front of her body tingled with Gordon's imprint as if she still had him pressed against her. She savored the feeling, enjoying the intimacy of his lingering presence, like the smell of fresh soap all over her body.

When the morning had made an official arrival, Rohini and Gordon sat down to eat breakfast with Tulsi Devi and the Colonel as if nothing had happened. They dressed all their desires in formalities and forced all sensitivities below the dining-room table where they couldn't be seen.

Rohini's father started telling Gordon about the tourist sights of Delhi. The Red Fort, Rashtrapati Bhavan, India Gate, Humayun's Tomb, Purana Qila just next door and then, of course, the Qutab Minar.

"If you can stretch your arms around the iron pillar at the Qutab Minar, you can make any wish you like and it will come true."

The only wish that Gordon could think of at that moment was the overwhelming desire to bed the Colonel's daughter. He found himself noticing a single curl that hung just below her ear and forced his mind back onto the tourist sights of Delhi. He mumbled about the sights he had seen in other cities of India, sounding quite unlike the exotic traveler of the night before.

All the while, the Colonel held the conversation, getting the reactions he required on the subjects that interested him most.

"Gordon, tell me something. Did your father serve in India?"

"No, but he blew up a few people in the last world war."

The Colonel felt embarrassed by the young man's turn of phrase, but dismissed it as youthful ignorance and turned the conversation back to the military as he knew it.

"Did you know Rohini is engaged to the son of a General?"

Rohini was watching Gordon's reaction to see if he looked upset. She wanted him to look upset. Then she would know that he really loved her. Gordon looked as if he had been dropped from a very great height and that pleased her. He congratulated her in such a coded, fraught manner that she delighted in his distress and told him casually that she would introduce the two of them.

"Why don't you take the car and driver to show Gordon around Delhi?" the Colonel suggested. "Show him the medical school and go to lunch at the Club." Rohini tried not to sound too enthusiastic, checking her timetable first to make sure that she would make it back by the late afternoon.

That day gave her such a taste for freedom she would never again be able to wear the shackles of her innocence. She told the driver to drive them to Chandni Chowk, where she would be far from anyone they knew. They sat in the back of the car, with feet intertwined so that the driver couldn't see any intimacy in his rear-view mirror.

"You didn't tell me that you were getting married," said Gordon.

"Well I am." She looked over at him, put her hand in his lap, low enough to be hidden from view, and whispered in his ear, "To you."

He smiled, completely taken aback at her proposal. When the driver let them out, Rohini gave him some money for lunch and told him they'd be gone some time. She led Gordon, weaving through the little gullies until they came to the wedding section of the maze, where grooms and brides came separately with their parents to drape themselves in the glittering, colorful future of married life.

The shops were brimming over with marriage bangles and gold kaleeras, bridal jewelery, duppatas, bindis, wedding turbans and sehra bandis. Rohini placed a ready-made wedding turban onto Gordon's head and laughed at her future groom. He pinched her behind, and she flinched. Then he delicately held her shoulder and kissed her just where her blouse started to reveal her neck. Openly.

Rohini turned around and faced him and they pressed their bodies tight in an embrace once more.

The shopkeepers shooed them away like untouchable lovers. He pulled, she followed, down a quiet alley where they could press, and kiss, and touch and melt with nobody else to disapprove.

Then they wandered some more, hand in hand, until the disapproval didn't matter anymore and they found themselves at the mosque, kissing on the stairs as Muslim women in purdah glanced over black veils, eyes dark with disapproval.

"We must find somewhere more private," Rohini urged.

Later that night, when Tulsi Devi and the Colonel were in bed, Gordon came into her bedroom.

"Is this private enough?"

When she saw him Rohini went to lock the door. She made sure there were no cracks in the curtain. She made absolutely sure that nobody could see them and there was not a single crevice for the outside world to peep through.

That was that. They were alone.

Rohini's heart was racing faster than when she had lain on that same bed thinking of him. He was real and everything they would do now would be real. She could sense the imminence of an initiation.

As they lay down on her childhood bed, Rohini could feel Gordon's experience in his confidence, in his hands, in his mouth, which all knew the shape of a woman's body even in the dark. It excited her and intimidated her at the same time.

But it did not stop her.

Like a wave that knew it would have to come to shore, she felt the sand already in her toes as he circled her navel with his fingers, freeing her from any ties to the womb and to her family.

Rohini was dizzy with desire for this English boy who had arrived in her life like an answer to an eternal prayer. Her longing to feel his skin next to hers was her passage into his world, where these things were permissible. Even worthy of approval.

"Are you all right to do this?" It was a simple invitation – words she would always remember, they stung her so deeply.

He lay on the bed, unbearably close, craving union. Just by wanting him, his wild, free world was opening for her now. They moved together. Rohini felt the closeness of his hips, their sheer reality under her fingertips. Their size, their tautness. It was so unfamiliar. So much more enthralling than she could have possibly imagined. This feeling of being in the reality of it. Unstoppable in her heightened responses. Deliriously strung to her senses.

Gordon started to reach places inside her that animated themselves for the first time, enlivening sensual reflexes all over her body. The fullness of him made her hold her breath. She held him there with her, with that breath, holding his Being in the core of her.

Rohini could have felt those waves all night. Her passions had been in an infinite gestation and now her river was meeting the sea at last. Their two bodies surged and gushed, waves lapping upon waves. She felt as if her body was made to be worshiped. As if all the oceans in the known world were hers. Gordon welcomed and lavished her with his fresh salty love until he could contain himself no longer.

Afterward the two of them lay together, Gordon watching to see if her body had changed. If there was any perceptible difference on her skin now that she had loved a man. Rohini felt at once a woman and a little girl, guilty that her parents were asleep down the corridor, unaware that she was feeling so thoroughly exalted.

They stayed there kissing, Rohini enjoying her newborn body, until some time later when her medical instincts took over.

"You realize that we could have just made a baby?"

He stared into her eyes with no regrets and assured her that he could handle it if she could.

It did reassure her. She felt it was the man in him talking. They lay together embracing, chest to breast, four legs as one, until they slept, body to body.

Rohini was still sleeping when Gordon woke and crept quietly back to his room. She slept on until her parents knocked on the door. In her dreams, the two of them were in England, searching for Jivan together.

Back at the breakfast table, the Colonel talked once more about seeing the sights of India.

"Have you seen the Taj Mahal?" he asked Gordon.

"No, but I'd love to." It was a lie. He had been avoiding the Taj Mahal precisely because it was where every visitor was expected to go. The Colonel, on the other hand, discovering that there was a place that his guest had not seen, offered to lend him the car and driver to make a day trip.

Rohini didn't say anything, but decided that she would have to work on her father to allow her to accompany Gordon. But she left it a day, so that she didn't sound too suspiciously enthusiastic. It was easy enough. She had been very nice to her father since Gordon's arrival and he was as malleable in her hands now as butter in the hot summer heat.

"Why can't I see the Taj too?" she asked. "Why is it that these ferengis get to see more of our own country than we ever do?"

The next few days after permission had been granted, she caught up on her studies and saw Gordon only in the evenings, when they waited until Rohini's parents had gone to bed to touch, share and join worlds. Often Gordon would tease her about the General's son and Rohini would giggle so loudly it almost woke up the household.

They set off for Agra one early morning, the car packed with enough provisions to last them a week. Getting out of Delhi, Rohini started to fantasize more about the possibilities of being together. Of joining him on his adventures and traveling like a gypsy in her own land. Now that she had been introduced to the adventures of the body, she wanted to share his adventurous spirit and travel even further. Go to places she had only ever dreamed of up till now.

That journey felt like the first one of many. She looked out of the window and saw the buffalo carts carrying sugar cane, the dhobis washing clothes in the river, villagers patting cow's manure into large piles for burning – the daily life of her country that eluded her in the sanctuary of Delhi. Gordon too looked out, but with the familiarity of one who had seen it all before.

While Rohini was thinking of India, he was thinking of how he loved this girl, and remembered a conversation with another traveler about how beautiful Indian women were. They had both agreed that they wouldn't stand a chance of getting one, because the girls didn't so much as lift their eyes in the street. Yet here she was now. This gorgeous girl Rohini, wrapping her leg around his and holding his hand discreetly under a cotton shawl. He looked at her curls tied back in a bunch, and then down at her swooping neckline – knowing he'd never again find a woman with quite as much class.

They arrived in Agra, making their way through the dirty over-crowded streets, and then they saw her – the Taj, looming over the ugly town like a lotus in a muddy pond.

It was a staggering sight. A monumental effort of love for a dead queen.

They were both silenced by the tomb's commanding presence. Its majesty. Its sheer proportions. As dumbfounded as if they were the first to ever see the sight. Only the driver talked, and talked, and talked, saying, "The statues you see in Delhi are so much smaller, hey nah?"

They got rid of the driver, telling him to go and guard the car. Entranced, they circled the Taj once, twice, three times, stroking their palms across the marble, looking up at the towering dome, up to the sky to see the vultures fly.

Round the back of the Taj, Gordon lined up with the other lovers to push his sweetheart against the stone to steal one of her forbidden kisses. The others in this lovers' hideout turned to look at the white boy kissing the Indian girl, openly demanding an explanation with their eyes. The two of them had to escape, and went inside the Taj, into the mausoleum.

Gordon thought about the act of love that had moved mountains of marble to these plains – all for the dead wife of the king. He looked over to Rohini and felt the tug of his own mortality.

"Will you marry me?" he asked, as if it would achieve some of his life purpose.

"I asked you first," Rohini replied, determined that she was going to have one up on him.

"Will you?"

Rohini said yes with her body. She pulled his hand around her waist and nuzzled into his neck. But instead of speaking the answer he wanted, she talked instead of the mausoleum that enveloped her.

"I want to see the Taj in the moonlight."

An idea occurred to her to make it possible. She remembered how on the way to Hardwar the train had broken down, and thinking fast she asked Gordon if he could somehow make the car break down.

Without hesitating they went back to the car, gave the driver some lunch money and told him he could take an hour off. When the driver was gone, Gordon took a piece out of the engine and threw it far away into the bushes.

"That will buy us one night of love," he told Rohini, and they went back to the Taj to eat their feast and have their photo taken – an image of two criminals of love. Young outrageous thieves.

They spent the night in a small hotel near Fatehpur Sikri. After seeing the Taj in the early evening, they went back to their cosy room, not wanting to waste too many precious minutes that could be spent nakedly and privately. Their stolen time together.

Here in a hotel like a married couple, Rohini felt entirely freed. There were no parents in the adjacent room, nor servants. Nobody at all who knew them. They had permission as never before to show themselves. Two bodies on borrowed sheets, on borrowed time.

That night, Gordon fathered his first child. And to ensure conception, the Taj sat a solitary night's vigil, the queen of the plains, bathed in the cold moonlight.

The driver spent the following morning in a panic, trying to locate a spare part for the car, whilst Rohini and Gordon spent the last few leisurely hours enjoying the independence reserved for fully grown adults.

When they got into the car and started getting closer to Delhi, they sensed their independence slowly slinking away. Rohini felt younger, powerless, compared to the woman who had so generously given of her body the night before.

In Sundernagar they were met with the expected exclamations of worry and had to retell the story of the car being robbed of its parts, playing innocent victims of fate. The Colonel apologized to Gordon, as if it were he who had stolen the car part, making Gordon feel all the more a thief for stealing his daughter's chastity.

The next day, seeing her parents were alone having afternoon tea,

Rohini went onto the verandah to announce that she and Gordon were going to get married.

"To hell you are!" her father said.

"But I love him."

"Love is a bucket of shit. You are like a newborn duck who opens its eyes for the first time and thinks that the first creature it sees is its mother."

"It's not like that with Gordon."

"Do you want to make a laughing stock of me? There will be no Gordon. He is leaving today. If you do not marry Rohan I will personally throw you out of the house." The Colonel's anger was giving him back the energy of his former years, making him grow taller once more with his words.

"And you will force me to marry him just like you forced Mama to give away my brother!" Rohini screamed as she stormed out, pushing past Dhruv who was cowering at the door.

The Colonel summoned the storms as he charged into Gordon's room and demanded that he pack his bags there and then. Gordon, knowing that his time of love was up, obediently, silently, placed his few clothes into his small cloth bag, walked a wide circle around Rohini's father and a straight line through the front door.

It could have ended there, his adventure with an Indian woman. It could have finished as a tale to be told to his mates back home. Along with the stories of the beggars, the trains, the sweepers and the crows. But as Gordon climbed into a nearby taxi, he knew that he would be back.

He knew that whatever else the future held, his story with Rohini had only just begun.

41

The cold war began again. Glaciers shifted around armchairs. Rohini was allowed out only to go to medical school and expected to return immediately afterward. Gordon waited for her outside the house a few days later, like a beggar at the gates. A beggar waiting to elope with a princess. Rohini saw him, climbed into the family car, looked through the window and said, "I love you."

It didn't sound right. What she felt was so much more complicated.

From that day onward a car dropped her off to her classes and a car was waiting for her when she finished. Her life in between was spent in a frosty, furious bedroom, demonstrating that she was not a part of the family that had shackled her.

Tulsi Devi tried talking to Rohini to make her family situation workable once more. "There's nothing wrong with Rohan," she said, attempting hard to balance the scales her daughter had kicked over.

But Rohini could think only of Gordon. Her mind always returned to him with the greatest fidelity, like a bee that has discovered the most exquisite pollen in one flower and can go nowhere else.

She rehearsed their future conversations, imagined his desperation without her, tried to work out what he was doing and what he was feeling at odd moments throughout the day. When he responded to her psychic pressure and appeared at the gates one day after a long break, her first reaction was not joy but anger.

"Jump in the car," she commanded, as if she were instructing one of the household servants. Instead of going to class, Rohini instructed the driver to take them to Gordon's hotel, where they found themselves in a room screened off from the others in a dormitory with high, open ceilings that listened.

They sat down on his bed and he told her that he was planning to go elsewhere, maybe to spend some time in Rajasthan alone. Rohini heard him out stoically at first, wondering where that left her.

"How can you leave me?" she asked.

"Because there's nothing for me to do here. And I'm never allowed to see you."

"You never make the effort."

"Listen. I'm only going for a month. I'll be back."

"If you loved me you wouldn't go for even a minute."

Rohini realized that they were having their first argument. A public one. She wanted to go home. To retreat to her world of fantasy where she could restage this drama and write her lines before she said them.

"I have to get home," she told him.

"Exactly! And if I go home with you they'll call the cops."

They looked at each other. One tear fell out of Rohini's eye and down her face.

"I've got to go," she said. "What's the time?"

From the other side of the screen came a voice. "Five-thirty, honey."

And they said goodbye again, because they had to.

Soon after that meeting Rohini went back to her world behind walls and Gordon left Delhi, as he said he would. This time to stay inside the fortress city of Jaisalmer near the North Western Frontier.

But nothing about India was the same now. He could feel the country slowly start to chew him up and spit him out. India irritated him. The chaos, the bureaucracy, the delays – all tested his patience and heated up his cool.

Three months ago he had cheerfully sat on a bus whilst the driver hijacked all the passengers and took them for a seven-hour detour between Rajasthan and Gujurat. They drove all over the country like happy hostages, helping the driver collect some bribes for a police fine. Now even a puncture delay of half an hour made him curse the Indian roads.

When he arrived in Jaisalmer, Gordon was no happier. The fortress city may have risen like a mirage out of the desert, but for him it was just another castle. One castle too many. He walked the streets without any joy or wonder as he looked up to see the intricately carved stone havelis with their magical pillars and courtyards. He kicked his bag impatiently while he waited for the hotel owners to boil up his water for a warm bucket bath. And when he was invited into the homes of the locals he made excuses to stay quietly in his hotel room. All this because he could not be with the girl he loved.

It worried him that here in the desert he was thinking of going back to England. Thinking about how it would be, to return to that far-off little island. And then what next? Would they ever understand that he'd changed? Would he ever be able to just settle down and narrow his horizons again after they had been so exploded by the East?

Rohini's time alone in Delhi wasn't easy either. A blood test under the name "Radha" confirmed what she had suspected. She was pregnant, and Gordon had gone. Who knows, maybe never to return? A month, he had said, and it was already six weeks. All her parents could talk of was bloody Rohan.

She wanted to spite them. To throw something in their faces so that they'd never mention his name again.

She chose her moment between split seconds to say it.

"I'm going to be having Gordon's child."

The words were out.

Tulsi Devi closed her eyes. Fear prickled her chest as she felt her own life repeat itself in her daughter. She shivered and looked over to Rohini's father, waiting for blood to be let, to pour freely like it had that night she had hidden from him, clutching her baby girl and her terrified, hysterical boy.

But the Colonel said nothing. Instead he looked silently down at his crutch, as if it might have some answer for him.

Rohini repeated herself, in case he hadn't heard; to rub it in further.

"I'm going to be having Gordon's child. For God's sake, say something!"

This time there was no storm. Worse, a hideous, wailing self-pity. Her father bowed his head down so low and wept so hard that Rohini thought he would collapse. He was knocked down. A cripple in body and spirit. He cried with the desperation of a man being killed slowly by the one he loved most in the world. He said nothing to Rohini, but went instead to lie down on his bed.

It was several hours before he was able to talk again. To speak the terrible words that were forced upon him by the return of the boomerang he had flung so far that night he'd finally rid himself of the burden of Jivan.

"We must find that wretch," he told Tulsi Devi. "We must force him to marry her and then I never want to see either of them again."

42

Rohini felt much better after she'd made her news public. She knew that her mother was obliged to be sympathetic. As for her father and Rohan, they could marry each other for all she cared.

It was Tulsi Devi who suffered most over those next few days. She felt compassionate, but her empathy was being squeezed from her by a snake that curled up on her chest and spat curses in her eyes. All she could see ahead of her was loneliness. A dead husband and two children in exile.

She was everywhere but where her body stood: in the past, regretting everything she had ever done; and in the future, a widow waiting for her curse to revisit her, wondering how it would next strike.

Sometimes when Tulsi Devi saw her daughter mooning around, she caught glimpses of herself as a young girl – her white convent sari floating on the surface of the Ganges, her belly patted lovingly by eunuchs. David De Souza's calculating hand laying her down on a bed of cotton …

And then Gordon showed up.

He met Rohini at the gates, kissed her eyes, her lips, her neck, her breasts, whilst the chowkidar watched, licked his lips and smirked.

"Let's go somewhere," Gordon said.

"How about to England?"

He stared at her. "You're not serious?"

"Gordon, I'm pregnant. We have to leave."

"Oh my God!' He loosened his grip around her to see if she was lying. No, she wasn't. He held her close again, but not tight. They walked out onto the main road and caught a taxi. He helped her in as if she were an invalid.

"Not to your hotel."

"No. We'll go to a real one to celebrate."

They were dropped off at the Imperial Hotel, famous for hosting important marriages. A palace compared to Gordon's backstreet hovel.

As they sipped tea and the bearers scuttled across the perfect lawns, they started to negotiate a future together in England.

"We'll go back to England overland by bus," Gordon suggested. "No, no. We can't. You're pregnant."

"If we go soon I'll be fine."

"Rohini, we can go tomorrow if your parents let us."

"They will, but we must get married first."

The wedding of Rohini and Gordon was nothing like the weddings celebrated at the Imperial Hotel. Or like the weddings Gordon had seen in the streets of Rajasthan. There was just enough ritual to make it legitimate and no pomp whatsoever, like her mother's own deflated version.

Gordon was summoned to a discussion to make formal arrangements, where his future father-in-law snapped his instructions.

"We'll buy you your clothes and then I don't want to set eyes on you again until the day of the wedding."

Tulsi Devi was more compassionate and offered to help him choose some clothes. She'd never stopped liking Gordon, but more than that, she was worried that he would back out now while he still had nothing to lose.

Rohini wanted to go shopping with them. To be near Gordon. The Colonel intercepted.

"You're not going to see this rascal again until the day of your wedding. He'd put another child in your belly if he could."

The man gave Gordon the creeps. What kind of a loving family would treat their daughter with such contempt?

It was beginning to feel like a wedding at gunpoint, with no romance, no respect and no love. His father-in-law would have been quite happy to see him walk around the fire seven times in handcuffs if necessary.

The day arrived and Gordon found himself catching a rickshaw to his own wedding, wondering if he was dreaming up this whole wife business.

He was dressed as instructed, but came without the usual fanfare of baraatis dancing through the streets. At the door he was ushered into the bedroom where he had stayed in the days when he was still a welcomed guest. Rohini's auntie Pyari gave him a warm hug, and tied a pale pink turban on his white head, followed by a curtain of little moongra flowers strung in short strands over his face.

"Is this so that they don't have to look at my face?" he asked, trying to work out if this aunt of Rohini's was on his side.

Pyari parted the flowers so that she could look directly into his eyes. "Indian, English, we are all the same. Our whole lifetime we spend hiding our similarities."

She pinched his cheek as if he were a young boy, innocent of all the crimes of which he stood accused.

Pyari brought him out and he saw her: Rohini, the goddess of the living room. A simple jewel placed on her forehead. Around her neck hung one of the most prized necklaces that Jyoti Ma had reserved for the wedding she had not lived to see. On each of his bride's fingers was a ring, with a chain linking to her bracelet. She wore a sari shot with purple and red threads and an elaborate gold border. Back in England she would have looked like a princess, but here in India she was just a little dressed up.

All Gordon wanted to do was kiss the bride, but all he was allowed to do was look. Rohini stared back at him. Not the coy glance of an Indian bride marrying an unknown man, but the sensual gaze of a woman who has seen every part of her lover. Kissed him naked, sucked him in, squeezed a child from his loins.

Only Pyari's family attended the wedding, but that was enough to fill the room, leaving only a small space for the pandit's fire in the middle. It was a short ceremony, with Pyari slowly translating all the Sanskrit promises. Promises that Gordon did not even have the choice to dispute. All the having and holding and paying for – lasting for lifetimes to come.

There was no dowry involved. None of the usual exchanges between in-laws. However, Gordon did receive one gift from Tulsi Devi. A large blue sapphire set into a gold ring. When it was handed to him Pyari whispered, asking if it was the correct stone for Gordon's astrology. Nobody seemed to know. Hadn't they realized that it was dangerous to wear a sapphire unless it had been prescribed specifically for its owner?

Nobody noticed the Colonel, who sat through the wedding procedure in body alone, looking down at his crutch instead of at his beautiful daughter. Then suddenly, after the couple had walked the havan fire seven times, the attention turned to him and he became the official father-in-law.

Gordon was sent to touch his feet as was the custom. Neither of them looked at each other. Gordon's hands lowered and then he hesitated. Should he touch the crutch as well? He did and the Colonel shifted it away swiftly, as if Gordon had touched an open wound.

When all formalities were through, the father of the bride stood up without saying a word and went off to his room to lie down. It was the last time the two men would ever meet each other face-to-face.

Part Four

Remember that in order to feel the full depths of life you must be empty. Bring Silence to the noise and you will hear the most subtle melodies. Always remember your Divine origins and you will live every moment with life in your hands.

43

Rohini and Gordon stayed at Pyari's house for the week between getting married and leaving India on a bus.

In that house they were received with great enthusiasm. They walked over patterns of flowers and petals to lie down together on their marital bed.

Pyari had utmost faith in their marriage and supported the newly-weds fully, taking Gordon aside and admitting that she too had made a "love marriage." But everyone, even Pyari, objected to the two of them taking off on a bus journey to England with Rohini pregnant.

They had been offered air tickets as a present, but Rohini was determined to do the journey that Gordon talked of so freely, even if she could only experience her country fully as she was leaving it. She wanted to make the most of this time when things seemed to be working out for her in her life. Even in getting pregnant she had created an escape route into a new world.

Last time she had gone to England over water. This time it would be over land.

The thought of returning to London was more exciting for her than for Gordon, who kept his reservations hidden beneath his outward love of freedom and adventure. He knew that when he arrived back he would have to make something of himself. He would soon have a family to support. His remaining days of freedom were too short for him to fully enjoy them; his parting from India too sudden for him to feel as if he had "found" the Truth, or whatever it was he had come searching for.

Boarding the bus was the start of the journey. It was like stepping into another world. There were travelers from all over Europe, all dressed like gypsies, carrying rolls of possessions just like the poorer Indian travelers on buses.

The inside of the bus looked like a gypsy caravan with rugs, colorful bedcovers, hookahs and tapestries traveling home with the foreigners returning to their old lives. There was even another pregnant woman (how Rohini would have loved to tell her family this), not just three months pregnant but seven months! And with her unmarried boyfriend.

Rohini could have felt quite out of her depth if it hadn't been for the friendliness of all the other passengers, who revered her because she was a part of the beloved India they were leaving behind. She was the one who had been given to them to make their transition into the real world easier. A living souvenir.

As the bus headed up toward the border with Pakistan, Rohini didn't look out of the window, but tried instead to acclimatize herself to the internal scenery. The culture inside the bus. She absorbed the philosophies, the language and the attitudes of these people as if by osmosis. Matching her vibration to theirs.

When she felt a part of it all, they traveled together as one in their own private time machine across continents.

She understood for the first time how Gordon was able to feel a part of the culture he was visiting, and yet still remain an observer. As they wove their way through different places she too felt like someone who observed and participated at the same time. An insider on the outside.

To ease herself into this new lifestyle, she experimented with their drugs, smoking and spluttering over hookahs. Gordon tried to stop her, but she scolded him for being so conservative. Even the baby didn't manage to blow the smoke from her lips. She wanted to experience everything. Now that she had agreed to this adventure she wanted it all, concentrated not diluted.

Gordon was amazed at how quickly she took to this life, knowing where she had come from, knowing what a leap she was making. His watchfulness distanced him a little from the others. Rohini was his to protect, but she seemed to be doing fine protecting herself.

Their bus, the friendly creature, took on a personality of its own as it made its way through different lands, passing people on the roadside who'd only ever lived their lives in one place. The Afghanis, Iranians and Turks stared at the bus as if it had come from outer space, a colorful graffitied wagon carrying an extraordinary bunch of tribal time travelers.

In every interesting place the bus driver – a Londoner named Reg – would stop if he felt so inclined. They took the time to wander around ancient cities, bathe in rivers, and wander through the local bazaars. Once in Afghanistan, one of the Cockney inmates, Joe, decided to lift a final souvenir from one of the market stalls. The tall Afghan in charge, with green eyes sharp enough to slice a lemon, caught him out and started threatening him. Joe dodged around the market, collecting all his fellow passengers for a quick and dramatic exodus. The bus left the scene of the crime like a thunderbolt, as if the vehicle itself was wanted for theft. The villagers watched as it flew over the mountain ranges and into the distance, everyone inside laughing and cursing Joe, singing songs and telling jokes about shoplifting.

They had adventures finding lost passengers, too. One single girl, Linda, had gone walkabout in Iran. The bus had to spend three days too long in the middle of nowhere to find her, and at long last someone recognized her behind black robes. She had fallen in love with an Iranian and was going to stay.

And so the bus moved on. Sometimes in the evenings, when Reg was too tired to drive, he would stop in the middle of a field and they would all pile out to stretch their legs and sleep under the stars. It was on one of these occasions around a campfire that Rohini learnt to play the guitar.

She took to it with flexible sitar-playing fingers. The notes were much easier to find than on the sitar. The melodies less complex. She found it easy to pick out the familiar ghazals she knew in Urdu and sing them to perhaps the most impressed audience she had ever had.

She realized that she was singing about her childhood dreams. But not even in her wildest dreams of love as a child had she imagined she would be where she was now, on her way to England, on this bus full of some of the best friends she'd ever made in her life.

Rohini was respected not only as the resident Indian and singer, but also, before too long, for her medical skills.

They were in the middle of Turkey in the mountain ranges when Rachel, the other pregnant girl on board, started to go into labor.

Rohini recognized what was happening before anyone else. She heard Rachel complaining of a stomach ache, saw her back arch with the pains. She'd seen it before. Then she noticed how low the baby was lying in Rachel's pelvis and worked out that it had reached its due date, even if its mother didn't know it.

She asked Michael, Rachel's boyfriend, if she could talk with Rachel for a minute. She felt her pulse, listened to her breathing and reassured her.

"Women in India give birth by the side of the road," she said, as some kind of signal that things had started.

"Is this it?" Rachel asked with trepidation.

"You'll have your baby in your arms in just a few hours," Rohini answered.

Then she went to the front of the bus and told Reg that they would have to stop and prepare for a birth.

Everyone except Rachel, Rohini, Michael and Gordon tumbled out of the bus, lit a fire and started making some dinner. From inside the bus they could all hear the campfire crackling, the guitars start playing and the singing of an enchanted and, for some time yet, footloose bunch of travelers.

Rohini had attended quite a few births but never as the person with the responsibility for making sure that the mother and baby came out alive. She felt confident, and felt the support of the child inside her own belly helping to bring its contemporary into the world. It wasn't medical knowledge, she realized, that was most important. It was her use of words. Her ability to make Rachel feel confident. She took to it with her intuition, loving the way they were cradled by the soft candlelight and lamps instead of the harsh hospital lights that she was familiar with.

Every now and then one of the travelers would come to the door bringing tea, snacks, hot water, incense – offerings of love to the laborers and the soul making its way into the world.

"Save your energy Rachel. Now breathe. A bigger breath when it's surging. Now make all the noise you want." It was as if she herself had gone through the process of birth, knowing it just from watching, and seeing the pattern now repeating itself. She remembered how Aakash had said to Ram that the body knew how to die – and she observed on this occasion that the body knew how to be born as well.

Rachel was in the most loving environment imaginable, without a thought for anything going wrong. She was managing it, knowing that she had a football team of supporters outside pitching for her. She needed to get through this for them as well.

After a while, as she and the night tired, she was no longer aware of anyone, even Michael. The pains were draining away her energy. It just wasn't possible to continue. She wanted help, drugs, anything to make it go away. Rohini reassured her, telling her that she was doing what millions of women had done successfully in the past. That all the women who had ever given birth were waiting for her to come out of it and through to the other side. It didn't matter where she was. Better here in the middle of nowhere than in a loveless hospital with nobody she knew to help.

Outside around the fire the others were quieter now. Lying down, unable to sleep, watching the stars and eternities beyond as they thought of Rachel. And then they heard a shivering shouting – a desperate sound in the Turkish night sky.

"Hold your breath now. Don't let the air out. You'll need it to push.

"Gordon. Go and get them to boil up some water and sterilize a knife." Rohini was totally in control.

Outside the excitement gathered and the travelers discreetly started looking inside into the front of the bus where Michael and Rohini were helping to hold up Rachel. The crease between her legs was gaping wide. She let out the most enormous grunt, then a yell which echoed against the quiet Turkish mountains.

The voices inside the bus continued talking hushed and calming words. Waiting for the first signs of life. And then it appeared – a silver gray head. She pushed some more. Ten more enormous pushes, with Rachel crumpled over her chin as she pushed down. The head came out. They all watched, holding their breath. This was it. One more push and the body followed.

The baby was a triumph. She was wrapped in cloths warmed by the campfire, and called Rohini after her impromptu midwife. After the birth Rachel was given massages by three different people and congratulated by grown men with tears in their eyes. She couldn't believe that it was all over, and that she had come out of it transformed into a mother, with a new human being that defied all boundaries of love and gratitude.

For Rohini it was the most magical and rewarding medical experience she had ever encountered. It would become a major influence in her later decision to practice home-birth midwifery in

England. Of all the births she had attended and marveled at in hospitals, none of them had quite held the sparkling humanity and compassion that they all witnessed at the birth of her namesake.

The bus stopped for three days in those mountains, for Rachel to strengthen and feel comfortable sitting. She was treated like the resident earth mother, and Rohini was made to feel like some sort of high priestess. The baby had the best start she could possibly have in life by being passed from person to person and absorbing the concept of independence.

Then they took off further into Europe, watching the scenery and lifestyles become more conservative as they edged their way westward. Slowly they were returning to the memories of their past lives. Returning to their previous reality which seemed no more real now than a comic strip. All of them shared the exact same feeling of displacement as they saw Westerners in their own countries, wearing drab clothes, living straightforward lives.

As they stopped off in different countries, they lost more of their passengers to the passing cities. In Paris, Jacques told the bus to pull up in front of a palace in Pont de Sevres and announced to all the passengers that this was his home. "What, this?" they all thought. "And that bugger was borrowing money from us all as if he were an Indian beggar!"

Halfway up the long drive that led to the palace, Jacques turned around and said, "Poisson d'avril, April Fool!" and made them all get back onto the bus. He was dropped off instead in front of a squalid building in the Latin Quarter.

They arrived in London in spring, when the crocuses and daffodils were sprouting out of the ground. Reg bought a round of beers for the remaining travelers in an olde worlde pub in Covent Garden and announced that it was the end of the journey.

Nobody quite wanted to leave. Nobody believed it. Their magic carpet had landed, and now it was being tugged from under their feet.

The barman had to declare closing time before the few remaining travelers faced the London air and made off in different directions, exchanging addresses and promises to meet again soon.

Rohini looked around. So much had happened to her since she was last in this city as a teenager. It didn't look as exciting as it had the first time. Nothing compared to the exotic towns and cities they had passed through on their journey from the East.

"Where to next?" Gordon asked. It was the resounding question on all their lips, and Rohini was still in a state of mind where she was happy to be taken, without questioning, in whichever direction the river flowed.

"Do you want to meet my parents, or see some of England?"

"Both. Why not?" *Why miss a thing?*

So they made their way by bus to just outside London where they could stand on a main road to hitch out toward Gordon's home in Dundon, Somerset.

Before they got there, they were going to visit Gordon's favorite place in England. He didn't tell Rohini where. It was a surprise.

Standing hitching at the side of the road, Rohini noticed how all the land around them was green; how the English fields snuggled up closely together. Unlike the starker landscapes that lay eastward, Gordon's world looked like a quaint little storybook.

"Will someone really stop for us?" Rohini asked, wondering how long it would take to hitch a ride.

A car pulled up, a corroded beast of a vehicle, driven by someone who looked familiar – a man who fitted into "the Beat generation" category, as Gordon described it. Together they drove further west and after nearly three hours Gordon told Rohini to look out as they passed over a hill.

"That's it. Stonehenge."

They abandoned their ride and made their way around grazing sheep and over clumps of grass to the center of the circle.

Rohini had never seen anything so primeval in her life. A temple made out of the land itself, dedicated to the land. No deity, but the sun entering it daily, blessing the sacrificial stone and moving on.

During her last visit to England she had seen only London, the capital of her country's former rulers. She had seen nothing of these Druid rulers from long long before the empire had even been dreamed of. She had no concept of ancient England – the wooded magical country of former years.

"Welcome to my home." Gordon bowed before her, the chivalrous Englishman.

"I'll live here any day. We'll buy some furniture for it!"

At Stonehenge they finally felt as if they had arrived in England. The undercurrent of the country was accessible here. The legend in the land. The wildness underneath the cosiness. The history that nobody could remember, because it spoke in symbols instead of words.

"Do you want to see Stonehenge in the moonlight?" Gordon asked.

He wanted it to be the perfect evening. They were the heroes of the age of Avalon. Gordon undressed Rohini under the sleeping bag and she shivered. He was Sir Lancelot and she was Guinevere. This was their land. She looked up at him and saw the stones circle his head, like a crown offering him its geomantic powers. He was set to prove that he was the land's best lover. He played with her, and then pushed into her and the earth that they laid on. She felt the ground under her and the stars caught in the circle above as part of her own body. A body with a kicking child inside it.

Soon after, some other travelers came along and set up some tents outside the circle, not wanting to intrude on their private shrine. Without thinking, Rohini got up and went over to make friends – and to invite them into the inner circle.

Gordon was silent. He had wanted to give Rohini a private introduction to England, but he was starting to accept that wherever she went, others would follow.

The travelers set up their tents next to Rohini and Gordon's makeshift bed, lit a campfire, played guitar, smoked a hookah. Gordon ignored them all evening whilst Rohini talked for hours, as if they were her soulmates. That night they all slept inside the stone circle, with giant stones at their heads, dreaming of lucid pre-historical images that would never be remembered during daylight hours.

Rohini awoke as if from a heavily drugged sleep. The sheep were bleating, the air was cold and their sleeping bag was wet with dew. This was unmistakably her first morning in England.

After saying goodbye to their companions of the night, they hitched again and reached Dundon, a small farming town built from the stone from that area. Gordon's family home, which he'd never spoken of, was the local mansion.

When Gordon caught sight of his parents' home he didn't just see a house, he saw his whole history behind those sad, suffocating stone walls. He saw himself as his parents did: a waster, a bum, a dropout. For a moment he wanted to turn back and spare them the disappointment of seeing him again.

Angela and John were upstairs packing their bags to go to Cornwall for a week when they heard voices downstairs. It was mildly irritating to have visitors just as they were about to leave. If it was the milkman they would pay him next week. He could wait.

Rohini walked into Gordon's house, feeling his trepidation in his tight grip on her hand. She looked at the stuffed partridges behind glass, posed in front of a background of the Norfolk Broads, and she felt the Englishness of her new in-laws before she met them. Nervous now, she wished that she wasn't wearing a salwar chemise.

Gordon kept telling himself that he was a free man, but everywhere he looked he saw stale memories of holidays from boarding school. Imprisoned years. He had broken free so why was he coming back for more?

"Act like you're just returning from the shops," he told himself. "You've grown up, man. They'll be glad to see you."

As soon as Angela got to the bottom of the stairs she saw her son, holding hands with an Indian girl.

She shouted out: "Good God, why didn't you tell us? Why didn't you tell us that you were going to go? Why didn't you tell us what you were up to over there? Why didn't you tell us when you were going to come back?" The questions came pouring out. And then: "Why didn't you come back earlier to get back to your studies?"

Gordon felt oppressed by his mother's unmet expectations. Rohini stood back, waiting for an introduction. She had never felt so foreign. Here was her new mother-in-law and she wasn't even able to touch her feet.

"Mother, this is Rohini." Gordon finally made his announcement and Rohini waited for more of an introduction. *I am your wife and also the mother of your child,* she felt like saying, but no further explanations followed.

Just then John came down with his bags in his hands. Seeing Gordon he first shook hands and then hugged him, stiff with formality.

Rohini was introduced to him, too, as just "Rohini." She waited to hear the word "wife" come from Gordon's lips, but he didn't let it slip even once.

"I presume we're canceling our trip to Cornwall, darling," John said at last as he picked up Gordon's old cloth bag and Rohini's suitcase and proceeded to show them into their separate bedrooms.

"Rohini, why don't I show you the bathroom so you can freshen up," Angela said politely. Rohini took it as an insult. *Your son is filthier than I am,* she wanted to say, but she knew that they were getting her out of the way so they could continue with their interrogation in private.

Later that evening Angela started making dinner. She gave her son the task of chopping vegetables and asked Rohini to feed the dog. Rohini said nothing. How could she explain to her new mother-in-law that she'd hardly been in a kitchen in her life, let alone kept animals or even eaten meat? She tried not to inhale whilst she spread out the offal for the German Shepherd fighting to get to the bowl.

"How did you and Gordon meet?" Angela asked, and Rohini waited for Gordon to tell the whole story. Instead he said, "Her mother is friends with Lily," and left it at that. Rohini excused herself and went to weep into the pillow of her single bed.

When dinner was ready Gordon went up to get her.

"I'm not coming down. They don't want me here," she told Gordon.

"Don't be silly, they love you."

"Why didn't you tell them we're married?"

"I will, just wait a while."

"And our child? Are you going to wait for the baby to announce itself, or are you going to say something?"

"Just give it time."

"Gordon, I don't think you realize. I've given up my country and my family for you, and you won't even tell them I'm your wife!" She was shouting now and Gordon was trying to calm her down so that his parents wouldn't notice the scene she was making.

Eventually Rohini came down and sat through a civilized meal of pork chops (left to the side of the plate) and vegetables (boiled with butter on them).

After dinner they talked around the open fire. Gordon told a docile version of his travels, and although he had always sworn he would never go back to his studies, he now started talking of his return to Cambridge.

Every so often Rohini noticed Gordon looking over at his father for approval. There was no mention of their marriage and no mention of their future life together. Disheartened, Rohini withdrew from the conversation, excused herself and went to sleep in her single bed, alone.

Angela went to bed soon after, to give the two men a chance to renew their friendship. She was tired and the events of the day had required such a monumental shift in the order of things.

Father and son continued talking by the firelight through the night, the sapphire in Gordon's wedding ring starting to sparkle a darker shade of blue.

44

Going back to Cambridge was something that Gordon did mostly for the sake of his father. If he could have put his father's name on his graduation certificate instead of his own, he would have done it just to please the man.

Back at Cambridge, Gordon's tutor at Trinity College was impressed. "Now that you've taken your education into your own hands what more can we teach you?" he asked, running his gaze down Gordon's attractive form.

"Sir, I would like to study Economics," he answered, feeling the pressure of those lascivious academic eyes.

"Well then, I'll be teaching you myself," he said, pleased to be spending some more time with this unusual student. Gordon, he felt, had more depth than the average boy who arrived at Cambridge straight from Eton or Harrow after only enough time to sample his mother's home cooking between leaving school and going to university.

Gordon felt his gaze. It was uncomfortable, but curious, and strangely enjoyable. He started describing his travels as if he had accompanied E.M. Forster on a grand tour of India.

To make university life more interesting, Gordon decided that this time he would have to get involved.

It was an effort at first, because he felt little affinity with the other students, who seemed to enjoy life at Cambridge with the frivolity of characters in an Evelyn Waugh novel. Nobody he met had experienced life as an adventure, as he had done. For him, Cambridge was a playground for overgrown kids, with its pranks on freshers and dons on dinner duty. The only place he found any joy was in the Anthropology Department. He spent many hours in the Museum there, looking at shrunken heads and dug-out canoes, artifacts which were neatly misplaced in a gallery with high ceilings and perfectly polished floorboards.

They had it good in the Anthropology Department. While he was busy studying complex monetary transactions in banks, anthropology students studied the economics of gift exchanges in tribal societies. Whilst Gordon studied supply and demand theory, they studied subjects like Death, Witchcraft, Love and Sorcery. Economics was the study of piles of coins in abstract. Anthropology was the study of Man. Better still, the study of Man embracing Woman.

Gordon saw the study of other cultures as a path toward "the radicalization of self-knowledge," as he called it. He started making a collection of ideas, which he would check out with Rohini to test her open-mindedness.

"Did you know that the Nuer in Africa are allowed to marry ghosts, and the Nayar women in South India are allowed as many husbands and lovers as they wish?"

"What are you suggesting?" Rohini asked. "Should I find a lover?"

"Not just one. Many. Why not? Marriage is a social construct just like any other."

Rohini looked down at her pregnant belly and burst out laughing.

No, she was not involved in this Cambridge world. There were never any pregnant bellies under those academic gowns. She was town and he was gown, and they only united when they were both undressed in bed.

She spent the days collecting things for their house (bought courtesy of John and Angela). He spent his days at Anthropology lectures. Her job was to wait and his job was to read Economics.

How often she blamed her loneliness on Economics ...

Rohini told nobody about her loneliness. Not even her mother. The only letters Tulsi Devi received from England were from Gordon's mother, Angela.

When the first letter arrived, Tulsi Devi opened the envelope with trepidatious fingers, expecting bad news. She was charmed, however, when she read it through. It told of a life quite unlike her own, and through these letters she made the acquaintance of relations in England whom she would never meet.

Tulsi Devi wanted to involve her husband in their daughter's life, so she decided to read that first letter out loud to the Colonel. When she reached the part where Angela invited them to go and stay in Somerset, he stopped her, saying, "She's gone, woman, don't you understand? Once I'm dead you can do what you want, but while I am alive, she is dead."

And then the letter arrived announcing that the dead girl had given birth to a daughter, named Saakshi. She weighed seven pounds seven ounces, had her eyes wide open at birth and a full head of hair.

On reading the news Tulsi Devi cried tears of joy and longing. Her desire to be in England with Rohini was as strong as her desire all these years to see Jivan, and she wondered – was she a grandmother already without realizing it?

A new surge of life was just what the house needed, for it was dying. Having lost one half of her life in her early years, Tulsi Devi had now lost her other half, leaving her with nothing but a rancid husband. Worse still, nowadays the Colonel was almost entirely bed-ridden and growing cataracts in both eyes through sheer refusal to look at his new world order.

No matter what, the letters kept arriving.

After a while, a desperate letter arrived from Rohini. "Mama," she wrote, "you have no idea how hard it is to look after a baby without an ayah. Saakshi is an insomniac. An angel in the daytime and a howling werewolf at nights. I am so exhausted I hardly have the energy to feed myself anymore."

Tulsi Devi took the letter to Pyari and read it out loud. Pyari, forever practical and reassuring, pulled some of the infinite numbers of strings at her disposal to start up a genuine puppet show: the sending of an ayah from Maharashtra, India, to Cambridge, England.

It was expensive, because a large deposit had to be given to the Indian government to send Vandana overseas, but there was no question of whether the money should be spent, just as there had been no question for Jyoti Ma about hiring Lily many years earlier at Prakriti. It simply had to be done. After all, Rohini hadn't so much as cooked a meal for herself before she left India. Until she was married she had never even picked her clothes up from the floor where they landed, and knew nothing of how those clothes returned nicely folded to her cupboards. Until the age of ten, for goodness sake, this child had never even had to bend down to do up her own shoes!

Vandana – a village woman with the face of a wicked stepmother – arrived in Cambridge escorted by a friend of Pyari's. She was instantly suspicious when she saw that Rohini's dwelling was humble, with none of the luxuries of the Sundernagar house. Here they sat on the floor on cushions, not on chairs. And this Indian girl was married to a foreigner. Why?

For Rohini the arrival of Vandana was a blessing. Gordon was out all the time at lectures, and in the evenings often with friends, escaping the responsibilities of parenthood. Rohini was besotted with Saakshi, but she fast realized that she was not a full-time mother. Her earlier life – the time before she discovered Gordon and freedom – suddenly felt like the most carefree days of her life. She was free in those days to do something for herself. To go to medical school instead of raising children for a man who was now doing all the studying instead of her.

She missed India. She missed her parents. She missed her father especially, knowing he was torturing himself with anger. She missed the warm weather in the wintertime. She missed her friends who were all at home now, either getting married or having children. It made her think about her brother Jivan, who was living in this cold country somewhere, maybe not so far from her. But how could she even start to look for him?

What she needed, she realized, was an occupation. Something she could throw her heart into. She could go back to medicine, but her qualifications to date were Indian, and useless. (How could the anatomy of an Indian be so different for them to insist that she start afresh?)

But did she really need to become a doctor?

After her experience delivering Rachel's baby in Turkey, she had an idea that she should study midwifery instead. There was something more intimate about midwifery. It felt closer to life than anything else.

With this plan in mind, Rohini started her studies once more, leaving Vandana to look after baby Saakshi. Many hours of the day she was out at the hospital, often staying with laboring women long after her shift had finished just so that she wouldn't have to hand over to another midwife in between her patients' contractions.

In complete contrast, there was one bow-tied obstetrician at the hospital who was hardly ever seen attending a birth, except in the last two minutes of second stage when he would arrive like a hero, catch the baby and claim all the glory. Once on a full moon, when the maternity ward was packed, he was left alone to handle a woman screaming through transition. Rohini went in to assist him just as he lost his patience and slapped the poor woman across the face to keep her quiet.

This doctor made Rohini even more determined to specialize in practicing home birth and stay away from the medical profession. He was also one of the main reasons why Rohini worked harder and longer at the hospital to see that her patients got the care they deserved.

Meanwhile the carer of her child was slowly going mad. Vandana had become suspicious of all white people. Whenever she was left in the house alone with Gordon she thought he was going to make a pass at her. She even slept with a knife next to her bed in case he did.

Every day she spent indoors, suspecting that all British men were rapists. As a result, for the first three years of her life Saakshi hardly ever left home. She stayed inside a two-bedroom house in Cambridge, England, learning songs from villages in Maharashtra, and speaking Marathi far better than English.

While Saakshi stayed indoors, Gordon went out, not like most fathers into the world of nine-to-five, but into a surreal playground with cobblestones and cloisters, sherry parties and tutorials. His feet hardly touched the ground as he parked his bicycle in a pile with all the others, and walked through the noble gates of Trinity College, past the Porter's Lodge and into Trinity Great Court in all its glory. There was something in those stone walls that allowed Gordon to deny reality, as thousands before him had; something in the spiral stone staircases, their steps worn down in the middle from the weight of England's aristocracy.

Then there were the men in bowler hats, called "bulldogs," who chased students outside college walls after hours. How could they be real? Or the mummers who performed plays in the street, like a spectacle from the Middle Ages.

Gordon appreciated Cambridge for its eccentricity. He accepted the fact that the air he breathed there was of mythological substance. But even so, Cambridge was a struggle for both him and Rohini. They were older than the other undergraduates, past their sell-by dates. They were biding their time and waiting for the pieces of paper that would qualify them for the world.

When Gordon sat his final exam in his third year, Rohini and Saakshi waited outside the regal examination hall with a bottle of champagne and a big question. "What next?"

Gordon had an idea that he shared with Rohini later as they quietly drank champagne on the back lawns of Trinity College while Saakshi splashed her feet in the Cam, watching the lovers, punters and pranksters celebrating the end of exams. It was an idea that would take them back to Asia. An idea that would involve a generous donation from Gordon's parents and a chunk of Rohini's inheritance from the sale of Prakriti.

"Saakshi, how would you like to go to India?" Gordon called out. Saakshi didn't answer. She was too busy watching a student with a bucket of water on Trinity Bridge, waiting to drench a kissing couple on a punt down below.

The idea was to buy goods in India and trade them in England. Regardless of what Saakshi might think of the plan, it settled well with the champagne in Rohini's head. She lay down next to Gordon on the prickly mown grass and kissed him as she took off his gown. They were free again. As free as they had been when they left Delhi on the bus that day on the way to a new life in England. She thought of their return. Tried to imagine the country she had left behind as she lay there in the pink Cambridge dusk, with a daughter in a world of her own, and a husband back in her world after far too long away.

They kissed again and held each other close and plans were made in love to return to the life they knew.

When Tulsi Devi heard of their return she felt sick with anticipation, but sick too with sadness that the man who needed to see Rohini most was too stubborn to realize it. She could not share her joy with her husband, and it was clear to all that Rohini's visit would have to be a clandestine one. Nonetheless, as soon as she had an arrival date, Tulsi Devi watched the clock for days, impatient with its slothfulness.

Rohini and Gordon reached India, this time respectably by air, and were picked up by Pyari's driver. Pyari herself was getting too old now to go to airports and the like. When Tulsi Devi received a phone call telling of their arrival, she slipped quietly out of the house.

"I am going to visit Pyari masi, she is not at all well," she told her husband as she left, trying to disguise her excitement.

"We're all half dead now," he answered, but nothing could dampen Tulsi Devi's feeling of joy as she made her way to meet with her daughter once more.

Rohini and Gordon waited near Pyari's gates, thrilled to be back in India, enjoying the luxurious scent of tuberoses that grew in the garden, breathing in the thick smells of Indian air, waiting to see Rohini's mother again.

As soon as Tulsi Devi's driver turned into the drive, Rohini climbed into the car and was given the warmest homecoming embrace.

Then Tulsi Devi saw Saakshi, who was clutched tightly in Vandana's arms. Not a baby but a little three-year-old girl. She had her mother's beauty. Not with jet black hair, but brown hair and blonde highlights. A little half-Indian girl. A stranger whom she loved instantly just for being her daughter's child.

Tulsi Devi coaxed Saakshi out of the arms of Vandana to sit on her lap.

"Who are you?" the little girl asked her grandmother.

"This is your nani!" Rohini exclaimed in child-speak, as if she were introducing her daughter not to an elderly lady but to the Mad Hatter or the March Hare. "Nani is Mama's mama!"

Watching her daughter with Saakshi made Tulsi Devi think about the time she had brought Jivan home to Prakriti. She remembered her own mother's alarmed reactions. The way Jyoti Ma had wedged distance between herself and her grandson. It made her think of Rohini's father back at home in bed, so near to his daughter yet unable to share the joy of meeting her again.

The reunion at Pyari's was small but precious. They all told stories about what had happened after their lives had parted, and Rohini was quite overwhelmed with nostalgia for the country that she now returned to. They talked about Cambridge, about midwifery, about Vandana (in English so that she couldn't understand). And then the conversation turned to the Colonel and his ailing health.

Once Rohini discovered that her father was going blind and was virtually unable to move from bed, she insisted on going back home to see him.

Tulsi Devi was protective. "Beti," she said, "if I see you pushed away again my heart will break and so will yours." She knew what it meant to be rejected. She knew it was something that could never be fully survived and she did not want her daughter to be forsaken. But after much persuasion Tulsi Devi finally did agree to a meeting – with one condition. Rohini could only see her father if she did not talk.

Tulsi Devi knew that the Colonel's cataracts had blinded him and that without any words he would not know the difference between his daughter and his wife. That his daughter would be as invisible as she had been all that time in England.

So Tulsi Devi, Rohini and Gordon left Saakshi behind and went to Sundernagar for the most understated homecoming ever. Entering her home like a trespasser, Rohini felt dispossessed and strangely alien in all the familiar places. Furniture had been moved around. The portrait that her mother had made her sit for in Simla was no longer on the wall. All the framed photographs of her as a little girl had been removed from the shelves. Only when an excited Dhruv appeared from the kitchen and touched her feet did she feel as if she was home. She wanted to hug him, but instead pulled him back up into a standing position and told him not to say a word to saab about her arrival.

Just then the Colonel shouted out, telling the beaming Dhruv to go and bring some curds and send in his wife. They all looked at each other. The Colonel called out loudly once more. Without a second look at her mother, Rohini got up and went to his door, walking into the semi-darkened room, a nervous but loving imposter.

"Just come and hold my hand," her father whispered, as if to his wife.

Rohini gladly went to hold her father's hand, looking into his blinded eyes. He said nothing whilst she stroked his hand. He just listened to the silence in the space that separated them, sensed the caring in her touch and the youth under her skin. After some time of just being there, saying nothing, Rohini gently put his hand onto his chest and left the room. Tears squeezed out from beneath the cataracts – the tears of a man imprisoned by his own love.

"We can go now," she told her two anxious conspirators in the living room. "I've said goodbye to Papa."

During that time in India, Gordon and Rohini made all the contacts they would need to start an export business. They met the Tibetan traders in Jan Path, and ordered boxes of turquoise jewelery, mandalas, rice paintings, masks, prayer bells, pipes and other desirables. They bought miniature paintings from Rajasthan, sandals from Kolhapur, pearls from Hyderabad, handbags, clothes, scarves, rugs, everything. They even met with a woman called Anjali and looked at a range of deity sculptures and temple carvings that she sold from her house.

"Who is this Anjali?" Tulsi Devi asked. "Is she tall and thin?"

"Yes, and very old and very stingy," Gordon added, not knowing what dust he was unsettling in his mother-in-law's memory. For a moment Tulsi Devi was a young girl again, adrift. A young girl in Anjali's house drawing pictures of pregnant nuns.

"You mustn't buy anything from her," Tulsi Devi said, her voice croaky and uncertain.

"Why not, Mama?" Rohini asked. "You'd love her collection."

"These statues must stay in India," she insisted. "Please promise me you will buy *nothing* from her," said Tulsi Devi, her face unyielding, her hands shaking.

It seemed like a strange request, but they both agreed that they would not buy from Anjali, even though they knew her sculptures would make the biggest profits.

They managed to take everything back to England with them. Everything except Vandana, who had taken a vow never to leave her country again for as long as she lived. Saakshi didn't want to leave her side. Their last two days together they sang Maharathi songs and cried in each other's arms. Vandana was told to go to the shops when the time came to leave so that Saakshi would not cling to her and refuse to go home with her parents.

At Pyari's gates, just as the three of them were piling into a taxi to go to the airport, Tulsi Devi took Rohini to one side.

"Try and find Jivan. Just see if you can."

It was a last minute request. To Rohini it sounded so cheap. So casual. So devastating. In an instant it left Rohini with a burden bigger than all the possessions they were taking back to England with them. She could feel her mother's desperation in those words. The longing and the remorse. And she felt guilty, too, for not having tried to find Jivan all this time herself. For not knowing where to start.

"Where do I find him, Mama?" she asked. "What is his surname? Where in England does he live? Is he even called Jivan anymore?" She wanted to add one more question through her tears. *Why the hell did you give him away in the first place?* But she couldn't bring herself to be so cruel. As it was she left a wide empty space behind her as the taxi pulled out of the drive to go to the airport.

45

Rohini and Gordon arrived back in London just in time for the dawn of the Age of Aquarius. Suddenly everyone was talking about India. Everything they sold was fashionable. The market stalls they ran in the early days in Camden Town, Portobello Road and Covent Garden were like temples for the hippies. Long-haired men and women in flowing robes would come and talk to them, feeling the silk scarves and holding up the hippy skirts with stars in their eyes. Hippy children with their addresses taped to their clothes would come and talk with Saakshi who played nearby. Everything Indian was hip, and they were the peddlers of the new era.

Rohini loved it, making friends with everyone she sold to. Gordon had his reservations. Going out to India had been wild before everyone was doing it, but now there was a trail that went there and back. Worse still, there were more and more people making money doing what they were doing.

But for Rohini, London was the place where everything was happening. She would sit on the stall wearing one of the kaftans she sold, and everyone would want to come and talk to her. She loved the hippies with their long hair and beards, looking like sadhus and yogis kidnapped from India and painted white.

During that era they went to open-air music festivals, be-ins and demonstrations. She discovered more and more about the counter-culture and its people. She learnt about communes and wanted to take her family to live on one. She also learnt about free love, perhaps the most dangerous lesson of all.

The friends that Rohini made were invited into their lives. They had a big house in Chelsea that Gordon had bought from a woman who had run it as a boarding house and brothel. After throwing out the debris, pulling down the partitions and cleaning out the condoms it became a cosy family home.

As soon as they moved in Rohini started turning her house into a gypsy caravan. There were tapestries from Gujurat in the corridor, wedding canopies from Orissa on the ceilings, rugs from Pakistan on the floors, and the walls were covered in paintings from Mysore and Tanjore. People would walk inside their house and immediately feel free to put on some music, light a joint, take off their clothes or go off into a bedroom with a lover. The house became the home of free love instead of paid love.

Rohini blossomed in that house, but Gordon felt as if they were losing their private space amid the collection of colorful people who gathered there. Some of them he really liked, but he hated the way Rohini's attention was always directed outward. The way he was considered uncool for wanting to spend the evening alone with his wife.

In place of Vandana, Saakshi was minded by a string of hippy friends. Her favorite was a man who called himself Seeker. Seeker used to sit her down and draw her portrait in charcoals, telling her about venereal diseases and reading her the problem pages in women's magazines. But the coolest thing about him was the way he saved his chewing gum on the side of his neck, attached to a few stray hairs so that it wouldn't fall off.

One summer Angela and John offered to take Saakshi for two weeks at Dundon. Gordon had planned it as his and Rohini's own personal summer of love. Saakshi left in the morning, and by the afternoon Gordon, Rohini and a couple of friends went to drop their first tab of acid in Hyde Park.

They were debating whether this stuff really worked when Rohini felt the grass at her feet start turning into a liquid green sea – and with it went the security of everything she had trusted as her reality. She was divorced from herself – her body felt like a puppet, her own limbs felt like strangers. The colors around her were so intense they scraped against her eyes. Gordon's voice became a speeded-up tape recorder. "You've turned into a cartoon," she told him and pulled out a mirror from her bag to prove it. Gordon started gazing into the mirror, slipping into a parallel universe as he looked into his own eyes and fell down a chute into the glass. Rohini looked at him watching himself in the mirror that he held right up against his nose. The whites of his eyes had turned black. "Stop it!" she ordered. Stop what? She was a hostage on this roller coaster now and forced to look at everything her consciousness conjured up for her.

They passed a soapbox at Hyde Park Corner. A long-haired bearded hippy with flared pin-striped pants and no shirt was dancing and preaching some garbled manifesto about love and freedom.

"I want this trip to finish," Rohini said, looking up as she felt herself being watched by a large tree with finger-like twigs. She could sense its frustration. It was an angry tree, hating how it had been anchored like that to the one spot.

She'd never felt so far from home, from everything she knew. And so lonely. Gordon was no help. He just kept saying, "Rohini, if you can't handle acid you can't handle yourself."

Coming down from the trip some hours later Rohini felt as if part of her was missing. She hated that experience of being rewired, unable to banish the warped field of reality that treated her perceptions as toys, laughed at her sense of sanity, gloated at the spirit that dwelled in her body. Gordon raved about the experience and sat down that evening to write an essay on his discoveries.

Somehow after that LSD trip Gordon grew to enjoy the constant flux of visitors that came to the house. Whilst Saakshi was still away they threw a party. They invited about forty people, but over two hundred turned up. All friends of friends who had heard about them and wanted to join the blast. One woman came wearing an amazing transparent crocheted bodysuit. On close inspection she was wearing nothing at all – her clothes had simply been painted on, just like her blue eyeshadow. By the end of the evening many of their guests walked around the house naked as they served themselves drinks and made themselves comfortable. Gordon was giving an impromptu lecture about re-educating the mind in the corner of the living room. A blonde woman had her hand on his thigh.

Rohini watched Gordon. He'd taken something – she didn't know exactly what. She saw him holding the hand of a woman who sat next to him, but instead of feeling sickened she felt strangely impressed, as she had been in India. Here he was, taking one step further over the frontier. Not one part of her wanted to go up and slap him. The vodka she had drunk was telling her to do the same. With anyone. It didn't matter. Just to experiment.

Gordon saw his wife conducting her experiment in the hallway, kissing a man neither of them knew. At first he was shocked and angry as he stood right next to them and Rohini continued her passionate kiss, unaware of her husband within breathing distance. Gordon felt like punching the man, but instead he left the house and took to the streets of Chelsea alone.

The next day he said nothing to Rohini about the party. He pickled his anger and stayed irritated with her for several days. All thoughts of free love turned to thoughts of confined hatred. Before Saakshi arrived back in Chelsea with Gordon's parents he turned the house upside down to eliminate any signs of their summer of love. He spent the whole afternoon with his father showing him a five-year plan for their business, whilst Rohini and Angela chatted about Saakshi's summer holiday.

During those days of advanced bohemia, Gordon busied himself with an exit strategy. He was one of the few people who realized that a house bought then for ten thousand pounds would be worth a million some years down the track. He bought a grand collection of houses in Chelsea, Bayswater and Fulham that their hippy friends would kill for in later years.

Looking back at this time in her life, Rohini never remembered Gordon's frustration. It was a golden era for them and for their marriage, or so she thought. They went backward and forward to India. Saakshi started speaking Hindi. They spent a lot of time out in the sun, so it must have been sunnier, and they must have had more time. Everything seemed easier. People stopped to think. To explore. To expand.

It was during this time that Maharishi came to visit London. Rohini took Saakshi with a group of friends to hear him talk. "This man," she told her daughter, "studied with my grandfather and uncle at the ashram of the Shankaracharya. He was a follower of Swami Brahmanand Saraswati, the Guru Dev you hear your nani talk about."

Maharishi sat cross-legged under a banner titled: "The Spiritual Regeneration Movement." A king of transcendence, garlanded with flowers, talking about the inner glories of life. "My mission in the world is spiritual regeneration," he said. "To regenerate everyone everywhere into the values of the spirit." His eyes glimmered as he told the audience that enlightenment was not just the birthright of yogis in the Himalayas, but the birthright of everyone who sat watching him in that hall.

His words gave his body a boundless presence. He radiated happiness. Rohini was awestruck, watching his fingers toy with some beads at the end of the mala he was wearing whilst the other hand held a flower. "The world is the Divine made active, everything rising as a wave on the eternal ocean of bliss consciousness," he said. Her eyes caught his for a second and she felt a rush of love for this person, as if he were family. Maharishi finished his sentence and started laughing in rapture. Laughing, perhaps, at how he had been tricked into coming down from the hills because of one single word he kept hearing in his head: *Bubaneshwar*. How from Bubaneshwar he had ended up on a wave that transported him around the world.

Rohini held her breath and then burst out laughing with him.

After the lecture she wanted so much to go and chat to him. To talk not just about his message, but about her grandfather and uncle. To catch up like family members. But she didn't have the patience to make it through the crowds of people who hung around, intoxicated by Maharishi and unable to leave.

On the way home Saakshi asked a lot of questions. She hadn't got the bit about enlightenment. What was it exactly?

"It's a higher state of consciousness, darling," Rohini told her daughter.

"Do you get enlightenment when you grow up?" Saakshi asked.

"Of course, darling," Rohini answered absent-mindedly, concentrating on the car that was doing a U-turn up ahead.

It was a turning point in Saakshi's development. Accidentally, she had discovered that enlightenment was her birthright. That she too could be like Maharishi when she grew up. It was just a matter of time before the magical man she had just seen would help her.

Soon after Maharishi's visit, Rohini was inspired to return to her practice of midwifery. She approached her re-found direction with trepidation as she remembered the bow-tied doctor who had slapped one of her patients; remembered how he had always made her hands shake as she stitched up the women who had labored in that Cambridge hospital. No, this time there would be no doctors to slow down her patients' progress. She made a decision and stuck to it: home births or nothing.

Amongst her network of friends nobody wanted to have their babies in stirrups anyway. Women had choices. They could have their babies in their own beds, in the garden or in the living room, underwater or under the stars, listening to chanting, with candles and incense burning and close friends around for good vibes.

Once her decision was made she was quick to find clients. Her rapport with women in labor was quite unique. She had shamanistic powers. A healing touch inherited from a grandfather she had never met. An appreciation of water births from a mother who had birthed a child in the Ganges. Rohini could communicate with women in labor like nobody else, meeting them at their threshold of pain and breathing them through it so that they could feel even more pain and welcome it. *Oh yes, she was alternative.* She would make women walk through the streets during labor without allowing them to show that they were in pain. She would climb into birth pools naked with her single-mother clients and embrace them as if she were the father of the child.

Delivering the next generation confirmed a principle that Rohini had always held as significant: *nothing about life is predictable.* Each child she delivered came into the world with a different story.

The most unusual babies chose her to be their midwife. And the mothers who came to her presented her with the most unexpected conditions. She was the only midwife she had ever come across who had delivered two babies from a woman who had two wombs.

There was one birth in particular that changed Rohini's focus from arrivals to departures.

Clare was four months pregnant when she came to Rohini, because, like all the other clients, she had heard amazing stories about this Indian midwife. Again, hers was no ordinary case.

Six months before getting pregnant, Clare had lost her mother. "Don't ask me why, but I'm convinced that the soul of my baby is my mother reincarnating as my child," she told her midwife.

Rohini offered total acceptance. Not because she was an expert in reincarnation. She had never given it much thought. She accepted Clare's story totally because what was important to her was her client's experience of the pregnancy and birth, not her own. And so she wrote down under Patient History: *Fetus of reincarnated mother normal size for 20 weeks.*

Clare invited her to a seance. At first Rohini went just to support her client. Nothing much happened that first time, but then she went with Clare to a spiritualist church where a medium got up onto the stage and started pointing at people in the audience.

"You, the Indian lady, there's someone standing behind you right now. Wait a minute, she's saying something." The medium put her hand to her head. "Something about an elephant! Does that make sense to you?"

"Yes, *yes!*" Rohini was so excited. This was better than the aghoris.

"She says she's your grandmother. Did she live on a farm?"

"Yes!" Rohini was gripped. She tried to imagine Jyoti Ma standing behind her and was transported instantly from the little suburban shed where she sat to the hills of Prakriti.

"She says that the elephant never forgets. He is the protector of your family."

It was the strangest experience ever for Rohini. Strange because of the place where she heard it and strange because it was not the sort of thing that Jyoti Ma would ever say to her. But stranger still, how could this medium possibly have guessed that her grandmother had lived on a farm? Let alone the fact that she had an elephant in her life?

Before the waterfall of questions could start pouring, the medium had moved on. "You, the gentleman to her left, I'm hearing something now about bowling. Did you have a brother-in-law who liked bowling?"

All the way home Rohini felt the presence of spirits and this feeling that her grandmother was helping her. She tried to work out what her nani had meant about the elephant always remembering, treating it like a riddle to be dissected.

When she got home she told nobody of the experience, but her mind was always on the spirits. She took a Ganesh statue from her collection of Indian artifacts and kept him near the front door to protect the household.

When it came time to deliver Clare's baby, instead of being fully present at the birth she tried to feel the presence of Clare's mother in the spirit world, or other helpers. She knew it was going to be a difficult birth. Clare was forty and this was her first child. She was the editor of a political magazine and totally open-minded – however Rohini knew all too well that it wasn't the mind that had to open for the baby to push through.

Rohini first heard that the labor had started when Clare rang to inform her, with mathematical precision: "My last contractions were ten minutes apart, the previous set were fourteen minutes apart. I think you should come."

As Rohini drove to Clare's home she kept asking herself, *how do I get Clare to let go*? She heard the answer as a voice speaking clearly inside her head. "Tell her a story," the voice said, "as if she were a little girl."

Rohini couldn't explain the incident – in those days she had never even heard of clairaudience. Nevertheless, she continued to listen for the voice as she held Clare's hand and wiped her forehead with cold flannels.

When Clare stopped progressing, Rohini, self-consciously at first, started to tell the story of "Little Red Riding Hood." Contractions started again with full strength, and after an hour of storytelling, Clare was fully dilated and delivered her baby to the story of "The Princess and the Pea."

At every birth thereafter, Rohini would try to feel the presence of spirits – even finding herself asking them for help whenever there were complications. It seemed to work, this telepathic arrangement. Once, when a baby was born blue, she asked the spirits to intervene, and as soon as she had, the baby started to push his blood back out to the peripheries of his body, like a butterfly pushing blood into its wings for the first time after leaving the cocoon.

It seemed natural for her that spirits would want to attend a birth, because the newborn was coming from their world and needed all the support it could get. Sometimes she would even ask the mothers she was delivering if they could tune in to the helper spirits. (If the British Medical Association had learnt about her new angle on home birth there would have been a veritable witch-hunt to stop her from practicing.)

Often during long labors Rohini would sleep for an hour whilst the woman labored on, and on one such occasion an older spirit appeared in her dream warning her about a tighter cord. Sure enough, the baby was born with its cord around its neck.

These things, little incidents all in all, amounted to a strong belief that the work she was doing was important. If the soul didn't die when the body dropped off, then the divide between the two worlds, she believed, was simply a window with one-way vision. A window that allowed the spirits to see what they needed to see and help when help was needed. For Rohini this window was always half open, and in later years all too much of her time was spent peering out toward infinite distances on the other side.

46

Saakshi always wanted normal parents so that she wouldn't stand out. She craved anonymity, but there was nothing ordinary about her. She never tried to hide when she was undressing for sports like all the other children. She never had anybody to talk to in the lunch hour. Instead she sat under the oak tree in the playground, her jumper stretched over her knees, hoping nobody would notice that she was unpopular. When it came to lunchtime she tucked into Indian food in an Indian tiffin carrier whilst the other kids ate sandwiches out of lunch-boxes.

"What's that? Dog food?" one little boy asked her once. "Mum says they always serve dog food in Indian restaurants."

In the junior school, when the children found out that her mother was Indian, they called her a "Paki" and asked her which corner store she worked in. She hated it and told them all that her father worked in an office. "What is he, *the cleaner*?" one vindictive little eight year old said snidely, whilst the other schoolkids tittered. Nobody was allowed to talk to Saakshi, everybody agreed she smelled. "How often do you take a bath, Paki?" they asked.

Saakshi always refused to cry in public. Instead she would go to the toilet in the cloakroom, sit down on the children's-sized pot and weep brave children's tears.

She made only one friend at her junior school, a girl called Dawn who told Saakshi that it was unfair to tease people because of their race. "You should never call black people black," she told Saakshi. "It's much more polite to call them tinted." Her one friend went to live in Manchester four months later, and when she had gone Saakshi decided that she would have no more friends and no more enemies. She even took two baths a day just in case being Indian really did make her smell.

When her mother dropped her off at school she would make sure that Rohini didn't come further than the end of the road, and then she ran the rest of the way so that none of the children could see her with her mother, brown skin and all. It was an entirely different story when Gordon came to pick her up. She would make him wait outside the gates holding her hand, whilst she pretended that she was waiting for her friends to come out. Needless to say, no friends ever came out. The children walked past her without even noticing that her father was white.

Saakshi's eighth birthday came along and there was nobody to invite to her party. She wouldn't have wanted anyone to come home even if she did have friends – then they would all know without a shadow of doubt that she came from a weird family.

Years later, when being different counted for something, she found herself blessing those kids for allowing her to escape the conformity of their circle. "Remind me to write and thank those naughty little English racists," she told her husband in another life. "If they'd loved me I'd be one of them by now and *god* would I be boring."

But without the wisdom of retrospect, being unworthy of her peers had a bad effect on Saakshi's studies. Gordon and Rohini kept changing her school to see if she'd be happy somewhere else, but her ninth and tenth birthdays came and went and there were still no friends to invite home for a party.

Everything changed when Saakshi went to high school – Godolphin and Latymer School for Young Girls in Hammersmith. She decided the day before the start of term that she was on an equal playing field. As she sat in the car on the way to her first day at school she told herself, *Nobody has any friends. Nobody knows I smell.* She imagined herself making more friends than anyone else. Winning friends as if she were in a race.

It worked. She was at the pinnacle of popularity. The girl that all the other girls wanted to sit next to in class – always up the back, being naughty, being brave, making her newfound friends laugh. She taught them how to have seances in the sick room during the breaks. She passed on all the wisdom about venereal diseases that she had learnt from Seeker, her babysitter. She was the only one with the courage to put her hand up and ask her elderly religious knowledge teacher, "Miss, are you still a virgin?" (Even though she regretted her question when her teacher admitted, through tears, that she was.) Saakshi was also the first to run out of school to the mosque for a smoke, the hallowed and most private smoking ground for the sixth formers. And then keep guard as all her friends took that first leap Out of Bounds.

She was still in her first year but she was determined to be the naughtiest girl in the school. By her third year she was regularly taking time off to go to Soho with her friends, put ten pence coins in the smut machines and giggle in the backs of the stores at peepshow obscenities shouting out, "Oh no, you've got to be joking. YUCK, that's disgusting!" The shopkeepers, who had seen it all before, would let her posse of friends continue perving, calculating that a handful of coins earned off schoolgirls in downtime wasn't anything to scoff at.

But those were innocent days, and the school was delightful for Saakshi. She started to do well, even though her home life was fast crumbling.

Her father spent much of his time overseas now, exploring new markets. India had been done to death. There was a smarter look coming in. Angular haircuts, high collars, padded shoulders, plain colors. It was

Zoo were fast asleep she was alone with the souls of those swamis, being guided through the knowledge that was her birthright. Enjoying the kind of Silence that speaks profound wisdom.

She even found a book of Maharishi's and inside saw a photograph of the magical man she had seen all those years ago and prayed to many times since. The sadhu with the flower and the beads who laughed like a man drunk on bliss. She read from the page where it opened: *That great, mighty current of evolution which is advancing the life of everything in creation is simply invincible – no one can resist it.* It was a portent. She knew then that she would have to jump into the current and swim. To bathe in the spring from which we all draw life. There was no other way forward for her. She had, after all, inherited her great-grandfather's questions.

Tulsi Devi had entered a silent spell after the death of the Colonel. It just didn't seem right to leave her there, staring off into empty space. Going home was out of the question. So Rohini rang Gordon to let him know of her plans to stay, booked Saakshi into a nearby school for one term, and settled back into Delhi life.

It was an education for Saakshi, quite unlike the one she had been receiving in London. Her new friends were Dia and Rita. They had never once smoked dope, run away from home in the middle of the night, or talked to strange people in the streets. But she loved their company anyway. They shared their own extravagances with Saakshi, such as Hindi movies, shopping, tailors and beauty parlors.

Rohini enjoyed revisiting her girlhood friends, and even managed to track down her best friend Damayanta who was now married with four children. Damayanta took Rohini to her club. Out on the lawns a familiar face started making his way over, keeping eye contact with Rohini. He came closer. She knew him, but from where? The man didn't look away once. He demanded recognition.

"Hello Rohini," he said, in a deep voice. "It's been so long." He knew her name. He looked at her as if he owned her.

"Rohini, you must remember Rohan," Damayanta prompted, seeing that Rohini had traveled more than just time and oceans to forget the face that now looked so intently at her.

"What all are you doing now, Rohini?" he asked, with the brash confidence that Delhi bestows on its menfolk. Then, without stopping for an answer: "I hear you are living in London." Rohini answered him, not failing to notice that he was more handsome than ever.

Rohan continued to talk about himself, the advertising agency he ran, and the glories of television campaigns for Doordarshan. Before going back to his wife and two teenage children further down the lawn, he gave Rohini his telephone number, and said, "Come, let's go out for a drink some time, yah?"

"He never got over you," Damayanta said, and continued with the gossip. "His father made him marry the very next person they found to save face for the family."

Damayanta wanted to know everything about Rohini's life. "How is it for an Indian over there?" she asked.

"Damayanta, I couldn't come back. It's my home now whether I like it or not."

"Of course you can come back if you want. You'll find work in a hospital here and Gordon will find some business."

But how could Rohini even start to tell Damayanta about her rift with Gordon. The mistakes she had made. How she had so thoroughly enjoyed making love with Taos. How she liked to deliver babies on the kitchen floor. Damayanta would only be able to imagine her own kitchen, complete with servant. Or maybe she was more open-minded. Maybe she wasn't giving her friend enough credit. Either way, Rohini was back at home with the taboos of India and happy to remember the way it used to be in her day.

Later on during that extended holiday in India, Rohini found birthday cards to her father that she'd made and he'd kept. They read more like love letters. All those years ago she had practiced love on her father, she thought, crying tears onto the faded paper that held her words. She also found old diaries and poems he had kept, all of them written by a young girl who had thought she would wake up to her fairytale future with a kiss from a handsome prince.

Rohini thought of Gordon, and how they had each been drawn to the culture of the other. She thought about how she had stretched her own culture like an elastic band until it had snapped back in her face.

She missed Gordon. She missed everything they'd had together. In that Sundernagar house every woman had her yearnings for elsewhere, for other, for beyond.

Tulsi Devi missed her husband, and thought of how they had grown old together. She remembered how easily he could be moved to tears – he who had been a stalwart of the British Army. She remembered, too, how he had fought his own demons to be worthy of her love. How eventually he had held no victory dearer than his wife's happiness. Over the years she had softened him, and he in turn had taught her how to expect more from a man than what was offered to her as a last choice. He had been her savior, first through suffering and then through love. He had saved her from her past, making her feel acceptable and respectable in her own eyes, and in the eyes of the world. All these things he had done for her, and only now was she able to thank him.

47

Gordon was enjoying his family-free time in London. He thought about Rohini as much as she thought about him, but absence was making his heart grow harder as he remembered only the most caustic moments they had shared together. Ironically it was one of Rohini's friends, Joanna, who made his time of separation so delightful. Joanna had taken him to a backstage party at a West End theater, where he had met Hilary, the leading actress. Hilary was an English rose, with strawberry blonde hair reaching down to her waist, the perfect smile of an air hostess, and large eyes of child-like blue. She was very English. The kind of fantasy girl he might have dreamed up when he was fourteen, before he looked up from his world to see that the sun rose in the East.

With many months ahead of him to enjoy the affair, Gordon felt like the free man he'd always preached he was. Free that is until a few nights before Rohini arrived home, when his pleasure, mixed with guilt and resentment, stirred up such a complicated cocktail of emotions that he vomited continuously for two days in anticipation of her arrival.

When his family returned from India, he told Rohini about Hilary the first evening they reunited, remembering how his wife had done him the kindness of being so direct and open about her affair with Taos. It was a moment he had been waiting for. Not just for some kind of churlish revenge, but because he knew that if he didn't confess, everything would come out in the wash anyway, dirty sheets and all.

"Isn't she that dull actress who always plays the bimbo?" Rohini had said casually, but inside her senses shrieked silently in frozen panic.

She tried to play it down. To make out that it was just a passing fling, like hers had been. But the very image of her husband lying naked with another woman left her so cold she could hardly bring herself to talk to him. Her indignation was futile, she realized, having been the first to trespass. So instead of trying to resolve things, she found herself being cruel. Gordon's response was to slam the door and go off to meet Hilary at a bar, at the theater, or at Ronnie Scott's. In Hilary's company, Gordon was no longer held hostage to the ideals he'd held dear a decade ago. He was a new man. An adored man outside the home and a hated one within it.

"You're a lousy husband and a pitiful father," Rohini told him as he left one day mid-argument. The door slammed. "You're deceitful, inconsiderate, heartless and I don't know why the fuck I love you."

Rohini's pain was so unbearable she could only spit poison at the man who was making her feel it. She too had been careless with their marriage, but somehow she felt that she had never betrayed him in her heart. Yet here he was, walking away, leaving behind no love in the home that they had shared all these years. Breaking the threads that had bound them, caring nothing for the little family that lay split open at the seams.

Whilst Gordon was busy conducting a very English affair, Rohini had never felt so close to India. She felt very Indian about this marriage, she realized, now when it was too late. She was Indian and an Indian woman only ever has one husband. If Gordon didn't already know that she would show him.

As their love soured, Gordon found the promise of Hilary sweeter and more alluring. Saakshi wasn't told about her for quite some time. But she felt it in their words, in their silences and in the distance between the two of them. She saw it in her mother's beautiful face when Rohini looked in the mirror, awaiting Gordon's return. And then in her bitter face when she saw him at the door, fresh and enthusiastic after a meeting with his new love.

Rohini often thought about how she could regain the stronghold over her husband's heart, but the cement between him and Hilary seemed to be firming up so nicely, she felt powerless to crack it. Only Saakshi had the ability to graffiti her name on that cement before it dried up. Only she could pierce his impenetrable heart. They would have separated there and then if it weren't for Saakshi.

For the sake of his daughter, Gordon dragged out the marriage, promising to leave one day in the future. It wasn't a date Rohini could put in her diary. For her there was nothing definite about it. Not like a due date for a baby. But this day of reckoning lay ahead, like a tempest on the horizon.

One day when Rohini was able to swallow her own bitterness and talk to Gordon, she found herself appealing to him gently, reminding him of the sanctity of their marriage.

"But I was forced to marry you at gunpoint!" he told her. "We were both too young to know what we were doing."

"It was still a promise for life."

"And you promised me that you would always remain my faithful wife," he replied, his voice a hard critical reminder of her own broken promises.

Sometimes Gordon would think about the consequences for Saakshi. He was choosing greater happiness for himself and sacrificing hers in the process. That much he knew. If Hilary hadn't given him all the time in the world to leave his wife, he would never have been so brave or so cruel.

Hilary moved into one of Gordon's houses in Chelsea and he started oscillating between her house and his bedroom in the office at home. Rohini would lie in their marital bed, willing him to come and join her, but he never slipped even once. Rohini even let herself into his office once, in a fit of desperation, just so she could be near him. He was disarmed in that moment and felt her softness as she cradled his hands in hers and said: "Don't you believe that if you've loved someone and shared some really special times with them, it's always possible to love them again?"

Gordon didn't answer. He knew she was speaking the truth. Rohini had touched him like no other woman ever could and he knew that if he softened now, he would break his resolve. She had the power to melt him if he surrendered now, but he had made a decision, mostly through fear, and he was very businesslike about the way he stuck to it.

"I'm not the right person for you, Rohini. You'll find someone. You will," he answered, putting the present moment between them and the time they had shared together in the past.

Rohini could have had any number of men to please her and fill the gap in her life, but she didn't. That was her decision. If she couldn't have her husband, she would have nobody.

The day of reckoning arrived when Gordon moved his wardrobe over to the other house. From then on he came only to visit Saakshi. Rohini saw how his eyes and hugs were only for his daughter, and felt envious. He seemed so thoroughly satisfied in his new life. Whenever she looked at Gordon she could see no reflection of her own suffering. Whenever they sat as a family over dinner, she saw him as if across the Great Divide, and found herself regretting that she had ever allowed him to steal her heart in India.

Rohini had never been a good loser. The only person who could replace the love she had lost now was Jivan, her brother. He was somewhere in England, she felt it. And she felt an urgent need to meet him – to restore a part of her own pride and happiness in this land that seemed so foreign now. He would understand her, because he was the only person in England who had known her before she had even fully opened her eyes.

Her tragedy could never match his, but she felt her own suffering demanded that she find him. And so she wrote a letter to her mother, saying, "Ma, I'm ready to look for Jivan now. Please give me all your support and love."

Several weeks later a letter arrived from Tulsi Devi. She had gone to the orphanage where Jivan had been sent, but the benefactors, Shiv and Rekha Kapoor, had long since passed away. She had written to Ram, her brother who was lost to the hills, and he had told her that Shiv Kapoor had promised to settle Jivan in a family of equal caste and affluence. "My beti, if you can find him, I will be able to die in peace," Tulsi Devi wrote. "Wherever he is, God give him strength. And God give you strength too."

All of that strength, but still no further clues.

Rohini often talked to Saakshi about going back to India to backtrack, to interview every living person in Delhi. Her mother was too old. She had given up holding out the lantern of eternal hope. It was Rohini's duty now to find Jivan. If she couldn't repair her own mistakes, at least she could attempt to repair her mother's.

Often when Rohini had a spare day she would drive from Chelsea to Southall. Would Jivan be there? Probably not if he had come to England with a very affluent family, but nonetheless, Southall was closer to home. She would lunch on channa chola followed by rasmalai, savoring the feeling of being an Indian amongst Indians. Then she would walk into sari shops, spice shops and sweet shops, asking people if they knew of a man named Jivan with a bad leg. Punjabi Sikhs, women who didn't speak a word of English, onlookers, would all join in. "Try the Gurdwara," one person suggested. But what was the point of asking in a Sikh temple? Jivan was a Hindu ... Rohini corrected herself. Jivan could be anything. Even a Mormon by now for all she knew.

Driving back from Southall one day, she started toying with the idea of Divine Intervention. The men and women of Southall couldn't help her. Her own mother couldn't help her. Only prayers could bring together two grains of sand washed off from the same rock. Maybe it wasn't so unreasonable to expect a miracle. Maybe miracles *required* some sort of expectation before they could manifest? Then it struck her. Why not ask a medium at the Spiritualist Church? Weren't the spirits always telling people to search for missing money in teapots and under floorboards? Surely there would be someone over there on the other side who could see through the illusion that separated her from her brother?

Rohini booked a private sitting with Dora Hindes, a medium who had been recommended by several people she knew. She was the best, they said.

The meeting started non-eventfully. The first thing that struck Rohini about Dora was her ordinariness. She was one of those women who didn't have a haircut, she had a coiffure. Her nails were painted coral, and an old-fashioned paste brooch clung to the lapel of her jacket. Raised in Tunbridge Wells, she had never been overseas, but she had traveled often over the waters that separated the living from the dead.

Dora wasn't young enough to be open-minded, and yet she was fully open in mind, body and spirit. So open that only a few minutes into the session she went into a gentle yet very powerful trance. Her eyes closed and her head hung low. When she lifted her face once more, it held the noble expression of someone in full command of the elements, a sheen over her eyes and a still gaze which took in not just Rohini, but everything else in the room, with equal focus.

"There's someone here who says that he's your grandfather," she announced. "He says that he has come out of the deepest silence to speak." Her eyes were still not fixed on any object in the room, but seemed focused instead on the space between all objects. One eye looked flat and glazed; the other was penetrating, its lid sinking low like a crescent moon.

"He says that he is finding the layer between absolute and relative values now. This is the layer of Truth, he says and he must talk to you only from this place."

Rohini interrupted, like someone speaking fast during an international call. "Tell him I am looking for my brother. If he isn't in the spirit world already, where is he?"

At that moment something even stranger happened. Dora's body started to shake, and Rohini went into a panic, terrified that it was her fault for disturbing the dead. Dora opened her mouth again but no words came out. Again she tried, and then a voice that was not her own articulated through her mouth. *"I will help,"* it said, speaking with the voice of Aakash. And then she lost him. He had gone.

After the session Rohini gave Dora twenty pounds. It seemed an odd exchange: the spirit of her grandfather for twenty pounds. And odder still, Dora refused the money. "This is the first time I have ever channeled a voice," she told Rohini. "I feel there's a reason why it all happened this way."

Dora sensed that Aakash would come back for her, too, and she was right. This was just the first meeting of many that would make Dora Hindes into one of the most famous mediums in the country.

Rohini was flattered and a little embarrassed. She wanted to know if they could summon Aakash back, because she wanted him to be more specific. But Dora had returned back to her normal self, and her eyes had fully recovered their everyday sparkle. She offered a cup of tea and Rohini found herself telling the medium what precious little she knew about her grandfather.

From that time onward Rohini felt resolved in her search for Jivan, fully trusting that Aakash would fulfill his promise and help her. She also asked the spirit of Aakash to help her in every aspect of her life. She asked him to help her by looking after her mother. She asked him to help give her strength to raise Saakshi. She asked him to help her find things that she'd lost, in the same way that the Catholics prayed to Saint Anthony. Everything that she had lost except Gordon's love.

One day Saakshi went missing. It was nine o'clock in the evening and she still hadn't come home from school. Rohini was speaking out loud to Aakash to help her find him as she rang a few of Saakshi's friends. They were all at home with their parents, alarmingly safe and with no idea of Saakshi's whereabouts.

Rohini started to blame herself. She imagined how she would feel if Saakshi did not turn up the next day. Or the one after. She thought about ringing Gordon, but didn't. What if Hilary answered? And then Gordon would blame her for being a slack parent. But Aakash could help. She begged him to aid her, knowing that from where he stood he could see everything, even the whereabouts of her missing daughter. After half an hour of psychic pleading, she received a phone call.

"Darling, where are you? I've been worried sick," she said.

"Mama, I'm at Bhaktivedanta Manor in Ilford and I'm staying the night here in the Hari Krishna temple."

"What?"

"I met some Hari Krishnas in Hyde Park and –"

"You're coming back to Chelsea right now. I'm phoning for a taxi and I want you to get in it as soon as it arrives, do you hear me?" Rohini's worry made her voice angry, and that puzzled Saakshi. Why should her mother be so worried? She was staying the night with a bunch of celibates who neither took drugs nor drank alcohol.

It had all started when Saakshi took the day off school to go to Hyde Park with a boyfriend called Ben, who had taken some acid. Out of nowhere a royal Indian chariot had appeared, carrying a deity. Over the green English grass it rolled, trailed by a band of pink-faced Hindus, dressed in dhotis and Indian shirts. It was the Jagganath Rathayatra – the festival when Lord Krishna is brought out of the temple and taken on a trip outdoors to look at the kingdom. And there, what should he see, but an eighteen-year-old boy on acid and a sixteen-year-old half-Indian girl on the lookout for love and spirituality.

Saakshi and Ben joined the procession, following the sounds of cymbals, enjoying the lunacy of the dancing, high as kites, with a band of gypsies singing "Hari Krishna, Hari Krishna, Hari Rama, Hari Rama."

Later, when the procession stopped for a while, Saakshi and Ben started talking with one of the Hari Krishnas. As Ben listened to stories of how Lord Krishna had fought evil serpents, he couldn't stop thinking, "I can't believe these guys are in my trip." Then one Hari Krishna started proselytizing, telling Ben and Saakshi that they lived in a Godless society: that life without God was an illusion, offering nothing but birth, death, old age and disease. The only redemption was to chant the name of the Lord so that he was always on the mind, and renounce all the senses. Stop taking drugs, stop drinking alcohol, stop having sex.

Saakshi remembered her Krishna stories from the vedic comics she had read as a child. Hadn't Krishna had thousands of wives and stolen clothes from the cow girls whilst they bathed in the river? What sort of a celibate was he? It was a bit of a letdown – all that fun for Lord Krishna and none for them.

One of the Hari Krishnas invited them both back to their temple to have some food. Saakshi looked over at Ben and saw him slowly greening out. When they met again a few days later, he explained that he had thought the Hari Krishnas wanted to take them back to the temple to eat them up.

So Saakshi went alone, back to the temple in Soho, a celibate's haven in a city of sin. It was staggering at first to see English men and women lying prostrate before a Krishna idol. Seeing English and American women with white saris and blonde hair, fanning a deity who would have been happier to sit next to a radiator should he have manifested in England.

The food was free, served from large buckets after being first offered to Lord Krishna, and strictly vegetarian, which was cool by Saakshi. Rohini had started eating meat occasionally since she arrived in England. "Spirit says it's all right to eat meat if you bless it first," she had told her daughter, but Saakshi could never bring herself to wrap her lips around something that tasted of blood and slaughter.

"Why should we kill an animal for just a few minutes of taste sensation?" one young Hari Krishna asked her.

"No reason," Saakshi said and looked closer at the man. He was about twenty-four and handsome. A Roman nose (or was it a broken nose?), bedroom eyes (not for display in the temple), and no hair, which only made his eyes even sexier. "What did you do before you became a devotee of Lord Krishna?" she asked.

"I was a truck driver," he told her, and she wondered what sort of a road he would have driven down to arrive here. What had gone wrong? A jilted love? Too many drugs? Too much traffic?

He told her his story. His name was Ishwar Das (previously Jim). He had always wanted more out of life. His soul was never fed at the truckstops when his belly was. Whenever he got what he thought he'd wanted, he found no satisfaction in it. Ishwar Das was looking for the meaning of life. He had some big questions but nobody wanted to listen to them.

The more they talked, the more Saakshi felt herself relating to his experience. It sounded like some kind of existential crisis. And it was a background feeling for her as well – a constant unreality behind a staged life.

She talked with Ishwar Das all evening, long after the other guests had left. Then Shanti, one of the women devotees, asked Saakshi to come with them to Bhaktivedanta Manor. So Saakshi went along for the ride, and enjoyed the eccentricity of the experience as the evening continued. She realized that she thought in a similar way about lots of things, and she found friendship in what they shared.

But then she rang her mother, and received her summons to return. As she went to tell Shanti she wasn't allowed to stay, she found herself exploding into tears.

Shanti put her arms around Saakshi. "You are going to be a devotee. Nothing can stop you. It will come to you. But you must obey your parents, even though they are living in ignorance."

Saakshi's tears were uncontrollable. It was as if her mother had told her that she could not step out on her own path toward enlightenment.

"You are a sincere searcher. Nobody feels this strongly after their first visit here. Wait and see, Krishna will look after you. It is your karma that brings you to Godhead."

When the taxi arrived, Saakshi climbed in reluctantly, dizzy with tears, disorientated by the day's events that had taken her from a babysitting adventure for a day tripper in Hyde Park, to a Hari Krishna temple on the outskirts of London. She watched the taximeter rapidly clock up the pounds as she backtracked toward Chelsea.

Rohini paid the taxi without any comment and instructed Saakshi to go to bed. They would talk about these adventures in the morning.

The next day Saakshi woke up with revenge in her heart. When her mother started to talk about the previous night's adventure, she started to sing loudly: "Hari Krishna, Hari Krishna, Hari Rama, Hari Rama."

"Saakshi, you left school in the morning and you didn't come home until nearly midnight!"

"Hari Krishna, Hare Krishna . . . " Saakshi continued, now onto the gospel version.

"Saakshi, you're not listening to me. If you won't listen to me, you'll have to go and live with your father."

"Send me. Anywhere is better than here."

"He'll be stricter –"

"Hari Rama, Hari Rama, Rama Rama, Hari Hari . . . "

That summer Saakshi became a Hari Krishna. Not a real one, but a closet one. It reminded her of the time she went out with some friends who were teddy girls and she dressed up in a puffed skirt for the night. They called her a "plastic ted." And now she was a "plastic Hari Krishna."

In the mornings she sold books in Oxford Street and gave away free meal tickets to invite people into the temple. Every lunchtime she ate with the other devotees, sitting on the Soho floor as the buckets went around. She chanted "Hari Krishna" at every spare opportunity to focus her mind on the life immortal that ran through her veins. And at no time did she ever tell her mother where she went.

Rohini met with Gordon over lunch and it was decided that Saakshi would live with her father over this difficult period.

The changeover coincided with an incident at the temple. One evening while the Hari Krishnas were performing their daily song and dance, Saakshi started dancing closer and closer to the men, particularly Ishwar Das, who danced closest to the Deity, his muscular legs flattered by his skimpy white cotton dhoti. Some of the women tried to encourage Saakshi toward the back of the temple where the women danced, but she kept going to the front where the brahmacharis danced, more ecstatic and buoyant than the women huddled together at the back.

After the Krishna party was over, she was taken to one side and instructed by a pale po-faced woman on her improper behavior. "You must stop talking to Ishwar Das," the woman said. "Can't you see that he's a practicing celibate and your attentions are distracting him?"

That was the end. From then on Saakshi swore that she would never go back to the temple. She felt insulted as a woman. All she wanted was a man who was as rich in spirit as she was, and they had humiliated her for this simple, primal desire.

Saakshi went to live with Gordon and Hilary just as the winter cold swept through London, causing people's happiness levels to sink a few degrees lower. She needed a break from Rohini, so they parted with consent, but as she walked out of the door with her father, Saakshi was hit by a wave of regret. She felt like a deserter, leaving like her father had. Leaving *with* her father no less. She knew that her mother's relief would soon melt into loneliness and she was right.

"Bye Mama," she said confidently. And when she realized that her mother wasn't going to answer, she added: "If we get killed around the next street corner, at least we'll know that we said goodbye! So long, adieu."

Gordon took Saakshi to her new home, six roads away from the one she was raised in. He was trepidatious. Saakshi was fully enjoying her disruptive phase, flaunting her mother's genes at their worst. He hoped that she would tread carefully in his house, get along with Hilary, and try not to upset the fine balance he'd spent the past two years creating.

To Saakshi's initial disgust, Hilary turned out to be the perfect stepmother. On the nights when she wasn't on stage she'd come and sit on Saakshi's bed and they'd have long talks together about serious subjects such as boys, drugs, music and love. As it turned out, Hilary was also the only person who took an earnest interest in Saakshi's future career. It was she who first took Saakshi around the art schools, bought her a decent camera and encouraged her to study photography. It was Hilary who set up a darkroom for Saakshi in the house and encouraged her to plaster the walls with her photographs (blown-up ants, grains of rice, parts of the body). Hilary would also try to get Saakshi talking about her feelings toward her parents – something that Gordon continually avoided.

"Do you miss living with your mum?" Hilary asked once, over a plate of sushi.

"Do you miss living with yours?" Saakshi asked back, making certain that Hilary got the message.

Saakshi was never prepared to talk things over adult style. Her parents were involved in a cold war, and she felt as if talking to Hilary would be like talking to the Berlin Wall. She could wail against the wall all she liked, pray to it that her parents would get back together, but the wall would still be a wall.

Whenever she thought about her parents and their relationship, Saakshi could feel the winter cold freezing them all into their various states of separation.

There were only a few shopping days left till Christmas. Men in duffle coats and fingerless gloves had already started selling roasted chestnuts on the pavements around London. The shoppers in Oxford Street smiled cheerfully as they knocked people over with their bags of presents. Mr. and Mrs. Santa looked out from shop windows, so jolly that everyone was spending well. It was that time of year. Women wrapped presents in a fluster of ribbons, paper, bells and candles. Carol singers sang of mangers and cattle in every central tube station. And Saakshi was faced with the terrible decision: where should she have Christmas lunch?

Rohini had planned Christmas lunch for the two of them back in November and Saakshi had agreed to spend the day with her mother, but now there was a better offer. Gordon and Hilary were spending Christmas in the Caribbean and they'd asked her to go with them.

When Saakshi went around to her mother's house to tell her the bad news, Rohini was alone. That always made her feel guilty. Rohini seemed to be alone all the time now. How could this have been the house Saakshi had grown up in, with strange bodies in every room each morning? The only social interaction Rohini appeared to have nowadays was with those Spiritualist Church people. Seances and the like.

When Rohini opened the front door her eyes lit up with joy, which made Saakshi feel all the more guilty about breaking the news. She gave away the consolation prize quicker than she'd intended. "Mama, will you come and hear me sing at the school carol service tonight?"

Rohini had nothing planned. She never did, unless one of her clients was giving birth; so that evening she sat in the school hall with the other parents. From the distance came the sound of angelic voices – *"On this day earth shall ring, with the sound children sing ..."* – and slowly the singing grew louder as the girls wove through the school corridors and into the darkened hall, each bearing a small candle.

Rohini was sitting next to the aisle and she picked Saakshi's voice as she approached, turning to see that her daughter had tears in her eyes. Rohini reached for her handkerchief and dabbed her own eyes dry before any of the other parents could see her being so sentimental. Then Saakshi's voice was replaced in turn by the different voices that passed by, singing *"Edeo o o edeo o o, edeo, gloria, in excelsis deo,"* and her daughter went up onto the stage with all the other girls to sing about the joys of Christmas.

It wasn't until after the concert that Saakshi told her mother that Christmas lunch was off. Rohini shrugged and started thinking about what sort of present would transport itself easily to the Caribbean. It was an invisible turning point in her life. From that moment onward, she started to push her daughter away, to protect herself from the disappointment that comes with heartbreak. Without being aware of it, she was propelling the very last person out of her life.

Rohini spent that Christmas in isolation, until the evening when one of her clients went into labor. If it hadn't been for that baby she delivered in the early hours of the morning, Rohini would have spent the whole day without seeing a soul, a midwife left on her own to celebrate a birth that took place nearly two thousand years earlier.

Part Five

When I lived my life, I lived amongst mountains. When we reunite, we will live together – you from the forests, you from the plains, you from the cities. We will live in harmony and abundance and we will invite the Gods to come and join us.

48

I didn't spend Christmas with Mama until ten years later, when I rang in early December to let her know that I was coming back home from Australia to introduce my man, Jason, to the family.

Even this time, I had a better offer.

We could have been celebrating Christmas on a beach house on the south coast of Australia. Next to a still lake surrounded by casuarina trees, dropping their needles onto a soft sandy bed for lovers to lie on. We could have been swimming naked in those still lakes with their black swans – nobody to disturb us but the ripples on the water and the tumbling grassy globes that roll over the beach. I could have been walking with Jason in the spotted gum forests that tower up the gentle hills, up toward Tinten and the Araluen Valley.

But I'm doing none of this. Instead I'm sitting on a plane with Jason, making a slow descent through the thick gray smog that hangs over Heathrow Airport.

"The weather in London is approximately five degrees centigrade. On behalf of the crew, I hope you enjoyed your flight with Qantas and we look forward to serving you again soon," sings the stewardess. It's the last Australian voice we're going to hear for some weeks, apart from Jason's. That much I know.

The plane is slowing down and my body is filling with anticipation. This is the country I have loved and hated, and left. This is the country I have managed to avoid for the past ten years. I'm ecstatic to be here, but also strangely deflated, if that's possible. London looks so grim from the skies. I'm tired. And nervous. I'm feeling so protective of Jason. I can't bear to see such a beautiful sun-kissed man forced to wrap a thick scarf around his neck. It doesn't seem right.

As we walk through Customs, Jason goes through the passageway marked ALIENS and I am ushered into another one for Britishers. "No, no, you don't understand. I'm an alien here," I tell one of the airport officials and jump over the rope that divides me from Jason, so that I can grip his hand and share my trepidation.

Jason is nervous too. "Do you think your parents will approve of me?" he asks.

"They're much more likely to approve of you than they are of me," I say, and we both laugh together, nervously.

Rohini stands anxiously in Arrivals. She has no idea what to expect of this man who is returning to England with her daughter. She's seen a photo of him. A big smile, big chest, big blue eyes and a curl garden sitting on his head. In the photo she's placed under a magnet on her fridge door, Jason has a large casual arm around Saakshi and a look of utter devotion in his eyes. But what if the camera had lied?

It looks promising, but Rohini can't help remembering the others before him. The Russian man in his forties whom Gordon called the "Loose Rouble." Saakshi had been crazy about him. And so surprised when he announced he was going back to live with his wife in Moscow. Then there was Peter, her boyfriend from art school, who ended up dumping her at a police station one night when they all got caught staying the night in a squat. And then Ben, who had threatened to take an overdose if she left him.

For so many years, Saakshi had preserved her naivety and optimism, going into every relationship as if she'd just met the man she was going to marry …

There's only a thin misty glass wall separating me from my mother now. I hold my breath as I turn the corner to expose my presence. We're walking down the arrivals queue now, searching a sea of eyes. At the very end of the line I see her.

There's only a split second to adjust to the changes the years have drawn on Mama's face, and before I've finished matching the mother I knew with this slightly older version, she's already hugging Jason.

"Darling, you look so much older," Mama comments.

"So do you, Mama," I answer, too late to screen my words.

"No, but it looks good on you. You look mature."

"Well, I grew up, didn't I? I'm allowed."

We drive back to Chelsea and Mama starts talking to Jason, not about England but about India.

"You must make sure that Saakshi takes you to India soon. My mother is getting very old, and you really ought to meet her."

"Mama, why don't you go back and live with her? Somebody has to."

"How can I?"

"Tell her, Jason," I say.

"What?"

"About India."

"Oh yes, there's this project that the Australian government is sponsoring – a complete redesign of the Delhi sewerage system. I've been offered a job on it next year if I want it."

"But Jason, that's wonderful, you'll love India. You must go. Everyone must go, at least once in their life."

"Mama, you should go too," I interrupt. "Nani needs you there now." Surely she can see this much.

Mama is silent. I know what she's thinking. There's no life for her there now. She's a divorcee. As far as they're concerned she's failed as a woman.

When we arrive at the Chelsea house I start making my way up to my old bedroom.

"No, not in there, darling. I'm putting you both in the middle room."

I walk around the house. It's haunted with memories from the past. There's a picture of me on Papa's shoulders in front of the Ajanta Caves. Then I see one of my "early works" from art school on the wall – a photo essay on my parents entitled "Commitment." God, I was cynical. What did they make of it? Oh, and here's another early piece. A painting made out of old rolled snot titled: "What's Art and what*snot.*" Delightful!

When I walk into my childhood bedroom I freeze over.

Not a corner of the room is lit. The light switch has been unhinged and a thick black curtain covers every inch of window. The four walls trap the impenetrable darkness around a long glass object in the middle of the room. I shiver and slam the door shut again to enclose that atmosphere, to seal it away.

"Mama ..." I'm trying not to show my panic, but I'm virtually screaming. "What's happened to my bedroom?"

"Saakshi, calm down, it's not your bedroom anymore."

"But what's been happening there?"

"It's our seance room. My circle sits there once a week or so –"

"It's become a spook's room!"

"Stop making fun of me. I've put you up in the middle room, all right?"

Later on, when Jason and I are lying together taking a rest, I ask him, "What do you think of my mama?"

"I like her. She's so friendly. I don't know, different or something."

"Is she like me?"

"Yeah, in some ways."

"So what do you make of her spook's room?"

"You've got to try to understand, Saakshi. Your mother lives alone . . ."

In the evening Jason takes us all out for dinner. Mama chooses the restaurant. An Indian place in Bayswater, but instead of the usual flock wallpaper there are skies painted onto the walls. I'm watching Jason impress my mother. He is so perfectly charming. Their meeting couldn't possibly be going better. The waiters make their way through the clouds like heavenly attendants and I'm flooded with a feeling of happiness.

"Does everyone have psychic abilities?" Jason asks Mama and she's off. She tells him about psychic artists, about past life therapists, about clairvoyants, psychic surgeons, and people who can read objects simply by holding them.

"I took Saakshi once to hear her great-grandfather talking through a medium," she tells Jason, carefully gauging how open-minded he is.

"Oh really?"

She continues. "His name is Aakash and he's channeled through one of the greatest mediums this country has ever known."

"She's called Dora and she does coffee mornings," I add. I can't help feeling a little embarrassed.

"I can play you some of the tapes of him talking if you like," Mama says.

"Mama. Aren't you interested in anything that we're up to? Don't you want to hear about my photography?"

"No, no," Jason continues. "I want to hear about Aakash." And then to Mama: "I'd really love to hear some of those tapes." He's searching for my hand under the table.

Mama tells Jason the whole story. How her grandfather went to live with the Shankaracharya of the North. How he became one of the most legendary sages in Uttar Kashi, a valley where saints were as commonplace as trees.

I would like to say something to Mama about our meditation practice, but she's too busy talking about spirits to want to know. I want to tell her that I too have been inspired to tread the path of my grandfather. That I remember the magical man with the flowers and beads whom she took me to see as a child.

On the way home from dinner, I make sure that Mama drops us off at Papa's house. He knows we're coming and if we don't make an appearance early on in the visit it won't look good. When we arrive we're met with an atmosphere so entirely different – so light and merry, like whipped cream on meringues.

Papa and Hilary are having a dinner party, and they greet the two of us as if we're long-awaited dinner guests.

I introduce Jason to the people I know and sit down next to Hilary to gossip, leaving Jason talking to drunk strangers who imitate his Australian accent and ask him what he's got against their Queen. After a while, I have to help him out, but it doesn't work. Somehow I end up throwing him into deeper water.

I nudge Jason. "Are you going to ask?"

"What now?"

"Go on. I dare you?"

Jason takes a deep breath and turns to Gordon.

"I'd like to ask for your daughter's hand in marriage."

I burst out laughing, I can't help it. So does Papa and Hilary and all their dinner party guests. They laugh and laugh, with Jason waiting quietly and seriously for an answer, looking so sweet and brave. They laugh until one friend of Papa's says, "Put the poor bloke out of his misery and say *yes* will you, mate."

After that party trick is well and truly squeezed for all it's worth, Papa says, "Really Jason, it's quite charming of you to ask me, but Saakshi's the one who has to live with you. Shall we ask her now?"

Later on, Jason tells Mama the same news about us getting married. Her reaction is quite different. She hugs Jason with tears in her eyes and says that she knew already. "Your marriage had been decided before either of you even met," she tells him. And she goes to find some cake in the fridge to sweeten his mouth, as is the tradition.

Before we leave to go back to Australia, Papa and Hilary announce that they too are getting married, as if they've caught some kind of contagious disease that's flying around. When their news is out, Papa comes round to give Mama back the sapphire ring her family presented to him on their wedding day.

And so this is the way it's all going to end?

Mama receives the ring stoically, but I can tell she's holding back the curses on her tongue. Not wanting to throw the ring out she puts it on her own finger, with the full realization that it will fall off soon enough. Accidentally, without her even knowing the exact moment her marriage has finally ended.

But get this. That ring does fall, and lands in the gutter not far from Mama's home. I am the one who finds it – I see it winking at me from under a car wheel as Jason and I are walking past. It's on a chain now under my shirt. Somewhere my mother can't see.

"Do you think it's unlucky to keep this?" I ask Jason, as I thumb the blue sparkles.

"It's your parents' wedding ring. Why not? If they hadn't met, I wouldn't have you now," Jason says. And so I keep my father's ring as a memento of the union that brought me into the world.

Sapphire, I've just discovered, is my lucky stone. It looks good on me; innocent. As far as I'm concerned, my parents may have ended their lives together but the love they shared is unretractable. It's alive and well in me.

I'm the one who has to make sure it never dies.

49

Near Safdarjang Enclave on the Ring Road in New Delhi there's a clock that ticks away the birth rate and population growth of India. HMT Watches, the sponsor, announce to the swarm of human life below that India's population is about to hit one billion. Babies are being showered onto this part of the earth literally every second. Neither floods, droughts, nor tyrannical rulers have been powerful enough to slow down the nation's growth. Even the hell-raising Delhi traffic can't seem to curb the statistics.

It's somewhere I always drive past on the way to anywhere. And I have to stop at the traffic lights, so I'm forced to look, knowing that in four months I'm going to be adding to the statistics. The baby in my belly will represent one more flick – one more blip on the inevitable surge toward one billion.

Last time I was at these traffic lights, on my way to see Dr. Khanna, I bumped into an autorickshaw full of chickens and found myself pulled up by two cops. They fined me one hundred rupees as a bad driving bakshish. Calculated into four Australian dollars, it didn't sound so bad, so I continued on my way, nauseous, vague and hormonal as usual.

My belly has started to scrape on the steering wheel. Nani tells me, "Saakshi, take the driver and go." And I try to explain to her that I trust my own driving instincts more than those of our driver. He likes to go the wrong way around roundabouts to save time. He likes to overtake on the inside lane. He gets out of the car and beats up other drivers if they do the same.

The only thing I am capable of now is surrender. I can do nothing about the Delhi traffic. Nothing about the nuclear testing in Rajasthan. Nothing about the freak heat that came in its wake. I can only feel the heat creep under my skin with the sun, and moan when the air-conditioner cools only one side of my body, leaving the other side weeping with sweat.

So why don't we just get on a plane and get out of here? Go back to Sydney where the sun stays friendly with the sweet sea breezes? I ask myself this question every day, but I know we won't return before the birth. And it's not just so that I can spend special time with my grandmother. If I went back now I'd be admitting defeat, giving in to all those people who thought I was crazy to come out here in the first place.

"You're so brave going to have your baby in India," people in Sydney said, and I laughed off their fears with the boldness of a midwife's daughter. "Childbirth in India is so terrifying, the women have only been able to produce around a billion babies," I boasted, leaning on the invincible power of nature to support my argument.

When I started looking around at the hospitals in Delhi, my bravado buckled and I found myself retreating, unable to maintain the faith I inherited from my mother. Here the clinics have stirrups that look like imports from a bondage and discipline parlor, and the obstetricians threaten old-fashioned persecution methods like shaves and enemas.

Mama rang to tell me to find someone here who's into natural birth. "Yes, birth is very natural," one doctor told me, showing me around her torture chamber with its tongs, syringes and sluice bowls.

I say, "No, no, I mean ... like an alternative birth." But how can I explain the sort of experiences I've been brought up on? The soft lights, the music . . . Who here would want to burn incense at a birth?! In India, of all places? Or give birth in the living room with all the servants watching?

I asked one doctor if he minded delivering babies underwater, and he said: "What? You want your baby to catch typhoid before it's even taken its first breath?"

Not even three months to go and I'm worried. Intensely, hopelessly worried. And all the time, I hear these horror stories. Sophie at the British Embassy had her baby here and they called in the sweeper boys to hold her legs apart. And then the sweeper women to clean up afterward, because it was too low caste for the nurses in that clinic!

Mama told me to make a birth plan and insist that the doctor abides by my wishes. This was the response I got. "Your problem is that you're not working. Most ladies are too busy to worry about what their births are going to be like. What for do you want to know everything?"

And when I'd asked for as little intervention as possible, another doctor told me, "But how can I say that I won't do any of these things? You see, every delivery is different."

"Yes, yes," I said. "I know that delivering a baby is a little less predictable than delivering a pizza, but at least you could give me some reassurances."

As soon as I get out of the car I'm in the blazing heat again. Nearly fifty degrees. It's the bloody nuclear testing. Every time I object to it, people give me long lectures on why India needs nuclear weapons. "The world will respect us now," they say. But I say, "India has become like a beggar who has chopped off her nose before going to beg the West for respect." Honestly, what can be so delightful about this great big bomb? When they dropped the first one, people were distributing sweets and dancing in the streets. "Now India has the bomb," they said, "Pakistan had better watch out!"

It makes me spew. Sometimes India is so hard to love.

I'm walking fast now to get out of the heat and back into an air-conditioned room before I cook in radiation waves. It's always a bit of a wait to see Dr. Khanna, but it's worth it, because he's the only obstetrician in the whole of Delhi who's agreed to do a home delivery. I really love him. He's very warm, empathetic and funny. I was going to tell him about the births that I attended when I was younger, but it didn't seem appropriate. Here is a man, after all, who's worked in the government hospitals where there are three laboring women in each bed, paying two rupees apiece for the privilege. How would I explain the concept of beanbags and cold compresses, the different birthing positions, the candles, the music? Where would the three-in-a-bed women find room for the luxury of all these things anyway?

"Mrs. Paloma next, please." I put down my copy of *India Today*.

The examination is easy. Dr. Khanna always smiles and makes a gentle connection with me before examining my swelling belly. He's more sensitive than the other doctors I saw before him who would lift my limbs and prod me like I was a cow with calf.

"Everything is going very well, Mrs. Paloma, you'll be pleased to know," he assures me.

"And you'll still be able to deliver my baby at home?"

"Why not?"

"Not everyone here is quite as open-minded as you, Dr. Khanna."

"In my nursing home or in your home, either way you'll have the best possible birth experience."

Doctor Khanna believes in birth experiences. That's what makes him so different. He's not the kind of obstetrician who has a knife in one hand and a clock in the other.

"Will I be all right to go up to the mountains for three weeks?" I ask.

"I don't see why not."

Dr. Khanna, you are so beautiful. That's just what I wanted – a go-ahead. Jason has been complaining that he never gets to see anything of

India, and I want to take him up to the hills to see where my great-grandfather once had his farm, Prakriti. All these years of visiting India and I've never been. My nani tells me stories of those glory days and on so many nights I have dreamed of Prakriti – have caught my soul traveling there, to that timeless other place where all those stories have their inspiration.

This time, I'll be going for real. The two of us. No, the three of us if you include the baby.

50

"If there is a paradise on earth, it is this, it is this, it is this." This crisp, cool relief of the hills of Himachal. Jason and I drove all the way up here via Kalka, five hours by car from Nani's house in Sundernagar. We've reached the hills now and I'm watching his reaction, because he's never been in the Himalayas before and I want to know exactly how they hit his soul. I'm holding the dashboard, because his unsteady eyes keep stretching off the road, up up to the heights ahead. "Oh my God, look over there," he says and I turn my head, unable to breathe it's so beautiful.

"I told you."

"I can't believe it's real. It's mind-blowing!"

"Let me read to you, Jason." I pull out a dusty sepia-covered book about Himachal Pradesh and start telling him about the maids of the mountains. "Comely and gay, fond of colorful attire, it is most agreeable to hear them, these winsome women, singing whilst they go about their daily duties in the fields."

"Oh my God, Saakshi, look over there!" I lift my head and my eyes meet a valley so rich in beauty I drop my guidebook.

Even I am unprepared this time. Unable to remember anything quite this beautiful. Was Kashmir this amazing? It's disappeared from my memory now. Here, layer upon layer of mountain fades into eternal white snowcapped peaks on the horizon. Jacaranda trees throw purple light onto the hillsides and the pines stand tall and wild. We're surrounded, taken utterly captive by the magic of the landscape. The beautiful wooden homes, the terraces, the distant mountain stream. Jason wants to take pictures, but I stop him. I know what cameras are capable of and I know that these hills don't lend themselves to snapshots. It's like asking an apparition of God to stand still and say "cheese."

"Let me read you some more about Kipling's Simla," I tell him. "Where sylphlike ladies in crisp crinolines, with blouses of finest silks, walked holding arms with gallant bewhiskered escorts, who strolled leisurely with studied nonchalance, under pines that whispered in the crisp, salubrious Himalayan air."

We're laughing now, laughing the landscape into our souls.

After a while, we stop to meditate. When after some time we open our eyes, we find ourselves in the holy hills, as if we were transported simply by closing our eyes. Out of nowhere comes a cow, almost mythological in its presence, nudging Jason with its horns, trying to steal the banana he's eating. Jason stands up: he's cornered against a boulder and all I can do is laugh.

Back in the car we go, and further up the hills toward Kasauli, which is where we plan to stay the night. When we get there we stop in front of a guesthouse, but checking in is a lot more difficult than anticipated, restricted as we are by the rules of the Public Works Division of the Indian Civil Service.

"You cannot stay here unless you are invited," a man tells me.

"How do I get invited?" I ask innocently.

"You have to write a letter."

I write a letter. We glance at each other, both knowing that we're doing the right thing. The man checks my signature, asks me about my family, and tells me that we're now invited.

Five minutes later we're being shown to our pretty holiday rooms which are surrounded by verandahs with a maharajah's view on either side. We're honored guests of the Indian Civil Service. The chowkidar, who's also the cook and the dhobi, brings us masala chai. This is bliss. Pure bliss. Everything is perfect and I'm wondering how my baby likes it here with its mama so properly indulged.

Some time later we take a walk through the old hill station. Up, up the hill. I don't know whether I'm gasping from dehydration, or from being pregnant, or from both. Jason, I need a Campa Cola. I'm thinking it, not saying it, because there are no shops around. Just old colonial houses. Large, sprawling Indian-style mansions.

We get to the old Kasauli Club at the top of the hill. We go inside, but an Indian bearer comes and tells me that we must leave at once because Jason is wearing kurta pyjamas and "only Western clothes are being permitted inside." I tell him we just want a drink. Campa, Limca, Fanta, anything.

"I am very sorry, madam, but you must be a member."

There's a twenty-year waiting list to become a member, and I'm really thirsty. Temporary membership will get us the drinks, but the Club Secretary isn't available to make the suitable enrollment. I'm trying hard not to be rude. I feel like helping myself from the bar. There's nobody in this club, after all. The rooms are filled only with fading light shining on old brown leather sofas.

"Can we leave?" I ask Jason. "I want to go to Prakriti."

The next day we're closer. I have the name of a small market town written in my notebook. Nani says it was the nearest village to Prakriti, and we've arrived now.

Already I'm more at home. There's a buzz here. Not just tourists from Delhi and Chandigarh. Here there are street people, interactions, bazaars. A bit of filth and a lot more life. There's an old North Indian-style church, colorful as a temple. Cobbled alleys with tiny shops facing each other, wooden balconies overhanging the shopfronts. Kids trailing us. We walk through the town, stopping only to buy a freshly cooked jalabi – beating the flies to our syrupy delight.

Down at the bottom of the market now, looking at faces, I wonder which of these people who look back at us now would know my family.

There are a couple of elderly people, I notice. They look at me and I smile. One of them looks as if she might be my grandmother's age, but she's far more nimble on her feet. She climbs up the cliff face at the end of town as if she were simply tackling a few flights of stairs, and she must be over eighty.

"Ask him," Jason tells me. I look up. There's an old man sitting on the steps of a shop that sells ayurvedic remedies. "Buy something first."

I follow his instructions, buy a tonic for breastfeeding mothers, and ask if he knows about Prakriti.

"Yes, yes. Very big people used to own it," he tells me. "Many years ago a white couple like you came and lived there too."

"You know about a man named Aakash?" I ask in Hindi.

"Oh yes. He was a very good man."

"Where is the farm?" I ask.

He tells us that the land has now been divided into many blocks. The main house has burnt down, but a large six-story building was built on the original site to house the Gurkha regiments, their families and other locals.

We follow his directions, which take us down to the bottom of the street and out along a flat road that hugs the mountainside. As we walk past a Ganesh shrine dug into one of the roadside cliff faces, the side of one mountain drops away and the Himalayas open up like a lotus around us, each petal reaching high into the skies. I feel swallowed up by the staggering beauty of this place, and wonder if I'm big enough to take it all in. Every piece of it, all the way up to the snows.

"Well, what do you think, Jason?"

"I can't believe your family owned all this. Why did they ever leave?"

Some chickens cluck from a nearby house and the noise ricochets against the sound of silence. We look out at the expanse of land that was once Prakriti. The vast and soulful mountain home that my great-grandparents called their own.

"I don't know. Aakash went to live in his ashram, I guess . . ." It sounds like a very simple explanation for a fall from grace.

"We should rent somewhere here for a couple of weeks," I suggest.

"But how? Ask one of the villagers to vacate their ancestral home for a few rupees?"

"We have to stay here, Jason."

We go back into the village and I start asking where we can rent a place to stay. People look blankly at us, but then one boy beckons and we follow him down a side alley, along an open sewer and into a long thin room, its roof just a little higher than our heads. There, lying down on a bed, is a very old man who looks as if he's around ninety. He wants to know why on earth we came to his village instead of Kasauli.

"We want to stay here because it's very beautiful," I tell him, revealing nothing about my family.

The man starts telling us how hard he has worked all his life. He drifts in and out, swimming in the confusion of rational thoughts and senseless images. I bring the conversation back to our question. "We hear that you have a place to rent around here."

He signals to his grandson, who comes over from the adjacent room and speaks in English. "Madam, I can take you to the building, but it is not a hotel."

This young man, Sudhir, takes us back down the road that continues out of the village, twisting around the mountains. We come to the same building we saw earlier: the six-story Himalayan high rise. It looks a bit unsteady, like it's been made without any plans. None of the bricks are overlapping as they should, but it's been standing for fifteen years now and it hasn't fallen yet.

"Has this land always been in your family?" I ask, knowing that it hasn't.

"No. Before it was a very big farm. My grandfather lived on it with his mother. We are just having this plot of land."

We are now being followed by a small group of villagers, all of them wondering why we are here, looking at these humble rooms for rent. Why aren't we in Kasauli like all the other big holidaymakers?

We enter the building from the top floor where it meets the road. The only place available is halfway down the building. Just one small room with some graffiti on the walls and a cement floor with paint smattered over it. A bare light bulb hangs low and there's a brick ridge about six inches high which squares off one corner of the floor – the basin.

"It's out of the question." Jason is whispering in my ear and smiling politely. "There's not even a toilet."

"We'll take it," I tell Sudhir and ask him how much. "Five hundred rupees for three weeks." Our neighbors on the corridor look shocked at how much we are being charged. It works out at twenty dollars – a figure he's had to invent quickly, because nobody takes these places for such a short time.

Jason and I spend the next three days in the market, buying things like fold-up beds, vegetables, cooking utensils, sheets, pillows and a few folkloric posters. It's a villager's dowry that we've accumulated for this three-week holiday and I can't help but wonder what the neighbors would think if they knew about the grand house in Sundernagar. The house back in Sydney, the Mercedes back in Delhi? What would they make of us if they knew that our family once owned the entire valley?

Our neighbors are curious, wondering why we need all these things for just three weeks. They've managed fine without pillows all this time. In the end I give up on them too, because I'm sure that ours have been filled with dust instead of cotton fiber.

Here we are, posing as peasants. We climb down three storys to use the squat toilet during the days, and at nights we just go in our wash basin in the corner of the room. We wash our dishes in the same basin, using Lux soap, the "Beauty Bar of Filmstars," which is always covered with wire hairs and organic food substances. To make the water go down the drain we used a grass broom. We sit on the floor like our neighbors, cooking our rotis and dhal.

But this isn't our life. How can it be? We aren't happy to throw our garbage over the balcony like everyone else in this building. The beautiful Himalayan gully just outside is strewn with plastic, paper and vegetables. There is nowhere else to put the trash because this paradise doesn't have a garbage tip. But still, we're not game to do as the Romans do. And so I spend my time collecting bags of garbage to take back to Delhi.

Out beyond the trash gully, at the end of our balcony, we have the most incredible view imaginable. Jason sits drawing it one afternoon, which makes a change from his CAD drawings of sewerage systems, but still it's impossible to capture. I sit with him, writing my diary, gazing out at the Himalayan heights, imagining how my family would have lived here in these dreamlike esoteric hills. How they would find it now, with this building where the farmhouse once stood, its litter trail following the mountain spring all the way down to the valley below.

Our neighbor to the left, a Nepali Gurkha's wife, sits all day outside her room with her baby. She looks over at my belly and tells me about the difficulties of her labor, the agony she was in. I don't want to know about it, so we don't make friends. But everyone else who comes in to watch us, we entertain. We offer them food whenever we are making any, and some of them accept it coyly. Others tell us, "No thank you, I am very well nourished." None of them seem to know much about the land or its history.

When the time comes to return to Delhi we go to visit the old man who owns the building, to return his keys. We sit on the bed opposite his and I ask him about his time at Prakriti.

"Translate it for me." Jason is keen to know what our landlord is saying.

"He says that his mother worked for my nani's mother. Her name was Bulbul. The farm was the biggest farm for miles around. The big people even had an elephant. Everyone wanted to work for Aakash Saab, because he was the most generous employer of his time ... Now he's saying something about someone going away. Yes, he's talking about Nani's brother Ram ... That plot of land he bought twenty years ago and it was right where the house used to be ..."

When we arrive back in Delhi I ask Nani if she knows about a woman called Bulbul who worked at the farm, but she doesn't. "There were so many servants coming and going in those days," she says. When I tell her about Raja, Bulbul's son, the man who owns the plot of land where the farmhouse once stood, she recalls nothing about him. But she wants to know what it looks like up there now. When I tell her that the farmhouse has been burned down she looks at me as if to say, "You just wouldn't know what that means," and she's holding back tears. The rest of the land I describe exactly as she remembered it – the same, except for the litter and the wobbly skyscraper.

Nani says she will never go back to Himachal now, because she is neither able nor willing. It was her past, she says, and the past can never be re-created.

51

This morning Mama goes and does it again. She rings me up and tells me that the soul of my baby belongs to my great-grandfather. I'm so angry with her. I wish she'd understand that she can't get away with it. This is my baby, not some kind of recycled person. I tell Nani and she laughs.

"And who all else has your mama been talking to in that spirit church?"

"She says she also heard from her papa."

"Saying?"

My nani never likes to admit curiosity about these things, but she always asks questions about her daughter's spirit interests whenever the opportunity arises.

"He says it's very important that she comes for the birth."

"She's your mother. She must come."

"But why? I've got a doctor. Would you have had your mother at your birth?"

That silences her.

The problem is, I know what my mother would be like at my birth. She would insist on doing everything her way. She'd have a group of naked people sitting around me chanting if she could, communing with the soul of the baby. We wouldn't be able to breathe for the smell of incense and I'd have the worst performance anxiety ever. Worse still, she'd be calling it Aakash as soon as it came out, even if it's a girl.

Mama is planning on coming anyway. There's nothing I can do to stop her. Nani has said that she won't allow a home birth in this house when there are perfectly good clinics all over Delhi. She claims that Mama would have died if she hadn't had doctors to help.

Mama is coming to talk Nani into it. If it's the difference between home or hospital, maybe she should be at the birth after all.

52

Mama arrived about a week ago. She says that the head's not engaged so the baby won't come on its due date. Doctor Khanna agrees. I wish they were both wrong. I wish I could give this baby to someone else to carry for a few hours. Just get it out of my body for a few minutes. A few seconds even.

I keep telling my mother my complaints, as if it's all her fault. Mama, I can't sit down for long enough to meditate. Every time I try to do some yoga postures I get a kick in the kidneys. My crotch hurts and I'm walking around like John Wayne. If this goes on any longer I'm checking myself into a hospital, because they're going to have to cut this baby out of me! Forget natural birth. Next time I'm going to get an epidural the minute I find out that I'm pregnant!

Mama tells me that it's going to get a hell of a lot more painful, so I'd better shut up and stop complaining. Thanks, Mama. Can you remember to tell me your worst birth stories just before I go into labor? We'll put some time aside, OK?

Jason's taking next week off. He's got to get his head out of the sewers at some stage, and time is running out. I've never felt so needy and I want him with me every second of the day.

It's too late now to turn around and go back home to Sydney, because they wouldn't let me on the aeroplane even if I tried.

My life is in limbo. All I can do is wait.

53

[CLICK]

"Silence is the mother of all existence . . .

"In Silence the universe gathers herself up and experiences the whole of creation. All galaxies and all souls spin toward that Still Silent Center.

"Here there are no polarities to split the perfect symmetry. There is a Divine consonance. A joy in the completeness of creation. A rich abundance of experience – all in its purest form. This is the home of the soul. And it is eternal . . ."

[CLICK]

Mama turns off the tape player and beams us a beatific smile. "These are some of the last words that Aakash spoke. I wanted to keep these tapes for you, Saakshi."

Jason, will you please stop looking so awestruck! "Mama, you weren't there to record his last words," I say. "You never even met him. That's a woman talking, putting on a man's voice."

Mama looks disappointed and Jason notices. "I'd like to copy the tapes if you don't mind," he says. Sometimes Jason is a lot better than I am at saying the right thing.

"We'll both keep them," I say, and before I can stop myself I'm saying, "I'm so sorry for being such a dreadful daughter, Mama. You've done so much for me. I'm so sorry."

I can't stop myself from crying. Mama gives me a hug and she's crying too. "I know, I know," she says. "I love you, Saakshi."

It's a pitiful sight. It's these hormones. Mama understands. She knows that this can't go on much longer. She knows that this baby is going to have to drop, come what may.

54

The minute I sit up in bed this morning my waters burst. I'm shaking with excitement and nerves. After waiting all this time I am face-to-face with the inescapable truth. This baby's time has come.

Mama's words come back to me. *You must never let on when your labor begins.* So I'm not going to tell Mama, or even Jason. I'm feeling delirious with my own excitement and strength. I'm going to do it on my own.

Quietly I take the keys to the barsati and go up onto the roof to walk, to make the pains stronger. It's going to get stronger. It's got to. If I woke Mama now she'd say that this is nothing. Not even pre-labor. *Don't make a fuss, Saakshi. Just stay centered. Feel the feeling.*

Up on the roof I look into the servants' quarters and see that they're awake. Soon the Sundernagar siren will start up and everybody will wake. The neighborhood will begin the day like any other. Yet this is my day. *Yes, this is my day.* I love this beautiful day!

I want to go downstairs now. I want to tell Jason. *The baby's coming. The baby's COMING.* I'm trying not to slip down the stairs and stumble with the weight of my excitement.

I can't wait to tell him. His eyes are still closed. I'm going to wake him with the news.

No. He's sick of me telling him I'm in pain. He'll think it's another false alarm.

But it isn't. My waters have broken.

It can wait.

No it can't. This is it. It's *his* baby too.

I'll wake him.

"Jason ... Jason." I'm holding his hand now so that it's not too much of a shock, but he can feel my excitement through my skin. "Jason! Jason! *The baby's coming!*"

His eyes open and he sits bolt upright, as if he's doing an emergency fire drill.

"Are you okay, Saakshi? Do you need something? Is it painful?"

I'm excited, but I have to relax him, because he's too energetic for me. We hug and he strokes my back. This is the way I've seen it happen, but always to someone else. This time it's me, in this moment, in labor. This is the birth of *my* child.

His hands follow my spine upward, collecting spasms under his fingertips, and I feel my belly cramping just under my chest. My back's sore, but nothing is quite painful enough. Mama says you're not fully in labor until you can no longer talk through your contractions. I'm still talking. I'm telling Jason how painful it is. I've got to stop it. *This is just the beginning, Saakshi.*

"Shall I wake your mother?" I look up at Jason and I see his perfection. This is why I married this man. This is why we're having this child together now.

"No. My mother goes to sleep during births that are far more progressed than this." I know she wouldn't so much as blink during this birth, but I don't want to wake her. This is our private time together. Jason touches my nipples to make the contractions stronger and it feels like we're play acting, but as soon as he does it I have another contraction. This time I can feel it take my breath away.

"Breathe Saakshi." I laugh. I've heard those words so many times before in my life and now I'm the one who's being told to breathe. Breathe. *Breathe.* But now I'm breathing and it's not necessary. Nothing is happening.

Mama walks into the room.

"Saakshi, are you in labor?" There's something uncanny about my mother. Sometimes I do believe she's psychic. Either that or she's seen all the signs a million times before.

"Yes, but nothing strong. My waters have broken."

She smiles. I've never seen her look so excited about a birth. The thrill of it is in her midwife's hands as she rubs them together in anticipation.

"This is going to be so special, Saakshi. And I have a feeling it's going to be easy for you."

No. Don't say that, Mama. You know as well as I do that anything can happen. We must be prepared for *anything.*

She continues. "If you like we can keep it just family and not call the doctor."

I knew she had a plan. I don't answer.

"Jason, Jason, it's hurting. Hold me."

"Saakshi, don't get excited. You won't be more than three or four centimeters."

That's not what I want to hear. I want to know that it's almost finished.

"Let's walk."

Mama walks on one side of me and Jason on the other. We leave the house and start walking down the road next to the zoo. I look up at the old fortress wall as if I'm hallucinating it. Nothing looks the same in this state.

I'm leaning more on Mama now, because I know she's used to bearing the weight of a laboring woman. I'm thinking for just one second about how it must have been for her when I was born. But another contraction seizes me and doubles me over. I forget about her. This is my time now. Not my mother's.

"Saakshi, walk through it. Nobody must know that you're in labor. That's the way to build up your strength for it."

I'm walking, but I can't believe her. I can't believe that anyone could walk through this much pain. The sides and the top of my belly are squeezing so tight I can hardly breathe. *There might be something going wrong.* I turn and start walking back to the house, sensing Mama's disappointment.

We get inside and Nani comes into our bedroom to see if everything is going all right. Mama tells her to go and rest. We need some quiet.

I want to get in the bath, but Mama says no. "You're not progressed enough, Saakshi. At this stage a bath will slow things down."

As soon as Mama leaves the room I tell Jason to call the doctor. Mama has no idea. She's treating me as if it's nothing. She doesn't know how bad it is.

I'm on the bed now. "Jason, call Mama, it's getting worse. No. Stop. Don't call her. I'll wait until the doctor arrives."

Just wait it out, Saakshi. "Jason, tell the doctor to hurry up. RING him."

Jason goes out of the room. I'm on my own and in a panic. The pains are searing now and there's no hand to hold. I need someone to hold my back when I arch up. I need someone behind me. *Jason, where are you?*

He comes back with Mama. I can't speak now. My eyes are closed. If I open them I see calm faces, but I can feel their nervousness. Mama puts on some music – Indian ragas or something. I ask her to switch it off. The music is distracting me from this feeling of going completely inside of myself. I want the doctor to arrive. I don't want my mama to deliver this baby.

"Speak to your baby, Saakshi. Tell the baby it's all right to come now."

I can't speak. I don't want to. I can't think of the baby. I can't think of anyone but myself.

There's a ring on the bell. The doctor's here at last. *Thank God.*

I feel a hand holding mine. It's big and soft and reassuring. I feel at last as if someone knows what's going on. I hope he's brought some pain relief in case I need some.

He puts on rubber gloves to see how far I've gone. I start a contraction and he pulls out. He tries again. It's painful. Like I've got something stuck up there.

"Eight and a half centimeters. Beti, you're doing so well." He puts his hand on my belly and the contraction squeezes underneath it. *Is this what it feels like to die?*

In between the contractions I can feel myself going to sleep. It's a very deep sleep and the room is quieter. Mama is saying something to the doctor. "This baby, I am told, is the soul of my grandfather reincarnating."

Jason holds my hand as the two of them talk. I'm in between a contraction so I listen. Doctor Khanna tells her a story about how he once needed pain relief for a village woman in labor and there was nothing, so he took some sweets he had in his pocket and asked God to bless them. Sure enough, when the woman ate the sweets, her pain started lifting.

Another contraction. My God, why are they talking? I want them to focus on me. I want help. I need help. And not just some sweets.

My mother continues as my hearing comes in and out in waves. "My grandfather Aakash was one of the great mystics of the hills. He left his farm to go and live in an ashram. He is coming back ..."

Now I hear Mama talking so loud she's almost shouting. And my doctor's voice too seems faster, traced with panic.

I'm scared. I feel so out of control. Another contraction heaves through my body till it numbs my brain.

"Jason, call Saakshi's grandmother," my Mama orders. Her voice is shaking now as she repeats my doctor's name: "Doctor Jivan Khanna." And then she calls out softly, as if to a baby in a cradle, "Jivan. My dear God."

There is Silence.

Jason tells me to open my eyes. I do. My mother and my doctor are in each other's arms. They are both in tears.

I can feel the surge. It's so strong. When it peaks I feel as if I'm losing consciousness.

And then the feeling turns.

I feel something else now. It's nothing I've ever felt before in my life. The very bottom of my belly is rising to the top. Every single muscle in my body is pushing, pushing, pushing this huge bulge out of me.

Mama starts talking to me again. "Put your chin down and hold your breath, Saakshi."

I open my eyes to see her. She is holding hands with my doctor. Radiant and excited.

Nani comes into the room, but I hardly notice. Everything outside is oblivion. I am inside my own body now. It's not so painful anymore. Not so much pain as a power so forceful it's awkward. It's pushing my insides out.

"Saakshi, you can do it."

I believe Jason for once. But every time I push I think the head will come out and it doesn't.

"Push harder next time," says Jason.

"No, don't push except when you really feel the urge," I hear my mama say, and feel like smiling at my amateur gynecologist of a husband, but I muffle out some words instead.

I look up and see my grandmother with tears in her eyes. She is sitting next to my doctor stroking his cheek, his hair, his bad leg. He has his head on her shoulder. Jason is crying too.

I'm feeling close to it. I can feel the head deep down in my body.

"Put your hand down and touch the baby's head, Saakshi." My mother is on the case again. Fully in the moment, I feel the power of her intention. Her focus, alertness and excitement. I try to put my hand down but it won't reach. And then I'm stopped by another contraction. It consumes me, leaving me unable to do anything but push.

"Now try again."

I put my hand down. The head is soft, round and slippery. I get a flutter in my chest. It's the first time I've touched my child. There's a baby in there. My child. *It's real.*

There's a force in my body more mighty than anything. It possesses me. It wills me – lending me its power. The head pushes its way out.

I take one more breath, knowing that I've done it already. And then another push comes from inside me. The body gushes out.

The room is swimming.

The doctor has my baby in his hands. I don't know why I'm surprised to see a real baby – what else could have been in there all through these nine months?

My nani. My mother. The doctor. Everyone is crying and hugging at the foot of the bed. Jason is cuddling me and telling me what a hero I am. I love him. I love the little slippery red creature that's handed to me.

My heart is racing.

When the baby is in my arms I feel I understand the whole mystery of life. He's a boy. (I wasn't looking. Jason had to tell me.) The baby's eyes are open. I feel the gush of love from the bottom of my beating heart and I breathe – this time from relief.

I can't believe that it's a real baby. A miraculous human being.

The baby has a red mark on his forehead, very little hair and tiny puckered lips. I kiss those tiny lips. And kiss Jason.

And from the distance I hear a calling – the trumpeting of an elephant heralding the new soul's arrival from its home over the garden fence – from way off in the heart of Delhi Zoo.

Reader's Guide to *The Seduction of Silence*

Author's notes—(some random thoughts at least) on *The Seduction of Silence*

The Seduction of Silence is not a tale about the ordinary life. It's about the human spirit—about life, spirituality, love, family, and journeys.

I wanted to start off the story from the other side of life, because I wanted to set the scope of the book with the broadest and most sweeping of all brushstrokes. To step right back, with a great and cosmic distance on the story.

And yet, I felt so sure that the reader would have to arrive very suddenly on solid ground, because life is like that. Spirituality is part of everyday life.

I knew that the story would end with a birth when I started working on this book. But just how much that birth would involve the characters, I had no idea. I had no inkling that Jivan would come back. I would not have written it, because it seemed too perfect an ending, except that Saakshi insisted. It was her birth experience after all. Who was I to argue?

The role of mythology

I have always been fascinated by universal laws and how they operate in the world of manifest differences. The point at which a myth becomes real, taking up parallels in the fiction of life. Ever since I read Joseph Campbell's work and well before that, when I studied Levi-Strauss, I've been fascinated by the role of mythology in fiction and real life.

For me, mythology starts at the point where the Absolute divides. There it leaves the world of archetype to find its true purpose in the world. If characters and stories can come fluidly out of this Source, then you have a potent starting point for fiction.

I wanted the beginning of Aakash's story to have the feeling of a great mythology. And his sudden disappearance from the plot, I believe, adds to his mythological status. I did not want to give a daily account of his life in Uttar Kashi, where he went to renounce the world. It was too personal and quiet an experience and did not bear any relevance anymore to the lives led by the characters that followed.

Good stories make good myths. The story of the Ramayana has always fascinated me. It is so rich in content and meaning that I felt compelled to use it as an anchor for a significant part of my story. It's lovely to have some way to return to this epic in my own writing.

The process of writing

Although this book took about eighteen months to complete, most of the writing for *The Seduction of Silence* took place over nine months. About the time of a gestation, with a particularly painful period just before final delivery!

So much of this novel touches on the theme of birth—probably because I started writing it while I was pregnant with my second son, and completed it while I was still breastfeeding.

A lot of the story came through as if I had no say in it. Nearly 90,000 words were written at a rate of 3,000 words a day (over one month). I would sit down in the morning and characters would write their own part in the story (even if they played no part in the original vision for the book).

It was so exciting to watch this story unfold. Overwhelming, too, because at times I had this feeling that the novel was going to be written with or without my assistance!

Last, I really loved working on *The Seduction of Silence* and I'm so thrilled that I was given the opportunity to share it with others.

Questions for Discussion

1. Characters such as Aakash and Ram are strongly motivated to renounce the world and devote themselves single-mindedly to spiritual practice. To what extent is spiritual progress possible "in the world." How do the spiritual and profane realms work together in life and in this book?
2. How do the births explored in this novel create turning points in the story?
3. Rohini observes that life and death are part of the same continuum. Do the themes of birth and death work as parallels or opposites in *The Seduction of Silence*?
4. How do the spiritual beliefs of the characters dictate their destinies?
5. How do the different characters reflect the theme of silence?
6. What is the importance of "belief" in this story? Is it necessary to share the same belief systems as the characters in order to understand the ideals represented in this book?
7. *The Seduction of Silence* takes place over 100 years in time, across different nations and different levels of consciousness. What are the threads that tie this story together and make it cohesive?

8. How do the past and the present work together in *The Seduction of Silence*? How does history make an impact on the experiences and emotions of the characters?
9. To what extent do the women in *The Seduction of Silence* break the patterns of their mothers? How easy is it to break patterns that are handed down?
10. The Himalayas are described by the author as the perfect setting for the soul. How important is the landscape to the spiritual sentiment of this book?
11. To what extent is *The Seduction of Silence* bound by time and place, and to what extent is its message universal?
12. Which parts of the book seem to be based on truth? Which parts are obviously "magical"? How is magic presented as real and how is reality presented as fiction? Is the difference between the two of any significance?
13. Which event is the most magical and memorable in *The Seduction of Silence,* and why?
14. *The Seduction of Silence* follows generations of one family as each person finds her own path to enlightenment. What spiritual journeys have your family members taken? Has anyone in your family stepped outside of tradition?
15. What does *The Seduction of Silence* say about the importance of a spiritual life, alongside a material life? How do you make time for your inner life?

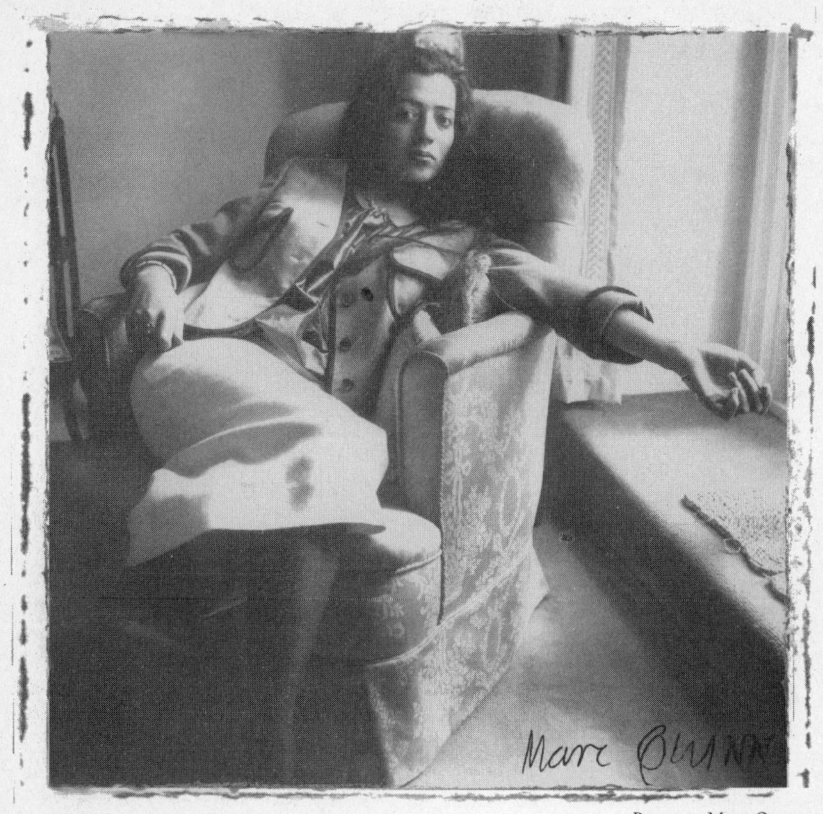

PHOTO BY MARC QUINN

Bem Le Hunte was born in Calcutta in 1964 to an Indian mother and British father. She left India as a young girl and was schooled in London, after which she studied anthropology at Cambridge. She has worked both as a writer and university lecturer since graduation, and currently lives in Sydney with her husband, artist Jan Golembiewski, and their two sons. This is her first novel.